Running on

Diesel

The Whiskeys

MELISSA FOSTER

ISBN-13: 978-1948868631

Cover Design: Elizabeth Mackey Designs
Cover Photography: R+M Photography

WORLD LITERARY PRESS
PRINTED IN THE UNITED STATES OF AMERICA

A Note to Readers

I have been waiting years to write Diesel and Tracey's book, and I am thrilled to bring you their emotional love story. I hope you adore Diesel, my roughest, gruffest hero yet, who withholds words as if he has a limited supply, and Tracey, the perfect mix of tough, sassy, and sweet to draw out Diesel's very own brand of romance. If this is your first Whiskey book, all of my Love in Bloom novels are written to stand alone, so dive right in and enjoy the fun, sexy ride.

For avid fans of the Whiskeys, while I'll be writing about the Whiskeys' Colorado cousins next (The Whiskeys: Dark Knights at Redemption Ranch), but the Dark Knights at Peaceful Harbor series is not ending. Isabel "Izzy" Ryder *will* be getting a happily ever after, as will Jon Butterscotch and others in the series. Stay tuned for more details.

You can download the Whiskey family tree here:
www.MelissaFoster.com/Wicked-Whiskey-Family-Tree

See the rest of The Whiskeys: Dark Knights at Peaceful Harbor series here:
www.MelissaFoster.com/TheWhiskeys

Sign up for my newsletter to make sure you don't miss out on future releases and sales:
www.MelissaFoster.com/News

For more information about my fun and emotional sexy

romances, all of which can be read as stand-alone novels or as part of the larger series, visit my website:
www.MelissaFoster.com

If you prefer sweet romance with no explicit scenes or graphic language, please try the Sweet with Heat series written under my pen name, Addison Cole. You'll find many great love stories with toned-down heat levels.

Happy reading!
~ Melissa

Chapter One

THE MURMURS OF the crowd at Whiskey Bro's competed with the sounds of billiards and the cold thunder of Desmond "Diesel" Black's mounting anger as he poured a round of shots for a customer, eyes locked on Tracey Kline. The hot little waitress was getting eye-fucked by a denim-jacket-wearing, spike-haired punk who had just strolled into the bar with two other guys. Tracey, being the sweet thing she was, batted her big hazel eyes, and with a flick of her pointy chin, sent her shoulder-length silky dark hair out of her face as she motioned toward a table. Her hair tumbled back down over one eye, which only made her sexier. The denim-jacket-wearing asshole must have seen it as an invitation, because while his buddies headed for the table, *he* headed for Tracey. Diesel gritted his teeth.

"Watch it, dude," Jed Moon, the other bartender, warned.

Diesel snapped around, glowering at him.

Amused, Moon nodded to the tequila Diesel was still pouring, which was flowing like a river off the edge of the bar, puddling by his black leather boots.

"Did you just *growl* at me? You're losing it, man." He tossed

Diesel a towel.

"Fuck." Diesel's eyes shot back to the asshole talking with Tracey as he mopped up the bar.

Tracey looked over, catching Diesel watching them. Her eyes narrowed, and the dickbag's gaze followed hers to Diesel.

Diesel rolled his shoulders back, breathing fire.

The asshole's face blanched, but as if he'd caught himself, an arrogant grin appeared, and he said something else to Tracey, then sauntered over to his friends. Tracey glared at Diesel, spun on her heels, and stormed over to another customer.

Moon sidled up to him. "I'm beginning to think you've either been here too long or you need to make that girl yours."

Diesel's eyes remained trained on Tracey. He wasn't about to make any woman his. He'd been a lone wolf since he was nineteen years old, when his mother lost a long, hard battle with cancer, and he'd left the only home he'd ever known in Hope Ridge, Colorado. At thirty-two, the only ties he had or wanted were to the brotherhood of the Dark Knights motorcycle club, of which he was a Nomad member—loyal to the club without claiming any chapter as his own. But Moon had a point about him being there too long. Diesel was a bounty hunter, and he didn't usually stay anywhere more than a few weeks before he got the itch to climb on his motorcycle and take off to another town or state. But he'd stuck around as a favor to the president of the motorcycle club's old lady, Red Whiskey. Her oldest son, Bullet, had run the bar for years, but now that he and his wife had a baby girl, he wanted more family time. Diesel had stepped in and taken over in the evenings.

Then there was the second favor Red had asked of him. The favor regarding Tracey, who had escaped an abusive relationship and had been a scared, broken bird without a nest—*She's a special girl, and I need you to watch over her. Keep her safe.* The favor, and the girl, had kept him there for nearly two years.

"I'd say fuck her out of your system," Moon said, jarring Diesel from his thoughts. "But Tracey's not like that. She's the kind of girl you settle down with."

No shit. Diesel dropped the towel and stepped on it to mop the liquor off the floor. "I'd split that pretty little thing in half."

Tracey might have come into her own these last two years and gone from a broken bird to a wise owl, but at six foot six and two hundred and fifty pounds of solid muscle, with a cock worthy of a hundred women kneeling at his feet, Diesel spoke the truth. Tracey was only a hair over five feet tall, and couldn't weigh more than a buck ten soaking wet. Not to mention that she was too damn sweet for the likes of him. But even that didn't keep thoughts of having her tight little body wrapped around him at bay. He didn't know how it had gotten to that point when he'd initially only been all about protecting her, but hell if she didn't send lust scorching through his veins.

That was the primary reason he was planning on getting the hell out of Peaceful Harbor for good soon. Usually, when the urge hit, he climbed on his bike and took off without giving anyone a heads-up, much less notice. But he couldn't do that to the Whiskeys. They relied on him, and he owed them time to find a replacement. He'd tell Red tomorrow that he was taking off after the holidays, which should give them time to find someone.

Tracey stalked toward the bar, shooting invisible daggers at Diesel.

This from the girl who hadn't been able to look him in the eyes for the first few months she'd worked there. She'd come a long way from the scared girl who lived in oversized flannel shirts and baggy jeans. His gaze dropped to the sliver of skin between the hem of the Whiskey Bro's T-shirt clinging to her perky breasts and her curve-hugging jeans. He imagined her spread out on the bar as he tasted that sliver of pale flesh on his way to the feast between her legs.

Tracey smacked her hand on the bar, snapping him from the fantasy he had no business entertaining. "*Stop* scaring off my tips."

"Pull your shirt down before you get yourself in trouble." The place was busy. She had plenty of tips coming in. She didn't need to advertise what she wasn't putting out.

She smirked, maintaining a challenging stare as she leaned over the bar, giving him an eyeful of cleavage and revealing a hint of black lace. "I think you have me confused with your biker hos. Just because they call you *Daddy* doesn't mean you can act like *my* father."

"Daddy," my ass. He wasn't into that shit. He leaned his forearms on the bar, bringing him nose to nose with Tracey, her enticingly feminine scent stoking the flames he was trying to ignore. He held her gaze, enjoying the quickening of her breaths, the nervous flutter of her long lashes as she visibly tried to regain her courage. He got a kick out of her newfound bravado, but she was liable to get herself in trouble acting like that.

"Getting a little mouthy, sparky," he warned. "Better check that."

She pressed her lips into a firm line and pushed from the bar, nervously looking at the customers climbing onto the barstools beside her. "I need a pitcher of Bud and three glasses."

He scanned the room as he filled the order, nervous energy jumping off Tracey like fleas. Diesel caught the asshole in the denim jacket checking her out and shut him down with another threatening stare as Tracey reached across the bar for the glasses. Diesel covered her slim wrist with his hand, his fingers covering her entire forearm. She was so small, it made him sick to think a man had ever raised a hand to her.

"What?" she snapped, fire igniting in her eyes.

"Watch yourself."

THE GALL OF this beast trying to tell me what to wear and how to act. There was a time when Tracey would have cowered under the controlling touch or warning glare of a man, especially one the size of a mountain who grunted more than he spoke. But she was no longer the weak, friendless girl she'd been when she'd escaped the wrath of her asshole boyfriend, Dennis Smoot, and she'd come too far to let anyone tell her what she could or couldn't do.

She held Diesel's dark stare, heat and fury warring inside her as the familiar and all-too-confusing clutch of attraction *or hate*—she could never tell which with him—dug its claws in deep. "I'm just trying to make a living," she bit out. "*You* watch *yourself.*"

Yanking her arm free, she gathered her order, sure smoke was coming out her ears. She stalked away, trying to calm herself down on her way to deliver the drinks. Why did she let him get under her skin? Her answer came as she passed Dixie Whiskey-Stone's side of the floor. Dixie was a tough redhead who handled the books for the Whiskey family businesses and waitressed a few nights a week. As always, her tables were packed with high-tipping men, while Tracey had two empty tables, and her other customers were mostly women, thanks to Diesel's *Don't go near her or I'll rip your arms off* stare.

The bastard.

Last Thanksgiving Tracey had finally figured out *why* Diesel scrutinized every male customer who came near her, and Red Whiskey had confirmed her suspicions. When Tracey had first started working there, Red had been worried Tracey's ex might come looking for her, and she'd asked Diesel to watch over her. But that was *two* years ago.

It was time to put an end to Diesel's bodyguarding, because it was either that or quit, and quitting was out of the question. She loved her job and she adored the Whiskeys. There was no way in hell she'd let that Neanderthal mess that up for her. No matter how insanely hot he was or how often she had sexy dreams about him.

The Whiskeys were her motorcycle-riding, tatted-up, leather-clad guardian angels. She'd met them through the Parkvale Women's Shelter, where she'd stayed after escaping her abusive ex. The shelter was run by another Dark Knights family, and Wayne "Bones" Whiskey, a physician, volunteered there. The Whiskeys had helped her get back on her feet, giving her this job, and more importantly, welcoming her into their large, though close-knit, circle of family and friends. Including her roommate, Izzy Ryder, whom she'd lived with since leaving the shelter. Izzy also bartended at Whiskey Bro's. The Whiskeys did so much for the community, it seemed like everyone in Peaceful Harbor knew them. Tracey had been isolated for so many years before getting away from Dennis, it had taken her a while to let her guard down, but the Whiskeys and their friends had been patient, making her feel safe and wanted, like she was part of a *real* family again.

Thoughts of her mother pressed in, bringing a wave of sadness. They'd had a falling-out when she'd moved away with Dennis, and now, six long years later, she didn't even know where her mother was. But she couldn't afford to get lost in that devastating swamp right now. She had five more hours of tips to earn.

She flashed a friendly smile at the slick-talking guy in the denim jacket, who was far too into himself, as she set the pitcher and glasses on the table. He and his friends were passing through town for a couple of nights, or so he'd said when they'd arrived. "Sorry this took so long, gentlemen."

"No problem. Seein' your pretty face was worth the wait." Mr. Slick lifted his chin in the direction of the bar. "What's the deal with you and Bigfoot?"

"If I had a dollar for every time I've asked myself that, I'd be a rich woman by now."

She glanced at Diesel, filling an order for Dixie, who was standing at the bar chatting, but Diesel's eyes were trained on Tracey, causing those funky feelings to claw at her again. He really was a mountain of grunting, scary-as-all-get-out muscle, tattooed from neck to wrist, with absolutely *no* people skills. The battered old black baseball cap he wore every day didn't fit with the rest of his tough-guy image, which made her curious about why he wore it. Did it have sentimental value? *Is it a trophy from a man you killed?* She laughed inwardly. When she'd first met Diesel, he was so cold and looked so lethal, she'd actually toyed with the idea that the man who was practically a legend in his own right for Lord knew what could be a serial killer. *A really great-smelling serial killer.* He always smelled clean and fresh, like a cold winter's day. But she'd learned the truth.

Desmond "Diesel" Black definitely wasn't Bigfoot or a serial killer. He was just a cold-blooded watch dog, and she was his charge.

"Hey, sunshine," Slick said, bringing her attention back to her customers.

"Yes? Sorry."

"So you and he aren't a *thing?*"

"No." *I like guys who can actually string together complete sentences.*

"What time do you get off?" He leaned closer, a creepy grin crawling across his face. Before she could get a word out, he said, "Let me rephrase that. What time can I pick you up and get you off?"

The two guys he was with chuckled.

Ugh. Between Diesel's ridiculously protective grab and this creep's entitlement, she wanted to punch something. "Sorry, but I don't date customers. Enjoy your drinks."

She went to help other customers, then headed up to the bar to place an order. *Eagle Eyes* watched her the whole way, igniting those confusing flames beneath her skin, which had been burning hotter ever since her friend Sarah and Bones's wedding several weeks ago. Diesel had been devastatingly handsome that night, all his muscles nearly busting out of his dress shirt and pants. Another friend's five-year-old daughter, Kennedy, had dragged him onto the dance floor, and the man who Tracey was sure had a heart of stone had twirled that sweet little girl and taken her into his arms with such tenderness, if Tracey hadn't already known him as the grunting pain in her ass that he was, her panties might have melted off.

She walked over to Jed's side of the bar. Jed was her friend Josie's husband. He was also a Dark Knight, but he was the antithesis of Diesel, with a warm demeanor, piercing blue eyes, and thick dirty-blond hair. Jed was a big guy, but not massive like Diesel, and he was madly in love with his wife and their seven-year-old son, Hail.

Jed flashed a warm smile. "What can I get you, Trace?"

"A back massage, a foot rub, and maybe a guy who actually knows how to flirt without being a jerk."

Jed cocked a brow. "Rough night?"

She eyed Diesel, who was setting a drink on the bar for a customer, his dark eyes sliding her way again. "Let's just say the guys my bodyguard doesn't scare off are the ones I wish he would." She placed the drink order and watched two couples leaving as she waited. The guys had their arms around the girls. One of them kissed his partner's temple, and Tracey sighed inwardly.

She'd never known what a good relationship looked like until she'd met the Whiskeys, but now she could spot them a mile away. Her mother had left her abusive father when she was only six, and she'd never seen her with a man after that. When Tracey was old enough to date, she'd met Dennis, and what she'd thought was love had really been a nightmare in the making. But these last two years, as she was embraced by the Whiskey family, she'd watched and learned. Biggs was a gnarly biker to his core, and Red was as tough as a biker's wife had to be to live in that world. They'd been married forever, and the love, trust, and respect they had for each other were insurmountable, resonating in everything they did and in the people around them. They'd raised three strong men who went by their road names—Bullet, Bones, and Bear—and a tough-as-nails daughter, Dixie. All four had hearts of gold and loved their significant others and friends like they needed those relationships in order to breathe.

Lately Tracey longed for that type of trust, friendship, and intimacy, too.

Jed pushed the drinks across the bar, catching her attention. "Hey, Trace, think you can babysit Hail Wednesday night? Josie's been working so hard to prepare for the bridal expo, I want to take her out someplace special."

Josie owned a gingerbread business. She and her sister, Sarah, a hairdresser, were sharing a booth at a bridal expo next month with Finlay, Bullet's wife, who owned a catering business, and worked part-time for the bar. Tracey and a few of their other friends were going to help them at the event. She mentally ran through her schedule as she put the drinks on the tray. Between her martial arts classes and waitressing, she didn't have all that much free time, but she loved watching Hail. "Sure. What time?"

"Does seven work?"

"Yeah," she said as Diesel closed the distance between them. "I'll be there."

"Be *where*?" Diesel's voice was rough as sandpaper.

She lifted the tray off the bar, determined to mess with him. "Not that it's any of your business, but Jed is setting me up on a mud-wrestling date."

Diesel's nostrils flared.

She couldn't help but chuckle. What kind of girl did he think she was? She couldn't resist tossing another barb. "Did I mention it's with *two* guys? There'll probably be some nakedness involved." She giggled as she walked away to deliver the drinks.

An hour later, the bar was packed, but Tracey still had free tables. She was fit to be tied over Diesel's stare downs and thrilled when Crow Burke walked in with Tex and Court Sharpe, three big-tipping Dark Knights.

"Hey, guys. How're you doing tonight?"

"Great, Trace. You?" Tex asked.

"You sure are lookin' fine." Crow raked his eyes down her body.

Tex elbowed him, giving him a chiding glare.

It was all she could do not to roll her eyes. Like she needed another babysitter? "I've got a table with your name on it right over there." She pointed in the direction of an empty table.

"You know we love you, Trace, but I think we'll sit at one of Dixie's tables tonight." Tex pushed a tattooed hand through his thick dark hair. "Diesel chews me out every time I flirt with you."

Furious, she planted her hand on her hip. "You're afraid of Diesel? Seriously? Aren't Dark Knights supposed to have each other's backs?"

"That's exactly why we're going to sit by Dix." Tex nudged Crow. "Let's go."

She looked at Court, the oldest of the three men.

"Sorry, Trace, but you know those two can't help but get themselves in trouble."

Anger simmered inside her as Court walked away, and she stormed over to the register where Dixie was ringing up a bill.

"Hey, girl." Dixie glanced at her as she punched in an order. "Whoa. What's got your panties in a twist?"

"Tex just told me that Diesel gave him crap for flirting with me. *Why* is Diesel doing that? It's like he wants me to quit. I mean *Tex*. Really? Like he's some kind of threat to my safety?"

Dixie parked her hip against the counter, giving Tracey a once-over as she crossed her arms. "You look hot tonight."

Tracey had always been petite, but now that her life was stable and she was happy, she'd put on a few pounds, and thanks to the martial arts classes she took at her gym, she even had some semblance of curves. It had only taken her close to twenty-six years to develop them. But she was onto Dixie's attempt to distract her with a compliment. "Compared to you, I look like a teenage boy with boobs, but you're not answering my question, Dix."

Dixie had the beauty, body, and confidence of Tess Carmina and the attitude of a badass biker who lived by her own rules. She dressed however the hell she pleased in Daisy Dukes, miniskirts, or like tonight, in a cropped Whiskey Bro's tank top, skintight jeans, and sky-high black leather boots. Nobody ever gave Dixie crap. Tracey wanted that respect from *Diesel*. Everyone else already gave it to her.

"Yes, I am, and you look nothing like a boy. You have great boobs, a cute ass, and a tiny waist half our friends would kill for."

"Thank you, but what does that have to do with my question?"

"I've been telling you for months that Diesel wants to fuck you. If that man looked at any other woman the way he looks at you, they'd be all over him." She arched a finely manicured brow. "If you ask me, you ought to drag his ass out back and ride him like a Harley. It's the only way to break the sexual tension between you two, and you know a man who looks like that fucks as hard and dark as he acts."

"I am *sick* of everyone telling me he wants me. It's like y'all have lost your minds. That man does not tiptoe around what he wants. He leaves the bar with a different woman two or three times a week. Fast women who drink too much and wear too few clothes. Women who are *nothing* like me, which is just fine, because chiseled features or not, he has absolutely *no* people skills, and I have zero interest in becoming some possessive, grunting biker's property." She was breathing too hard, anger and adrenaline coursing through her veins. "You know what? Forget it. I'm sick of this, and I'm going to put an end to it right now." She stormed toward the bar, pushing through the crowd, Diesel's eyes drilling into her as she pointed at him. "You. Kitchen. *Now.*"

She didn't wait for a response, making a beeline through the double doors, into the empty kitchen, where she paced, her nerves rattling with the reality of what she was about to do. She shook out her hands, gulping in air as the beast walked through the doors, eyes narrowed.

It was now or never, and she couldn't afford *never*.

Her legs ate up the space between them. He hulked over her, appearing much bigger from that perspective than when he was behind the bar. But that didn't stop her. Hands fisted, her fury burst out. "This overprotective crap you're doing has got to stop! I know Red told you to look after me, and maybe I needed it two years ago, but that's done. *Over.* You're relieved of your duties. I don't need you scaring off my customers, or telling me what to wear, or scaring off guys who I might want to go out with. I'm *never* going to meet a guy, much less make friends, with you *King Konging* me every time guys look my way."

He made a growling noise low in his throat, shoulders rising.

"I can take care of myself. *Stop. Watching. Over. Me.*" She poked his chest to emphasize each word, unable to stop spewing venom. "I spent years living under some guy's thumb, and I will *not* have you ruining my life. Back *off*, Diesel. Do you understand?"

His dark eyes drilled into her, jaw tight. "You done, sparky?"

"I am *not* your property. *Stop* calling me that. I'm not your *anything*. You work here. I work here. End of story. You do your job. I'll do mine. Are we clear?"

He made a half grunt, half scoffing sound, that maddening, cold stare turning into something much darker, as terrifying as it was seductive. He stepped closer, and she stepped back, bumping into the counter. He boxed her in, placing his tattooed hands on either side of her, and lowered his face to within an inch of hers, sucking all the oxygen from the room.

"You want me gone, take it up with Red," he grated, low and deep, and then he rose to his full height and walked back into the bar, leaving a cold draft in his wake.

The air rushed from Tracey's lungs, and she pressed a hand to her chest, shaking all over. Slow clapping rang out from the back of the kitchen, and she spun around, mortified at the sight of Bullet Whiskey, a brooding, tattooed, bearded biker whose size rivaled Diesel's. He was clapping, and beside him Finlay, a petite blonde, held their eight-month-old daughter, Tallulah.

"*Bullet,*" Finlay chided, handing him the baby. "Can't you see she's having a hard night?"

"Ohmygod, you guys. I can't believe you saw that. I had no idea you were here." Tracey was mortified.

Finlay rushed to her side. "Lulu was cranky, so we took her for a ride, and we just stopped by to pick up my planner for the expo. But, Tracey!" Finlay hugged her. "You *finally* stood up to him. I'm so proud of you. Are you okay?"

"I don't know." Tracey glanced at Bullet, panic burning in her chest. The Whiskeys might treat her like family, but Diesel was a Dark Knight, which meant he was even more their *family* than she was. "Am I going to be fired?"

A deep laugh rumbled out of Bullet. "Not a chance, sweetheart. We don't fire family."

"But...?" Tracey didn't know what to say.

"Diesel's a big boy. He can handle himself," Bullet said. "I didn't realize you were having such a hard time with him. I'll talk to him."

"No," Tracey said quickly. "This is my mess. I'll clean it up."

"Honey, you're shaking." Finlay rubbed a hand down Tracey's back. "Want me to make you some tea or something before we go?"

"No, thanks. I need to get back out there." She blew out a breath, her heart pounding frantically. "What if I just poked the bear? We have hours until we close. What if he's even worse now?"

"You can't think that way." Finlay gave her hand a squeeze. "You showed him what you're made of. Now, you go out there and prove it. Hold your head up high and be strong. Heck, I did that to Bullet. Right, Bullet?"

Bullet nuzzled the baby, softening all his hard edges. "I've never seen anyone stand up to Diesel and live to tell about it."

Finlay glared at him.

"What?" Bullet's brow furrowed. "I'm talking about guys, not pretty little gals like Tracey. I've never seen *any* sweethearts stand up to that man."

"Great. If I don't show up for work tomorrow, you'll know why." Tracey pushed through the double doors with her heart in her throat, feeling the intensity of Diesel's stare like a laser beam on her back as she went to check on her customers.

Dixie fell into step beside her. "What did you say to him? He looks like he's ready to kill someone."

"I told him to back off. Bullet and Fin saw us. It was *so* embarrassing."

"They're *here?*"

"They just stopped by to get something." Slick flagged her over to the table. "I gotta go."

"That guy was looking for you a minute ago. Seems like a real douche."

"Tell me about it." Tracey went to see what he wanted. "Hi. Can I get you something?"

Slick arched a brow. "I thought you said you and that guy weren't a thing."

"Sure looked like you went in through those doors for a quickie," the biggest of the three guys said.

Slick cocked a grin. "We'll show you a better time than that asshole."

"Don't you dare talk to me like that. I'll be right back with your bill." She turned to leave, and the denim jacket guy grabbed her wrist, tugging her down so his face was right in front of hers, sending chills racing down her spine. She yanked her arm free. "Don't you ever—"

Diesel's hand shot in front of her and grabbed the guy by his shirt, hauling him to his feet, then higher, his legs dangling beneath him. Diesel got right in his face, muscles bulging, teeth gritted. "Get the fuck out of here. If you ever come back, they won't find your body." Those cold eyes slid to the others, who were now on their feet. "That goes for you assholes, too." He dropped the guy he was holding, and the guy stumbled back. Diesel took a step toward him.

"Let's get out of this shithole." Slick sneered.

Diesel stood guard until they left, and then he turned around, pinning Tracey in place with a piercing stare. "Still wanna have that talk with Red?"

"*Yes.* He was just an arrogant jerk. I could have handled him."

"The same way you handled me?" he asked gruffly, but it was clear he wasn't looking for an answer as he lowered his face toward hers, just like he'd done in the kitchen, the same thrumming heat and dark warning vibrating off him. "You do your job and let me do mine."

He walked back to the bar, leaving her fuming once again.

Diesel watched her even more closely after that, but it was the prolonged stares of a different kind he was giving her that wreaked havoc with her nerves. Or maybe she was imagining the way he was looking at her because of the things Dixie had said. Either way, by closing time, she was more than ready to go home.

"Thanks again, Trace," Dixie said as she and Jed headed out for the night.

"Anytime," Tracey called over from the pool table area.

Dixie was trying to cut back her evening hours now that she was married, and she had been interviewing for new waitstaff all week. But Tracey never minded sticking around a little later to do the extra cleanup. After all, while Dixie's husband, Jace, was waiting for her at home, Tracey had nothing but an empty house waiting for her. Izzy was out of town, visiting her family for the weekend.

When she finished cleaning, she put away the supplies and went to grab the trash, but Diesel had already taken it out to the dumpster. She pulled her phone from her pocket, focusing on ordering an Uber since her car was in the shop, rather than looking over at Diesel as she walked out the front door and into the warm August night.

She leaned against the railing to wait and tipped her face up to the starry sky, wondering if she'd done the right thing by confronting him. Diesel didn't come to Dixie's rescue when guys got handsy with her. He stepped closer, but he let Dixie handle things herself. Why couldn't he do that for her? Minutes passed in peaceful silence, broken only by the sounds of the cars driving by, the balmy air hugging her skin. Her phone vibrated, and she sighed as she read the message indicating her Uber had canceled.

The door opened behind her, and she felt the wooden floorboards dip beneath Diesel's weight. "Where's your car?" he asked as he locked the door.

"It's in the shop until Sunday."

He stepped beside her. "I'll take you home."

"It's okay. I'm ordering an Uber. The last one just canceled."

"You're not getting in an Uber with some stranger. Let's go. Get on my bike."

She put a hand on her hip, her gaze lingering on his chest and biceps straining against his T-shirt, before she realized she was staring and broke her trance. "Why do you think you can tell me what to do all the time?"

His dark eyes held hers, the muscles in his jaw bunching as he walked down the steps to his bike and grabbed the helmet. "You think I'll let you get in the car with a stranger after what happened tonight?"

"I'm *fine*." Okay, maybe a *teeny-tiny* part of her was nervous about it, now that he brought it up.

"You think you're fine. But that sliver of doubt you're feelin'? Guys sense that shit." He motioned to the bike. "Get on."

She crossed her arms and lifted her chin, holding her ground just for the point of it.

"*Jesus.*" He set down the helmet and walked over to the steps. When she didn't move, he reached up, grabbing her by the waist, and lifted her off her feet, carrying her to his motorcycle, despite her flailing legs and hollering.

"*Diesel!* Put me down!"

He plopped her onto the bike, ignoring her complaints, and stuck the helmet on her head. He climbed on in front of her, reached behind them with one massive hand, and pushed her forward, so her inner thighs were against his ass. He grabbed her hands, wrapping them around his thick body. "Hold tight."

"This is kidnapping, you know. You're too big to hold on to. I have to cancel the Uber…"

The roar of the engine drowned out her voice. Her pulse skyrocketed, and she clung to him for dear life as he drove out of the lot and onto the main drag. She'd never been on a motorcycle before, and she hadn't believed her girlfriends when they talked about the vibrations being better than foreplay. Not that she had a lot of foreplay experience. After the first year or two, Dennis hadn't bothered with that. She pushed thoughts of that ugly relationship away as they cruised through Peaceful Harbor, taking in the lights illuminating the marina and the scents of the sea whipping around them. The town looked different than it did from within a car. It was even more beautiful. The trees seemed brighter, the air crisper. She felt freer, too. With her chest pressed to Diesel's back, the heat of his body mixing with the warm air caressing her skin, and the delicious rumble and roar of the engine working its way up her core, she could see how it might feel romantic with the right person. The ultimate turn-on, even.

If she hadn't been forced onto the bike.

When Diesel pulled up in front of the house she and Izzy shared, he cut the engine, but her body continued vibrating as he climbed off and reached for her helmet, stopping short, those dark eyes softening the slightest bit as they moved slowly over the length of his bike, lingering on her. His Adam's apple jumped, and those muscles in his jaw bunched again as he removed her helmet and lifted her off the bike. He must have known her legs were wobbly, because he didn't let go. His large hands remained wrapped around her ribs, his thumbs pressed just below her breasts, his fingers on either side of her spine.

Her eyes flicked up, the raw desire staring back at her, turning those confusing feelings into turbulent gusts, whipping and mounting like a violent storm. A flash of something cold and hard to read registered in his eyes, and he released her like he'd been burned.

He scanned the yard before his attention returned to her. "I'll pick you up tomorrow evening for work."

She blinked several times, trying to get her brain to function. "What? No. I can get an Uber."

"Be ready by five." He pushed a hand into the front pocket of his jeans and pulled out several bills, pushing them into her hand. "For tonight's Uber."

What the…? "You don't have to—"

"Get inside so I know you're safe." He climbed onto his bike, his heavy boots rooting him to the pavement.

Too frazzled to argue, she headed up the walk and glanced over her shoulder at the arresting and confusing man watching her as she unlocked the door. She gave a quick, awkward wave and walked inside. Only then did he start his bike, but she heard him idling out front while she washed her face and got ready for bed. It wasn't until she climbed under the covers and turned off her light that she heard him drive away.

Chapter Two

SWEAT DRIPPED DOWN Tracey's temples as she punched the pads her martial arts instructor, Lior Levy, was holding. She'd been studying under the ex–Navy SEAL for a year and a half, and she was mentally and physically stronger for it. But today her thoughts were all over the place, and she was having trouble focusing on the workout. Diesel had messed with her head far more than the jerk at the bar had last night. She'd spent half the night picking apart the looks Diesel had been giving her lately and the other half battling dirty dreams in which he'd *shown* her exactly what those dark looks meant. Her dreams had been so vivid, she could still hear his gruff commands, still feel the heat of his flesh and the weight of his massive body as he drove his hard length into her. She'd woken up sweaty and on the verge of orgasm twice and had been forced to ease the tension herself. When she'd closed her eyes, it was his chiseled face she'd seen and his gruff demands that had pulled her over the edge.

"Come on, Trace. Get your head in the game," Lior encouraged, jarring her from her thoughts. "Explode into each strike."

She felt her cheeks burn and tried to focus, but *right jab, left cross, right hook* warred with a combination of Diesel's gruff commands from her dream—*Suck harder. Take it deeper*—and the memory of his hands around her middle as he'd plucked her off the steps at Whiskey Bro's like she was as light as a butterfly and plunked her down on his bike. He was cold, *brutal*, not at all the kind of guy Tracey imagined herself with, so *why* was he the only man she'd dreamed about for the last few months?

Right jab, left cross, right hook.

Suck harder. So fucking good.

Right jab, left cross, right hook.

Ride me faster.

Tracey's insides clenched with desire. *"Ugh!"* She threw her hands up, trying to walk off her frustration. "I'm sorry, Lior. I need a minute." She grabbed her water bottle, taking a swig as she paced.

Lior set down the pads, watching her stride across the floor. He was in his late thirties with hair shaved nearly to his skin, deep-set gray-blue eyes, and though he was probably only about five foot ten, he had the type of authoritative presence that made him feel much larger. Tracey knew he was scrutinizing her mental state, looking for clues in her behavior, the way he and his wife, Eliani, who was now six months pregnant and no longer teaching, had taught her to.

"What's going on?"

"Nothing really. Work stuff."

"Still having trouble with your big-ass babysitter?"

"Something like that." She'd told Lior about Diesel after Bones and Sarah's wedding, when she'd come in for a lesson and had attacked the heavy bag with a ferociousness she'd never felt before. One of Bones's friends, Dr. Rhys, had been checking Tracey out at the wedding, and she'd sent him a few flirty glances. She hadn't realized Diesel had seen them. When Diesel had strode across the dance floor toward her, his expression different than it was at work, a little softer, appreciative of her dress, maybe, she'd thought he might actually try to have a conversation with her or ask her to have a drink with him. But the closer he'd come, the darker his stare had turned, and then he'd simply inserted himself between Tracey and the handsome doctor, staring the poor guy down. Before Tracey could say anything, Izzy had snapped, *Stop cockblocking Tracey and ask her to dance already.* Diesel hadn't taken his threatening stare off the doctor as he'd said, *I don't dance.* When Izzy had pointed out that he'd danced with Kennedy, the man who answered to no one had grunted and had remained an immovable wall between Tracey and the rest of the male species.

Lior crossed his arms. "Want to talk about it?"

"No. I want to beat the hell out of someone." *And I want to show Diesel that he doesn't control any part of me.*

A glimmer of *fight* shone in Lior's eyes. "Now we're talking. That's why you ought to consider helping me train while Eliani is off the floor."

Eliani was the reason Tracey had chosen their program. She was from Israel and had been a victim of domestic abuse prior to coming to the United States and meeting Lior. She understood what Tracey had gone through and had helped her bridge the gap from fearful to empowered. Lior had been nudging Tracey toward becoming a trainer ever since Eliani had stopped teaching, but Tracey wasn't sure she was ready.

"You've got what it takes to help a lot of people, Tracey."

She set down her water bottle, too edgy to think straight. "Not in this mood I don't."

"Fair enough. Then let's practice some takedowns."

Tracey spent the next hour unleashing her frustrations on the man who had taught her that her body, though small, was a weapon, not a battering ram. With every strike, every knee and kick, she shattered those ridiculous dirty dreams, regaining her resolve to show Diesel Black exactly where she stood.

Later that afternoon, she took her time picking out the perfect outfit to solidify her plan, settling on a red-and-black plaid miniskirt, a black Whiskey Bro's T-shirt with capped sleeves, and her favorite black chunky lace-up boots, which Izzy had given her last Christmas. She added the leather bracelet she'd splurged on at the spring festival and sat down on the edge of her bed to make the phone call she'd been putting off all day.

Tracey's stomach knotted as she navigated to Red's contact information. Once she made the call, everything between her and Diesel would change. She was stepping out from beneath his protective wings. She tried to imagine a world in which he *wasn't* always looming over her. She knew she could handle herself, but there was no denying the nervousness moving through her. She drew upon what Lior had taught her, that strength came from within. If she didn't believe in herself, how could anyone else?

Gathering her courage like a cloak, she made the call.

"Hi, Tracey. How are you, sweetheart?"

Red's warm greeting brought a pang of guilt. Red had become the mother Tracey had missed so desperately, doling out hugs and advice, making sure she knew her door was open anytime, day or night, and always—*always*—having Tracey's back, which was more than Tracey could say for her own mother. Although that wasn't a fair assessment. If Tracey had learned anything in the past few years, it was that she was responsible for her own decisions. She knew exactly what she'd been giving up when she'd walked out of her mother's house six years ago.

She pushed those thoughts away, focusing on the conversation ahead. She knew the Dark Knights watched out for everyone, and she hoped Red wouldn't take what she had to say the wrong way. "I'm well, thanks. How are you?"

"Doin' great, hon. Bear and Crystal were here with Axel, and we had a wonderful visit." Bear and his wife, Crystal, had named their baby boy after Biggs's youngest brother, Bear's late uncle and mentor, Axel. "I still can't believe he's a year old already. It's funny how the little ones are getting older, but I just stay thirty-five forever." Red laughed. She was a young Sharon Osborne lookalike, from her short red hair to her penchant for wearing black, and she had the energy of a woman half her age. She babysat all her grandchildren—biological and surrogate, like Hail, Kennedy, and Kennedy's younger brother, Lincoln.

"I'm sorry to bother you, but do you have a minute?"

"Darlin', I always have time for you. What's going on?"

Tracey ran her finger along the pattern on her skirt, choosing her words carefully. "I hope you know I'm grateful for everything your family has done for me and how much I *love* my job."

"I do, honey."

"Okay. Good." She exhaled with relief. "Because I need to talk to you about Diesel."

"Go on," Red said carefully.

"Red, I appreciate you asking him to watch out for me when I first started working at the bar. I needed that support. But I'm stronger now. I can handle myself."

"I know you can. I have total faith in you."

"Thank you. I do, too, and that's a really good feeling. But Diesel's breathing down my neck and scaring off customers. Well, not scaring them off from being at the bar, but from sitting at my tables. I asked him to back off, but he said I had to take it up with you. Would you mind telling him that I can handle myself? I have to be allowed to stand up to customers or flirt with them. That's how we make tips—you know that—and I would *never* cross any lines."

"Tracey, I told him that months ago. Whatever he's doing now has nothing to do with me."

"But..." Tracey was at a loss for words. Had she misunderstood what Diesel had said? He was pretty clear about it being a directive from Red. *"Really?"*

"Yes. Now, keep in mind, when Diesel took over for Bullet, it was for his brawn, not just his bartending abilities. He helps keep riffraff out of the bar. Could that be what you're feeling?"

"Maybe. We had an incident yesterday, so that kind of makes sense."

"Dixie went through the same thing with Bullet for a long time. And you *know* she can handle herself. She's a fire-breathing dragon when she wants to be. But, honey, the men in our world are protectors through and through. They're as fierce as they come, and backing off is not easy for them. *Especially* when they care about you. If you'd like, I'll speak with Diesel again."

"No, it's okay. Maybe you're right, and he's just doing his job and being who he is. I'll just keep letting him know that I can handle it. Hopefully we'll find a middle ground. I'm sorry to have bothered you with this."

"You are never a bother, honey. The good news is you won't have to worry about Diesel for long. He came by to see Biggs this morning. He's leaving right after the holidays."

The knots in her stomach tightened. "Leaving? To go where?"

"Wherever the wind takes him. We're lucky he's stuck around this long. We usually don't get to see him for more than a few weeks at most, and some years not even that long." Red sighed. "I've enjoyed having our big, broody boy around. But this is what you want, right? For Diesel to get out of your hair?"

"Uh-huh," Tracey said halfheartedly, feeling oddly like her legs had been kicked out from under her. He was leaving. That was good, right? So why did she feel like she needed to hold on tight to the one man who made her crazy?

DIESEL CLIMBED OFF his bike in front of the cute house where Tracey lived. A picture window overlooked a small garden, and above that, a single window was centered in the gable. Since when did he think in terms of *cute*? That chick had been fucking with his head since she'd first walked into the bar, those doe eyes pleading for safety. He'd felt it then, the unstoppable pull in his gut to watch over her, and that metal-to-magnet feeling had only intensified since. He could have killed that man who'd grabbed her last night. That was when he'd known his time in Peaceful Harbor needed to end.

He climbed the steps to the minuscule covered porch, pushing aside the unease that had been gnawing at him since he'd spoken to Biggs that morning, and knocked on the door.

The door swung open, and holy hell, Tracey stood before him looking like a sex kitten in a fuck-me plaid miniskirt and thick-soled black boots that made her look edgy and rebellious. Her hot little body taunted him as much as the challenging look in her eyes.

Fighting the urge to back her up against the wall and fuck that smirk off her face, he gritted out, "You gonna change?"

"Nope. I'm all set." She stepped onto the porch, her ass brushing against him as she turned to pull the door closed, stirring the monster in his jeans. She planted her hands on her hips, eyes narrowing. "I talked to Red."

"You got a point?"

"I *know* she already told you to back off."

He probably shouldn't take pleasure from her scowl, but when she got fiery like that, cheeks pink, eyes shooting fire, it only made him want to get up close and personal with those flames, feel them lick their way up his body. "Just keeping trouble out of the bar. You do your job, I'll do mine."

"You." She poked his chest as she'd done last night. "Are." *Poke.* "A." *Poke.* "Pain." *Poke.* "In." *Poke.* "My." *Poke*—

He captured her hand beneath his, holding it against his chest, and she gasped. "You want to touch me, baby girl? I prefer it much lower."

She yanked her hand away. "You're so…*God.* I don't want any part of your disgusting revolving bedroom door, *Unleaded.*"

"Your loss."

Heat and frustration simmered in her eyes.

"You can't ride on my bike in *that.*"

"Watch me." She flashed a victorious grin and pushed past him.

That tiny flick of a woman was going to be the death of him.

DIESEL SLID TWO drinks across the bar to a busty brunette and a twiggy blond. "Twelve even."

"Would you mind running a tab for us?" The brunette tilted her head with a flirtatious smile. "I have a feeling we'll be here for a while."

He gave a curt nod, making a mental note to watch their consumption so he didn't have to get their drunk asses home at the end of the night. There were a few men and women on that list, as there were most weekend nights. The bar had been too busy to do much in the way of keeping obnoxious guys away from Tracey's tables, but Diesel had kept a close eye on her, despite her annoyed sneers.

"Thanks. You're sweet," the brunette said playfully, touching his hand. "See, Annie? I told you he wasn't mean."

Diesel pulled his hand away. He didn't like to be touched unless *he* initiated it, and even then it was always on *his* terms—how, when, and where he allowed it.

Moon laughed, shaking his head as he served another customer.

Diesel was not in the mood for bullshit, and he had no interest in fucking the two women who had practically offered themselves up on a silver platter to every man who had looked their way tonight. He looked past them at Tracey prancing around in that damned miniskirt with a newfound air of confidence that rivaled Dixie's. But she *wasn't* Dixie. She didn't carry a rough and craggy chip on her shoulder from which to draw strength and ire, hardened from years of fighting to be heard over three tough older brothers. Tracey's chip was newly plucked from the ground, scuffed and scarred for sure, but she'd only just found the strength to put it on her shoulder, and she had yet to test it further than getting into a verbal scuffle with Diesel. He hadn't been surprised she'd spoken to Red. That newly plucked chip had definitely fueled the fire in that pretty little chick's belly. It was a good thing he was on his way out, because this new good-girl-gone-bad vibe she was rocking was damn hard to resist. Hell, she was hard to resist anyway, like a pristine, unrideable road still wet from the pour, glistening in the sunlight.

Fuck.

He needed to get laid before he did something stupid, like plowing through the barriers he'd erected to ride that sweet little piece. But when it came to Tracey Kline, riding and claiming would be one and the same, and he wasn't about to get tangled up in that barbed wire.

As if Tracey heard his thoughts, she glanced over her shoulder, and their eyes collided with the same cock-tempting heat that had been thrumming between them for far too long. He clenched his jaw against the desire working its way deep. In a few months, she'd be nothing but a memory.

She lifted her chin defiantly and strode up to Biggs Whiskey as he came through the front door, cane in hand.

A stroke had stolen Biggs's ability to ride motorcycles years ago, rendering his left side weak, his left hand clumsy, and his speech a little hard to understand. His grandfather had founded the Dark Knights, and Biggs was a biker to the core, from his black leather vest with Dark Knights patches to his leather boots and every tattooed inch of leathery skin in between.

Diesel couldn't hear what Tracey was saying, but Biggs stroked his scraggly white beard, his wise eyes shifting toward

Diesel. Diesel lifted his chin in acknowledgment, trying to read Biggs's expression, but he wasn't giving anything away. Not one for picking apart situations, Diesel went back to serving customers.

A few minutes later Biggs sidled up to the bar. All the stools were taken. Diesel looked at Crow, a fellow Dark Knight sitting in front of him, and motioned for him to give his seat to Biggs. Crow climbed down and headed across the room toward the guys who were playing darts.

Diesel wiped down the bar as Biggs climbed onto the stool. "What'll it be, old man?"

"A Guinness and some conversation." Biggs nodded hello to Moon, where he was serving customers at the other end of the bar.

Diesel scoffed and filled a glass. Biggs knew he wasn't a talker, but Diesel figured he was there to talk about his leaving town. He set the glass in front of him and leaned his hands on the bar, holding Biggs's gaze.

"I caught wind of some trouble here last night," Biggs said in his slow drawl.

"I handled it."

He took a drink. "And you handled it *well*, from what I heard."

Diesel glanced at Tracey, who was using the register by the office, wondering if she'd said something about the incident.

"She didn't say nothin'." Biggs took another drink, and the right side of his beard lifted with a knowing grin. "At least not about *that*. How'd she handle it? Was she shaken up?"

"She gave me shit for stepping in."

Biggs chuckled. "She's a tough little gal, and she's come a hell of a long way. Gotta give her that."

Diesel didn't react. He'd learned long ago that most reactions were wasted energy.

Biggs looked around the bar. "You helped get her there, son. We all did in our own way, but you've played the biggest part here at work. Even if you scared the shit out of her for the first few months, it was your presence, your unspoken promise to keep her safe, that allowed her to grow into the confident woman she's become."

Diesel shoved that praise down deep. He wasn't a man who needed praise to feel good about himself, but Biggs didn't dole it out often or lightly, and because of that, his words carried extra weight.

"By taking over for Bullet and taking on the drive-bys at the women's shelter for the club, you've given my family a chance to grow, too." The Dark Knights watched over the women's shelter, and they drove by at various times to show their presence, so gangs, drug dealers, and other troublesome folks would know not to mess with the ladies at the shelter. Diesel coordinated those efforts and took his turn driving by a few times each month. "We'll miss you when you're gone, son, but I know what it's like to crave the open road. I was never a lone rider, like you. I've always needed the anchor of family. Tiny used to ride with me, and when Axel got old enough, he came, too."

Biggs was the oldest of his siblings, followed by his brother Tiny, sister Reba, and his youngest brother, Axel, who passed away a few months before Diesel's mother. Diesel had never met Axel, and he'd met Reba only a handful of times, when he was visiting the Bayside chapter of the Dark Knights in Cape Cod, which was run by her husband and brother-in-law. But he had great respect for Tiny, one of the founders of the Hope

Ridge, Colorado, chapter of the Dark Knights. Tiny ran Redemption Ranch, a horse rescue that also gave troubled souls a second chance. They hired ex-cons, recovering addicts, and people with social and emotional issues, all of whom worked on the ranch as part of their therapy program, while undergoing traditional therapy from psychologists on the ranch like Tiny's wife, Wynnie, and a host of other medical professionals, mostly composed of Dark Knights and their family members.

Diesel had gone to school with Tiny and Wynnie's kids and had worked as a ranch hand while he was growing up. Diesel hadn't been a troublesome kid, but any time he'd leaned the wrong way, Tiny had reined him in and had taught him how to channel his energies in the right direction. Diesel owed Tiny a lot. He was the reason Diesel had become a Dark Knight, and he'd set Diesel on the right path, connecting him with the right people, to become a bounty hunter, which enabled him to live the nomad lifestyle he enjoyed.

"Then Red became my back warmer." Biggs's eyes filled with the warmth they always did when he talked about family. "I always thought I was strong, but a man who can go his whole life without giving in to the love of a good woman is a stronger man than me. Axel was a lot like you. He never could settle down with one woman. Lord knows plenty of women tried, but he battled demons. He lost his first love when they were out on a ride. Someone ran a red light, and she was thrown. Died on impact." Biggs shook his head, pain rising in his eyes. "We don't talk about that much. The accident wasn't Axel's fault, but he was never the same after it. Drinking, getting into fights. Spent years tryin' to outrun the pain."

"Sorry to hear that." Diesel was cut from that same cloth. He'd spent most of his life trying to outrun pain, too.

"That was a long time ago, and he's at peace now." Biggs finished his beer and pushed to his feet. "I'm going to miss you when you're gone, son. Are you heading to Colorado to see the boys?"

"Yeah. I told Tiny I'd come see them first, check on the cabin, touch base before taking off again." He'd kept the cabin where he'd lived with his mother and stayed there when he returned to Colorado.

"I'm sure he'll be glad to see you. Well, son, at least we'll have the holidays with you. You know you've always got a place under our roof."

Diesel nodded curtly, trying to ignore the thickening in his throat that often accompanied his talks with Biggs. "Thank you, sir."

"*Sir* my ass. Now get back to work." With a wink, he headed across the room, slowing to drop a kiss on the top of Tracey's head, then talking with Dixie for a few minutes. His and Red's kindness reminded Diesel of his mother. She'd had a heart of gold, too, and enough love to blanket the state. Even all these years later, the pain of losing her still cut like a knife. But Diesel had become an expert at ignoring that pain. He pushed it down deep, then beat the fucker into submission as Tracey approached the bar, eyeing Moon, who was busy serving a group of guys.

With a reluctant sigh, she headed over to Diesel, tilted her too-fucking-pretty face up at him, and her eyes went soft. Christ, that was sexy.

"You okay, there, Unleaded? You look like you want to kill someone."

He didn't respond, as he didn't to most nonsensical questions that people didn't want real answers to.

Tracey went up on her toes and leaned across the bar, beckoning him closer with a crook of her index finger, giving him an eyeful of cleavage as he leaned in. When they were nose to nose, her eyes darkened, the air between them sizzling and crackling. She probably thought he didn't notice the slight widening of her eyes, as if the heat shocked her every time it ignited, or the way her eyes then narrowed with determination. This sweet little miss had something to prove, and *man*, he wanted to tear her clothes off with his teeth and let her use his body to make her point.

She whispered, "Didn't your mama ever teach you that you attract more bees with honey?"

She was going to keep testing his resolve, throwing that sexy-as-sin innocence and newfound bravado his way, if he didn't put a stop to it. He had to nip this in the bud. "Why would I want bees, when I like lappin' honey?" He threw in a lewd tongue gesture for good measure.

"*Ugh.*" She pushed away from the bar with a look of disgust.

This was too much fun. He couldn't resist pushing her buttons. "Jealous, baby girl?"

"In your dreams. You're a *pig*. I can't believe you get any women at all."

"Oh yeah, sparky. Jealousy looks mighty good on you."

She rolled her eyes. "Give me a pitcher of Coors and two Jack and Cokes."

When she stalked off with the order, Moon sidled up to him. "You'd better stop that shit, D. You two are liable to make this whole place go up in flames."

Yeah, he was pretty well fucked. "You know what they say. It's best to go out in a blaze of glory."

Chapter Three

TRACEY HUSTLED FROM one table to the next, taking drink orders, chatting with customers, and raking in tips. She could hardly believe Diesel was actually lightening up with his overzealous watchdog behavior, but she wasn't a fan of his raunchy tongue gesture. *Geez.* What made him go from grunting to *that*?

She didn't have time to overthink it as Bones walked into the bar with Dr. Rhys, and they sat at one of her tables. This must be her lucky day. Like all the Whiskeys, Bones was tall, dark, and built for a fight, though he was leaner and had fewer tattoos than his brothers. He was also as kind as the day was long. Dr. Rhys possessed a different type of good looks. The kind that made her stomach nervous and fluttery as she headed over to them. He was tall, too, with short dark hair and eyes that exuded warmth and compassion with an underlying seductiveness that belonged on the big screen.

Sure, she'd cast a few flirtatious smiles his way at the wedding reception before her broody bodyguard had stepped between them, but now that she was standing a foot away from him, his boyish smile aimed directly at her, she had trouble remembering her own name.

"Hi, Tracey." Dr. Rhys's smile widened. "You look beautiful tonight. How are you?"

Beautiful? She couldn't remember the last time a guy had called her that. If one ever had. "Good. Fine. Thanks. You, Dr. Rhys?" *Oh my gosh. Ramble much?*

"Please, call me Damon, Tracey," he said charmingly. "I delivered a healthy baby girl this afternoon, I'm having a drink with a good friend, and I get to see you again. I'd say I'm doing great."

Her cheeks burned, and she was sure she was grinning like a fool. In an effort to stop the blush from spreading, she turned her attention to Bones. "And how are you, Bones? How're Sarah and the kids?" Bones had adopted Sarah's three children from a previous relationship; Bradley, who was five, Lila, who was almost three, and their youngest, Maggie Rose, who was a year and a half.

"Everyone's great. Sarah's with Penny right now, trying to figure out how to do her hair for the wedding." Sarah and Josie's older brother, Scott, had just proposed to Finlay's younger sister, Penny, who was three and a half months pregnant. They were having an intimate wedding in the spring after the baby was born.

Tracey waved a hand. "Penny will look gorgeous no matter what she does with her hair."

"Another wedding?" A glimmer of interest shone in Damon's eyes. "I'm going to have to get an invitation to that one, so I can dance with you."

Oh boy.

Flustered but enjoying his flirtation, Tracey didn't know how to respond, so she took a stab at humor. "I can't give out invitations to someone else's wedding, but I can get you a drink. What would you like?"

Amusement rose in Damon's eyes. "I'll have a whiskey, neat, please."

"That sounds good to me," Bones agreed. "I'll have the same."

"Okay. I'll be right back with your drinks." She turned to head up to the bar, and her eyes caught on Diesel's brooding stare, sending those flutters into a full-on tsunami.

Why couldn't her panties get in a twist for the charming, well-mannered doctor instead of the dirty-talking, rough-necked biker? Not that she cared about a man's job, but *come on*.

She made a beeline for Moon and spent the rest of the evening trying to avoid Diesel's stormy, all-too-appealing eyes. After closing for the night, she and Dixie cleaned up, and she went to get a trash bag from the storage room. When she came out, she plowed right into Dixie. "Sorry."

"It's okay. You've been all over the place tonight. I was just going to do that," Dixie said.

"I've got it. Go home. I've got to wait for Diesel anyway."

"Oh? You're *waiting* for Diesel?"

Tracey rolled her eyes. "Not like that." She went to gather the trash with Dixie on her heels.

"See you next week, ladies!" Moon waved from the other side of the room.

"Bye," Tracey and Dixie said in unison.

"Spill, girl," Dixie said as Tracey pushed through the ladies' room door, following her in.

"It's nothing. You know my car is in the shop. He insisted on driving me to work, so he's driving me home."

Dixie let out a little squeal. "I sense a little *boom chick a wow*

wow."

Tracey gave her a deadpan look. "You have *lost* your mind, woman. Diesel and I are oil and water, and he's leaving town after the holidays."

"Well, that makes him even more attractive. You haven't been with a guy since you left Dennis. You need some practice."

"I need practice flirting, too. Dr. Rhys—Damon—was flirting with me. At least I think he was, and I rambled like an idiot. How about you help me with that instead?"

"That man is *hot.* You definitely need to drink that tall glass of champagne, but he's probably a slow lover, like all finesse and shit." Dixie flipped her hair over her shoulder and leaned against the counter.

"You say that like it's a bad thing."

Dixie arched a brow. "Have you ever been taken against a wall in a fit of passion? Been eaten out in an elevator? Had sex in a meadow?"

"Um...?" She shook her head. *Holy crap.* "In an elevator? They have cameras, you know."

"Yeah, that's half the fun. Finesse is beautiful and sensual, but if you haven't been fucked senseless, you are missing out. You should totally take this opportunity to have a little no-strings-attached fun with Diesel and hone your sexy skills."

"I'm not like you. I have no sexy skills." She giggled, but her mind tiptoed into dangerous territory, thinking about her dream and Diesel in all his naked glory. She knew *what* to do with a guy, even if she hadn't enjoyed it in the past as much as she wished she had. But what Dixie described was a world away from what she saw herself doing.

"I'm sure he won't mind showing you the ropes."

"Diesel is a total womanizer, and he can't even hold a normal conversation. Can you imagine the pillow talk with that man? Nothing but grunts and growls."

"Hey, grunts and growls are hot in the bedroom. But I think your pillow talk would go more like this." She thrust her hips, speaking breathily. *"Yes! Harder. More. Oh, oh...Yesss!"*

Tracey laughed as she gathered the trash. "You're a mess. Go home and have your way with Jace."

"Okay, but at least *consider* the possibility."

Tracey rolled her eyes. "Sure."

"You're a sucky liar." Dixie strutted out of the bathroom.

Tracey finished cleaning up the bathroom and went to get the trash from behind the bar, passing Diesel on his way to the kitchen with a tray of glasses.

"Put the bag by the back door. I'll take it out."

"You're busy. I've got it." She had to hand it to him. For as little as he talked, at the end of the night, he never failed to offer to help.

He gave her a narrow-eyed look, like he was going to argue with her, the way he usually did when she took the trash out, but then he shook his head and pushed through the kitchen doors.

Thank God for little favors. She wasn't in the mood to argue.

After collecting the trash, she headed for the back door to put it in the dumpster. As she stepped into the darkness the oppressive humidity made the air feel sticky. The dull bulb by the back door of the bar lit her way as she crossed the gravel lot toward the dumpster. Her attention fell on Diesel's old jacked-up truck parked out front of the Dark Knights' clubhouse behind the bar, a rough-looking two-story wooden building with blacked-out windows. He stayed in one of the rooms upstairs. She'd heard stories about bikers sharing women and doing all sorts of things she didn't want to think about. She also knew the Dark Knights were as loyal and as fierce as they came, but they didn't share their women. At least the men she knew well—the Whiskeys, Jed Moon, Jace Stone, and the others she'd met through the bar—didn't. Who knew what Diesel was like?

She reached up to open the dumpster and heard something to her right. She jerked her head in that direction, half expecting Diesel to give her crap about taking the trash out, but she didn't see anything and searched the shadows for movement.

"Thought there was nothing between you and Bigfoot."

Tracey whipped around at the chilling voice, coming face-to-face with the creepy guy in the denim jacket who had come to the bar last night. She dropped the trash bag. The hair on the back of her neck prickled as he stepped closer, and she stepped back, panic spreading like wildfire through her chest. Her back hit another man, and she gasped, turning as her brain kicked into gear. She drove her elbow into his gut. He keeled forward, cursing. She grabbed his shoulders, driving her knee into his groin, and bolted for the door. But they were too fast. The guy in the jacket grabbed her arm and threw her against the dumpster. Her face smacked against metal, and she saw stars, crying out as she collapsed to the ground. Pain seared through her body, and she tried to crawl away, but they were on her in seconds, dragging her backward, pulling her to her feet. One guy slammed her against the dumpster again, sharp metal digging into her back. The other guy tore at her shirt, groping her as she flailed and kicked, screaming and cursing. Someone hit her across the face, and she cried out again, fury surging inside her. She jerked her arm free, clawing at one guy's eyes. He grabbed her by the hair, yanking her back so hard she shrieked, pain searing down her back as he seethed, "You little bitch. I was gonna play nice last night. Now you'll play by my rules."

"Fuck you." She spat in his face, unwilling to go down without a fight.

He cocked his arm, and suddenly he was torn from her and thrown backward through the air, landing with a *thud* in the darkness. Fear and confusion rocked through Tracey as Diesel's face came into focus, cold black eyes locked on the other man, who was holding her arm so tight her fingers were numb. Seconds passed in a blur of animalistic noises as Diesel's fists flew, and the guy stumbled, doubling over. Diesel nailed him with an uppercut, sending the asshole flying backward. Diesel stayed on him, fists flying. The other guy came out of the shadows, the blade of a knife catching the light.

"Diesel!" Tracey shouted, backing up as Diesel's fist connected with the first guy's jaw, sending him careening to the pavement.

Diesel spun around, hulking toward the armed man who was waving the knife with a sinister expression. In one swift move, Diesel grabbed his wrist, turning his massive back to the armed man's chest, and flipped him over his shoulder. The knife skittered across the pavement, and Diesel was on him in the space of a second, landing blow after blow, until the man on the ground lay limp as a rag doll.

Diesel pushed to his feet, arms arcing out from his body, chest heaving, dark eyes scanning the pavement. He swept Tracey into his arms, his heart thundering as furiously as hers. She clung to him as he one-handedly pulled out his phone, eyes locked on those lifeless men as he put the phone to his ear, his voice as cold and dire as death itself. *"Booker.* Two guys assaulted Tracey. Back lot at Whiskey Bro's. Come get 'em before I put them six feet under."

He pocketed his phone, his rough hand brushing something wet from her face.

Clarity came in jagged, painful bursts, the blur of panic giving way to a mix of fear, anger, and embarrassment as Diesel's voice filtered in. "Bleeding...get you cleaned up..."

The men lying motionless in the shadows came into focus, anger clawing its way to the surface, until Tracey felt like she was going to explode. She pushed out of Diesel's arms, storming over to one of the men in a fit of rage, hands fisted. She kicked the guy wearing the denim jacket in the ribs. "Asshole!" *Kick.* "Don't you *ever*"—*kick*—"come near me again!" Gulping air into her lungs, she stalked to the other guy, unleashing more fury. "Motherfucker!" *Kick!* "I am *not* your victim!" *Kick.* "I hate you!" *Kick.*

Diesel grabbed her arm, but she continued kicking and screaming. He tugged her into his arms again, holding her tight and safe, but she couldn't stop the anger from spewing out. "I *hate* them! I know how to fight! I should have been able to fight them off!" Sirens blared in the distance, and she was vaguely aware of Diesel's phone ringing, but she was bleary-eyed and shaking, years of anger erupting from someplace deep inside her. She didn't even know what she was shouting, but she couldn't stop the hatred from coming out. Furious tears spilled down her cheeks.

Two police cars flew into the lot, followed by an ambulance, and within seconds Moon was running across the field that separated the bar from his property, shouting to Diesel, who held Tracey in a vise grip. A motorcycle roared into the lot, followed by Biggs's car. Bullet flew off the bike, running toward

them, fists at the ready. It took a minute for Tracey to process
why they were there. Then she remembered Booker was not just
a cop, but he was also a Dark Knight, and any time police were
called to the bar, he notified Bullet and Biggs.

Suddenly there were people everywhere, lights flashing, and
Diesel was leading her inside. He got her a shirt from behind
the bar, and then time became a blur of relaying what had
happened to the police as she filed a report, insisting she was
okay and didn't need to go to the hospital. She was furious with
herself for not being able to fend off those men, and she was
even angrier at her attackers for seeing her as someone they
could attack. She struggled against tears, refusing to let any more
fall, and looked at Diesel's hard features. How many times had
she asked him to back off? If he hadn't been there...

Diesel stuck to her like glue, even as the EMT checked her
out, cleaning up the gash on her forehead and tending to her
other cuts and abrasions. Every time she flinched, Diesel
growled, stopping the EMT with a dark stare until Tracey said,
"I'm fine. Just let him finish." But when Diesel looked at her,
those cold eyes changed to tortured. That was the only way to
explain what she saw in them. It was as if he felt her pain as his
own, and she didn't know what to make of that.

She felt like she'd been run over by a truck. Policemen
milled around, Bullet and Moon were on their phones, and
Diesel looked like he was going to murder someone. His
knuckles were red, two of them bloody, but he wouldn't let the
EMTs clean them up. Biggs's expression told her he was right
there with Diesel. When Bullet's brothers, Bones and Bear,
showed up, Tracey knew that soon the rest of the Dark Knights
would be there, too. She might not be a Dark Knight, but she
was part of that family. She gripped Diesel's hand. "I don't need

a cavalry. Please take me home."

"Why don't you come home with me, darlin'?" Biggs suggested. "Let Red and me take care of you tonight."

"Thank you, but I'm okay. I just want to go home."

"I've got her." Diesel left no room for negotiation.

Bones and Moon looked over, and Bones said, "Tracey, if you're going home, Moon and I will go take care of our kids so Sarah and Josie can be with you tonight. They're worried sick."

Tracey's heart swelled, but all she wanted to do was get cleaned up and climb into bed. "Thanks, you guys, but I really just want to be alone and try to get some sleep. Can you let them know I'm okay and I'll talk to them tomorrow?"

"Sure," Bones said. "I'm really sorry this happened to you, Tracey."

Diesel looked at them, then at Bullet and Bear, a round of nods passing between them, as if they'd communicated telepathically. There was a flurry of activity as more Dark Knights came through the door, and Bullet went to get Diesel's truck for him from the lot by the clubhouse.

Diesel drove Tracey home with Bullet, Bones, Bear, and Moon following on their bikes. Within minutes, at least a dozen other motorcycles had joined them. She'd heard about the Dark Knights doing that kind of thing when there was trouble, but she'd never seen it. Tracey had been alone for so long, facing evil at the hands of her ex, being the one they were watching out for brought waves of unexpected emotions. She struggled to hold them back as Diesel helped her out of his truck, keeping one arm protectively around her as the other men parked in front of her house.

"Are they staying?"

He nodded.

"Why?"

"Sending a message. In case those bastards have friends."

Panic gripped her. "You think they know where I live?"

"Let's get you inside."

"*Diesel.* Do you think they followed us home last night? Wouldn't we have noticed?"

"I would have noticed. But they could've singled you out before last night. We're not taking any chances."

She looked around, imagining awful men hiding in the bushes. Thinking back to last night, she said, "There was a third guy with them last night. Remember?"

"I'm tracking him down."

"How? You haven't left my side."

The muscles in his jaw bunched. He didn't respond as he guided her up the walkway.

Bullet fell into step beside them. "You okay, Trace?"

She nodded, although she was holding herself together with Scotch tape.

Diesel took her keys and opened the door. "Stay here."

Bullet stayed with her on the porch as Diesel checked out the house. It was like they had been doing this type of thing forever, and she was pretty sure they had.

"Do you think they're going to send someone after me? Diesel said he's tracking down their friend from last night, but he's been with me this whole time. Did he say that just to make me feel better?" Granted, she'd been too rattled to pay attention to Diesel's conversations with Booker, Biggs, Bullet, and the rest of them, but still. Tracking someone down seemed like a big job when you have no clue who that someone was.

Bullet shook his head. "Diesel doesn't waste his breath. He gave directives; the brotherhood is carrying them out."

"You sound like the mafia."

Diesel appeared in the doorway and nodded to Bullet as he came to Tracey's side.

Bullet turned to walk away, and Tracey touched his hand, stopping him. "Thank you. Please tell the others I appreciate their help. I feel bad keeping you guys from your families."

"You are our family," Bullet said, and headed down the walk.

Those emotions she'd been holding back lodged in her throat as she and Diesel went inside. He locked the door behind them, taking up the entire entranceway, making the house seem even smaller. Tracey didn't know what to do with herself as he followed her into the living room, and she noticed he'd closed all the curtains. She thought she'd feel safer there, but after what Diesel had said about those guys possibly watching her before last night, with the curtains drawn like she was in a safe house, she felt like a *victim*, and she hated that feeling.

"You don't have to stay. With all those guys out there, I'll be fine." As soon as the words left her lips, she wanted to take them back. The second she'd seen him in the darkness, she'd known those men couldn't hurt her anymore. She'd never felt safer than she had in his arms, but that brought more confusing feelings, and it pissed her off that she'd needed saving at all.

He crossed his arms, stepping closer. "I'm not going anywhere, baby girl."

Her pulse quickened. She was riveted in place, held captive by the storm of emotions whipping between them. All that energy uncapped the fear, confusion, and anger she'd been holding back, and it bubbled up to the surface, threatening to tumble past the painful lump in her throat. She couldn't let him see her fall apart and choked out, "I'm gonna shower."

She hurried down the hall on trembling legs, making a beeline through her bedroom, into the bathroom. She turned on the shower and angrily, shakily struggled to tug off her boots and socks and strip off her clothes. She wanted to burn those clothes, to get as far away from what had happened as she possibly could.

Catching a glimpse of herself in the mirror, tears welled in her eyes. A butterfly bandage stuck out from under her bangs, covering the gash over her left brow. She had scrapes on her cheeks, bruises on her arms, and she was sure there were some on her back and hips, too. But it was the fear in her eyes that pummeled her, too reminiscent of the weak girl she used to be. The person she vowed never to be again. She was *not* weak. She was *not* helpless.

Anger roared inside her as she stepped into the shower, trembling so badly her teeth chattered. The warm water stung the cuts and wounds peppering her arms, back, and legs. Fear and pain swamped her. She crossed her arms over her chest, willing herself to be strong. She closed her eyes, memories of the attack slamming into her, drawing the tears she'd been holding back. She could still feel their hands on her flesh, still hear their voices cutting through the night. Tears fell like rivers as she poured bodywash onto a washcloth and tried to scrub the memories away. She scrubbed her arms hard despite the stinging and the pain, sobs escaping as she tried to scrape the feel of her attackers off her flesh. The pain was immense, but the heartache of feeling like in one night those men had obliterated all the progress she'd made was even more devastating. Anguished cries tore from her lungs, and her legs gave out. She crumpled to the shower floor and tucked her knees to her chest, rocking as the water rained down on her and giving in to the pain, the anger, and the grief of a night she hadn't seen coming.

DIESEL PACED THE living room, emotions raging through him as he waited for Tracey to finish her shower. He never should have let her take the trash out. What if he hadn't heard her scream? What if he'd been a second later? *Fuck.* He couldn't go there.

He checked the time. She'd been in the shower for twenty-five minutes. That was too damn long. He went down the hall to check on her and called through the open bedroom door, *"Tracey?"* Had he ever called her by her name before? He stepped into the room. The bathroom door was open, and he heard the shower running. His chest constricted at the sound of Tracey sobbing. His hands fisted by his sides as he stepped closer, standing outside the door with his back to the bathroom. "Trace?"

Her sobbing continued.

Fuck.

The water had to be cold by now. There was no steam, no warmth. He went into the bathroom, stepping over the pile of clothes and shoes on the floor, and grabbed a towel. "Tracey, I'm going to turn the water off."

Her sobs came from down low, and he realized she was sitting on the shower floor. Christ, that killed him. Keeping his eyes trained high, he reached behind the curtain and turned off the water, then pushed a towel through to her. "Can you wrap this around yourself, baby girl?"

She took the towel, and he heard her pushing to her feet,

her sobs intermixed with painful winces. He wanted to kill those fuckers. When the EMT was checking her over, Diesel had seen cuts on her back and legs and bruises blooming all over her pale skin. He looked around the bathroom for clean clothes, but she must not have brought any in, so he tugged off his shirt and handed it through the curtain. "Put this on."

A few seconds later she pulled open the curtain. She was wearing his shirt, which hung to her knees, and the towel was on the floor by her feet. Her face was bruised and scraped, makeup smeared beneath her eyes, running down her cheeks, and she looked so fucking sad, it killed him. He grabbed another towel and wet the corner of it to clean her up. Her lower lip trembled, fresh tears spilling down over his fingers as he wiped off her makeup.

"I can fight," she said shakily.

"I know you can." He knew she spent time at a gym and took one-on-one martial arts classes with an ex–Navy SEAL, and he also knew how useless that training was if not practiced at a level that mirrored real life.

"I hesitated." Her voice cracked, more tears falling, but her underlying anger came through. "I should've—"

"*Stop.*" He tipped her chin up. "You are *not* going to beat yourself up because two assholes got the upper hand." He dropped the towel to the shower floor and lifted her into his arms as gently as he could, which apparently wasn't gently enough because she winced, which cut him to his core as he carried her into the bedroom.

He lowered himself to the edge of the bed with Tracey on his lap and brushed her hair away from her face. "Listen. Anyone would have hesitated." He wiped her tears with the pad of his thumb. "They're *done*, Tracey. They're going to jail, and

I'll get that third guy. But right now you need to rest." He laid her on the bed.

"*Ow.*" She sat up. "My back and shoulder are too sore."

He shifted on the bed, resting his back against the headboard, and motioned for her to come to him. She gave him a wary look. He cursed under his breath. "Do you really think I'm going to try something? Especially after all you've been through? I'm just going to hold you so you can sleep without pain."

Those big hazel eyes turned apologetic as she moved beside him. Her left side had taken most of the trauma, so he tucked her right side against him. She was so petite, he had to slide lower to lessen the angle of his body so she could drape herself over him comfortably without putting pressure on her back or shoulder. His hand settled on her hip. "Does that hurt?"

She shook her head against his chest.

He rested his head back, taking in the white walls of her bedroom and the cheap dresser and nightstand that looked secondhand. The bed was definitely a double. He barely fit on it. A blue blanket was folded at the bottom of the bed on top of a plain white bedspread. There was one framed photograph on the dresser of Tracey, all knobby knees and pointy elbows, probably twelve or thirteen years old, taken with a petite dark-haired woman who could only be her mother. They shared the same almond-shaped eyes, perky nose, and pointy chin that brought the words *elfin magic* to mind. Diesel's mother's voice whispered through his head. *We need a little elfin magic, Dezzie. What d'ya say? Go get our paints.* He was just a boy in that memory, seven or eight maybe, and he remembered running out to the shed to fetch the bucketful of little paint cans and paintbrushes so they could add to the hobbit-and-elf-themed walls of the hobbit room they'd started when he was too young to remember.

A stab of longing moved through him, and he shifted his gaze around the room to try to distract himself from the ache tiptoeing in with another memory. This one from when his mother had been too weak to move. He'd carried her to that elfin-magic room, which by then was covered floor to ceiling with elves and hobbits, wizards and forestry.

Where were Tracey's favorites? Nothing in that room spoke of her uniqueness. She'd lived there a long time, and there wasn't one picture on the wall or even any of those fancy throw pillows most women liked.

He looked down at the beauty sleeping against him, her warm breath floating in soft puffs over his skin. She jerked in her sleep, whimpering, legs kicking. He held her a little tighter. "*Shh.* You're safe. I've got you." The tension eased from her body, and he pressed a kiss to the top of her head, pulling the blanket over her. Unfamiliar sensations slithered through his chest, different from the ones that usually had his cock saluting when he was near her. These were protective urges, bigger and more powerful than anything he'd ever felt. These sensations made him want to bolt, and at the same time, they made him want to nail his fucking boots to the ground.

What the hell?

Chapter Four

MORNING CREPT IN with stages of awareness of all the places Tracey hurt, which was pretty much all over, of cool air between her legs, and of Diesel's arm wrapped protectively around her, his hand cupping her ass through his shirt that she was wearing. All the parts of her that were resting on him were hot. He was like a freaking furnace. She swallowed hard, her nerves pinging like a pinball. How could she have forgotten to put on underwear? She lay still, her cheek on his bare chest, his heart beating steady and sure against it, his thick arm keeping her tight against him even in his sleep. This from the man who everyone knew hated to be touched.

Maybe he didn't have a heart of stone after all.

She must have kicked off the blanket in the middle of the night, because it was bunched up at the bottom of the bed. Her gaze slid down the length of him, lingering on the dusting of hair leading south from his belly button and disappearing beneath the waist of his jeans. She couldn't help but notice the bulge behind his zipper or the outline of what looked like a mammoth erection trailing down his pants leg.

Lord have mercy.

She forced her gaze lower. His feet reached the end of the bed. He'd slept in his black leather boots. She'd bet he still had his hat on, too. Memories of last night trickled in, bringing the faces of the monsters who had attacked her and the menacing look in Diesel's eyes as he'd come to her rescue, so different from the compassionate looks he'd given her last night. How had he known she'd been rooted to the shower floor, unable to pull herself together? How was it possible that the man beside her was the same man she'd thought might have a bevy of bodies buried somewhere? She couldn't be more grateful for his helping her when she was attacked or for keeping her safe last night.

His hand pressed harder on her ass as he stretched, his back arching. She stole a glance at his face, that strong jaw and eyes clenched tight, neck and shoulders pulling back with the stretch. His baseball cap was firmly in place. She had a feeling he didn't even realize his hand was on her butt. She tried to lift the rest of her body off him, but his hand remained firmly in place, holding her still, making her second-guess her assumption.

Her eyes darted to his, and she found them brimming with concern.

"How do you feel?" His voice was even rougher than usual.

"Sore." She wanted to thank him for all he'd done, but now that she was fully awake, she couldn't think past his hand on her ass, the fact that she wasn't wearing underwear, and everything she'd gone through last night simmering just beneath the surface, waiting to be dealt with. She needed to get her head on straight. But first she had to get off that bed. "And like someone's fondling my *butt*."

He moved his hand, and she pushed slowly to her feet,

wincing in pain.

His brows slanted. "Where're you going?"

"To the bathroom to get dressed." She made her way to the dresser and fished out underwear and her most comfortable shorts and T-shirt. "You didn't think I'd lie there without underwear on all day, did you?"

He smirked.

She headed into the bathroom, convinced that he was the hardest man in the world to read. When she saw her clothes and shoes on the floor and her battered face in the mirror, those thoughts were replaced with the anger from last night clawing its way free. Her cheekbone and brow were scraped and bruised, and she had a small cut above the left side of her lip. She peeled off the butterfly bandage from above her brow, revealing a red, crusty gash. She took off Diesel's shirt, her body complaining with her movements. Black-and-blue patches marred her left side, hip, and shoulder. There were finger-sized bruises just above her elbows where those awful men had grabbed her. She turned around and peered over her shoulder into the mirror, her stomach seizing at the sight of more scrapes and bruises. Her mind trampled back to the bad days with Dennis, when he'd come home drunk and out of control, and she'd borne the brunt of his wrath.

She reminded herself that *this* was different.

She knew in her head that it was, but it took a few more reminders for it to sink in. With Dennis, she'd felt trapped, like she'd had no choice but to stay with him. But last night she'd fought, had tried to get away, and she reported the assault to the police. She didn't just run away as she had from Dennis. Those assholes were going to pay for what they'd done. It sickened her that she hadn't pressed charges against Dennis, but that was a nightmare she couldn't afford to get tangled up in right now. She had to get dressed and deal with the complicated man waiting for her in her bedroom. How did a person thank someone for saving their life? Words didn't seem like enough, especially when she'd spent so much time giving him crap at work.

She carefully washed around her wounds, thinking about how gentle Diesel had been when he'd cleaned her face last night. She found the small first aid kit under the sink and went to work applying ointment to her scratches. She bandaged her forehead, brushed her teeth and hair, and dressed. She gathered her dirty clothes from the floor and put them in the hamper; then she picked up Diesel's shirt and pressed it to her nose. It smelled like him, rugged and manly, with hints of her bodywash from last night's shower. The combination was strangely comforting.

She picked up her boots, took a deep, fortifying breath, and went to thank him for all he'd done.

The bedroom was empty and the bed was made, her blanket folded neatly at the foot of it. She put her boots in the closet and followed a savory scent toward the kitchen. On her way through the living room, she peeked out the front windows and saw two guys on motorcycles.

Diesel stood at the stove with his back to her. He was shirtless, jeans riding low on his hips. His muscular back and lats formed a perfect V to his thick waist. A tattoo ran down the back of his neck and between his shoulder blades. It was a naked man superimposed in two positions within a circle and a square, one with his arms and legs apart, the other with his arms apart and his legs together. Tracey had seen the image before, but she didn't know what it meant. She was curious about all of his tattoos, but more so about the meaning of that tattoo and why Diesel had the face of a fairy tattooed on the back of his left arm. But while his arms and chest were thoroughly inked, there were no other tattoos on his back, and *boy oh boy* did he look delicious.

But it wasn't his beautiful body that had her pulse quickening, or the tattoos or lack thereof that had her stepping toward the man who hated to be touched, and despite the consequences, wrapping her arms around him from behind. She pressed her cheek to his hot skin, one hand flat on his stomach, the other still holding his shirt. His muscles flexed, rigid with discomfort, but she was powerless against the overwhelming gratitude swamping her. She would be a whole different person today if he hadn't saved her last night. Would she even have survived whatever those men had planned to do to her?

He inhaled deeply, his body puffing up to what felt like twice its normal size.

"Thank you," she said softly, and lowered her hands, taking a step back.

Diesel didn't move, tension wafting off him like the wind.

"I'm sorry I made you uncomfortable. I just appreciate everything you've done for me." She had so many questions. Why did he let her sleep on him last night but flinch when she hugged him? Had she been too out of it to realize he'd been uncomfortable all night, too? Did any part of him think she'd caused those men to come back?

No, she wouldn't let herself believe that.

Silence stretched between them for so long, she was pretty sure he was trying to keep from exploding at her. Why did he hate being touched?

He turned with two plates in his hands, his face a mask of

seriousness. One plate was piled high with French toast, and the other had a mountain of scrambled eggs on it. The strangeness of Diesel doing anything domestic was too much. Nervous laughter fell from her lips. "You *cooked*? Is that for the guys out front?"

"They're fine. You need to eat." He lifted his chin toward the kitchen table, where she was surprised to see two place settings, complete with glasses of orange juice and two mugs of coffee, a bottle of syrup, and a stick of butter on a plate.

"Were you a chef in a previous life?" She set his shirt on his chair and sat at the table.

He didn't respond, just set the plates in the middle of the table, pulled his shirt on, and sat across from her. When she didn't immediately fill her plate, he loaded it up with two slices of French toast and more eggs than she could possibly eat. His knuckles were scraped and red, and they looked painful, but he didn't seem to notice as he piled four slices of French toast and the remainder of the eggs onto his plate and began eating. He shoveled mounds of eggs into his mouth and ate each piece of French toast in only two bites, like a human vacuum. The man was like a machine checking off a to-do list—*Wake up. Feed wounded girl. Feed self*—and she was mesmerized. What other secret talents did he have?

He eyed her over a forkful of eggs. His gaze moved to her plate, then back to her face, and he lifted his chin, his silent message received loud and clear. *Eat.*

She wasn't very hungry, but he'd gone to so much trouble, she poured syrup on the French toast and took a bite. *Holy cow.* It was mouthwateringly good, fluffy with a hint of vanilla and the perfect amount of cinnamon. "This is delicious."

He gave one curt nod, accompanied by a manly sound that

was neither a grunt nor a growl, but wholly *Diesel.*

She continued eating, savoring every bite. "*Mm.* Seriously, this is amazing. Where did you learn to cook?"

Those dark eyes flicked to her for half a second as he finished eating, but he didn't answer. He drank his juice and immediately guzzled his coffee. *Juice. Check. Coffee. Check.* It was like eating with a really talented caveman.

He piled the two empty plates on top of his, pushed to his feet, stabbed two fingers into his empty juice glass, two into his empty mug, and carried it all to the sink, where he promptly started washing them.

"I can do those."

"I've got it," he said gruffly.

As she ate, she watched him moving efficiently from one task to the next, washing and drying everything by hand, including the pans and mixing bowls, and putting them back into the cabinets where they belonged. He turned and reached for her plate, which was still loaded up with eggs.

His brows slanted. "You need the eggs for protein."

"I ate some. They were good, but I can't eat that much."

He dragged his eyes down the length of her, as if he didn't believe her.

"*Diesel,* I ate enough. I promise. Now step away from the sink so I can wash my dishes, or I might never let you go home."

She stood with the plate in her hands, and he took it from her. "Drink your juice."

"You really do have a daddy complex, don't you?"

His jaw clenched. "Vitamin C helps reduce inflammation."

"Who knew you were such a sweet-talker?" She leaned against the counter to drink her juice as he washed her dishes.

"Thank you for making breakfast and cleaning up."

He dried the plate, eyes narrow and serious. "I called Red. She and some of the girls are coming over."

"Why?"

"I've got to take care of some business, and you shouldn't be alone."

"Diesel, there are two beefy bodyguards outside. I don't need to bother everyone else. I'll text them."

"Your phone broke. The cops found it on the ground last night. I'll pick you up a new one. You need to see the girls. They've been blowing up my phone. Josie's going to drive your car over from the shop so you'll have it. She can catch a ride home with Red."

She crossed her arms, but it hurt her shoulder, and she winced, dropping her hands. A flash of pain shone in his eyes, like it had last night. As much as she wanted a little girl time, she didn't want to *feel* like a victim any more than she already did. "I don't need them to come over, and I can call an Uber to take me to get my car."

"The girls are coming over, and you're *not* getting in an Uber with a stranger," he said emphatically. "And once you're healed up, I'm going to teach you how to fight."

He had a point about not riding with a stranger. "I know how to fight. I've been doing martial arts for a year and a half. I just hesitated, and there were *two* of them."

"If you want to protect yourself, you've got to be trained the right way. Doing martial arts in a studio is great for getting the basics under your belt, but it's worthless unless you've been trained to handle situations with pricks like the ones from last night." He stepped closer, those all-seeing eyes challenging her. "Unless you're afraid to try?"

She scoffed and lifted her chin, ready to slam him with a sassy retort, but all that came out was "Do you really think I can learn to protect myself against guys like that?"

"I wouldn't waste my time offering to teach you if I didn't. You may be small, baby girl, but you're fierce."

His belief in her bolstered her waffling confidence, and his use of *baby girl* brought a whole different range of emotions, and awareness, like of his thighs brushing against her.

"If you put half as much energy into learning to fight as you do into giving me hell, you'll do just fine." The side of his mouth quirked up with the tease, but just as quickly, that teasing smirk morphed into something darker, bringing with it a jolt of electricity.

Butterflies swarmed in her belly. "I'm sorry for giving you a hard time at work. I know you were just looking out for me. The truth is, I hate feeling like I need protecting at all, in any situation, but I'm thankful you were there for me last night."

He looked like he wanted to say something more, his emotions so potent, she could *feel* him struggling to hold back whatever it was. She opened her mouth to ask at the same moment he lifted his hand and brushed her hair away from the bandage above her brow. It was such an intimate, tender touch, words failed her. His expression softened, his eyes trailing over the bandage, the scrapes on her cheeks, and gazed so deeply into her eyes, she thought he was going to kiss her. A heaviness pulsed around them like nothing she'd ever felt before. Her heart raced, and she held her breath, silently willing him to do it, or to say whatever he was feeling. A knock sounded at the front door, startling her and breaking their connection. Diesel's jaw tightened, his expression chilled, and he stepped back, restacking that wall of bricks around him.

"That'll be Red and the girls," he said gruffly. "I'll get out of your hair."

He headed for the front door, and the air rushed from her lungs. Her mind was a fog of confusion. She'd never met a man so *hard* and visceral he could sweep her into his vortex without a single word and leave her feeling like a different person when he walked away.

The sounds of her friends' voices and fast footfalls heading toward the kitchen jarred her from her thoughts just as Josie and Sarah burst into the room with Dixie, Finlay, and Crystal on their heels, enveloping her in a group hug that made her wince with pain.

"*Ow, careful,*" Tracey pleaded.

"Sorry," Sarah said. She was the older of the two sisters, a little taller and blonder than Josie.

"We've been so worried about you." Josie was holding a bag from her gingerbread shop.

"Are you okay?" Finlay asked.

Dixie planted a hand on her hip. "Diesel should have killed those bastards. I knew they were douchebags."

"How about you give her a second to breathe, ladies?" Red said as she walked into the kitchen with Penny and their other friends, Roni and Gemma. Red took Tracey's hands, holding them tight. "I'm going to hug you very lightly, because Biggs said you got thrown around pretty badly, but my mama heart needs to do it, okay?"

How could words alone make Tracey feel like crying? Not for the first time, and she was sure not for the last, she wished she'd had someone like Red around when she'd been with Dennis. Maybe if she had, she wouldn't have stayed for so long.

Tracey nodded, and Red embraced her, whispering, "I'm so

glad you're okay, sweetheart."

"Thank you. I wouldn't be if it weren't for Diesel." As they headed into the living room, she looked out the front window and saw him talking with the two guys who had been out there earlier. He looked over his shoulder, and she swore he was looking right at her, an inescapable current running between them.

As everyone sat down, Josie opened the bag she'd brought and began handing out gingerbread cookies that had *Feel Better Soon* written on them in pink icing.

"You made me cookies?" Tracey took one, her heart filling up.

"I was so worried about you, I couldn't sleep, so I baked." Josie ran her gingerbread shop out of the renovated garage at her house.

"I'm glad it's not just me," Finlay said. "I was up half the night baking a cake for you. But when I got up this morning, Bullet had already eaten half of it with his coffee. That man has the appetite of a buffalo."

They all laughed and ate their cookies.

"Bullet said Diesel stayed with you last night," Finlay said. "I can't imagine he was much comfort, but at least you were safe."

"He is pretty stoic. I was afraid of him when we first met." Roni tucked her dark hair behind her ear. "But after the way he helped Quincy and Simone, I have nothing but respect for him." Roni's fiancé, Quincy Gritt, was a recovering drug addict, and he ran Narcotics Anonymous meetings, which Simone Davidson, who was also in recovery, had attended. When Simone's ex, a drug dealer, made it too dangerous for her to stay in the area, Diesel arranged for her to stay at Redemption

Ranch to continue working through her recovery. He'd escorted her there last December to be sure she arrived safely.

"I'm really thankful Diesel was there." Tracey sat in an armchair and tucked her feet beside her, thinking about when she'd fallen apart in the shower. She hadn't even been nervous when she'd heard him come into the bathroom. She'd been relieved that he'd somehow known she shouldn't be alone. "I've never seen anyone fight like him. He didn't hesitate. Not even when he saw the guy with the knife. He went at both of them with everything he had."

"Of course he did," Dixie said. "What he lacks in comforting skills, he makes up for in beast mode."

"Actually, I kind of lost it after I got home," Tracey admitted. "He knew exactly what I needed, and he stayed by my side all night. He was pretty amazing, you guys. He even made me breakfast this morning."

"Diesel cooks?" Finlay asked.

"Yeah, really well, too," Tracey said.

Josie said, "I'm so glad he took good care of you. Jed thinks the world of him. I know Diesel drives you crazy at work, but he can smell trouble a mile away."

"That he does," Red said. "He's a bounty hunter when he's not bartending."

"He is?" *I guess he really can track people down.* Tracey looked around at the other girls, who were just as shocked. "I didn't know that."

"Yes, ma'am. He's one of the best. That's what he does when he travels, and he put his life on hold to help our family at the bar," Red said. "He will be sorely missed when he leaves."

A pang of sadness or disappointment, Tracey wasn't sure which, moved through her.

"Diesel's leaving?" Gemma and Crystal asked in unison. The brunette besties ran Princess for a Day boutique, where children could spend the day dressing up as different types of princesses, including everything from glittery gowns to tomboy-princess attire.

"He's stayed a lot longer than we thought he would, but he's ready to hit the road," Red explained.

"Oh no. Kennedy's going to be so sad." Gemma was married to Quincy's older brother, Truman, who worked at Whiskey Automotive. Truman and Quincy's mother had overdosed a couple of years ago, leaving behind their much-younger siblings, Kennedy, who was now almost six, and Lincoln, who was now almost four. Truman and Gemma had stepped in to raise them as their own.

"So are half the women who come into the bar," Dixie quipped.

A niggle of jealousy clawed at Tracey. "He drove me crazy for so long, but now I can't imagine going back to work without him there. Especially after last night."

"Are you afraid to go back?" Finlay asked.

"I would be." Penny put her hand over her tiny baby bump.

"Me too," Roni and Gemma agreed.

"Last night was terrifying, and maybe I should be afraid to go back, but I'm not. I won't be taking the trash out by myself anytime soon, but I'm not going to let them keep me from living my life. I won't do that again."

"Attagirl. But you know, if you want time off, you've got it," Red said.

"Thank you, but I don't. What I need is to heal so I can learn to better defend myself."

"That's exactly what you need," Dixie agreed. "You've come

way too far to let those bastards drag you down."

All the girls talked at once, sharing support and cheering Tracey on.

Dixie's phone rang. "It's Izzy on FaceTime. I hope that's okay. She really wanted to talk to you." She answered the call. "Hey, Iz."

"Is she okay? Let me see her!" Izzy demanded, and Dixie handed the phone to Tracey. Izzy's worried eyes stared back at her. "Are you okay? I'm sorry I'm not there. I'll be home later tonight."

"I'm fine. Really."

"Oh, Trace. I should have been there for you. When I get home, I'll spoil you rotten. I promise."

Tracey held up a cookie. "The girls are doing a great job of that already, and as much as I appreciate it, I don't want to be pampered, or even talk about what happened anymore. It gives too much power to the guys who attacked me. Can we please just act normal and talk about something else? Kennedy and Lincoln's birthday party, or your husbands, or Penny's wedding, or something?" Kennedy and Lincoln's party was a little more than a month away.

"Are you sure?" Dixie asked.

"One hundred percent," Tracey assured her. "I know you guys are willing to talk about it, and I promise if I feel the need to, I will. But right now I just want to talk about something happy and pretend life is normal."

"You heard the woman," Izzy exclaimed. "Let's get chatty!"

Tracey leaned the phone against a set of books on the coffee table, and as all the girls gathered around, a cacophony of conversation erupted. For the first time since last night, Tracey heard herself laugh. She looked at the women who had become her family and realized Diesel had been right after all. She *had* needed time with them. But there was no denying the part of her that wondered if—*hoped*—she'd get more time with him, too.

Chapter Five

THE WIND WHIPPED against Diesel's skin, and the sun beat down on his shoulders as he drove his motorcycle back over the bridge that separated Peaceful Harbor from the rest of the world late Sunday afternoon. It seemed fucked up to him that the sun was still shining with all the shit going on inside him. He remembered the first time he'd come over that bridge the month after his mother died, when he'd driven cross-country, trying to shed the sadness that had clung to him like a second skin. It hadn't worked then any better than it was working now. Only this time it wasn't sadness eating away at him. It was a dire need to see Tracey, to make sure she was okay, and a plethora of other feelings he didn't want to dissect. He'd tracked down the third guy who had been with the assholes who had attacked her. The pussy had hightailed it back home to West Virginia the minute he'd gotten wind of his friends' arrests.

That was all well and good, but it wasn't enough.

Diesel had paid him a little visit to ensure he'd never cross that bridge again. The fucker admitted to knowing what his friends had planned to do to Tracey and had done nothing to stop it. He was lucky Diesel hadn't killed him. Diesel had left him begging for his life and swearing he'd never step foot in Peaceful Harbor or go near Tracey again, which was exactly how Diesel had left Dennis Smoot two years ago, when he'd hunted him down and made him pay for what he'd done to Tracey.

Diesel had made damn sure neither of them would come near her. He'd hired his buddies out their way to keep an eye on not only those pricks but also their known associates.

He stopped at the clubhouse to shower, then climbed into his truck and headed over to Tracey's house. He'd been twisted up over her all day. One minute he was thinking about the way she'd mewled and whimpered in her sleep, and the next he was seeing those big hazel eyes imploring him as they had earlier that morning.

As he pulled up in front of her house, concern and desire tangled into one hell of an ass kicker. He grabbed the bag with the new phone he'd bought for her and climbed out of his truck, heading over to talk with Tex, who had taken over for the guys who'd been there that morning. Tex was a good guy, even if he flirted with Tracey too damn much. "Any trouble?"

"Nah. It's been quiet since the girls and Red left."

"Great. You can get out of here. I've got her."

"A'right. Let me know if you need anything." Tex climbed on his bike. "See you at church tomorrow night." Church was what they called the meetings of the Dark Knights, which took place Monday nights at the clubhouse.

Diesel nodded and headed up the walk. He knocked on the door, leaning against the frame as he waited. The door opened slowly, and *damn*. She was such a pretty little thing in those skimpy shorts, but those awful scrapes and bruises made him want to take her into his arms and protect her from the world, to kiss her, breathe his strength into her, until she felt more resilient, safe.

"Hi." A small smile curved her lips, but it was the flush on her cheeks that stirred those emotions he was trying to ignore.

"I brought you a phone." He held out the bag.

"Thanks." She opened the door wider. "Do you want to come in?"

Hell yes. He wanted to come inside *her*. He gritted his teeth against that urge, but there was no turning off the desire to be near her. "Did you eat dinner?"

She shook her head, her hair falling into her eyes. "I'm not very hungry."

"Get your shoes on. We're going to eat."

"Diesel—"

He leaned in close, and her eyes brightened, her sweet scent wreaking havoc with him. "Don't waste your breath, baby girl. Let's go."

"Remember the whole bees and honey thing?" She pushed her feet into black Converse sneakers.

He smirked, because obviously *she* didn't remember the details of that conversation, while he never forgot a damn thing.

Her brows knitted, and her memory must have returned, because she said, *"Shoot,"* under her breath. "Never mind." She grabbed her purse and walked outside, moving easier than she had last night.

He pulled the door closed behind her, checked the lock, and followed her down the walk. "How's your pain?"

"Trailing about two feet behind me."

He snickered, loving her sass. It was good to hear her getting back to being herself. The time with the girls must have helped. He went around the truck to open the passenger door and helped her in.

"You know it's customary to *ask* a person if they want to go out to eat." She reached for her seat belt. "Not force them against their will."

He closed the door without responding and went around to the driver's seat.

As he settled in behind the wheel, she made her voice deeper and said, *"Why, yes, Tracey. I do know that. I was just…"* She threw her hands up, eyes rolling. "I can't even think of a reason for you to act that way."

He glanced at her as he started the truck, getting a kick out of her efforts to figure him out. *Good luck, baby girl. I can't even figure out my own fucking self.* "You don't want to go eat?"

"I didn't say that. I said there are nicer ways to ask if I want to go."

"So you *do* want to go?"

"I guess. *Yes.*"

He pulled away from the curb. "A'right, then. Save your breath."

She groaned. "You are *so* frustrating."

If that wasn't the kettle calling the pot black, he didn't know what was. She sat there too fucking gorgeous for her own good, taunting him with those toned legs and that kissable mouth. He had dirty fantasies about that mouth of hers, and if he kept thinking about it, he'd get them both in trouble. He did his best to push those thoughts away as he drove past the marina and the heavily commercialized, wealthier parts of town, to where fancy strip malls and high-end restaurants gave way to roadside barbecues and warehouse-style shops.

He pulled into the gravel lot by a narrow strip of beach and parked in front of Paolo's Pizza Shack, a walk-up restaurant that had seen better days. The small red weathered-wood building was indeed a *shack*, with a handwritten laminated menu nailed to the wall beside the ordering window and a few picnic tables out front beneath strings of lights. It wasn't much, but it was all Paolo Russo and his twelve-year-old son, Adrian, had, and it was enough to keep a roof over their heads and smiles on their faces.

Diesel threw open his door and went around the truck to help Tracey out.

"I've never been to this end of the Harbor." She looked around the parking lot. "There isn't much here."

"How much do you need?"

"That's a weird question."

"Is it? Or have you just never thought about it before?" He had a feeling she'd thought about how much she needed plenty of times, considering she'd gone from a horrible situation to staying at a shelter with very little to her name, and she didn't strike him as the type to forget what it was like to have nothing once she was back on her feet.

She seemed to mull over his question as he reached into the glove compartment and grabbed the book he'd bought for Adrian.

"What's that?" she asked.

He closed the truck door and held up the book. Her brows knitted. "*The Two Towers*? Do you like to read while you eat?"

"It's not for me. It's for him." He motioned behind her to Adrian, the skinny, dark-haired, sharp-minded bundle of energy wheeling his wheelchair around the side of the building.

Adrian's eyes widened with excitement. "Diesel!"

"*Wheels*, my man. How's it going?" Diesel and Adrian did their secret handshake, smacking palms, gripping each other's fingers, then bumping fists, making an explosion sound as they pulled their hands back.

"Great! I'm almost finished with *The Fellowship of the Ring.*" Adrian looked curiously at Tracey. "Are you his girlfriend?"

Tracey's eyes widened.

"Christ, kid," Diesel grumbled. "Don't ask her that."

Adrian looked confused. "Why not? You've never brought a girl here before."

"Because it puts us in a weird position."

"Why? She either *is* or *isn't* your girlfriend. What's weird about it?"

Tracey laughed, and man it was good to hear after all she'd been through.

"I'm not his girlfriend," she said. "But I like the way you made him squirm. My name's Tracey. What's your name?"

"Adrian, but you can call me Wheels if you want. That's my road name. Diesel gave it to me. You don't have a road name because girls don't have them, right?"

"Um, yeah. That's right."

"What happened to your face? Did you fall? When I fell off the trampoline, I had to get stitches on my head. I was six. That's how I ended up in the wheelchair. Do you have stitches?"

Diesel's heart broke for the boy every time he talked so matter-of-factly about how he landed in that wheelchair, and from the look in Tracey's eyes, he could tell she was just as affected.

"No, just a few cuts, but I'm okay," she reassured him. "So, you like to read?"

"Boy, do I ever. Diesel got me hooked on *The Hobbit*. He's read it, and *all* the Lord of the Rings books, and he said after I read them, we can watch the movies together. Have you read them? They're so good..." Adrian went on about the stories, and Tracey smiled and chatted about the book she had never read.

When Adrian took a breath, Diesel handed him the new book. "Here you go, buddy. The next in the series."

His face lit up. "Awesome. Thank you!"

The ordering window opened, and Adrian's father, Paolo, a dark-haired, olive-skinned man in his midforties, stuck his head out. "Hey, Diesel. Good to see you. Adrian, I thought you were heading over to see Marnie?"

"I *am*," Adrian hollered. "I just stopped to talk to Diesel and Tracey. She's *not* his girlfriend."

Diesel gritted his teeth.

Tracey laughed, turning a sweet smile to Adrian. "Is Marnie your girlfriend?"

"No. She's my best friend. Her mom works over there." Adrian pointed across the parking lot to the craft shop. "I want her to be my girlfriend, but Diesel says that's a big responsibility and I need to make sure I'm ready for it. So I'm working through my list."

"Your list?" she asked.

"Yeah. Diesel came up with a bunch of things I need to think about before I can have a girlfriend. Like, am I ready to be there if she needs me? Am I sure I won't accidentally hurt her feelings by saying something stupid? He says girls take everything different than boys, so I have to think before I talk. And other stuff, like do I want to be interrupted by her texts when I'm reading? Diesel said you have to answer girls' texts or they get mad. Is that true?"

"I think that depends on the girl." She looked at Diesel with a glimmer of amusement and something new in her eyes, as if hearing about that list made her see him differently. "But it sounds like Diesel gave you some pretty good advice. You should pick flowers for her, too. Is that on your list?"

"Flowers? No." Adrian looked at Diesel. "You didn't say anything about flowers."

"That's okay," Tracey said. "He isn't really a flower type of guy. But definitely add it to your list. Flowers tell a girl she's special and that you've been thinking of her."

"I think about her all the time," Adrian said. "I'll add it to my list. Diesel, if you ever want a girlfriend, you should add it to your list, too. I'd better go."

"Do you want me to push you across the lot?" Tracey offered.

"No thanks. Number five on my list is that I can handle my current responsibilities, and being independent is one of them." He beamed at Diesel. "Thanks for the book. You should make Tracey your girlfriend. I like her."

"Christ, kid. Now I gotta make you a new list. *What not to say around chicks.*" He ruffled Adrian's hair. "Get outta here, kiddo. Have fun with Marnie."

As Adrian rolled away and they headed up to the ordering window, Tracey said, "So, you like hobbits and you make boyfriend lists. Diesel Black, you just got a lot more interesting."

He scoffed.

They ordered pizza, and Tracey talked with Paolo while they waited for the pizza to cook. She was so easy and warm and sweet, she reminded him of how his mother used to talk to people she'd just met like she'd known them forever.

When their pizza was ready, Paolo gave him an approving look. As if he'd sought approval for a damn thing in the last twenty-plus years?

Tracey plunked her hot little self down *right* beside him at a picnic table. "I love pizza." She took a bite and closed her eyes. "Mm. *So* good."

He imagined her saying that when they were naked and he was buried deep inside her. He cleared his throat and took a bite of pizza to try to fend off those dirty thoughts.

"How do you know Adrian and Paolo?"

"Adrian was getting bullied at school, and his father reached out to the Dark Knights. I shadowed him to classes and after school for a while, made sure nobody gave him hell."

"And did it stop the bullying?"

"Yeah." He finished his slice, remembering how awful it was to see that great kid in so much misery.

"How does that work? Intimidation? Isn't that the same thing as bullying?"

"I like to see it as opening the kids' eyes. When kids pick on who they consider to be an underdog, we go in and show them that they're the underdogs. We're not there to scare them. We're there to teach them."

"What do you mean?"

"There are three types of bullies. Bullies who learn the behavior from their parents, those who use it to get attention, and those who bully out of fear. The kids who bullied Adrian did it out of fear. My being there took the negative interest off him and replaced it with curiosity, which opened the door for conversations. Kids are afraid of what they don't understand. Hell, so are adults. Two of the kids had known him before the trampoline accident left him paralyzed from the waist down, and the other had just moved into town. They see a smart kid who looks and talks like them, and they worry that if he ended up in a wheelchair, they could, too. They didn't hate Adrian. How could they? He's a great kid. They hated the wheelchair."

She picked a mushroom off the pizza and ate it. "How'd you get past that?"

"We talked to the class about bullying and how it makes the other kids feel, and as they got used to seeing me and Adrian together, they asked questions about why I was there, that kind of thing. It's all about communication, making people see how their actions affect others. Once they got past their fears, they realized how cool Adrian is and backed off."

"How long ago was that?"

He picked up another slice of pizza. "Six months, maybe."

"And you still come to see him? That's nice."

"I don't take friendships lightly. Who could be there for a kid and then disappear?"

She was quiet as they ate, and he took a moment to really look at her, as he'd done while she'd slept last night. He was intrigued by far more than her looks. Tracey didn't do the fake shit most women did around him. She dove into the pizza without hesitation, while most women pretended they existed on air, and while she never wore much makeup, even with those damn scrapes and bruises she was gorgeous without it. She hadn't worn makeup when she'd first started working at the bar, and he'd never forget when he'd first seen her all dolled up. She'd always turned heads, but makeup gave her a classy look, like an old-school actress who stood out among all the rest. It was impossible to look away from her, like at the wedding, when he'd been riveted by her.

"When do you think we'll know if the guys who attacked me will be let out on bail?"

He stuffed his thoughts down deep and took a drink. "They

won't be. Court found out that they had outstanding arrests in West Virginia for assaulting two other women. They'll be behind bars for a long time. I tracked down the third guy, and he won't be coming over the bridge again in this lifetime."

She bumped him with her shoulder. "You didn't kill him, did you? Because I'd hate to have to visit you in prison."

He gave her a wry look. "I wanted to. Same with the other assholes. But I'm a dick, not a murderer."

"You're not that big of a dick. You took great care of me."

Not good enough. Those assholes got to you.

"Does this mean everyone can go back to their normal lives, and I don't need anyone sitting outside the house anymore?"

"Yeah. I've got eyes on the third guy. He won't get anywhere near Peaceful Harbor."

She exhaled with relief. "Thank you. I just want to put last night behind me and keep moving forward. I spent enough years living in fear. I never want to live that way again."

"How'd you get mixed up with that Dennis guy, anyway?"

Tracey reached for another slice of pizza. "I was young and stupid."

"How young?"

"I was a junior when we met, and he was a senior. He was the cute, popular boy that all the girls liked, and I was the stupid girl who met him at a party and fell hopelessly in love with him and all of his charms."

If he had a buck for every dickbag who had charmed a girl into thinking he was something he wasn't, he'd be a rich man. "What'd you like about him?"

"He made me feel special. I wasn't one of those girls with low self-esteem or anything like that, but I was a little shy. I played soccer, and he came to all my games. I worked as a hostess after school, and he'd drive me to and from work. He talked me up to his friends like he was the luckiest guy in the world to be going out with me. *Me.* I mean, I know I'm not special, but he paid a lot of attention to me."

"The hell you're not."

She rolled her eyes. "I know I'm not ugly, but you know what I mean."

"Yeah, I do, and you're *wrong.*"

"Says the guy who leaves the bar with a different leggy woman three times a week."

She bit into her pizza, and he stewed on that comment.

"*Anyway,* for as smart as I was academically, I was an idiot when it came to boys. We lived in Virginia Beach, and he went away to school in Pennsylvania. He called all the time and saw me when he came back for breaks, and there were signs, but I ignored them. He started getting jealous my senior year, but he told me he loved me all the time, so I wrote it off as him just being really into me."

Diesel ground his teeth together, wishing he'd been there to open her eyes.

"My mom couldn't afford to pay for college, so after I graduated, I worked full time and took a few classes at the community college. He got even more jealous about that. He'd call and ask a million questions about the guys in my classes, and we'd fight or break up. Then he'd show up and apologize, professing his love for me, promising he'd stop being jealous, and I'd take him back. Eventually I stopped taking classes because they weren't really getting me anywhere, and it wasn't worth the fights. We were on again, off again for years, and then, right before my twentieth birthday, he quit school and said he had a great job offer and was moving to New Jersey. He asked me to go with him, and he promised me the world. Not that I wanted or needed him like a sugar daddy or anything. He said we'd have a great life, and he talked about all the things we'd do together."

She shook her head, staring vacantly across the parking lot. "He had such big plans, and I was stupid enough to believe him. I should have listened to my mother. She saw all the warning signs and begged me not to go with him, but I actually thought the woman who had left my abusive father to save me from him didn't know what she was talking about. She told me if I left with him not to come back with bruises and a broken heart and expect her to pick up the pieces. Talk about being a fool."

Her eyes glassed over, the pieces of her painful past taking shape like shards of glass. He fought the urge to pull her into his lap and comfort her.

Comfort her? What the ever-loving hell was that all about?

There was only one woman he'd ever wanted to hold to take her pain away, and she'd up and died on him.

He cleared his throat again, as if anything could scrape those feelings away. "Your father was abusive?"

She nodded. "But my mom got us out when I was little. He found us a few weeks later, broke in when I was asleep and beat her up pretty bad. He was arrested, and we moved and started over in another town."

Diesel made a mental note to track down her asshole father.

"I told you I should have listened to her. But I didn't, and I can't change that. Things were great with Dennis for a while. I got another hostessing job, and he was training as a marketing rep. But that didn't last. Something would happen at his work, and he'd blow up at me, or go out drinking and come back drunk and angry." She lowered her eyes. "At first he'd just yell, or accuse me of ridiculous things, like being with other guys. I didn't even know anyone except at work. Then one day he shoved me against a wall."

His hands fisted beneath the table. It killed him that she'd had no one to protect her.

"I should have left right then, but where could I go? I had no savings. I didn't even have a car, and I wasn't about to go crawling back to my mom with my tail between my legs. The truth is, I didn't even think about leaving that night. I was so crushed by his actions, I think I was in shock. I remember yelling at him because I couldn't understand how he could tell me he loved me and then shove me like that."

"Because he didn't fucking love you. He wanted to control you."

"I know that *now*. But I was a different person then. I couldn't see past that to deal with the real issues because I *wanted* to be enough. I wanted him to love me so much that he couldn't hurt me. But when you're in that situation, it's all so crazy. The abuse feels personal, like he wouldn't have been that way with anyone else, when in reality, I could have been anyone and he would have done the same thing."

"That's part of the pattern of abuse. They make you feel that way so you'll stay and blame yourself."

"I know that now. Now that I know what love is and what a healthy relationship looks like, I know we never had that. But back then, I was too close to see it. He cried later that night, and he seemed genuinely sorry when he promised to do better. I wanted to believe him so badly. The next day he brought me flowers, and for weeks he was kind and attentive, as close to perfect as a boyfriend could get. But eventually it happened again, and he showered me in apologies and promises. He always said he'd get help, and I'd stay, hoping he really would, but he never did. He'd canceled my cell phone a few months after we moved because we couldn't afford it, and I kept saving for a new one, but I couldn't keep a job because he'd show up and accuse me of flirting or make a scene for no reason. I sound stupid, but the times in between the abuse were so good, I let them sway me. I believed I could change him, that my love was enough to change him. I became his enabler, allowing him to use me as his punching bag. Sometimes I wonder if I wanted to fix him just to prove to my mom that she was wrong, which is also really messed up. I look back, and I don't even recognize who I was then."

The sadness in her voice was too much. He put his arm around her, pulling her gently against his side, and hell if she didn't fit as perfectly as she had last night, as if he were meant to shelter her. "I didn't know you then, but I'd have recognized you. You've got a big heart, baby girl, and he took advantage of that."

She turned her beautiful face up to him, those scrapes and bruises twisting him up inside. The need to protect her and the desire he fought so hard to ignore were so strong they blended together. How could he ignore the desire brimming in her eyes? Pulsing between them like a living, breathing entity? It happened so often with them, so fast, he should be used to it. But he had a feeling there was no getting used to this type of connection. It was different from seeing a chick across the room and wanting to bang her. Tracey had gotten deep under his skin, awakening parts of him he'd never known existed. She made him want more than a quick fuck. She made him want to pay homage to every inch of her body, to learn every dip and curve, to take away the pain of her past, and pleasure her so thoroughly, he obliterated every bad thing that had ever happened to her.

Her mouth was so close, so tempting, he felt himself leaning in, the need to taste her, to take her face between his hands and kiss all that sadness out of her system, overpowering. Her lips parted on a needy sigh, and *Christ* that was sexy. But he knew it wouldn't end there. One taste would never be enough, and he was *not* what she needed. She'd spent two years putting down roots, nurturing friendships, and building a family among her friends. He didn't know the first thing about that shit. He'd been there for the same amount of time, had known those people years longer than her, and he still felt like an outsider.

He knew where he belonged.

The road didn't just call his name—it *owned* him.

It took everything he had to lower his arm and put space between them. "Don't beat yourself up for past mistakes. Keep your eyes on the road ahead." He added that last part as a reminder for himself as much as for her and guzzled his drink.

TRACEY BLINKED SEVERAL times, trying to pull herself out of the lustful place she'd fallen into and make sense of what just happened. What was it about Diesel that drew her in like a moth to a flame? She was all revved up, as if she hadn't just been spilling her guts before that moment when their eyes had connected. Just like earlier, when she'd have bet her life he'd been about to kiss her or say something *big* before they were interrupted. Why was he holding back? He didn't have to stay in her room last night, let her sleep on him, or make her breakfast. He didn't have to take her out for pizza tonight. With the sun dipping from the sky and the lights strung above them blooming to life, it felt almost romantic sitting by his side at the picnic table, just the two of them, talking about something so intimate. Now that she knew he'd never brought any other woman there, it sure felt like he cared about her.

I don't take friendships lightly.

His words brought a troubling thought. Had she totally misread his caring for a friend as wanting more? That hit her like a cold shower. This was all too confusing, and she had to say something, to break the tension. "Spoken like a true biker" fell nervously from her lips.

"Born and bred."

She grabbed hold of that and ran with it to distract herself from wanting him. "Are your parents bikers?"

"Nope." He ate half a slice of pizza in one bite.

Back to the nontalker then.

"What made you finally leave that asshole?" he asked gruffly.

She was surprised he wanted to know. "If I tell you, you'll think even less of me."

He glowered at her. "Only a prick would think poorly of a woman who had been abused. Nothing you tell me will come close to the shit I've seen, and if it does, then I'll track that fucker down and kill him with my bare hands."

Was this Diesel's brand of romance? That he'd kill for her? Or was she seriously losing her mind? "You just said you weren't a murderer."

His dark eyes hit her with the heat of the summer sun. "I'm not, but anyone who could look at your sweet face and hurt you doesn't deserve to walk this earth."

Okay, then.

"What made you finally leave?"

"Things went from good, to bad, to worse. We'd lived to-gether for almost four years, and his jealousy was out of control. He was coming home at different times during the day, as if he might catch me doing something. And then one night he punched me in the face." She absently touched her cheek with the painful memory. "He'd never hit me in the face before. I don't know why that felt like it was a measure of anything, but something inside me snapped that night. I'm ashamed to say it, but when he fell asleep, I stood over him with a kitchen knife. I *wanted* to kill him. That's when I knew I had to get out of there. Isn't that sick? I had to hit rock bottom to escape *his* abusive behavior? The therapist at the shelter had to work really hard to help me accept that I wasn't a total loser."

"That's survival, baby. That's not uncommon in those situa-tions. You'd been beaten down, emotionally and physically, and you were looking for a way out, to reclaim your life."

"I know. It's just embarrassing to admit that I let myself be treated that way. When I was young, I had dreams of learning to play the guitar and visions of sitting on the grass at festivals with my boyfriend, maybe jumping on a bus together with a guitar strapped to my back, visiting cool towns. I never had dreams about being abused, stealing my boyfriend's wallet and keys, and driving the car I'd just stolen from him to the bus station. But I got out, and I am proud of that. I was so afraid he'd report the car stolen and find me, I left it a few blocks from the bus station and bought a ticket to the farthest place I could with the money I had, and that was Maryland. Once I got off the bus, I asked a lady if she knew of any shelters for women, and she told me she didn't know of any around there, but that she was heading to Pleasant Hill to see her cousin. She said she could take me to the Parkvale Women's Shelter, which she knew was a good shelter. I would have gone to the moon if she'd said I'd be safe there. I'm so grateful she brought me there. That's where I met the Whiskeys, and they changed my life."

"*You* changed your life. You were brave to escape. The Whiskeys just helped you get back on your feet."

"I don't consider myself brave. I stayed in a horrible situation for years."

"Do you have any idea how many women never get out? How many die at the hands of their abusers? You were fucking brave, sparky. Own it."

He said it so vehemently, she wanted to own it. "I guess I did learn something from my mother after all. I was too young to remember when we left my dad, but maybe the memory of leaving him is lodged in my subconscious."

"Why haven't you seen her?"

His question gave her pause. "How do you know I haven't?"

"Baby girl, when Red asked me to watch out for you, it became my business to know where you went. You haven't left the Harbor since you got here."

She arched a brow. "So you've been *stalking* me?"

"Do I look like a stalker to you?"

"You look like a badass biker." She smiled. "Or a serial killer, but that's beside the point."

He laughed.

"Was that a *laugh*?" She leaned closer, and he schooled his expression. "Damn, Diesel. For a minute there, that hard-core facade of yours cracked, and you actually showed some happy emotion."

His jaw tightened again, as if he wouldn't allow himself that pleasure. "Your *mother*, sparky. Why didn't you go back home after you escaped?"

"Because she told me not to."

"*Jesus*. People say all sorts of shit they don't mean when they're scared and angry. I'm sure you said things you didn't mean, too."

"So many things." Her heart ached at that truth. "I miss her. Before I started seeing Dennis, my mom and I would get up early Sunday mornings and drive around looking at gardens in people's yards, around churches and hotels, and we'd drive by special gardens that you had to pay to get into. Sometimes we'd stay out all day just driving around. This time of year, she always found gardens with zinnias, my favorite flowers. Gosh, that feels like a lifetime ago."

"What the hell are you doing, baby girl?" Pain rose in his eyes. "You *don't* turn your back on family. Their love is unconditional."

"You don't understand. It's not that easy. I never returned her calls after I moved in with Dennis because it was after the abuse started, and I didn't want to admit that to her. And now it's been too long." Tears welled in her eyes. "Besides, I think she meant what she said when I left, because a few months ago I just wanted to hear her voice, and I called her, but her number was disconnected. I tried to find her, but I couldn't."

"What do you mean you tried?"

"I called the landlord we rented from, but he said he hasn't seen her in three years. I even checked on social media. Not that I expected to find anything. She was always afraid my father would find us if he got out of prison, so we never used social media. It's like she never existed. I just hope nothing has happened to her." She looked up at the sky, blinking against tears, trying to push the sadness aside. "I know I was stupid for avoiding her, but if she *is* okay, too much time has passed anyway."

"There's no such thing as too much time." His eyes bored into her, and he bit out, "I'd give my fucking life for one more *hour* with my mother."

Her heart lodged in her throat. "You lost your mom?"

He looked into the distance, adjusting his baseball cap. "Thirteen years ago."

"Oh, Diesel." She touched his arm, and he flinched. But she didn't let that stop her. She spread her hand over his forearm. It wasn't much, but she didn't think he'd accept a hug, so it would have to do. "I'm so sorry. Do you want to talk about her?"

The muscles in his jaw were working overtime again, but he remained silent.

"What about your father? Is he still around?"

"Never knew him."

"Oh." Her heart broke for him. "Do you have other family? Brothers or sisters? Aunts or uncles?"

"No." He pushed abruptly to his feet and gathered the empty pizza box and their plates. "We should go."

She carried their empty cups to the trash can, knowing she'd hit a nerve and wishing he'd open up to her. What had his relationship with his mother been like? They were obviously close, given how badly he wanted to see her again, but had he ever talked with her, or had he always kept to himself? Tracey didn't know how old Diesel was, but her guess was early thirties. If his mother passed away thirteen years ago, he'd been alone for a very long time.

He remained quiet on the drive back to her place, jaw

clenching, dark eyes sliding her way once or twice, which only made his jaw clench harder.

Izzy's car was in the driveway when they arrived. Diesel came around to help Tracey out of the truck, and she shifted on the seat, facing him, and put her hands on his shoulders. She swore every bit of him flinched, even his eyes, but she was getting used to that. "I know you don't want to talk about your mom, but everyone needs a friend they can trust. I may not be a Dark Knight, or a guy, or whatever defines *trustworthy* in that bullheaded mind of yours, but if you ever want to talk about her, I'm a really good listener."

His expression didn't change, but he adjusted his baseball cap, the way he had when they'd talked about his mother at the picnic table. Had his mother given him that hat? That would explain why he wore the ratty old thing all the time. She tucked that thought away to revisit later, just as she had the other tidbits she'd learned about the elusive biker, and quickly pushed to her feet on the running board to keep the moment from getting awkward.

She expected him to help her down, but he wrapped his thick arms around her and touched his forehead to her chest, stealing the oxygen from her lungs. The embrace lasted only a few seconds. She might have imagined it if he hadn't left coolness in his wake as he pulled back and lifted her off the running board.

"Let's get you inside," he said gruffly, as if he hadn't just shocked the living daylights out of her.

She climbed the steps to the porch and realized he was no longer beside her. She turned and found him standing at the bottom of the steps. The storm of emotions whirling between them had formed a barrier, or more likely in his gruff mind, a warning. The steps brought them almost eye to eye. Tracey could barely think past her racing heart, so she didn't even try to think, and let her emotions lead. "Thank you for pushing me to go out tonight. I had a good time." She leaned in and kissed his cheek, whispering, "You can trust me with your secrets." When she drew back, his hard eyes met hers. A tough pill to swallow. "I guess I'll see you at work tomorrow."

"I'll be out here."

It took a second to realize what he meant. "But Izzy's here, and you said I don't need to worry or have anyone watching out for me anymore."

"I'm staying."

"Diesel—"

"I'm not doing it for you, Trace." He turned and walked away, leaving her baffled.

As she went inside, she had a feeling that might never change.

Izzy bolted to her feet on the other side of the living room, wearing a tight gray minidress, her feet bare. Her straight black hair swung along her shoulders as she ran to Tracey and threw her arms around her. "I'm so sorry I wasn't here for you."

Tracey winced, but hugged her back. "It's fine. I'm fine. How was your visit with your family?"

"They're amazing, and Susan's pregnant! I can't wait for her baby shower. I'm going to spoil that baby rotten." Susan was married to Izzy's oldest brother, Jeremy. Izzy took Tracey's hand, leading her to the couch. "More importantly, how are *you?*"

"I'm okay. I was shaken up pretty bad, but I feel better now. Diesel said the guys who attacked me aren't going to get out on bail. I don't know what he did to their friend, but I guess he took care of him, because he said I don't have to worry about him coming back to town."

"Good. I hope he broke his legs. Are you sure you're okay?"

"Yeah, just a little sore. It's funny what being abused for years will do to a person. As scared as I was, I think I was even more angry. But I'm fine. I promise."

"Okay." Izzy let out a breath of relief. "Then give me the good stuff. What did I just witness between you and Diesel? It looked like he *hugged* you by his truck. Did you crack that stone?"

Tracey glanced out the window and saw him pacing by his truck with his phone pressed to his ear. "I don't know what's going on with us." She told Izzy about the last few days. "But there was a moment this morning, and again tonight, when I swear he was either going to kiss me or tell me he wanted to."

"Don't kid yourself. That's not a man who hesitates or asks permission to kiss a woman. He's the kind of guy who bends you over the pool table and takes what he wants."

Tracey wrinkled her nose, not wanting to think about what he does with other women. "I thought so, too, but I'm telling you, I felt something big. Something *different*. Like that embrace you saw out there. What the heck was that? And to just act like he didn't do it afterward? I swear it's like he opens up a tiny bit, and then he snaps closed again. I want to dig my fingers into that crack and pry him open."

"You and every other able-bodied woman," Izzy teased. "Many of whom are already *prying* open his zipper."

"Don't remind me." Tracey felt a little nauseated at that. "I know it's nuts, but I want to get inside him and see what makes him tick."

"Oh, *Trace*. I know he looks at you like he wants to eat you for dessert, but you really like him, don't you?"

"He got to me." Tracey shrugged. "But he confuses me. I mean, right before I came inside we argued because he said he was staying out there tonight after telling me I didn't need anyone standing guard. You know what he said? That he wasn't doing it for me. What does that even mean?"

"He said that?"

"Yes!"

Izzy flopped back against the couch cushions and kicked her feet up on the coffee table, crossing her ankles. "I think the boy's got a crush on my girl."

Tracey groaned and fell back beside her. "A crush? What does that mean in the biker world?"

"Hell if I know. That you might get bent over a bed instead of a pool table?"

They both laughed.

Tracey rested her head on Izzy's shoulder. "What am I gonna do?"

"You could go with friends with benefits, like me and Jared." Jared Stone, Dixie's husband's hot, arrogant younger brother who never sat still for more than five minutes, was a world-renowned chef and restaurateur. He and Izzy had been hooking up for as long as Tracey had known them.

"No offense, Iz, but I don't think I'm wired for that."

"I'm not sure I am anymore, either. Everyone is so happy and in love, I'm starting to want more, too."

"I've always wanted more." She thought about Diesel and the longing in his voice when he'd talked about his mother. He'd been alone for so long, she wondered if he ever got lonely. "Do you think Diesel will ever settle down with one woman?"

"Sorry, Trace, but that would be like caging a grizzly. Dix

told me he's leaving town after the holidays. Did you know that?"

"Yes." Tracey sighed and stood to look out the window again. Diesel was leaning against his truck, arms crossed, eagle eyes trained on her, like he sensed her every move. Her pulse quickened. She could stare at him all day long trying to figure him out if not for the desires making her body hot. She sat beside Izzy again. "Of all the guys in the world, why is he the only match that lights my fire? Why can't I turn off my feelings for him?"

"I keep asking myself the same thing about Jared."

"What's wrong with us?"

"Nothing. You're into a big, off-limits, growly guy, and I'm addicted to sex with Jared." Izzy grinned. "Nobody fucks like Jared Stone. The man is legendary. I think he has a magic dick."

Tracey rolled her eyes.

"I'm serious. That sucker comes near me, and I get all twitchy and excited. I'm going to start calling him my personal *orgasmatron*."

"You should put that on a T-shirt for him," Tracey said through her laughter.

"I just might do that. But seriously, we need to find you a nice guy with a magic dick. Was Dennis good in bed?"

"How would I know? I have nothing to compare him to. But I don't remember it being magical."

"He's the *only* guy you've ever been with? How did I not know this about you?"

"Because it's not something I go around telling people." She lowered her voice. "Want to know another secret?"

"If it's juicy."

Tracey nudged her. "Hey, you don't want to hear my *sappy*

secrets?"

"Save those for Josie. She's all about that flowery jazz."

"She *is*. I love that about her. She's so in love with Jed, it practically oozes off her."

"Right? So give me the juice, baby."

Tracey couldn't believe what she was about to admit, but the dreams she'd had about Diesel brought it all to the forefront. "I've never had the big O with a guy."

"What?" Izzy sat up. "Are you kidding? That asshole hurt you and didn't even have the goods to satisfy you? That's it. I'm going to find you a great guy who will treat you like gold and pleasure you with his magic dick."

How about a growly guy with a magic tongue that likes to lap up honey? Tracey clamped her mouth shut to keep the thought from flying out. She needed to stop this craziness before she ended up bent over a pool table.

A thrill darted through her.

She tried to ignore the sizzle and burn of desire, but it was like trying to stop a raging bull.

Chapter Six

DIESEL HAD SPENT so many years avoiding personal connections, he'd thought he was a master at it. But in one weekend he'd completely fucked it up. It was Monday evening, and he'd been giving himself hell all day. What had he been thinking, spending all that time with Tracey? The need to protect her, to know she was safe, had left him unable to walk away last night. If that wasn't bad enough, he couldn't stop thinking about how incredible she'd felt sleeping across his body, like she belonged there. He kept seeing her adorable smirk when she teased him and the way she'd looked at him when he'd talked about his mother. *God*, that had hit him like a truck, snapping something inside him that made him want to be even closer to her. He never made mistakes, especially not with women. But a thousand men couldn't have held him back from that embrace. Now everything was messed up. She had walked in for her shift tonight with eyes full of hope, flashing that secret look women gave men when they had a special bond, and he'd fucking loved it so much he'd smiled like an idiot.

There was no denying the magnitude of his mistakes. He'd needed to take a giant step back, no matter how much it killed him. It was torture putting up walls between them again, but that space was vital to keep Tracey from getting hurt. Their connection was too potent for anything less, even if after two hours of avoiding eye contact, he was ready to ask Bullet to beat him to smithereens. Maybe that would make it easier.

Tracey was heading up to the bar, her almond eyes sliding nervously to him. He fucking hated that he made her feel anything other than safe and happy. *Or hot and bothered.* There was no denying the way her sinful innocence got to him when she got flustered. It was by far the sexiest thing he'd ever seen. But that enjoyment had to be something of the past. He wanted to tell her he was sorry, that he had no business taking her out last night. But he knew if he pulled her aside, none of the right words would come out. He wanted her too badly. If he opened his mouth, his next move would be sealing it over hers, getting himself into even deeper trouble.

Church was starting in twenty minutes, the perfect excuse to get the hell out of there early. He looked at Tracey nearing the bar and shot a glare at Izzy, who had been bitching at him since she'd come in for her shift. "You take her. I'm outta here."

Izzy glowered. "What crawled up your ass and died to-night?"

It wasn't his ass that had been affected. It was that fucking organ in his chest, which was more dangerous than a machine gun. He turned away, but not before he saw the shattered look in Tracey's eyes. He'd gone up against some of the toughest guys around, and not one could take him to his knees the way that sexy little waif did.

As he headed for the front door, Jeanette, a tall blonde he'd hooked up with earlier in the summer, walked in with two of her girlfriends, dressed to impress in tight jeans, high heels, and cleavage-baring shirts. Jeanette's eyes locked on Diesel. She tossed her hair over her shoulders, smiling seductively as she sauntered up to him, stopping only when her breasts brushed against his arm. "I'm glad you're here. Now I can have a *really* good time."

"I'm on my way to a meeting."

"That's okay. I need time anyway. I'll text you for a ride later." She winked and went to join her friends.

Diesel uttered a curse as he left the bar and headed around back. He blew through the doors of the clubhouse, heading straight for the fridge as his buddies called out greetings. He opened a beer and guzzled it down. It was times like these he was glad he'd set up a gym in the back room. He needed the outlet now more than ever.

Bullet sidled up to him with Bear on his heels. "What's got your balls in a knot?"

"Nothin'." He tossed the empty bottle in the trash and pulled out another.

Bear clapped a hand on Diesel's and Bullet's shoulders. "How's it going?"

Diesel eyed Bear's hand on his shoulder.

Bear stepped back. "Sorry, man. I forgot you don't like to be touched." He cocked a grin. "I gotta ask. How does that work with the ladies?"

"However the hell I want it to." Diesel took another drink, biting back thoughts of how much he'd liked being touched by Tracey, and it hadn't even been sexual.

Bear nudged Bullet. "Sounds like someone needs to get laid."

Diesel glowered at him. "I'm not in the mood, buddy."

"Sorry, man." Bear's expression turned serious. "Anything I

can help with?"

The only thing that'll help is hitting the road, putting miles between me and that sweet little temptress. "Yeah, I need to talk to you guys about the bar. Have you thought about who to replace me with after I take off?"

"We're tossing around some ideas," Bullet said. "What're you thinking?"

"That you can't hire a pussy. Someone's got to keep the girls safe."

"We're putting the word out at the meeting tonight, but I'll fill in until we find the right person," Bullet said. "Don't worry, man. We'll keep her safe."

He shouldn't be surprised that Bullet knew he was worried about Tracey. He had great instincts. As far as filling his position went, Diesel trusted Bullet's and the other Dark Knights' instincts, but short of them, other people's were a crapshoot. "Good. I bought some spotlights for the back of the bar and the front of this place. I thought I'd hook 'em up later tonight."

"I'm all in with the back of the bar, but you want to put spotlights on the clubhouse?" Bear asked.

Diesel finished his beer and tossed the empty bottle in the trash. "If those assholes were smarter, they'd have broken the light by the door. Having a backup plan can only help."

"That makes sense. It's not a bad idea," Bear agreed. "We can run it by everyone tonight."

"Need help installing them on the bar tonight?" Bullet asked.

"Nah. I've got it. Thanks."

Bones waved them over to a table by Moon, Tex, and Court, as more Dark Knights filed into the clubhouse. Biggs headed up to the table at the front of the room with the other club officials. As a Nomad, Diesel wasn't required to attend church, but these were the connections that mattered most, and he made a point of attending when he could out of respect for the brotherhood. Regardless of which chapter he was visiting, his fellow Dark Knights always had his back.

The meeting started, and as Biggs discussed club business, Diesel's mind traveled across the parking lot to Tracey. He was doing the right thing by putting space between them, but that didn't mean he'd leave her unprotected.

Biggs opened the floor to the members, and Bullet let them know about Diesel leaving and the opening for a bartender. A number of guys said they knew people who would be interested. *People* weren't Dark Knights, but he had to trust that Bullet would choose wisely.

When Bullet finished, Diesel took the floor. "You all know there was trouble at the bar two nights ago. The two men who attacked Tracey Kline had outstanding warrants for assault, so they're taken care of. I dealt with the third guy, and I've got eyes on him. I don't think Tracey or her roommate is in imminent danger, but I want to set up drive-bys for their house and keep up a club presence."

There was a murmur of agreement and nods. Biggs held up his hand, and the room quieted. "That sounds like a good idea. I assume you'll be coordinating it?"

"No, sir. I want some space from this one." Diesel gritted his teeth as some of the guys wondered aloud about his decision, and Biggs gave him a scrutinizing stare, asking the silent question, *Are you sure about that?* Diesel nodded.

Biggs's raised a hand, silencing the room. "A'right. Do we have any volunteers to coordinate the efforts?"

"I'll take it on," Moon offered, looking curiously at Diesel. "Anyone who wants to volunteer can talk to me after the meeting."

"I've got another suggestion," Diesel announced. "I think we ought to put spotlights on the front of the clubhouse."

Questions rose around him, and Diesel spoke louder. "Hear me out. Nothing is more important than the safety of the women who work in that bar. They have jobs to do, and sometimes that means going out the back door." He fucking hated the idea of Tracey ever going out there again. "If you don't want lights on the clubhouse, we can erect poles in the parking lot and direct the lights toward the back of the bar, but that area needs to be lit in a way that assholes can't knock them out easily. We can put the lights on a timer, so they come on at nine and go off an hour after the bar closes. It won't cost the club a penny. I've already bought the lights. I'll install them and pay the additional electrical costs each month."

Everyone spoke at once, but Biggs was quick to silence them. "We'll take a vote on this, but before we do, I want to say something. My daughter works at that bar, and you know Dixie's tough."

"A fucking ball breaker," Crow called out.

Biggs nodded. "That's true, but what happened to Tracey could easily have happened to Dix or to any one of your daughters or wives. So before you vote, think of the women in your life."

"More importantly," Bullet said gruffly, "think of the reason this club exists." He pushed to his feet. "We're here to protect this community, and while what Diesel has suggested directly affects our bar, it also sends a message to dirtbags not to fuck with our community."

"You got that right," one of the guys shouted, and there was a round of agreement.

"Vance and I can put poles in the lot if you want to go that route," Vaughn Bando offered. He and his brother, Vance, owned a concrete company. "We just need a day or two to get it done."

Biggs took a vote, and the lights were approved. The Bando brothers agreed to get permits and erect poles in the lot.

Diesel sat down as another member took the floor, and Bullet leaned closer, speaking low. "Something happen between you and that sweetheart that I should know about?"

Yeah, just not what you think. Diesel shook his head.

Moon leaned in from the next table, eyeing Bullet. "Do the fireworks between them count?"

Diesel shut him down with a dark stare.

After the meeting, some of the guys went to play pool, while others played darts or sat around shooting the shit. Diesel played a few games of pool with the guys and talked with Vaughn about the work he was going to do. He was heading across the room to sit down when Biggs intercepted him.

"That was a good idea you had about the lights," Biggs said.

"Thanks."

"But are you sure you want to give up control of those ride-bys?" Biggs asked.

Diesel didn't like anyone knowing his business, but he wasn't about to lie to Biggs. "It needs to be done."

"I respect that."

Diesel's phone vibrated, and he pulled it out of his pocket to read the message, biting back a curse at the sight of Jeanette's name on the message. *Ready for that ride?*

"Everything okay, son?" Biggs asked.

"I gotta take care of something at the bar."

"Does that *something* have big hazel eyes?"

Diesel pocketed his phone, his gut churning. That hazel-eyed girl was the only one he gave a damn about, and he was starting to wonder when the last time was that he'd done something that *didn't* have to do with her. But as was his way, he didn't see a need to respond. "See you around, Biggs."

He left the clubhouse and headed back into the bar. His eyes found Tracey like a GPS missile. Jeanette walked into his line of sight, her face lighting up as she hurried over to him and said, "I knew you'd come!"

Jeanette touched his arm at the very moment Tracey looked over. His chest constricted at the hurt rising in her eyes and eating up the space between them. He yanked his arm away from Jeanette.

"Sorry. I forgot. *No touching*," she said playfully.

"Let's get out of here." He pushed open the door and followed her out, chased by the soul-crushing sadness he'd left behind.

Chapter Seven

TUESDAY AFTERNOON, AFTER a night of bitching with Josie and Izzy and stuffing her face with ice cream, Tracey was still fit to be tied. That in and of itself infuriated her. It wasn't like there was anything real between her and Diesel. It was a good thing she was working the day shift, because if she had to work with him, she'd lose her frigging mind. She'd been an idiot to think they'd had some sort of connection. She'd bet the big jerk didn't even know the meaning of the word *connection* beyond when his dick was inside some drunk woman.

She pocketed her tips and cleared a table, chastising herself for letting him get her so riled up. She couldn't afford to be off her game today. She was the only waitress working the lunch shift, and they were beyond busy. She was headed for the kitchen when she saw Damon and Bones walk into the bar. Damon waved, flashing his megawatt smile right at her.

"Hey there," she called out, hands full. "There's a table in the back. I'll be right over." She'd gladly serve the two hottest, nicest doctors around.

She pushed through the kitchen doors and put the dirty dishes on the counter by the sink, where Ricardo was busy washing dishes. Ricardo was nineteen and part of the Young Knights mentorship program run by the Dark Knights. He worked as a dishwasher, but was also taking cooking lessons from Finlay, with hopes of one day becoming a chef.

Ricardo reached for a plate. "Still busy out there?"

"Crazy busy."

"Tracey, you're just in time." Finlay was transferring something from a tray to a cooling rack.

"In time for you to wipe my brain clean? Because I'd really like to delete a few things from my head right about now."

"I was going to say to taste test Ricardo's latest creation." Finlay turned with a little chocolate cake on a plate and an empathetic expression on her face. "Are you sure you don't want to tell me what's bothering you?"

As much as Tracey wanted to tell anyone who would listen exactly what she thought of Diesel, she also didn't want to. She hated the way she felt about him right now, and she still had to work with him. It wasn't his fault she'd built things up in her head and couldn't shake off the hurt of his ignoring her. She was seriously toying with the idea of looking for a new job. It was only August, and he wasn't leaving until January. That was a long time to subject herself to watching him with other women night after night. Keeping the details of her disillusionment to herself, she said, "Have you ever felt like you had your feet planted firmly on the ground, and then a gust of wind suddenly sweeps you up and leaves you drifting? And all you want is to make sense of things, to land again so you can start over, but that wind keeps blowing the ground just out of reach?"

"Sounds like a Katy Perry song." Ricardo began singing "Fireworks."

Finlay wiggled her shoulders to the beat.

Tracey couldn't help but laugh. "Well, Katy must have been thinking about me when she wrote it."

"Sounds like whatever you're going through is pretty confusing," Finlay said.

"That's putting it mildly."

"I'm sorry you're going through a hard time, but this should help." Finlay handed her the plate. "It's lava cake. Ricardo made it. Take a bite while it's still warm. It's guaranteed to put a smile on your face."

Tracey ate a bite, and the rich chocolate melted in her mouth. "Oh, Ricardo, this is heavenly. You're going to make an amazing chef."

"Thanks. Fin's a good teacher."

"Can I get a dozen of those to go so I can drown in them tonight?" Tracey took another bite, then set the plate down. "I have to get back out there. Bones and Damon just got here."

Finlay lowered her voice. "*Go.* Dr. Rhys could put a smile on anyone's face."

Tracey headed out of the kitchen. She stopped by a table to check on customers on her way to Damon's table and noticed Bones talking to a group of guys at another table. She felt the heat of Damon's appreciative gaze as she approached. "Hi. Sorry I took so long."

"Not a problem." Damon's expression turned serious as he took in the yellowing bruises on her cheek. "I heard what happened the other night. I'm so sorry. How are you feeling?"

"I'm okay. The soreness is easing up. Thanks for asking."

"I hear you fought a good fight."

"Not quite good enough," she said softly.

"But you're okay, and that's what really matters." Damon

leaned closer, his voice low and sexy. "You know, I've been thinking about you since the wedding. How'd you like to go to dinner with me? We could check out Nova Lounge in Pleasant Hill on your next night off, share a nice dinner, get to know each other better." Nova Lounge was the most expensive restaurant around. It was co-owned by Jared Stone and business mogul Seth Braden.

Her nerves pinged, and her thoughts raced back to Diesel, bringing renewed hurt. She was *not* going to pine for a man who was no good for her when this gorgeous gentleman was asking her out on a proper date. "I'd like that."

"Great." His face lit up like he'd won the lottery. "When's your next night off?"

The last time someone had been that thrilled about going out with her, she'd been a teenager. She'd forgotten how good it felt to be wanted. "Thursday."

"Fantastic." He took out his phone, and she gave him her number and her address as Bones returned to the table.

Damon made a big deal out of Tracey going out with him, and Bones seemed happy for both of them, although he gave Tracey curious looks that she couldn't read. After taking their orders, she made a beeline for Izzy at the bar.

"Why do you look like the cat that swallowed a canary?" Izzy teased.

Tracey leaned closer, whispering, "Damon Rhys asked me out!"

"*What?*" Izzy slapped her hand on the bar, then lowered her voice. "The orgasm gods were listening! This is *amazing*. I want all the details. How did he ask? When are you going? Where's he taking you?"

Tracey told her everything. "But I have no idea what to

wear to a place like that."

"Something sexy but not sleazy. You can borrow one of my outfits, but it might be more fun to go shopping and splurge on something new. After all, this is your first date since Dennis. It's a big occasion, *and* it's with the hottest doctor around."

Tracey wanted to say her first date had been with Diesel when they'd gone for pizza, but that wasn't a date, and why the heck was she letting Diesel ruin this for her, anyway? "Yeah, I think I'll do that. I have tomorrow afternoon off, and I'm not babysitting Hail until seven. Are you free? Do you want to come? I'll ask Josie, too."

"I have to work, but definitely text me pics before you buy anything."

Izzy's excitement pumped up Tracey even more. If only it could quell the dull ache in her chest that Damon wasn't Diesel.

BY THURSDAY AFTERNOON Diesel felt like a wild animal ready to charge. The last few days had been worse than hell. He knew he was doing the right thing by putting space between himself and Tracey, but he fucking missed everything about her. He'd thought they'd still be able to work together civilly, but she'd been giving him the cold shoulder since Monday night, rarely even looking at him. When he did catch her eye, she looked like she wanted to murder him. He missed her sass and the sweet and sinful way she used to look at him that twisted him up inside. Even the way she used to bitch at him was better than being treated like he didn't fucking exist.

Why the hell couldn't he let her go? Moon was coordinating

the drive-bys at her place, but Diesel still found himself driving over there in the middle of the night, needing to see that all was quiet with his own eyes. The worst part of it wasn't even that trying to let her go was like driving ice picks beneath his fingernails. It was knowing *he'd* caused her to go from sweet and sassy to cold and tough, and that drove those damn ice picks directly into his heart.

Finlay came out of the kitchen and set a plate with two sandwiches and chips on the bar. How'd she know he'd forgotten to eat? "Thanks."

She followed his gaze to Tracey, who was talking with customers by the pool tables. "You're going to bore a hole through her if you keep staring like that."

Diesel didn't respond, and he didn't look away from Tracey. She was getting off in a few hours, and if he didn't fix things between them, he was going to explode. He turned his back to the floor and crossed his arms, futilely trying to shove his feelings for Tracey away.

"You know, I always thought you were like Bullet," Finlay said sweetly. "But you're not. He may be crass, but at least I always know what he's thinking. The very first time he spoke to me, before we were even properly introduced, he asked if I wanted to take a ride on the Bullet train." She giggled. "Can you imagine?"

Diesel gritted his teeth, because yeah, he could fucking imagine. "You got a point?"

"Yes. Communicate with her, Diesel. If you want sex, tell her. She's a big girl. She can handle it. You might be surprised by her answer."

"I don't want to fuck her, Finlay," he said harshly. If that was all he wanted, it would be easy to move past. But if he got inside Tracey, the emotions that were eating him up would pour out like lava, and there'd be no turning back.

"*Oh,*" she said with surprise. "Well, this tension between you two is like quicksand, and if you're not careful, she'll slip right between your fingers."

He chewed on that for the next few hours. When the lunch rush was over and the bar had nearly cleared out, Tracey stalked up to the bar with daggers shooting from her eyes. "The couple by the pool table wants a round of Cokes, but I'm going to clock out. You can bring them over." She turned on her heel and headed for the office.

Adrenaline surged through his veins. *Fuck this.* He rounded the bar and followed her into the office, closing the door behind him. "What's up your ass?"

She spun around, fury flying from her lips. "What's up *my* ass? You take care of me, sleep in my bed, cook for me, and take me out for pizza, earning my trust and treating me like there's something between us. Then you stop speaking to me without any explanation, and you have the gall to ask what's up *my* ass?" Her words cut like knives. "It's okay for you to pretend I don't exist, but the minute I give it back to you, you get mad? Fuck you, Diesel. I was stupid for even thinking there could be something between—"

He crushed his lips to hers, hauling her against him, taking the kiss deeper, wanting to climb inside her. He only meant to shut her up, but holy hell, the way she kissed him back was fucking nirvana. He couldn't stop devouring her, and she was right there with him.

Until she pushed at his chest, cheeks flushed, and snapped, "What was *that*?"

"You were stuck in a rant. I had to shut you up."

"So you *kissed* me?" She looked appalled, but she sure hadn't kissed that way.

"That sexy mouth of yours was going off on me."

"Of course I was going off on you! You've been treating me like I did something wrong, and *you're* the one who left with some drunk chick the other night."

He leaned over her, so he had her full attention, seething, "I didn't fuck her this time. And I don't answer to *anyone*, Tracey."

Her nostrils flared, eyes so full of hurt and anger, he could swim in them. "And I don't kiss guys who don't respect me enough to answer to me. I'm *so* glad I accepted a date with Damon for tonight. I'm *done* with you."

"You're going out with *Rhys*?" he fumed as she threw open the door and stormed out, leaving him seeing red, a string of curses raging out as his fist flew through the wall, and that ice pick in his chest sank deeper.

Chapter Eight

TRACEY MUST BE losing her mind. Nova Lounge was built on a bluff overlooking Pleasant Hill. It was the most glamorous restaurant around, and *she* couldn't stop thinking about kissing Diesel. How did that man overshadow marble floors, a mix of brick and elaborately carved wooden walls and columns, high ceilings with metallic, patterned panels, and sparkling gold lights raining down over each table? That wasn't even the worst of it. The fancy surroundings were nothing compared to the gorgeous, thoughtful gentleman sitting across from her in his crisp white dress shirt, looking at her like she was some sort of princess.

Damon was not only good-looking, but he was also thoughtful. He'd called to say he'd be late because one of his patients had gone into early labor. He'd brought Tracey a bouquet of flowers, and he must have told her a hundred times how beautiful she looked. Thank goodness she and Josie had gone shopping yesterday and found the cutest black minidress. It was classy but not clingy and had a built-in bra, which made it extra comfortable. The spaghetti straps weren't too thin, the neckline dipped rather than plunged, and the skirt flowed nicely to the middle of her thighs. She'd even found a pair of inexpensive strappy sandals to go with it.

She'd been a nervous wreck before their date, but they were halfway through a delicious tortellini dinner and he was so open and easy to talk to, she couldn't even remember why she'd been nervous about their evening together. He told her he'd become an ob-gyn because his father had been one, and that his father had loved his job so much that even when he'd come home at three in the morning after a difficult delivery, he still glowed from bringing life into the world. Damon tossed jokes into his stories, so comfortable in his own skin, a stark contrast to the herculean efforts it took to learn anything about Diesel. Her body flooded with heat at the thought of Diesel and that kiss...

God, that kiss. She'd relived it a hundred times. Her thoughts started to drift to how it had felt to be crushed against his hard body, to be devoured by his desire. What was she doing? Diesel was a no-go, and if she wasn't careful, thoughts of him would ruin her date.

She tried to push thoughts of Diesel away, scrambling for something to say. "So, how many of your patients hit on you?" She cringed inwardly. It was the first thing that popped into her head, no doubt because Izzy and Josie had been begging her to ask him.

He laughed and sipped his wine. "I don't notice that stuff."

"Come on, everybody notices that stuff." She had a feeling this attentive man noticed everything.

He smiled. "I'll sound conceited or arrogant if I admit that."

"You just admitted it," she teased. "Curious minds want to know. Spill it, Doc."

"Fine, but remember, *you* asked. The first thing single women look at is my left hand. Once they notice there's no ring, that's when things change, and they go from nervous to flirtatious."

"I can just imagine the conversations." She made her voice higher. *"While you're down there…"*

They both laughed.

"You're not far off, believe it or not."

"I believe it. So, why are you still single?" She ate a bite of tortellini.

"I'm old-fashioned. I want what my parents have, and I guess I haven't met *the one* yet." Heat flickered in his eyes.

She took a drink, silently urging the butterflies she'd felt toward him the other day to swarm or goose bumps to chase up her limbs, but there wasn't even a flutter. *Diesel must have broken me.* A flutter stirred in her chest with the thought of the brooding growler, and she nearly choked on her wine, coughing and clearing her throat. *Damn you.* She sipped her water.

"You okay?" Damon asked.

"Mm-hm. Yes. Thanks."

"Now it's my turn to ask the uncomfortable questions. Wayne hasn't told me much about you. Where are you from?"

"I grew up in Virginia Beach."

"That's a nice area. What brought you here?"

She debated not telling him about her past, but he'd been so honest with her, she didn't want to lie. She already felt like he was way out of her league, despite her girlfriends insisting there were no leagues, and she was about to reveal just how far. "I'm not proud of this, but I got out of an abusive relationship and ended up at the Parkvale Women's Shelter. Bones—*Wayne*—volunteers there. That's how I met the Whiskeys, and Red offered me a job."

"Oh, Tracey. I'm sorry to hear that."

"It was two years ago, and I was young when I got involved with the guy."

His expression was serious. "It was a long-term relationship?"

"Yes. Too long. But I'm not the same person I was then." Why did she feel the need to defend herself?

"What's changed for you?"

"Gosh, everything. I was only sixteen when we met. I've learned a lot about life, love, valuing myself. I won't settle for less than I'm worth. I'm stronger now, emotionally and physically. I'm taking martial arts, and I can't wait to get back to it next week." Diesel's voice whispered through her mind. *And once you're healed up, I'm going to teach you how to fight.* Her stomach knotted.

"Martial arts. Now, that's impressive."

She reached for her glass, and Damon lifted his in a toast. "Here's to new beginnings."

Their conversations turned lighter as they finished dinner. When they left the restaurant, Tracey couldn't help but think about how nice it was to be with someone who actually talked with her. She knew more about Damon after two and a half hours than she'd learned about Diesel in two years. But as he walked her to her door, there was no denying the lack of sparks between them. Damon felt like a friend, the way Moon or her other male friends did, and she blamed Diesel for that damn kiss.

"Thank you for tonight," she said on the porch. "I had a great time."

"Me too. I can't remember when I've had this much fun on a date."

He leaned in to kiss her, and she closed her eyes, silently

hoping she might feel sparks. But all she felt was the sweet peck of his lips. *What* was wrong with her? Damon was honest to a fault, handsome as could be, and looking for forever love. What more could she want? Diesel's face bloomed before her eyes, and that passionate kiss came rushing back, infuriating her.

"I'd love to see you again." Damon's voice brought her mind back to the moment. "We could take my boat out this weekend."

"I had such a great time, but—"

"*Uh-oh.*" He cocked a brow, his voice full of disappointment.

"I'm sorry, Damon. You have to know how wonderful you are. I mean you're literally every woman's dream guy."

"Except yours, apparently."

"It's me, not you." As the words left her lips, they both laughed. "I know how that sounds, but it's really true. I like you a lot, but..."

"It's okay, Trace. Is there someone else?"

She lowered her eyes briefly, then met his gaze. "Yes and no."

"Sounds complicated."

"To say the least," she said softly.

"Well, I hope he knows how lucky he is. But you'd better stick to your guns about not settling for less than you're worth, because you're a pretty spectacular woman."

"Right now I feel a bit like a dummy."

He laughed. "You're following your heart. There's no harm in that. Thanks again for a great night. I'll see you around."

As he walked away, the anger simmering inside her rose to a boil. If only Diesel hadn't followed her into the office. If only he hadn't kissed her like she'd never been kissed before.

But it was so much bigger than that. It was two years of getting under her skin, making her obsess over the things he did. Two years of making butterflies nest in her stomach, all those heart-racing moments that snuck into her dreams, and then turning all that sizzling heat into something more, something that felt special and deep, after she was attacked.

If only Diesel didn't exist. That might solve her issues.

She was so mad at him, at herself, at the situation, she debated hunting him down and giving that beast a piece of her mind.

DIESEL POUNDED THE heavy bag at the clubhouse, trying to drown out thoughts of Tracey on her date with pretty-boy Rhys. But it was like trying to silence the fucking roar of a train. Rhys was the guy who had made Diesel realize how much he felt for Tracey at that damn wedding, and now Diesel was making plans to leave town, practically handing Tracey to him on a silver platter.

Fuck.

He stalked away from the heavy bag, tearing off his gloves and throwing them to the floor. He lay on the bench, the weights already loaded on the bar. As he did a set of presses, his mind traveled back to that kiss. He'd been replaying it all night, trying to figure out if he'd fabricated her kissing him back, but he could still feel her tongue thrusting over his, her eager mouth devouring him. He could also still hear the venom in her voice. *I don't kiss guys who don't respect me enough to answer to me. I'm done with you.*

He gritted his teeth, pushing the bar up, his arms shaking under the weight of it. Dixie had seen the hole in the office wall and had peppered him with questions until he'd finally had enough and snarled, "Fucking Tracey. That's why I punched the wall." Dixie had gotten a kick out of that, which had only pissed him off more. He'd patched the damn hole after he'd closed the bar, and that had only amped up his anger.

He pushed out one more rep, set the bar on the rack, and sat up. This was so messed up. He wasn't some dumbass kid with a crush. He took off his baseball cap and raked a hand through his hair, looking at the hat he'd had forever. Tracey's face appeared before him. *You can trust me with your secrets.*

His chest constricted, and he put his hat back on, rising to his feet.

"Diesel Black, get your butt out here!"

He snapped around at the sound of Tracey's angry voice. What the hell? He headed down the hall to the main meeting room, where he found her pacing, hands fisted by her sides, gorgeous in a sexy little black dress. A dress she'd worn for the goddamn doctor.

"I am *so* mad at you!" she seethed. "You ruined my date! I was with the perfect guy, and all I could think about was *you*."

He should probably feel bad for the pleasure that brought, but there was no hiding the grin tugging at his lips.

"You and your stupid grunts and growls and that *kiss*!" She groaned, still pacing furiously.

He stepped closer. "Yeah?"

"Don't *yeah* me. You're ruining everything! You've got my head all messed up."

"Mine too." He took another step closer.

"I had a *great* time tonight with an amazing guy who actually talked to me like a regular person and asked me to go out on his *boat* with him. And I felt *nothing.* Not one little spark when he kissed me or complimented me, or *anything.*"

Thank fucking God. Diesel moved closer. "Good."

She stopped pacing and stared at him. "It's not good! It's a disaster! I swore I would never get involved with a guy who was bad for me again, and I can't stop thinking about *you.* You're the worst guy on the planet for me."

"You're not wrong."

She laughed incredulously. "*Great!* I'm a frigging bad-boy magnet, but at least I know I'm right when I say I'm heading down the wrong path. *That* makes me feel better."

"I'm not a *boy.*" He closed the remaining distance between them. "And I'm definitely not what you need."

"I *know!*" She was breathing so hard, her chest brushed against his bare chest with every inhalation. "Why are you shirtless?"

"I can't get you out of my fucking head either."

"*Stop* thinking about me!"

His jaw clenched.

"All I want is a nice guy who respects me and wants to have a happy life with me."

"You want more than that. You want this." He lowered his mouth to hers, wrapping one arm around her tight little body, pushing his other hand into her hair. She was right there with him, feverishly devouring his mouth. *Oh yeah, baby girl, neither of us can deny this.*

When their lips parted, she wobbled, and he held her tighter. "You can't do that," she said breathily. "It screws with my head."

"That's what you want, baby girl. You want what Dr. Fuck-face can't give you."

She narrowed her eyes. "Don't call him that. He's a great guy."

"He is, but it's true. He doesn't make you wet like I do, or make your knees weak, does he?"

"*No*, okay?" Her cheeks flushed. "I told you. I felt nothing, and it's *your* fault. Did the woman the other night make you feel like you do when you kiss me?"

"I didn't let that woman put her lips on me."

"Yeah, *right*. I can't do this with you." She sounded on the verge of tears, and that killed him. "I don't want to be a notch on your belt, and you don't answer to anyone."

He tightened his hold on her. "I've never answered to anyone, but I answered to *you*," he growled. "I told you I didn't fuck her."

"But you followed it up by drawing a line in the sand, telling me you don't answer to anyone."

He lifted her up and set her on the pool table, wedging himself between her legs, and grabbed her chin, angling her face up so she had to look into his eyes. "Listen carefully, because I don't have time for grammar games. If I don't touch you soon, I'm going to lose my fucking mind. I said I didn't fuck her, and then I *explained* that I don't answer to anyone but I was answering to *you*."

"*Oh,*" came out as a stunned whisper.

He pushed his hands up her outer thighs, brushing his thumbs over her damp panties, and she inhaled a sharp breath, desire brimming in her eyes. His cock jerked with need. "I've got nothing to offer you, baby girl, but the shirt on my back. But I want *you* like I've never wanted anything in my life, and if you're in my bed, there won't be anyone else."

"But you're leaving."

"I was leaving to escape *this*." He pushed a thumb over her clit, working it in slow circles through her panties, and her breath rushed out. "Plans can change."

"They can?" she panted out, eyes wide.

Her sweet innocence, all breathy and needy, slayed him. "Hell yes. I need you in my bed. Tell me you want me, baby girl."

"Take me—"

He crushed his mouth to hers and lifted her into his arms. Her legs wound around him as he strode toward the steps, taking them two at a time. She felt fucking perfect, tasted like sweet desire and sinful pleasure. Devouring her mouth, he pushed his hands beneath her panties, stroking over her wetness, earning a lustful moan. She was so wet and ready, he couldn't wait to get his mouth on her. He pulled her dress strap down her arm as he carried her into the bedroom, and heard a *rip*. She gasped.

"*Wait.* It's new." She tried to reach the zipper.

He set her down and moved behind her, unzipping the dress. It puddled at her feet, revealing bruises on her back and side, unleashing all the emotions he'd been holding in. Protectiveness and possessiveness battled for dominance. His chest constricted against that tangle of barbed wire he'd tried to avoid. But there was no more avoiding the sharp points digging into his flesh, claiming him as he was about to claim her. He reached around her from behind, palming her breasts, rolling her nipples between his fingers and thumbs, earning one sinful moan after another, and touched his forehead to the center of her back. The hatred he had for those fuckers who had hurt her carved through the darkness inside him. He imagined every slice severing a tether that had chained him down and had kept him from her. He fought against the hatred, pushing it to the cellar of his soul, focusing on the beauty who had come to him, *chosen* him over the man who was better for her. *Fuck*, that turned him inside out.

He pressed a kiss between her shoulder blades, all those unfamiliar warm feelings boiling and burning, until his entire body ached with them. He tore down her sexy black panties, leaving her in only her heels, and quickly shed his boots, socks, and clothes, needing to feel her hot flesh against his. He pressed his body to her back, his cock against her ass, caressing one breast, his other hand sliding between her legs. She was waxed bare, and the feel of her drew a growl from his lungs. "So fucking beautiful."

He sealed his mouth over her shoulder, sucking and biting, as he ground against her ass and pushed two fingers into her slick heat, using his thumb on her clit.

"Oh *God*." She grabbed his wrists, craning her neck to the side, giving him better access. *"Don't stop."*

Her pleasure drove his need deeper. He worked her quicker, thrust his fingers deeper, sucked harder. She rose onto her toes, her body trembling, her ass cheeks soft and perfect against his raging cock. She dug her nails into his wrists, panting and moaning. So fucking hot. He bit down on her shoulder, and her hips bucked, her sex clenching around his fingers.

"Diesel" flew from her lips, lustful and urgent.

The sound sent heat racing through his core, and he didn't relent as she panted and gasped, her body shaking and shuddering through the very last pulse of her climax, his cock throbbing to get in on the action. She went boneless in his arms, trying to catch her breath.

"I've got you, baby girl." He kissed her neck, nudging her legs open wider with his knees. "Hands on the bed."

"*Diesel...?*" She looked nervously over her shoulder, her body going rigid.

"I'm not going to fuck your ass. But I *am* going to make you come so many times, you'll forget how to walk. Unless you want to stop." It would kill him, but he'd gladly die for her.

"*No.* I don't want to stop."

He kissed her over her shoulder, slow and deep, feeling her tension ease from her body. When their lips parted, she bent over and put her hands on the bed. What a sight, seeing the woman he'd craved like a drug for too fucking long spread wide for him, gorgeous ass there for the taking, pussy glistening. The urge to drive his cock into her was strong, but the desire to pleasure *her* was even stronger. He kissed his way down her spine and grabbed her ass with both hands, nipping and kissing down her perfect pale cheeks and along the curve of her ass. He'd waited so long to taste her, he was salivating at the heavenly scent of her arousal. He held her cheeks open wide and slid his tongue along her sex. Her sweet essence spread over his tongue, and she shuddered against him. He did it again, harder this time, dipping the tip of his tongue into her as he worked her clit with his fingers, and her moans had him quickening his efforts. She thrusted her ass back as he devoured her, but he needed *more*, and slicked his tongue from her pussy to her ass. Her cheeks clenched.

"Give yourself to me, baby girl. I won't hurt you."

She fisted her hands in the blanket as he licked and teased, until her body relaxed and she was moaning and rocking, begging for more. He suddenly, desperately needed to see her face. He pulled her up to her feet rougher than he meant to, taking her in a mind-numbing kiss. She kissed him back like she wanted to live in his mouth, and fuck, he wanted to live in hers. He lowered her to the bed, took off her heels and tossed them to the floor as he moved between her legs. Perched on his knees, he had the view of a lifetime despite the bruises, his girl willing and wanting beneath him, her hair fanned out around her beautiful face. But it was the trust in her eyes that made his insides go soft and his cock grow impossibly harder.

He dragged his hand along her wetness, covering his hand with her arousal, and gave himself a few tight strokes. "You're so fucking sexy, baby girl."

She reached for his cock, and he grabbed her hand, holding it against her belly as he lowered himself between her legs and took her clit between his teeth, teasing it with his tongue. Her hips bucked, and she touched his head with her free hand. He grabbed that wrist, moving it to her belly with the other, and held them both with one of his hands as he feasted on her. He *took* and *gave* and took some more, until she writhed and moaned and cried out his name as she came. That glorious sound tugged at him.

Sweet Jesus, this woman would be his undoing.

As she came down from the peak, panting and shaking, he crawled up her body, slowing to suck her nipple into his mouth, rubbing his hard length against her wetness. Fuck that felt good. He reclaimed her mouth, kissing her rough and greedy, and she was just as eager, clawing at his shoulders. He pinned her hands beside her head, feasting on her luscious mouth. Desire mounted inside him, pounding its way to the surface, until he couldn't take it anymore. He drew back, reeling from the emotions swimming in her eyes—filling the fucking room—so thick he could drown in them.

"My turn," she said so sweetly, it stole his breath.

He wanted to crawl over her and drive his cock down her throat, but his heart wouldn't let him, not with those bruises on her back. "As much as I want to fuck that pretty little mouth of yours, it's going to have to wait. I need to be inside you."

A seductive smile curved her lips.

He snagged a condom from the nightstand and tore it open as he went up on his knees. She watched him roll it on, doe eyes soft and affectionate and so damn beautiful he took a moment just to savor the view. She reached for him as he came down over her, and he gently pinned her wrists beside her head as he aligned their bodies, nestling his cock against her entrance.

"Wait," Tracey pleaded.

He stilled, hoping she hadn't changed her mind.

"I want my hands free so I can touch you."

"No," he said gruffly. He'd long ago locked his heart behind a lead door, chained it down, and threw away the key. She was already taunting that keyhole with some kind of magic. He didn't need to test those boundaries. But the hurt in her eyes nearly bowled him over. He dipped his head beside hers, "It's not you, baby girl."

"Then what is it?"

He didn't respond, just clenched his teeth, wishing she'd let it go. But this was his feisty girl, and he knew she wouldn't settle for silence.

"Is my touch too intimate?" she whispered over his cheek.

He lifted his head, and one look in her eyes drew the truth in the form of a nod.

"I *want* intimate," she said softly. "I don't want to feel like a prisoner in your bed. I felt like that with Dennis, and I don't ever want to feel that way again."

Gutted, his forehead fell forward. "Fuck, Trace. Is that what you feel like?"

"You don't look at me like you don't care, and you weren't touching me like that. But this"—she tried to lift her wrists, which were pinned to the bed—"feels cold. I mean, at some point it'll feel sexy and *hot*, but this is our first time, and it kind of feels like I could be anyone, and I don't want to be just anyone to you."

He released her wrists, pissed at himself. "If you were just anyone, I would've fucked you a year ago and moved on. But you're not. You're in my *bed*. Most women never make it past the pool table."

"You should have stopped after *in my bed*." She sounded a little mad and a little hurt, but the amusement in her eyes overrode both.

Amusement gave way to something softer, kinder. She reached up and caressed his cheek. Her pleading eyes held him captive as her fingers trailed down his neck and along his shoulder, alighting sensations unlike anything he'd ever felt, and it took everything he had not to swat that hand away.

"I know you have demons, and you don't have to share them with me," she said softly. "But don't lock us in a dungeon *with* them. We'll never survive. I had to trust you to let you touch me. Maybe you can try to trust me, and we can move past your demons together."

THE PAIN IN Diesel's eyes was so unexpected, Tracey wished she hadn't said anything. She could feel his muscles tensing and steeled herself, for fear he was going to climb out of bed and put an end to them.

"I don't know if it's possible to move past them," he said gruffly.

Something told her she was seeing a side of him no one else ever had, and that trust made her want him even more. "Do you want to?"

"For *you?* Fuck yeah."

"Then I know you will." He might not be eloquent or romantic, but if she'd wanted only that, she'd be with Damon. Not the man whose emotions were as real and powerful as the sea. She leaned up, whispering, "Kiss me."

His mouth covered hers, rough and demanding. His big hands moved down her hips, lifting her bottom as he thrusted, entering her fast and hard. For a moment she couldn't breathe for the overwhelming pressure and unfamiliar sensations filling her up. But he didn't stop, and she loved that he couldn't hold back, because for the first time in her life, she didn't want to, either. She bent her knees, opening her legs wider as he took her deeper with every thrust, his thick cock driving, stretching, *claiming*, filling her so completely, she could barely think. But she didn't want to think; all she wanted was to feel. She reveled in the weight of him, the thundering of their hearts, and that magnificent feeling of a perfect fit as he buried himself to the hilt and stilled. He put his arms around her, kissing her passionately, the pressure inside her mounting until it was exquisitely painful.

He tore his mouth away, gritting out, "Fuck, Trace...*Fuuck.*"

Thankfully, he reclaimed her mouth, because she was so caught up in the feel of him, she needed his breath to breathe.

Lord, this man knew how to love a woman. Every thrust of his hips sent shocks darting through her body. She clung to his arms, ran her hands down his back, his muscles bulging and flexing beneath her fingers. She grabbed his ass, and damn, like the rest of him, it was incredible. But he flinched. She smacked his ass, and he jerked, breaking their kiss.

"What the…?"

"It's like a shock collar. I want to grab your ass. If you don't want a smack, don't flinch."

A half growl, half laugh tumbled from his lips as he reclaimed hers, driving into her harder, greedier. Their teeth gnashed, tongues dancing to a frantic beat, and all thoughts fell away. Their bodies grew slick from their efforts, every pump of his hips taking her closer to the edge. She dug her fingernails into the backs of his arms, earning a low, sexy growl, which sped through her, sparking fires beneath her skin. They moved in perfect sync, creating their own symphony of moans and hungry sounds, their bodies sliding, damp skin smacking, and *God*, it was incredible. She never knew sex could be like this, all-consuming, like they were one person.

He tore his mouth away with a carnal look in his eyes, so potent, she was sure he could feel everything she felt as he slowed them down, intensifying the sensations with every thrust. She whimpered, gasping, clinging to him in desperation, hanging on to her sanity by a fast-fraying thread. And then all at once he lifted her bottom, driving his hips forward, and catapulted her into ecstasy. *"Diesel"* flew from her lungs as she soared through fireworks, hot, vibrant, and *explosive*. She could barely see, but *oh*, could she feel, as he abandoned all restraint, and surrendered to his own powerful release, gritting out her name, his body flexing and jerking.

When they finally came down from their high, she was floating, her head spinning. He grabbed her hands, pinning them to the mattress, and took her in a long, sensual kiss, sparking renewed flames.

His thick fingers laced with hers, and he brushed his lips over her cheek, whispering, "Smack my ass again, and you'll face punishment."

She laughed.

When he gazed down at her, he was smiling, and *holy cow*. Diesel was always handsome, but that smile lit *her* up from the inside out. Okay, maybe that was his cock, which was still twitching inside her, but Lordy, that smile was glorious.

And it disappeared as quickly as it had come.

His muscles tensed and he rose onto his forearms, studying her face. Tracey's nerves caught fire as he climbed off the bed and headed to the bathroom without uttering a word. Was that his way of saying he was done? Should she get dressed? Leave? Her stomach knotted, and she pulled the sheet up to her chest. He stopped at the bathroom door, and she held her breath as he glanced over his shoulder.

"Don't even *think* about leaving that bed, baby girl." He winked and headed into the bathroom.

The air rushed from her lungs, an unstoppable smile stretching her lips. She put her hand over her racing heart, telling herself to get used to the epic highs and heart-stopping unsurety of the roller coaster that was Diesel Black. She had two clear choices: step away from all that he was, or throw her arms up and go along for the ride.

She swallowed hard at the thought of giving herself over so completely to any man, much less one as hard as Diesel. But no part of her wanted to walk away from what they'd finally found.

When he came out of the bathroom, those dark, predatory eyes locked on her as he strode toward the bed, his formidable cock swaying between his thick thighs. He tore the sheets back, and her heart nearly stopped as his eyes moved slowly, lasciviously, down the length of her, leaving flames in their wake.

"Mm-mm." He crawled over her, his shaft hardening against her belly. "You're finally *mine*."

"You don't *own* me."

His jaw tightened. "The minute you walked your fine little ass into this clubhouse lookin' to *claim* me and I brought you into my bed, you became *my* girl. I don't own you, but I sure as fuck am not going to share you."

She'd been wrong about having only two options. There was a third one. A better one. This was *their* roller coaster ride, and her voice needed to carry just as much weight as his if they were going to stay on track through the highs and lows. "That goes both ways, *growly one*."

"You got that right."

She wound her arms around his neck, happiness bubbling up inside her. As his lips came hungrily down over hers, he made one of those growling noises, and she realized where that noise came from—that big heart he protected with everything he had.

Don't worry, my growly guy, I'll protect it, too.

Chapter Nine

DIESEL AWOKE TO the feel of Tracey's naked body nestled in his arms, her hair tickling his chin, and her breath warming his chest. Her hand rested on his stomach, delicate and pale against his olive skin. He'd known sex with Tracey would be hot, but he'd never imagined anything as powerful as the emotions that had consumed him when their bodies had come together. For the first time since he'd left the notion of *home* behind, he'd been swamped by feelings of being *exactly* where he was always meant to be. Those feelings had stuck with him through the night, swelling and intensifying with every kiss, every touch, and now waking up with her in his arms felt so fucking right, he never wanted to move. The nomad in him fought back, wanting to climb onto his bike and drive as fast and far as he could. But he shut that asshole down, holding her tighter.

She stirred in his arms, evoking the warmer, softer feelings he'd had, and he pressed a kiss to her head. She tilted her face up, her beautiful eyes hitting him like a heat wave.

"Hi," she said softly, pulling the sheet over her bare ass.

He kissed her forehead. "I bit that bare ass last night. You're not hiding it from me." He threw the sheets off, moving over her, loving the blush on her cheeks so much he kissed one. "Why're you blushing?"

"Because I'm not used to waking up naked with the guy I've been crushing on."

He kissed her neck. "You've been crushin' on me, sweet thing?"

"Shut up." She wrinkled her nose, whispering, "I can't *believe* I'm here."

"Why not?"

"Because of your revolving bedroom door. I never pictured myself as one of your *bed bunnies*."

"The door doesn't revolve as often as you think."

"*Please.* I see you leaving the bar with women *all* the time. You don't have to pretend otherwise. Just don't go doing it now that we're together, or you'll never have me in your bed again."

He fucking loved her confidence, but he needed to set the record straight. "You think I fucked all those women?"

She shrugged, looking vulnerable and sweet enough to eat.

"I'm not an asshole, Trace. I don't take advantage of drunk women. I drove most of them home, and yeah, I screwed some of the sober ones. But that's *all* they were, quick and dirty, mostly clothed, fucks, and they knew going into it that it wouldn't be anything more."

"And how many of them have gotten to wake up in your arms?" She turned her face away and closed her eyes. "*Don't tell me.* I don't want to know. I hate sounding jealous. I'm sorry I asked."

"Baby girl, when it comes to you, I wrote the book on jealousy." He kissed her cheek, and she opened her eyes, beaming up at him.

"Yeah, you kind of did." She laughed.

"There's only one woman who's woken up in my bed *or* in my arms, and I'm lookin' at her."

She rolled her eyes. "Come on, Diesel."

"Don't question my word, sparky. You might not always like what I have to say, but I respect you too much to lie to you. You *know* how I feel about being touched. Do you really think I'd let someone I don't care about sleep in my bed all night?"

She shook her head, grinning like she'd won a prize. "You let *me* sleep on you the night I was attacked."

"Damn right I did. Doesn't that tell you something?"

"Yes. It tells me a lot. But *this* tells me even more." She reached up as if she were going to put her arms around him, but she put her hands on his cheeks instead.

His jaw tightened, and he fought with everything he had against the knee-jerk reaction to pull back. He *wanted* her touch, *craved* it, and the emotions staring back at him were worth the struggle. He brushed his lips over hers and bit her lower lip, giving it a not-so-gentle tug.

"*Good.* Now stop bringing other people into this bed, and let me show you just how much I want you here before we have to go to work."

As he kissed his way down her neck, she said, "I don't work until six, and you're not scheduled until four."

"*Exactly.*" He grazed his teeth over her nipple, and she arched beneath him, sucking in a sharp breath. "If I have to keep my hands off you from six till midnight, I'm going to need reserves."

"Then stop talking and get busy." She giggled, and he sucked her nipple into his mouth, turning the sweet sound into sinful moans and seductive pleas that he knew he'd hear in his sleep.

"YOU KNOW YOU really screwed up letting Tracey slip through your fingers." It was almost six o'clock, and Izzy had been tossing barbs at Diesel since he got to work. "She went out with Dr. Rhys last night, and she *still* hadn't come home when I left for work this morning."

"That so?" he said evenly, smirking inside as he made a drink for a customer. Fucking Rhys had nothing on him.

"Yup. She was into you, but you blew it." She started putting clean glasses away. "I don't know what is wrong with guys like you, overlooking the best women around and taking the raunchy ones home. Rhys knows a good thing when he sees it, and he knows how to treat a woman. He took Tracey to Nova Lounge. She looked *hot*, too, in a slinky black dress, eyes made up all pretty."

The dress I ripped when I took it off her? "No shit?"

The door to the bar opened, and Tracey walked in with Moon, her eyes darting to Diesel. He winked, and her cheeks pinked up. She was a sight for sore eyes in a black-and-white floral miniskirt, a black Whiskey Bro's tank top tied at her waist, and black high-tops. He watched her pretty little ass sway as she and Moon headed to the back to clock in. She was going to drive him out of his fucking mind on purpose; he just knew it.

"Did you see that smile on her face?" Izzy said. "That's the glow of a well-fucked woman. Bet your girls don't look like that the next morning."

I only have one girl, and she fucking glows brighter than the stars. He and Tracey had fucked like jackrabbits all damn day, stopping only to refuel with brunch so they had enough energy to keep going. He gritted his teeth to keep a gloating grin from breaking free, and when he didn't respond, Izzy went back to what she was doing, chatting about the applicant Dixie had brought back for a second interview for the waitressing position. They were in the office now.

A few minutes later Tracey and Moon came out of the back room and headed up to the bar. Diesel couldn't take his eyes off her, remembering just how good she tasted and felt. His body ignited with her every step.

"Get over here, Tracey," Izzy demanded. "A text that says *we'll talk later* does not cut it. I want details."

Tracey's eyes shot to Diesel as he strode to Izzy's end of the bar, leaned his forearms on it, and growled, "Get your fine ass over here, baby girl."

"Baby girl?" Izzy exchanged a curious look with Moon as Tracey sauntered over to Diesel grinning like the beauty she was.

Tracey lifted her chin defiantly, despite the heat simmering in her eyes. "You talking to me, Unleaded?"

He fucking loved her snark. He leaned over the bar, grabbed her shirt, and hauled her off her feet for a kiss, taking it deep and slow. It felt fantastic to kiss her when he wanted to, and it took everything he had to set her on her feet and not do it again. "Pink cheeks and dreamy eyes look hot on you, baby."

Tracey trapped her lower lip between her teeth, but it did nothing to hide that sexy smile as Dixie and the middle-aged, keen-eyed brunette she'd been interviewing approached with shocked expressions.

"What the hell just happened?" Izzy asked, wide-eyed.

Diesel met her incredulous gaze. "That didn't clear things up for you?"

"Are kisses like that part of the benefits package?" the brunette asked. "If so, I'm *in*. I can start right now."

The girls laughed.

"No, kissing is *not* part of the package." Dixie looked imploringly at Diesel.

He lifted his chin. "Tracey's my girl." The hell with kissing. Claiming her was as freeing as the open road.

Tracey blushed a red streak, but there was no denying the happiness in her eyes.

"About damn time you came to your senses." Dixie smiled approvingly.

"Wait." Izzy looked at Tracey. "You went on a date with the hot doctor and spent the night with *Diesel?* You little ho. I'm so proud of you."

Diesel glowered at Izzy.

"Do you have to say that so loud? I didn't *do* anything with Damon." Tracey eyed Diesel flirtatiously. "How could I when *Unleaded* had me all tied up in knots?"

"Oh, the grunter is into bondage?" Izzy teased.

The brunette and Moon laughed.

Dixie held her hands up. "Okay, enough, you guys. You're going to make our new waitress quit before she starts."

"Not a chance," the brunette said. "Y'all are a fun bunch. I think I'm going to like it here."

"We hope so." Dixie gave them a serious look. "You guys, this is Dana Everton. She's starting Monday. Dana, this is Diesel Black, Izzy Ryder, Jed Moon, and Tracey Kline."

They all greeted her.

"If you have any trouble with customers, just tell Diesel or Jed, and they'll take care of it," Dixie said.

"I raised three football-playing, troublemaking boys and tossed out a cheating husband. I think I can handle myself," Dana reassured her.

As Tracey chatted with Dixie and Dana, Izzy went to clock out, and Diesel went to serve a customer.

Moon came behind the bar to start his shift. "I take it I can nix those drive-bys at Tracey's?"

Diesel grunted in agreement.

"How'd this happen, man? I thought you were hands-off because you were leaving town. Does this mean you're staying?"

Diesel didn't have an answer, and as the Friday-night rush started, he didn't have time to figure one out, which meant it would continue to eat away at him for who knew how long. He motioned to two guys at the other end of the bar. "You got customers."

"Right, well, for what it's worth, I hope you stick around. I'm used to your grumpy ass."

Diesel looked across the room at Tracey talking with a group of guys, three of whom were openly checking her out. That clench in his gut was still there, jealousy gnawing at him like a rabid animal. But knowing she was *his* made him feel less like he wanted to kill them and more like he wanted to go over there and stake his claim. He never thought he'd want to claim a woman again after the way he'd been fucked over by the girl he'd dated for two years and had trusted with his deepest feelings, but hell if he didn't want to shout that Tracey was *his* from the rooftops.

As the night wore on, Tracey taunted him every chance she got, strutting around in that sexy skirt, flashing him heated glances. It was all he could do to keep from hauling her into the back to have his way with her.

He was fixing a drink for a customer when she headed up to the bar near closing time. He handed the customer a drink and went to the far end of the bar, where Tracey was waiting for him.

"See that table of women looking over here?" She motioned toward the back of the bar, where three attractive women were watching them. "They think you're hot. They wanted to know if you were single." She lowered her voice. "I think I know how you feel when guys hit on me. So I told them you were married…to a guy."

"What the hell, Trace?"

She laughed. "I'm kidding."

He looked over at the women, lifting his chin in acknowledgment of their appreciative glances. Their smiles widened.

Tracey scowled as he strode out from behind the bar. "You'd get pissed if I did that."

He hauled her into his arms and kissed the hell out of her. "Shut that shit down from now on. I said I'm yours. Fucking own it."

"I think you just did. You can't kiss me like that in front of customers."

"The hell I can't." He looked at Dixie, who chuckled.

"I may not get fired, but my tips will suck."

He leaned down, speaking directly in her ear. "There'll definitely be sucking going on tonight, but there'll be a hell of a lot more involved than just the tip." He kept her close, aroused at the thought of her mouth on him.

Heat flamed in her eyes. "How am I supposed to work the rest of my shift with that in my head?"

"The same way I'm going to while picturing you on that bar, your pretty little skirt pushed up around your thighs and my mouth between your legs." He squeezed her ass. "You got an order to place, baby girl?"

She blinked several times, crimson staining her cheeks. "Um, yeah. Two bottles of Coors and a fresh pair of panties, please."

Thoughts of what he'd described burned into his mind for the rest of the night. Tracey's flirtatious taunts, which often were followed up by bashful blushing, amped up his desire. By the time they closed the bar and Dixie and Moon headed out, Diesel was consumed with desire. He was locking the front door when Tracey came out of the back room carrying her purse.

"Where do you think you're going?" He closed the distance between them.

She lifted one shoulder. "Home? I wasn't sure if you *really* wanted to see me tonight, or if you were just playing around."

"Fuck that. You're mine, Trace. You damn well know I want you in my bed every night."

Her eyes widened. "*Every* night?"

"Hell yes, and you're going riding with me Sunday."

She set her purse on the bar and slid her finger into his belt loop, looking up at him seductively. "A girl likes to be *asked* if she's free, not told where she's going."

He lifted her and set her on the bar, pushing his hands up her thighs. "This is me asking." He brushed his thumb between her legs, teasing her through her panties, and lowered his mouth to her neck.

A sigh left her lips. "*Mm.* I like the way you ask. Maybe I can be free for a ride Sunday, but we'll have to see about sleeping arrangements. I might want to be in my own bed some nights."

He bit her shoulder, just hard enough to earn a surprised sound. "Then I'll be in *your* bed, too."

She trailed her fingers down the center of his chest. "That's very presumptive of you."

"Damn right it is." He pushed his thumbs into her panties, teasing her wetness with one, her clit with the other. Her eyes fluttered closed. "You got a problem with that?"

"No," she panted out as he pushed two fingers into her tight heat. "Oh *God.*" She grabbed him by the shirt, looking nervously toward the door.

"It's locked."

"What if Dixie or Moon come back?"

"They *won't.*"

He continued kissing her neck, earning one needy sigh after another.

She flattened her hand on his chest, pushing him back. "Wait. It's *my* turn to make *you* feel good."

She slid off the bar and took his hand, leading him behind it, and pushed him back against the bar. "That was too out in the open for me." She worked the button on his jeans free.

Fuck. Yes.

Her eyes never left his as she tugged his jeans down his thighs, freeing his erection. Heat surged through him. She fisted his cock, licking her lips, and holy hell, he'd never *wanted* as desperately as he did right then. He grabbed her hair, tugging her into a rough, demanding kiss, craving the connection, the taste of her before she got a taste of him. She kissed him hungrily, stroking his cock as they feasted on each other's mouths. He didn't want to stop kissing her, but he'd fantasized about fucking her mouth for so long, he *needed* to do it before she made him come with her hand.

He tugged her hair, breaking their kiss. "I fucking *love* kissing you, but I need your mouth on me, baby."

Her smile lit the fire in her eyes, and man, that tore at something deep inside him. He reclaimed her mouth, fierce and possessive, the way he wanted to fuck her mouth. Then he brushed his lips lightly over hers. "Once I'm in your mouth, baby, I'm not pulling out. You cool with that? And don't worry, I'm clean. I always wrap it before I tap it." Her eyes were so full of lust, he could taste it.

"You took all of me. I want all of you."

Her words hit hard, taking root beneath his skin as she sank lower, licking him from base to tip, lingering on the broad head of his dick. She dragged her tongue around and over it, driving him out of his mind. "Look at me." He tightened his hold on her hair. Her eyes flicked up to his, lust and deeper emotions coalescing, drawing his needs like confessions. "Work it good, baby girl. Make me *yours*."

She took him greedily into her mouth, her lips stretching around his thickness. He slid one hand to her jaw, caressing it as he watched his cock drive in and out of her swollen lips. "So fucking beautiful."

She cupped his balls with one hand, stroking and sucking, dragging a groan from his lungs. His chin fell to his chest, eyes locked on hers as she worked him with her hand and mouth, pulling back every few strokes to slowly tease the head, taking him right up to the verge of release. He buried both hands in her hair, hips pumping to match her rhythm, taking her deeper, thrusting faster. She moaned, eyes filled with pleasure, bringing a slew of emotions he couldn't grapple with. He struggled to push them away and focus on the pleasure she brought. But with his sweet girl loving him with her mouth and *enjoying* it, stroking him faster, tighter, so damn perfect, his entire body ached with the need to come. Heat seared down his spine, and his hips shot forward as he found his release.

"*Fuck*, baby—" His climax tore through him like a runaway train. He clung to her hair, hips rocking, grunting with the mind-numbing pleasure. She stayed with him, taking everything he had to give until aftershocks rumbled through him. When she drew back, lips swollen and glistening, she pressed a kiss just above the base of his cock, eyes so full of emotions, he felt them wrapping around him, the pain of the past coalescing with the pleasure of *Tracey*.

He lifted her to her feet, and the truth came tumbling out. "You destroy me, baby girl."

"I don't want to destroy you," she said softly. "I want to make you whole."

The world screeched to a halt. How could two small sentences rock him to the core?

He wasn't ready to analyze any of that, so he tossed it onto the mountain of other things he wasn't ready to think about and gritted out, "And I want to make you come."

He crushed his mouth to hers, urgent and rough, trying to outrun the mountain looming over him. He lifted her onto the bar, tearing off her panties as they kissed. He pulled off her shirt and bra, and she shot a glance at the door again. "Don't get shy with me, baby girl. There's *nothing* we won't do together."

He pulled her to the edge of the bar. His eyes traveled down her heaving breasts to her glistening sex. He brought her fingers to his mouth and sucked them, loving the hitch of her breathing. He moved her fingers in and out of his mouth and stroked his cock with his other hand. When he guided her hand to her clit, she stilled. "Do it for me, baby."

Her fingers moved tentatively as he put his hands on her thighs, pressing her legs open wide. "Christ, I could come watching you do that."

"I could come watching you, too," she said shakily.

Jesus. She was his every fantasy come to life. "And one day you *will*, but first you're going to come on my mouth." He cupped her jaw, brushing his thumb over her lower lip. "Tell me you want that."

"More than you could know."

Her sinful and shy whisper was so damn hot. "That's my sexy girl." He dug his wallet out of his pants and tossed a condom, and the wallet, on the bar. "*Then* I'm going to fuck you, so every time you come into the bar, all you can think about is my face between your legs or my cock buried nine inches deep."

The breath rushed from her lungs, her fingers quickening on her clit as he lowered his mouth between her legs, making good on his promise. After she came, she clung to the edge of the bar, trembling, trying to catch her breath as he sheathed his length.

"Hurry," she panted out.

He lifted her into his arms, guiding her legs around him as he took her in a long, sensual kiss. She couldn't know that he'd *never* kissed anyone the way he kissed her, that he'd never *craved* anyone the way he craved her. But *he* knew, and that knowledge scrambled up to the top of that looming mountain as she slid down his body, and he thrust every inch into her. She whimpered into their kisses, and he leaned back. "Too hard?"

"No. I just never knew it could be so good."

Neither did I hung on the tip of his tongue, but he swallowed it down, reclaiming her mouth with renewed fervor. They both went a little wild, clawing, thrusting, nails digging, teeth biting. They were swept into their storm, battered by pleasure too intense, *need* too immense to hold back as their orgasms crashed over them. They cried out, voices echoing off the walls, every thrust stealing a piece of him and giving it to her. There was no use fighting it.

There was no escape from the thing that was *Tracey and Diesel*.

They rode the highs of their passion, and when they finally, reluctantly descended from their peaks, Tracey collapsed in his arms, burying her face in his neck with a contented sigh. He leaned against the bar to combat his shaking legs, still buried deep inside her. Heat pulsed in the air around them, their hearts thundering, and he felt high as the damn sky, reborn. He didn't know what the hell was going on, but one thing was for sure. He was overcome with the power of *them*. It took everything he had to shove those feelings onto that towering mountain, praying it wouldn't come crashing down.

Or maybe hoping it would.

He didn't fucking know about that, either.

All he knew was that whenever Tracey was in his arms, there was no place else he'd rather be.

Chapter Ten

TRACEY DUG THROUGH her clothes late Sunday morning, choosing an outfit for her motorcycle ride with Diesel. She put on a T-shirt and jeans and was just about to sit on the bed to put on her sneakers when her phone rang and Josie's name flashed on the screen. *Shoot.* Diesel was going to be there any minute. But they'd played telephone tag all day yesterday, and she wanted to share her excitement with Josie.

She sat down and put her phone to her ear. "Hey. Sorry I forgot to call you back. I had a class with Lior yesterday, and we ended up talking about the attack and everything that's happened since, and then I worked an eight-hour shift, and—"

"You and Diesel got lost in the sheets?" Josie teased.

Tracey laughed and finished tying her laces. "Pretty much."

"Yay! Please tell me he's worth blowing off your bestie."

"He definitely is, but I *am* sorry."

"Don't be. I get it. But I want *all* the dirty details. One minute you're going out with Dr. Rhys, and the next Jed's telling me that Diesel kissed you and you two are a couple! *What* is going on? How did this happen?"

"I don't *know*," Tracey said a little giddily. "I went out with

Damon, and he was funny and charming. You know how he is."

"I know he's one of Peaceful Harbor's most eligible bachelors and Diesel barely strings full sentences together, so keep going."

"I had a great time with Damon, but there was no spark, and I couldn't stop thinking about Diesel."

"That's what wanting a guy for nearly two years does to a girl."

Tracey flopped onto her back on the bed. "I'm sure that's part of it, but I think the night he took care of me was the beginning of a change between us. He was so gentle and kind, I can't unsee his empathy or unfeel his compassion." She told Josie about some of their quiet, more intimate moments. "It's like I keep getting peeks beneath his armor, and I know there's a lot more to him than the glimpses I've gotten. But to be honest, I went to the clubhouse to give Diesel hell after my date with Damon, and I don't know what happened. The second I saw him, I had butterflies and goose bumps, and I *wanted* him like I've never wanted anything before. I yelled, we talked, and somehow I ended up in his bed, which is where I spent the last three nights."

"*Three* nights? Wow."

The hesitation in her voice gave Tracey pause. "What? Just say it."

"You were worried about his revolving bedroom door. I like Diesel, you know that, and Jed thinks he's the greatest guy around, but I don't want you to get hurt."

"I know, but he's not like we thought. I mean, he kind of is. He's not a talker, and he's been with a lot of women, but not as many as we thought." She told Josie about Diesel driving the drunk women home and not sleeping with them. "Don't worry.

I'm going into this with my eyes wide open. But he said he's with me now and he's not going to be with anyone else, and I believe him."

"I guess he's not if he's keeping you in his bed every night."

"You don't hear me complaining. The man must snack on Viagra." They both laughed.

"Does he know how to be loving in bed? I picture him being rough and, I don't know, like a biker."

"You're married to a biker." Tracey didn't mean to sound so offended, but she felt protective of Diesel.

"I know, but Jed is sweet, and Diesel is rough."

"He is, but with me he's sexy rough, not mean rough. And I know without a shadow of a doubt that he would *never* hurt me physically." They'd showered together each morning, and when he'd washed her back, he'd kissed each of her fading bruises. She'd reveled in every second of it.

"Is he still leaving after the holidays?"

"He hasn't said, and I don't want to push it right now. I know he's not promising me the world, but he makes me feel special, which is weird, because it's not like he's spouting sonnets. The man withholds words and emotions like he has a limited supply. I don't know how to explain it, but when we're together, whether we're eating breakfast—which he cooks, by the way—or I'm in his arms, I feel safe and happy, and the way he looks at me is…" She sighed, trying to find the right words.

"Like you're his next meal. We've all seen it."

Tracey laughed. "Yes, but it's different now. He still looks at me like he wants to tear my clothes off, and butterflies are permanently nesting in my belly, but it's like he's seeing more of me. Or maybe like he's seeing me for the first time or something. I don't know how to explain it, but we have a connection that feels good, and even if it takes a while to really get to know all of him, that's okay. I want to see how this plays out."

"Oh, Trace. I'm so happy for you."

"Me too."

"So tell me, what's the clubhouse like inside? Are there pictures of naked women everywhere?"

Tracey laughed. "In some of the other bedrooms, I'm sure there are, but thankfully not in Diesel's. He's a neat freak, too. His room is spotless, clothes folded perfectly. I was shocked. But the clubhouse is like a giant man cave with pool tables and dartboards. It smells like guys and leather, kind of like the bar, but different. The fridge is packed with beer, but Diesel uses one shelf for his groceries, and those items are perfectly organized. He puts me to shame, that's for sure." A knock sounded at the door, sending those butterflies into a flurry. "I have to run. He just got here. We're going for a motorcycle ride."

"He's formally claiming you to the world as his woman. That's a *huge* deal."

"What?"

"That's what it means when you ride on the back of his bike. You're his old lady."

"I'm twenty-six. I'm not anyone's *old* lady. But I am his *girlfriend*." A little thrill raced through her. "So weird, right?"

"Weird and wonderful. Does he know you're helping me at the bridal expo in a few weeks? Because if he thinks he's going to monopolize *all* of your time, I'll have to give him a stern talking-to."

Tracey laughed. "I haven't mentioned it, but I will."

"Thanks! *Go.* Be safe. Wear your helmet and use condoms."

"Yes, *Mom.*"

She ended the call and hurried to the door, excited to see Diesel. When she pulled it open, Diesel dragged those sexy eyes down the length of her, heating her from head to toe, and in one quick sweep of his arm, he lifted her off her feet, holding them chest to chest as he kissed her.

"Ready to go for a ride, baby girl?"

She didn't even know where they were going, and she didn't care. She'd be wrapped around Diesel, and that was the most glorious feeling in the world. "Am I ever."

DIESEL WAS IN paradise. There was no better feeling than cruising the open road with his girl at his back, the sun on his skin, and for the first time in years, happiness in his heart. If they didn't have commitments, he'd keep driving straight out of the state, take her someplace far away for the night, then climb on his bike tomorrow morning to do it again, and the day after that, and every day thereafter until she'd seen the whole damn world.

But they had commitments, and an hour into the ride, he pulled off the highway, heading for Cleary Farms, the first of the gardens he'd found online and mapped out for their ride. He wound through rural roads to the crest of a hill, where acres of vibrant sunflowers came into view. Tracey held him tighter, but he felt her chest lift off his back, her excitement crackling around them as he cruised down the hill and turned into the entrance. He'd called the manager of the farm to arrange their visit, as he had with each of the other places he was taking her today. Following the instructions he'd been given, he turned off the driveway, down a narrow dirt road that ran between two sunflower fields, and followed it up a hill and around a bend, driving slow so Tracey could enjoy the view.

After leaving Cleary, he got back on the highway and headed to Burton's Gardens in the next town over, where they drove along the service path, winding through fifty acres of burgeoning blooms and flowering trees. He drove slowly, letting Tracey bask in the beauty of the flowers. When they finally headed back to the highway, visiting the next garden, and the next, making their way through each one, Tracey held him tighter. He could feel her adrenaline as if it were his own.

McKinley Gardens was the halfway mark on his list. He drove down the service path, bordered by more colorful gardens, followed it up to a small group of pink and white flowering dogwood trees, and parked beneath them. Diesel couldn't remember ever being as excited about flowers as he was at that moment. He climbed off the bike and turned to help Tracey, but she was already tugging off her helmet and scrambling off the bike.

She launched herself into his arms, kissing him *hard.* "This is amazing! How did you find all these gardens? And how did you get access to drive through them?"

He shrugged.

"Oh *no*, mister. You're not going to shrug at me and get away with it when you've done something this wonderful!" She went up on her toes and pressed both hands to his cheeks, kissing him again. "I haven't seen gardens like these in years. And the sunflowers! Oh my gosh, Diesel." She squealed, kissing him again. "Thank you! I had no idea you were so romantic."

"I'm not. You're my girl. You like flowers. It's about time you saw them again."

She laughed. "You're *wrong*. This is epically romantic."

He didn't need praise, but he loved seeing her so happy. "It's not a big deal. Come on, let's walk down to the water."

"Not only is this a big deal, but *you're* a big deal, too."

"You're the big deal, babe." He draped an arm over her shoulder, and they went to the crest of the hill, which gave way to gorgeous views of a shimmering pond surrounded by more bountiful gardens and flowering trees. A deck led to a gazebo in the middle of the pond, with flower boxes lining the railings.

"Oh my goodness, *Diesel.*"

She looked awestruck, her radiant smile lighting up her face. Her bruises were almost gone, the cut over her brow was healing, but he knew that even after the visual remnants of that awful night had disappeared, he'd never forget the changes they'd brought. He pressed his lips to hers, and they headed down a footpath that cut through flower beds toward the pond.

"Oh, look! Those are zinnias, my favorites."

As if he'd already forgotten?

"See those white ones? Those are lilies." She pointed to flowers as she spoke. "They're my mom's favorite. And those are dahlias. They're our second favorites."

She continued pointing out flowers the whole way down the hill, telling him about visits to gardens with her mother and how much she'd missed doing it. He'd been trying to track down her mother, but he'd hit one roadblock after another. But he wasn't about to let that door close without getting the answers Tracey needed, and more importantly, deserved.

They walked along the dock to the gazebo, where a picnic table set for two and a basket of food and sparkling water waited for them.

Tracey's jaw dropped. "Is this for *us?*"

"You gotta eat."

"Diesel." She buried her face in his chest, squealing with delight, and beamed up at him. "Now I know why you're so big."

He cocked a brow.

"You need a big body to fit your gigantic heart."

He laughed. She couldn't be cuter as she raved about the gardens over lunch, going on about the types of flowers they'd seen and how magical the day had been, as dreamy-eyed as she was overzealous. He didn't tell her they still had four more gardens to see, because he was into her no matter what her mood, but her excitement lit up everything around her, including *him*, resurrecting parts of him he'd thought he'd killed off long ago. He wanted to stay in her light, to soak it in and become a part of it.

He wrestled with the edginess that desire caused as they finished lunch and headed back to the bike. Tracey gazed up at him, her hazel eyes dancing with happiness. She patted his chest, smiling when he didn't flinch at her touch.

"I sure like you, growly guy." She rose onto her toes and kissed him.

He helped her onto the bike, and when she wrapped her arms around him, he felt like a fucking king.

The rest of the day was just as exhilarating, and later that evening, as they drove over the bridge into Peaceful Harbor, the sun skimming the mountains in the distance, Diesel wasn't ready for their ride to end. He knew Tracey was going to be tired from using muscles she hadn't even known she'd had, but it would be worth it. *Kind of like the last few nights.* He grinned to himself, savoring the memories of not just the incredible sex they'd had, but of holding her while she'd slept, feeling her nestle in as close as she could during the night, as if she were trying to burrow beneath his skin in her sleep, and of the indescribable sensations that filled him each morning when her beautiful smile was the first thing he saw.

He cruised past the bar, continuing beyond the road that led to Tracey's place, heading to the other side of the Harbor. He drove the rural roads he knew by heart, meandering through the foothills of the mountains, and pulled into the entrance of the place with the best view in all of Peaceful Harbor. He climbed off the bike to open the old metal gate blocking the gravel driveway, which looked like it led into the heart of the majestic mountains. He straddled his bike and drove down onto the property, which was flanked by acres of overgrown pastures, and parked in front of the small log cabin at the base of the mountains. The windows were boarded up, the roof littered with leaves and branches from the tall trees. The porch steps and floorboards were warped from age, and a large tree stump sat in the middle of the overgrown grass out front, seedlings sprouting out like surprises.

A familiar sense of peace came over him as he helped Tracey off the bike.

"I knew today was too good to be true." A tease rose in her eyes. "You got me high on all those beautiful gardens and riding on the open road and brought me to an abandoned property to slaughter me and get rid of the body, didn't you? I was too chatty over lunch, wasn't I?"

He cocked a brow. "Baby girl, you've got a twisted sense of humor. This is the old Whiskey place, where Biggs and his brothers and sister grew up." He set their helmets down and gazed up at the mountains. "Tiny told me about it when I first came out this way."

"Why don't you stay here instead of the club?"

"Because I'm not a Whiskey."

"Oh, sorry. I think of the Dark Knights as one big family, and you're part of them. The Whiskeys treat you like family."

"The club is a brotherhood, and the Whiskeys are friends, not family."

"But—"

He shut her down with a glare.

She sighed, and he could tell she wanted to argue the point, but she relented. "Fine." She looked up at the cabin. "So why are we here? It's all boarded up."

"I don't know. It reminds me of home, and I guess I wanted you to see it."

"I've never heard you talk about where you're from." She wrapped her arms around him, her smile reaching all the way up to her eyes. "Careful, growly boy. Your armor is cracking."

It was crazy how much he craved her touch, her smile, and he had a feeling it was those desires that had led him there. "My armor will never crack, baby girl." He kissed her and slung an arm over her shoulder, walking toward the path he'd worn in the woods over the years. "Let's go down by the creek."

"I like creeks. There was one by my house growing up. Was there one where you grew up?"

"Yup." He pulled back a branch as they made their way through the woods.

"Where was that?"

"Hope Ridge, Colorado. Same place as Redemption Ranch. I went to school with Tiny's kids."

"And...?"

"And nothing." They made their way past thick patches of ferns, their leaves shaking as creatures skittered along the forest floor. He pulled back more branches blocking the clearing by the creek and followed Tracey into the grass, which was peppered with wildflowers.

"Come on, Diesel. Tell me *something*. Anything. Why did Tiny tell you about this place?"

"I don't know. We're close. I mean, I worked at their ranch for a while and joined the Dark Knights because of him. My mom and I used to go to the ranch for Friendsgivings and other gatherings. When I took off, he said I should check out the view from here."

"It's nice he thought of that. It sounds like he really cares about you." She looked up at the mountains on the other side of the creek. "It's pretty here. Is this what Hope Ridge looks like?"

"Some parts of it." They went to a boulder by the creek and sat down.

She put her hand over his. "You know everything about me, and you gave me the best day today because you knew it would make me happy. I want to know more about you, so maybe one day I can do something special for you."

"I don't need anything special. My past isn't full of flowers or meaningful moments worth recreating."

She curled her fingers around his. "My past is pretty ugly, and I trusted you with it."

He turned his hand over and squeezed hers, wishing he could erase those parts of her past. "There's not much to tell, babe."

"What was your childhood like? Did you play sports? What do they do in Colorado? Ride horses? Rope cows?"

He shook his head. "I went to school, hung out with friends. I've never been big on sports or roping cows, but I can ride horses."

"So you had a good childhood?"

"Some parts of it."

She leaned against his side. "Like…?"

"I don't know. Times with my mom before she got sick. We took walks in the woods like this, caught minnows in the creek." His throat thickened with longing for those times. He only let himself think of her when he came to the cabin.

"What was she like?"

He didn't share details of his mother's life with anyone, and he was surprised to realize he wanted to share them with Tracey. "She was all heart—spontaneous, happy. She saw the best in everyone, and she played the guitar. She liked playing it outside, like you wanted to."

"You remembered?"

"I don't forget much." It was a blessing and a curse. "My mother had shitty parents. They never let her forget that she was an imposition they hadn't asked for. A *mistake*."

"That sucks. That's so hurtful."

"Yeah, but she was tough. She left home after graduating high school, traveled around. She was artistic, and she loved *The Hobbit*, elves, that kind of thing. She used to take me to a hobbit shop that sold all sorts of *Hobbit* paraphernalia."

"She's the reason you gave Adrian those books, isn't she?"

"Yeah. She didn't read me children's books when I was little. She read *The Hobbit* and *The Lord of the Rings*. I practically know them by heart. Hobbits and elves were her thing. She really dug their love and respect for nature. She thought it was cool that elves could only die from a mortal wound or a broken heart and that elves and hobbits lived simple lives, free from greed. She used to tell me that we needed more elfin magic in our lives."

"I love that. What else?"

"She loved painting, and we had a whole room she called the elfin-magic room. It was pretty cool, actually. The damn thing was covered floor to ceiling with elves, hobbits, wizards, forestry. We were *always* painting. Year after year." His chest constricted with the memories. "I think she started when I was about six, and she had a zillion reasons to paint. If she was trying to make a tough decision, she'd paint. If I was in a bad mood, *we'd* paint. I suck at painting, by the way, but she praised me like I was Michelangelo."

"Those seem like meaningful moments. You two must have been really close."

"Damn meaningful. It was us against the world. When I was a boy, she read to me, and when she got sick, I read to her. That fucking circle of life, Trace, it's a killer."

"I know. I'm sorry." Tracey moved closer. "What was her name?"

"Ruth. *Ruthie.*" He realized he hadn't said her name in years.

"That's a pretty name. Did she give you the nickname Diesel?"

"No. That's my road name. Tiny and the guys gave it to me when I became a Dark Knight. She called me Dezzie, for Desmond."

"Aw, that's sweet. Did she work as an artist?"

He shook his head. "She was a waitress at the Roadhouse, a biker bar."

Trace lowered her chin, looking up at him through those long lashes. "You realize you're going out with a waitress who works at a biker bar, right?"

"Yeah. It's a coincidence." He leaned in and kissed her. "Don't make it weird."

"I won't if you won't. Did she go out with a lot of bikers?"

"Never. I asked her why once, and she said she had her fill of them at work, and while she liked Tiny and the guys, they weren't her type."

"Guess your father wasn't a biker."

Diesel scoffed. "Definitely not. She never really dated anyway. She busted her ass for us at work, and when she was home, she was all about making my life great. So when she got sick, I busted my ass for her."

THE PAIN IN his eyes betrayed his matter-of-fact portrayal of what must have been a horribly difficult time. Tracey's heart broke for him anew, and his love for his mother drove Tracey's feelings for him even deeper.

He pulled out his wallet and withdrew a picture, looking at it for a long moment before handing it to her. "This was taken when I was fourteen."

She recognized the face of the pretty young woman with hair a little lighter than Diesel's pinned up in a messy bun, curly tendrils springing free on the sides. It was his mother's face tattooed on the back of his left arm. In the picture, she wore a colorful top with bell sleeves, faded jeans, and an effervescent smile that matched Diesel's. Tracey would give anything to see that smile on him now. He and his mother were sitting on a wooden bench, and he was wearing denim shorts that came to his knees and a yellow T-shirt. His hair was side parted, long on top and messily falling over one brow. His forearms rested on his thighs, and he was holding a leaf between his hands. There was nothing tense about the boy leaning into his mother's embrace, his head resting against her cheek, like she'd hugged him all the time. That made her ache for him even more.

"She's beautiful. You have her smile, the same straight nose."

"Yeah, she always called me her *major me.*" He almost smiled as he put the picture back in his wallet. "You know, like *mini me*, but bigger."

"I get it. I love that. You look happy and relaxed. I can't even imagine you like that."

"I was in a good place back then. My buddy Seeley, Tiny's oldest son, took that picture. He's a veterinarian now and goes by his road name, *Doc.* We used to go there for Friendsgivings and other events. The picture was taken two years before her diagnosis. My mom and I had just come back from riding horses with their family at the ranch."

"She looks so young."

"She was only twenty-two when she had me." He wrung his hands together. "Her mother died from cancer when she was pretty young, too."

"It must have been terrifying for both of you when your mom was diagnosed. Did you have anyone to lean on? Tiny and his family?"

"It was rough. I had a girlfriend, Debbie, and I talked to her about shit. I didn't want to burden Tiny's family with our nightmare. His wife, Wynnie, is a therapist, and she talked with my mom a lot. She offered to talk with me or connect me with another therapist, but I wasn't into that. I'd been working on the ranch since I was fourteen to make a few extra bucks to help out with the bills. I baled hay and cleaned stalls to get that shit out of my system. My mom's boss at the Roadhouse, Alice, would bring dinners by and offer to take my mom to her treatments. But she was *my* mother, *my* responsibility. I took her for treatments and cared for her when she got sick. When she went into remission, we thought she beat it. But about a year later she was getting short of breath, and we found out the cancer had spread to her lungs."

Tears dampened Tracey's eyes. "Oh, Diesel, you must have been devastated."

"We were. But my mom put up a brave front. She never cried in front of me. Even when she went downhill. The treatments took their toll, and the meds made her blow up like a balloon. The pain had to be unbearable, but she was so damn strong."

His jaw muscles bunched and she reached for his hand, but he lifted her into his lap, putting his arms around her. "I haven't even said her name in years until tonight. That feels like a betrayal, like she wasn't important. But she was. She *is*." He spoke low, his voice full of pain. "I want you to know about her, Trace, because you're important, too."

Tracey opened her mouth to speak, but her man of few words had rendered her momentarily speechless. She finally managed, "You're important to me, too."

He kissed her then, slow and sweet, and she felt another change happening, a door opening a little wider, a chance for them to get closer.

"You *should* say your mom's name, talk about her, relive the good times, and even if it's hard, think about the painful memories, too. Otherwise you've buried her whole life with her, and it sounds like she worked hard to make it a good life for both of you. You don't have to talk about her now if you don't want to, but I know what it's like to miss someone and to try not to think about her. It's really hard, so when you're ready, I'd love to hear more and see more pictures if you have them. I bet little Dezzie was adorable."

A mix of pain and relief washed over his features. He looked at her for a long silent moment before saying, "I'm ready, Trace. But I don't have more pictures. I couldn't go through her stuff after…I left everything behind."

"That must have been hard to do, leaving your life behind. But I get it. You were trying to run from the reminders of what you'd lost."

"*God,*" he said, more to himself than to her. "You really do get me."

"There's a lot of you to *get*, and I have a feeling I've only scratched the surface. But I want to understand all of you and what you've been through."

"There's no easy way to tell you about what happened, but you can imagine what it was like. When my mom got too sick to work, I took on hours at the Roadhouse as a busboy and a dishwasher. Tiny's boys and I hung around the Dark Knights doing their grunt work, and some of the guys would give me odd jobs to make extra money. I didn't care if it was shit work. But it still wasn't enough. Then I met this guy Doug Wallace at the bar. He was a tough dude, a few years older than me, and we got to talking. He seemed like a good guy, like I could trust him. He told me he'd lost his father to cancer, and I told him about my mom. It turned out he was an underground fighter, and he brought me into the ring. That's where I made our money. I quit school to take care of my mom, got my GED along the way, and fought to keep a roof over our heads and pay the bills."

"What's an underground fighter?"

"Illegal fighting. No rules."

"Oh my God, *Diesel*. Isn't that dangerous?"

He scoffed. "Yeah, but I was big even then. I was doing manual labor at the ranch and working out in their gym with the guys. I wasn't as thick as I am now, but I was pissed off at the world. That and my size were a deadly combination."

"I'm sure they were. That scares me, and I wasn't even there. I thought the Dark Knights didn't break the law. Did your mom know? What about your girlfriend? Were they okay with you fighting? Was Tiny?"

"My mom didn't know, and my girlfriend thought it was cool. Tiny hated it. He offered us money more times than I can count. But I wasn't going to take handouts from anyone. My mother had always supported me. It was my turn to support her."

"That was incredibly noble of you, but you were just a kid shouldering adult responsibilities."

"You sound like Tiny. He and I argued about that a lot, but sometimes life deals you a shit hand, and you gotta play it out. He knew that, and he respected my decision. He still mentored me to become a Dark Knight, stood behind me when I was a prospect, and voted me in six months before my mom died."

"You did so much, all while you were losing your mom. Did you get hurt fighting?"

"Sometimes, but never more than the guys I fought."

"Did you *kill* anyone?"

"No, but I put a few guys in the hospital. That's the job, babe. They knew when they stepped into the ring what the risks were, just like I did. I could have killed them, but I chose not to. I wanted the money, not to end someone else's life."

"Did Debbie watch you fight? I couldn't have watched."

"She did, but she was nothing like you. She got off on that stuff."

"How long were you with her?"

"A couple of years."

"I'm glad you had her to lean on while your mom was sick." Tracey wished she could have been there to help him through his loss.

"Sort of. At first she'd come home with me after the fights and help me take care of my mother, but after a while she stopped. She said she wanted to stick around and bet on other fights, not take care of a dying woman or listen to my bullshit."

"You mean your *grief* over it?"

He nodded.

"That's ridiculous. How can anyone choose betting on a fight over supporting their boyfriend?"

He shrugged. "I didn't think much of it. Her family didn't have a lot of money, either, and I knew I was dragging her down with all the crap I was going through. Besides, I didn't mind. It gave me time alone with my mom."

"Who was with your mom while you were fighting?"

"When she got sick enough to need someone there, Tiny, Wynnie, or Alice would help out. But during the last few months, Tiny's brother Axel was diagnosed with lung cancer, and he and his family were back and forth from Maryland. Axel died a month before my mom. But they were there during the last few hellish weeks. Tiny, Wynnie, and Alice hovered near the end. My mom was taking so much medication, she slept most of the time. She wasn't eating. I was afraid to fall asleep, afraid she'd be dead when I woke up. I'd carry her into the hobbit room to see the paintings and sit with her in the rocking chair. She was too weak to move, but she'd manage a smile and then conk out. Eventually we moved her bed in there." He lowered his eyes, shaking his head. "One night after a fight, I forgot my phone and wallet, and when I went back to get them, I found Doug balls-deep in my girlfriend on the side of the building."

"That's *awful*. You trusted them *and* your mom was dying." No wonder he tried so hard not to let anyone in. "I hope you beat him up and gave her hell."

He shook his head. "They weren't worth it. I grabbed my things and got out of there. Alice called on my way home and said my mom had taken a turn for the worse." Tears glistened in his eyes, bringing tears to Tracey's. "I ran faster than I'd ever run in my life, blew through the front door."

Tears spilled down Tracey's cheeks.

"It wasn't like you see in the movies, with last words and all that shit. She was delirious, and it was like she was fighting death. I climbed into bed beside her and held her, told her it was okay to let go. I don't know how long it took, but she fought with everything she had, and then..." His jaw tightened. "At least she died in her elfin-magic room, surrounded by her favorite things."

His glassy eyes drew tears from hers. "I think *you* were her favorite thing."

He nodded and pulled her into an embrace. "I miss her every minute of the day."

She missed her mom, too, but she would never compare her ache to his pain. She didn't know if her mother was alive or dead, but she knew one thing for sure. Diesel never would have chosen a woman over his mother and walked out on her the way she had. "Thank you for telling me about her. Now I know where you learned to be such a good man."

He drew back with a perplexed expression. "I fought illegally, and as soon as I buried my mother, I climbed on my bike and took off. That's not a good man."

"You did everything in your power to make ends meet for the woman you loved most in this world. You were betrayed by people you trusted, and you didn't take vengeance on them. You taught a little boy to make a boyfriend list, and you taught other children that bullying was wrong. You, *Dezzie* Black, are the very definition of a good man. I bet your mother is up there in heaven, painting elves and hobbits and bragging about you to anyone who will listen."

LATER THAT NIGHT, as Tracey slept in his arms, Diesel reflected on how good it had felt to open up to her, to share the memories he'd been running from for what felt like his whole life. She made thinking about his mother less painful, something he hadn't thought was possible. But he was learning how wrong he'd been about that, and about himself. He loved his nomad lifestyle, but being with Tracey was better. He could practically see her collecting the bits about his life he'd shared, tucking them away like treasures. He'd wasted a lot of time trying to stay away from her, and he was starting to think she was the best thing that had ever happened to him.

He pressed a kiss to the top of her head, and she stirred.

"Can't sleep?" she whispered.

"I didn't mean to wake you."

"You didn't. I was awake." She folded her arms over his chest, leaning her chin on her hands, her smiling eyes holding his. "I was just thinking about you and your mom."

Of course she was. She was too thoughtful to have just let those thoughts go. He kissed her forehead.

"That's her tattooed on the back of your arm, isn't it? The fairy?"

She didn't miss a thing. "Yeah, that's her."

"Do you have any other tattoos for her?"

"That tattoo is not for her. It's for me."

She smiled at that. "You know what I mean—others that represent her? What does the one on your back mean?"

"The *Vitruvian Man*? Da Vinci used it to show the connection between the human form and the universe, bridging the gap between spirit and matter."

"I didn't know you were so deep."

"I didn't know you were so curious." He squeezed her butt.

She giggled. "Tell me what the others mean."

"You really do want to know all my secrets."

"Every last one of them," she whispered, and kissed his chest.

He fucking loved that she wanted to know all his secrets. "That's gonna cost ya." He rolled her onto her back, moving over her, and heat shimmered in her eyes.

She dragged her fingertips over the Dark Knights emblem on his left pec, a skull with dark eyes, sharp brows, and jagged fangs. "I know this one is for the club." She ran her fingers over the lighthouse tattooed on his neck. "What will it cost me to learn the meaning behind this one?"

"That's a hefty fee involving my dick in your mouth." He kissed the corner of her smiling lips.

"*Hm.* Really?" She licked her lips, arching beneath him, rubbing against his cock. "What about this one?" She ran her index finger along the tattoo on his forearm.

He gyrated his hips, wetting his cock with her arousal. "It's expensive. It involves me buried deep inside you in this position." He rubbed the head of his erection against her center. "And an encore with you on all fours."

"You drive a hard bargain," she said breathlessly.

"Damn right I do." He nipped at her neck. "Buckle up, baby girl." As his lips neared hers, he said, "I'm about to drive you into next week."

Chapter Eleven

TRACEY SAT AT her kitchen table Wednesday morning eating banana pancakes with Diesel's hand resting on her leg, watching him shovel food into his mouth like there was a timer on him. She had a feeling that would never change, and she was falling so hard for him, she'd come to see that as one of his lovable quirks. He'd been a little more relaxed since telling her about his childhood. They'd stayed at the clubhouse Sunday night, but he'd come over after church Monday and they'd stayed at her place the last two nights. Last night it was his turn to drive by the women's shelter in the middle of the night, but he took her key with him and slipped into bed with her when he got back so she could wake up in his arms again. Even though those drive-bys took him away from her for a little while, she was proud of him for giving the women at the shelter peace of mind that there were good people looking out for them.

News had traveled fast about that claiming barroom kiss that had rocked her world. Red had stopped by the bar yesterday and had confided in Tracey that she'd sensed Diesel's feelings for her since they'd first met, but she'd said that now they burned brighter than ever. The guys had given Diesel a hard time for waiting so long to make a move, but Diesel had shut them down with one of his glares. He would always be her watchdog at work, but now those times were interspersed with discreet touches, taunting winks, and stolen kisses.

She had no doubt that trusting her with his painful past—and now with his healing heart—was bringing them closer together, making their relationship stronger. Their nights were incredible, but nothing compared to mornings, when it was just the two of them, the walls around them keeping the rest of the world at bay. It was in those hours when Diesel was the most unguarded, when they were braided together like mating snakes, their hearts beating as one. When he'd whisper her name out of the blue, run his fingers along her hip or back, or tighten his hold on her and brush his lips over her cheek or forehead, as if he were saying *I'm glad you're mine* in his own way. She cherished those moments, and mornings like these, when he'd whip up a delicious breakfast and sit in the chair closest to her so he could hold her leg or nuzzle against her neck as they ate.

Diesel would never be a teddy bear, and she wasn't waiting for him to change who he was. He was hard and untrusting because he'd had his heart broken in the worst ways, and those wounds may never fully heal. But buried beneath all that hurt, he had a lot of love to give, and she was the lucky recipient. Her man of few words showed how much he cared by his actions, like coming to her gym this afternoon after her class with Lior to teach her more aggressive self-defense.

He finished his pancakes and downed his juice in one gulp, then leaned in and kissed her neck. "Why're you lookin' at me like that?"

"I'm just glad we're together. Thanks for making breakfast."

His eyes darkened, and a wicked grin lifted his lips. "Thank *you* for breakfast in bed."

Her stomach flip-flopped as those sexy memories rolled in. He leaned in for a kiss, and she heard Izzy come in the front door.

"What smells so good?" Izzy breezed into the kitchen wearing the same dress she'd worn to work last night. "I'm the one hooking up with a chef, and you get banana pancakes? *Someone* needs to up his game."

Diesel motioned to a plate of pancakes on the counter. "Those are yours."

"You're my hero." Izzy hurried over to the counter and carried her plate to the table.

Diesel gave Tracey a quick kiss and guzzled his coffee.

"Trace, wanna share?" Izzy waggled her brows.

"I've still got half a pancake on my plate."

"I meant *him*." Izzy grinned.

"No," Tracey and Diesel said in unison, making Izzy laugh.

Diesel glowered at her and got up to wash his dishes.

"Don't worry. I'm not into threesomes." Izzy ate another bite of pancake. "I'm glad you're together. Diesel is a lot easier to work with when he's all sexed up."

"Izzy." Tracey glared at her.

"What? He is. I almost saw him smile yesterday, and he hasn't threatened to kill anyone in a week. By the way, thanks for the earplugs you left on my bed Monday night."

Diesel glanced over his shoulder at Tracey, brows slanted in confusion.

Tracey's cheeks burned. "We're not exactly quiet."

"Aww, look at you all rosy cheeked," Izzy teased.

"Ohmygod. *Stop.* Did you have fun with Jared?"

"I always have fun with him, but the way you two flaunt your coupledom is messing with my head." Izzy ate a forkful of pancake.

"What do you mean?" Tracey asked.

"I mean, Jared's not taking *me* out on his bike to see gardens. I keep having these thoughts, like wondering who else he's been with." Izzy slumped in her chair. "I need to stop hooking up with him, but I really *like* hooking up with him. Tell me to stop being stupid."

"I'm outta here," Diesel said gruffly.

"Did I scare you off with girl talk?" Izzy asked.

He glanced at her but didn't respond. Instead, he put one hand on the back of Tracey's chair, the other on the table, leaning in so close her pulse quickened. "You're sure you're healed up enough to fight in class today? Promise you're not in any pain?"

He cared so much, he'd asked her the same question a dozen times over the last few days, and touched her yellowed bruises, just to be sure. "I promise."

"Okay. I've got business to take care of. I'll see you at the gym later." He took her in a toe-curling kiss, leaving her a little light-headed as he nodded at Izzy and headed for the front door.

Izzy fanned her face. "Where can I get one of those?"

"You can't. He's one of a kind."

TRACEY GOT TO her class a little early and began warming up on the heavy bag, trying to get her head out of the clouds. She'd never been the type of girl to have her head *in* the clouds, and she was surprised how difficult it was to stop daydreaming about Diesel.

"There's the toughest girl around."

Tracey turned at the sound of Eliani's voice and let out a squeal. "I've missed you!" She hugged her pregnant friend. "Look at that baby bump! How is it possible that you still look like Gal Gadot? Shouldn't your face get puffy or something?"

"Everything about me is puffy. Even my hair has new life." She shook her head, sending her thick dark hair swinging over her shoulders. Her expression turned serious, and she put her hands on Tracey's shoulders. "Lior told me what happened. How are you?"

"I'm fine now. Almost all healed up and ready to learn to fight better."

"Yes, he told me that, too. And that you are with the grumpy one."

Tracey laughed. "I *am*. But he's gruff, not grumpy. I think an even better word is *guarded*, but not so much with me anymore. He's a really great guy, Eliani. I feel safe with him, and you know what? I think he feels safe with me, too."

"I'm happy to hear that." Eliani glanced over Tracey's shoulder as Lior walked into the room. "And there's *my* great guy."

Lior slid his arm around Eliani's waist and kissed her cheek. Then he dipped his head and kissed her belly. "Are you ready to get started, Tracey?"

"Yeah, sure. I'm so glad I got to see you, Eliani. Will you be around when we're done?"

"She's sticking around to help with your training." Diesel's voice boomed through the room.

Tracey spun around, her pulse quickening. "Hi. You're

early. What are you doing here?"

"Teaching you to fight." He dropped a kiss on her head and held a hand out to Lior. "It's nice to see you both again. Thanks for letting me come in today."

"Wait. You *know* Lior and Eliani?" Tracey asked.

Diesel nodded. "After I told you I'd teach you to defend yourself, I reached out to them because you trust them, and I want to go over two-on-one scenarios so you're never caught off guard again. They can help me show you how to use the skills I teach you in conjunction with what you've already learned."

"When Diesel suggested we bring in Eliani to get a woman's perspective, the three of us got together to make sure we'd work well with each other and to figure out the best way to handle it. I asked Diesel to come in early because you're skilled enough to *teach* martial arts, Tracey. It's a much better use of your time to train with Diesel, which is why I suggested we use your class time plus the hour after."

Tracey looked at Diesel, a little hurt that he'd done all that behind her back. "Thank you for going to so much trouble, but why didn't you tell me?"

"I'm sorry, babe. Sometimes having too much time to think about this kind of training is a detriment. It allows you to set up expectations and come up with ideas that would end up being barriers and holding you back. I didn't want you to go there. I had planned on mentioning it at breakfast this morning, but then Izzy showed up, and she seemed to need your attention. But if you're not comfortable with this, that's okay. We can work one-on-one, just the two of us."

"No, it's okay. I want to be able to defend myself, and you're right. I would have overthought it and probably ended up being really nervous. Now I'm just a little irritated, which isn't a bad thing for this situation."

Lior and Eliani laughed, but Diesel remained serious.

Tracey pointed her gloved hand at him. "For the record, I don't like when people go behind my back."

He nodded curtly. "Understood."

"But you had a good reason, so you're forgiven. Now, let's get started so I can flip you or something."

"There won't be any flipping going on," he said firmly. "I'm going to teach you to fight dirty, which is harder than you think. You need to get rid of any ideas you have about fancy kicks and trying to flip a guy twice your size. We're going for creating openings so you can get the hell out of there."

"Getting away didn't work very well last time," Tracey pointed out.

"That's why we're doing this. Lior says you're great in the studio. Now it's time for the next level." Diesel began removing her gloves. "You're not going to wear gloves or pads on the street, so we're not going to practice with them. We're going to work on controlling your position and movements against *two* attackers, so nobody can get behind you. I'll show you what targets to go after, which ones put you in danger, and when and how to strike. I know you've learned about kicks and punches, but the truth is, during an attack, fear takes over, and most strikes miss their targets and leave you vulnerable. We'll work on that and on perfecting open-hand strikes, which are less likely to injure you and more likely to land where you're aiming. I'll also teach you to neutralize holds in close contact, using techniques that give you enough power and space to get the hell out of there."

"I can do a thumb lock," she said.

"That's good, babe, but perfecting a thumb grab at high

speed isn't easy. Especially with a size disadvantage. You're used to a very controlled environment, and by the time we're done, you're going to see the difference between a walk in the park and a run through hell."

Her nerves prickled. "You're making me nervous."

"Good, because if someone grabs you, you're going to be scared for your life."

"Yes, I remember it all too vividly."

"I know. That's why we're doing this. You need to know how to fight when you're in that condition. We'll take it slow at first, but I want you to feel the fear and have to fight through it. That's the *only* way you'll be able to do it in real life."

He tossed her gloves aside, and Tracey's annoyance gave way to anxiety, remembering the attack in detail, the fear that had consumed her. Diesel must have seen it written all over her face, because he took her hand and said, "Excuse us a second." He led her away from Eliani and Lior, his eyes serious. "You're scared."

"Yeah, kind of."

"You should be. That's another reason I didn't let you know ahead of time. This isn't going to be easy. I'm going to push you, baby, and I'm going to scare you, but only because it's the best way for you to learn. What we're doing today, and every other chance we get until this type of self-defense is second nature for you, is going to test you mentally and physically." His jaw tensed, a storm of emotions in his eyes. "You might hate me after this."

Now she understood why he'd wanted to make sure she was fully healed. "I could never hate you." Knowing he cared deeply enough to do this for her endeared him to her even more.

"I hope not, baby girl. You sure you're up for this?"

She was determined to make him—and herself—proud. "Absolutely."

"Remember, the goal is *not* to pretend you'll get the upper hand and slay a dragon, but to stun it just long enough to escape." They started slow, just as Diesel had promised. "The first thing you need to do is be aware of your surroundings every minute of every day. Whether you're at work surrounded by people or in a dark parking lot alone, you're still at risk. Always be aware of who and what is around you and know your escape routes. Size up customers and passersby, because you never know who's a little off their rocker. Don't count on safety in numbers. If you're with your girlfriends, be aware of which of them is the weakest, because she may need your help if something goes bad."

Did he realize how much that told her about *him*?

They worked through the mental side of sizing up opponents and controlling her proximity to two attackers, making sure she understood where to position herself—never between the attackers, always to the outside edge, facing them—and how to do so. Practicing was nerve-racking. He and Lior came at her slowly, but even at that pace, as she tried to evade them, her fear was real. She moved quickly to keep them in front of her as they tried to take control. Diesel wasn't playing around. He gained control every time, not giving her an inch and, at the same time, firing her up. *Think aggressively. Be fiercer. Use your head, Tracey. Overcome that fear. Your life depends on it.*

He taught her to lower her center of gravity by bending her knees if grabbed from behind, then exploding up all at once, and other tactics, like going limp to get her attacker off-balance, which went against every iota of her being when fear was fueling her. Every effort ended with a sprint away from her attackers, and every practice move got harder, not easier.

This was nothing like her classes with Lior. There was no laughter, no calm between attacks, no water breaks. The better she got at her footwork, the more they ramped up their efforts. Eliani stood off to the side calling out advice, showing them different moves Tracey could try since she was so small, like ducking instead of pivoting. Tracey was sweating, her heart racing, as Diesel and Lior surrounded her time and time again, grabbing her, saying mean things that attackers might say. The more she tried to punch or kick, the harder they combated it and the louder Diesel roared. *You're wasting energy. Focus. Where's your escape?* He stalked closer, and she threw a punch, but he evaded it. *Escape, Tracey*, he commanded. It was *so* real, fear consumed her. She fought harder, trying to get out from between them, kicking and punching, her head swimming. When Lior grabbed her from behind, she struggled futilely, just as she had the night of her attack. Tears of anger burned as Diesel stalked toward her.

"I can't do it!" she seethed. "I'm sorry!"

Diesel lowered his face beside hers, speaking gruffly. "You *can* do it. This is your live or die moment. Are you going to let some asshole take that away from you, or are you going to get the fuck away and come home to *me*?"

Something inside her snapped, and she bent her knees, taking Lior down with her, throwing him off-balance enough to get an elbow to his gut and loosen his hold. She tore out of his arms and ran, but Diesel caught her by the wrist, yanking her toward him. She threw her palm toward his nose, clipping his chin enough to send his head back, and kicked him in the groin. He stumbled, and she yanked her arms free, sprinting to the other side of the room, shaking, gasping for breath, tears falling down her cheeks, as Eliani and Lior cheered her on.

Diesel closed the distance between them, covering his crotch with one hand.

"Sorry," she panted out, swiping at the sweat dripping down her cheeks.

"You nailed it, baby girl."

"I'll never be able to do that in a real-life situation. I almost gave up." She hated admitting that, but it was true.

"That's why we're going to practice every chance we get. Twice a week with Lior. The more we practice, the more confident you'll become. This is supposed to be hard, to take you to the brink. But you've got this, and you've got me." He wrapped her in his arms, holding her tight. "I'm not going to let anything happen to you."

"You won't always be here. You told me you might not stay."

His jaw clenched, eyes narrowing. "It'd take someone ripping my fucking heart out for me to leave you."

Was she delirious? Had she heard him wrong? "Diesel...?"

"I protect what's mine." He gave her a quick kiss. "Let's get back to work."

How was she supposed to fight when he'd just romanced the hell out of her...*Diesel style.*

Chapter Twelve

THERE WERE MORE than a hundred exhibitors in the ballroom of the hotel overlooking the harbor at the bridal expo. Tracey replenished a tray of gingerbread cookies, taking it all in. She'd never seen so many bridal gowns, wedding cakes, or wedding planners. It seemed everyone who had anything to do with weddings was there representing destination venues, travel agents, limousine services, photographers, and dozens of other bridal services. Josie and Finlay's booth was decorated to perfection in white, yellow, and pink, with touches of lace, greenery, and fresh flowers. Tracey had never dreamed about white weddings or fancy honeymoons, but being surrounded by all this wedding fanfare and excited brides-to-be and their giddy friends could make anyone dream of magical moments and happily ever afters.

Especially after the last several weeks.

Tracey could hardly believe she and Diesel had been together for almost a month. The two and a half weeks since he'd started teaching her to fight had passed in a blur. Busy days blended into intimate nights, sometimes spent at his place, sometimes at hers, but always in each other's arms. He'd carved out time every Wednesday and Saturday to work with her, Lior, and Eliani, making sure Tracey was getting stronger and more confident, pushing her until she believed in herself as viscerally as he did. They'd seen Adrian last weekend, and he'd been thrilled to hear that she was Diesel's girlfriend. She'd had fun listening to them chat about all things Tolkien, and Adrian insisted that she start reading *The Hobbit*, so she could watch the movies with them after he finished reading all the books.

Tracey had never been happier, felt more respected, cherished, or *loved*. That was a big word she was pretty sure Diesel would never say, but how else could she explain the way he looked after her before himself or anyone else? They didn't take long walks by the seashore or stargaze and share hopes of a fairy-tale future, like some couples did. He hadn't promised her the world, or anything in so many words, beyond his vow to protect her. But he shared himself and his past, which was more meaningful than empty promises, and she felt his love for her in all the little things he did. Like the breakfasts he made for them every morning and the zinnias in a beer-bottle vase she'd found in her cubby at work. She felt it in the motorcycle rides they took on Sundays, each of which had included strolls through gardens and making out behind the cover of bushes and trees.

A group of girls swarmed Josie's table, drawing Tracey's attention.

"Look, you guys!" exclaimed the one wearing a white sash with BRIDE TO BE written on it in gold. "Bride and groom gingerbread cookies. What a great idea!"

"Feel free to try them," Tracey offered, and the girls each grabbed one.

Their booth had been busy all morning. Josie and Tracey wore matching GINGER ALL THE DAYS T-shirts, and Finlay and Izzy wore FINLAY'S CATERING shirts, making it easy for customers to know who to ask about their offerings. Finlay was going over a wedding cake brochure with another bride-to-be, and Izzy was schmoozing the girl's mother-in-law, who was raving about Finlay's elaborate wedding cakes. Josie chatted with a group of women about her display of wedding-themed gingerbread houses, and Sarah had set up a hairdressing chair at one end of their booth, where she was doing free bridal hairstyles. There was a line ten women deep waiting to sit in her chair. Tracey had never thought much about having a real career, but as she watched her friends building their businesses, she wished she had something more, too.

She didn't have much time to think about that as the group of girls moved on to the next booth, and Penny, Dixie, and Roni burst through the crowd in their shorts and cute tops, giggling and stuffing their faces with cupcakes.

"It's a madhouse in here. Want some?" Roni offered Tracey the last bite of her cupcake.

"No thanks," Tracey said. "I've eaten about ten cookies already."

"I do!" Penny snagged the piece off Roni's napkin and popped it into her mouth as Finlay finished with her customer and joined them.

"You finished *both* of yours already?" Dixie asked.

Penny put her hand on her barely there baby bump. "Don't cupcake shame me. It's the pregnancy hormones. Sex and food are all I think about these days."

"I see I'm going to need to make extra cupcakes for Kennedy and Lincoln's birthday party," Finlay teased. "Scott can take care of your *other* needs."

Kennedy and Lincoln's birthday party was next Sunday.

Tracey was still deciding what to get them. Diesel had such a soft spot for the kids, she wondered if he'd go shopping with her.

"You guys know I hired Trixie to bring miniature horses to the party as a surprise for the kids. That's why the party is Western-themed." Dixie snagged a gingerbread cookie. Her friend Trixie Jericho owned a miniature horse therapy business in Pleasant Hill, where she lived with her fiancé, rancher Nick Braden.

"Bones and I are already prepared for the kids to beg for a pony after the party," Sarah said. "They *love* them."

"I can't wait to see Kennedy dragging Diesel *all* around the party," Tracey said as Josie and Izzy finished with their customers and joined them. "Remember when she made him a Valentine's Day heart with their names in it? Don't tell him I told you, but he kept it. It's in his sock drawer. I saw it when I stuck a note in there for him."

There was a collective "Aww."

"I know, right? I melted on the spot when I saw it, but I didn't tell him, so mum's the word."

"That's super cute," Dixie said. "But I guess you haven't heard the latest about Kennedy and her crushes. I took her to see the miniature horses on Nick and Trixie's ranch to make sure she wasn't afraid of them, and she followed Nick *everywhere*. She took his hat right off his head and wore it all afternoon. It was the cutest thing."

"Aw, poor Diesel," Tracey mused.

Izzie nudged her. "I think your man's *very* well taken care of these days."

There was a murmur of agreement.

"It's too bad Gemma and Crystal had to work today. They

would have loved all this," Josie said as an announcement rang out through the loudspeakers about the fashion show starting in ten minutes on the main stage, featuring Jax and Jillian Braden.

A cacophony of noise rose around them, and it seemed everyone in the place hurried toward the stage. Nick's brother Jax was a famous wedding-gown designer, and his twin, Jillian, was not only well known for her unique dresses but also for the Leather and Lace clothing line for female bikers, which she'd designed with Dixie's husband, Jace.

"Do you think I'll get to see any of the show?" the woman whose hair Sarah was doing asked.

"Yes. I'll be done in two minutes," Sarah reassured her. The women waiting in line looked fretfully toward the stage. "I'll be here all day, ladies. You can go enjoy the show and come back later."

The women practically ran after the others, and as promised, Sarah finished with her customer quickly, and the woman thanked her profusely before rushing toward the stage.

"This is nuts. If I ever want to get married, remind me to elope." Izzy plucked a cookie from the table and took a bite.

"Not me," Roni said. "I know Quincy and I aren't engaged yet, and between his recovery and getting my dance company off the ground, we have a few years before we'll be ready to take that step. But one day I hope to see him standing at the other end of the aisle, looking at me like I'm all he ever wanted, and I want all of you guys there to celebrate with us. We don't need a big, expensive wedding, but after everything Quincy has been through, he deserves a celebration, and all this just makes me want it more."

"Well, it's a good thing you want one," Dixie said. "Because Quincy can't wait to see you walk down the aisle."

"I loved our wedding, and I'm glad we waited until Maggie Rose was born and our lives were settled," Sarah said.

"I'm glad we're waiting until the baby is born, so I can fit into a wedding dress," Penny said.

"Keep eating those cupcakes and you might not," Finlay teased.

"Pen, you have a busy year coming up with the wedding and the Sweet 'n Savory Dessert Festival," Tracey said.

Penny owned Luscious Licks ice cream shop. She had been trying to get an invitation to exhibit at the festival for years, and Scott was instrumental in making it happen. They were all excited for her.

"Don't forget our *babymoon*." Penny rubbed her belly. "I think I'm going to need to hire more people for the ice cream shop."

"I'll help when I can," Josie offered. "Your life is going to be crazy once you get that little baby home and realize you can kiss sleep and long hot showers goodbye."

"But that won't matter," Finlay reassured her. "Because you and Scott will be so in love with each other and the baby, that's all you'll think about."

"Did you find a wedding gown?" Sarah asked.

"She found about fifty of them," Dixie said. "Jax has an enormous booth near the stage…"

As her friends talked about weddings, babies, and business-es—all the ways in which their lives were moving forward—Tracey's thoughts trickled back to having something more for herself. Her heart belonged to Diesel, but she wasn't ready to think about a wedding, much less babies. She still had parts of her life to figure out before she could make a lifelong commitment to someone else. She tried not to worry about whether

Diesel could ever really settle down in one place, or if he'd get restless and end up resenting her. He was a bounty hunter and a nomad, after all. She wondered if he missed the excitement of the work, the open road, or the freedom of his single life. He didn't act like he did, and he'd been there for two years, so she hoped he would have felt the urge to take off before now. But still, those worries lingered in the background, cushioned by all the wonderful feelings she had for him and the belief and trust between them. Only time would tell with Diesel, but maybe it was time for her to start thinking about a real career for herself, finding a way to make a difference in other people's lives the way her friends were.

"Earth to Tracey." Josie waved her hand in front of her. "Daydreaming about Diesel again?"

"He *is* delicious to think about," Tracey admitted.

"I knew he'd give earplug-worthy orgasms," Dixie said with a smirk.

Tracey looked imploringly at Izzy.

"*What?* It's true," Izzy insisted. "I came home the other night, and I could hear y'all as I walked up to the front door."

"You could *not*," Tracey said with a laugh.

Izzy gave her a deadpan look.

"Okay, *fine*. It's true. *Geez*." Tracey looked around the quiet room. "Where are all the brides-to-be when I need them?"

DIESEL CLIMBED OFF his bike late Sunday afternoon, missing Tracey like he hadn't seen her in a month. That was messed up, but hell if he could do anything about it. The crazy thing was, he didn't want to. He liked the way she made him feel, the way he longed for her to be warming his back when he was on his bike and in his arms every night. But today he was tied in knots. He'd finally gotten a solid lead on her mother and had driven to Annapolis to check out the information. He'd found the petite brunette with whom Tracey shared a perky nose and pointy chin. Only Michelle Kline was now Michelle Kline-Braham, with a new family and a seemingly perfect life.

One that didn't include Tracey.

He'd spent a long time watching her with her family at one of her two teenage girls' soccer games, and he'd paid close attention to her husband's behavior. The handsome Black man had cheered on his daughter and hugged Tracey's mother and his other daughter a number of times. When the game was over, he'd high-fived the daughter that had played and had spun her around in an embrace, which seemed to embarrass her. Did they have room in that shiny life for one more?

He hoped he wasn't leading Tracey toward heartache. He knew she'd be pissed that he'd tracked them down behind her back, but that hadn't been his intent. He hadn't wanted to give her false hope—or worse, have her tell him *not* to try to track down her mother. He couldn't have done that, knowing she had that gaping hole in her life. Now he had to find the right time to tell her, and he had no idea how he'd know it was the right time.

But he trusted his gut to clue him in.

He pulled out his phone as he headed into the clubhouse and saw a text from Tracey on the screen. *Hope you're having a great ride. Miss you.* She'd added a kissing emoji, and that ridiculous thing made him smile. *A fucking emoji.* He'd always hated them. *Until Tracey.*

She was making him question everything he thought he knew about himself with her elfin magic, and she wasn't even trying. She never asked for a thing, didn't bitch about who he was or how he acted, and she accepted him for the man he was, faults and all. That made him feel things he had trouble keeping inside and want things he'd never imagined wanting, like to show her the world. Just the two of them on his bike, cruising across the country, enjoying the mountains, plains, gardens, and whatever else her sweet heart desired.

He sent her a text on his way upstairs. *Hey, babe. When are you wrapping things up?*

He headed into his bedroom, where a small pile of Tracey's clothes was folded neatly on the chair and her hairbrush sat on the dresser beside a note she'd tucked into his sock drawer at some point. He'd found it earlier that morning—*Thinking of you. xox, T.* He pictured her hiding it while he brushed his teeth or slept. Like always, those thoughts led to more, of her sweet whispers when she wanted his attention, of her sexy mouth and the scorching things she did with it, and her gorgeous hazel eyes that said *I trust you, please don't hurt me,* and *I want you,* all at once.

Just thinking about her got him fired up.

His phone vibrated with her response. *I'm leaving in a few minutes. How about you? Are you still out?*

He thumbed out, *Just got back to the clubhouse. Jumping in the shower. Come up when you get here.*

Okay. See you soon. She added a heart emoji.

The damn emoji made him smile again. He hadn't smiled this much since he was a kid. He tugged off his shirt and called Tiny on speaker as he sat down to take off his boots.

"D, my man. How's it going?" At three hundred plus

pounds, with his thick salt-and-pepper hair and scraggly beard, Tommy "Tiny" Whiskey might look doughy, but he was one of the toughest men Diesel knew, and like Biggs, one of the most generous, too.

"Pretty damn well. You?" He pulled off his boots and socks.

"*Eh.* Sasha and Cowboy finished expanding the paintball field, and Doc's got himself another dog. Dare's got a bug up his butt about running with the bulls in Spain, and Birdie's on a mission to marry off Cowboy. Other than that, things are going fine." Tiny and Wynnie's three sons were Dark Knights and went by their road names—Doc, Dare, and Cowboy. Their oldest daughter, Sasha, an equine rehabilitation therapist, lived for those paintball battles as much as Birdie, the youngest, lived for her made-up missions.

Diesel chuckled. "Sounds like nothing's changed."

"Nope. But I heard things might be changin' for you. Wyn talked to Red the other day. She says you've got yourself a sweet young thing. Put her on the back of your bike and everything. Sounds serious."

Diesel headed into the bathroom to turn on the shower, his gaze moving over Tracey's toothbrush beside his, her shampoo and body wash in the shower. *Yeah, it's serious.* "That's why I'm calling. I know you were expecting me after the holidays, but I'm sticking around for a while." He'd already told Bullet there was no need to hire another bartender.

"Damn, son. You ain't had a girl by your side since you were a teenager. What's Biggs puttin' in the beer out there?" Tiny laughed. "This sweetheart got a name?"

"Tracey. She's as tough as she is sweet. But she's had it rough, and I don't know, Tiny… For the first time in my life, something's speaking louder than the open road."

"That's good, D. Good for your soul. I'd love to meet the little gal who's keepin' your boots on the ground. But I'm not going to be the one to tell Birdie or my old lady that you're not coming out after the holidays. That's on you, boy."

Diesel laughed. "Fair enough. I'll take care of it. I gotta run."

"Be safe, son."

"You too." Diesel ended the call, stripped off his jeans, and stepped into the shower.

He hadn't seen the guys from Hope Ridge since last December, when he'd taken Simone to the ranch. It'd be good to touch base with them. Maybe he could head out there with Tracey after the holidays. An uncomfortable feeling trampled through him. He hadn't brought anyone into the house he'd shared with his mother since she'd passed away, but he knew his uneasiness was about more than that. *For the record, I don't like when people go behind my back.*

He put his hands on the tile wall, letting the water rain down the back of his neck, hoping he hadn't fucked things up. He heard a noise and opened the shower curtain just as Tracey stepped out of her jeans and walked into the shower, her sweet smile calming his discombobulation. He swept his arm around her, tugging her in for a kiss. She tasted like sugar, gingerbread, and her own unique taste, the taste that had become a part of him. "I fucking missed you," he growled against her lips.

"You did?"

"Hell yes." His hands skimmed down her body, and he palmed her ass, kissing her again, deeper, more passionately.

"Tell me again," she whispered.

It took him a second to understand what she was asking. "I missed you, baby girl." As he said it, he realized he'd never said those words aloud to her before this, which was fucking insane since he'd felt them a hundred times when they were apart. Her smile was like a vise to his heart as she went up on her toes, meeting him in another scorching kiss. She rubbed his back as their tongues danced. Those loving touches turned him inside out.

"Your muscles are so tight. Hard day?"

"It was a hell of a day, but it's better now."

"Let me get some body wash and I'll massage your back." She turned to get the bottle, and he began kissing the back of her neck.

"I don't need you to rub my back, baby. I need to touch you."

He slid his arms around her, one hand moving between her legs, the other to her breast, and lowered his mouth to the base of her neck, giving it a hard suck. She moaned, and her head fell back against his chest. He teased her nipple, sliding his fingers into her tight heat and using his thumb where she needed it most. His cock ached to get in on the action. She pressed her hands to the tiles, riding his fingers, sinful noises sailing from her lips. So damn beautiful. So damn *his*. "Give me your mouth, baby."

She looked over her shoulder, and he crushed his mouth to hers, grinding against her ass, teasing her into a needful frenzy. Her fingers dug at the tiles as her orgasm claimed her. She cried out into their kisses, but he didn't relent. He lived for this, to feel her rapt with desire, to hear her sexy noises. He kissed her harder, more demanding, using his thumb on her clit to extend her pleasure as she mewled, her hips thrusting, sex clenching. As she came down from the peak, lost in a haze of lust, and so damn beautiful he ached for her, it was impossible to harness his desire. He deepened the kiss, loving her mouth the way he wanted to love her body, until he was out of his mind with need, and growled, "I need to fuck you, baby. Are you on birth control?"

"No," she panted. "But you can pull out."

"Fucking dangerous." But even as he said it, the idea of her slick pussy wrapped around his cock with nothing between them had him salivating.

"I trust you."

"Spread those beautiful legs, baby." He aligned their bodies, entering her in one hard thrust. She cried out a loud, surrendering moan. He cupped her sex with one hand, teasing that swollen bundle of nerves as he drove into her, fast and hard, then slow and tender, heightening their arousal with each thrust, until they were both moaning. The pleasure was so intense, so utterly exquisite, he couldn't think, could only *feel*.

"Don't stop."

He quickened his actions, teasing her nipple with his free hand, earning sharp gasps and needy pleas. When he sank his teeth into her shoulder, his name flew from her lips, her inner muscles clenching tight and perfect around his shaft, nearly drawing the come right out of him.

"You feel so fucking good, baby." He pressed his hand against her lower belly, holding her tight against him as he slowed himself down, trying to stave off his release, but he kept climbing, higher and higher, until he was barely hanging on to his control. The need to see her face, to kiss her lips, clawed at him.

"Fuuck." He withdrew, turning her roughly, one hand clamped on the base of his shaft.

His mouth claimed hers as she stroked his cock, as urgent

and demanding as the need coursing through him. He wrapped his hand around hers, squeezing tight, pumping his hips, using his other hand between her legs, working both of them faster, tighter, *harder*, until they crashed into oblivion. He tore his mouth away on a curse as he came on her stomach, sounds of pleasure filling the air, every jerk of his hips dragging a grunt or growl from his lungs, until he was milked dry, and they collapsed into each other's arms, breathless and sated.

"Jesus." He gathered her in his arms, his sticky mess smearing between them. "You fucking kill me."

She giggled.

He turned them and leaned his back against the wall, sinking lower so they were eye to eye. He was so full of emotions, full of *her*, the truth came tumbling out. "I'm free-falling for you, baby girl."

She touched her cheek to his, whispering in his ear, "I know."

"You *know*?" He laughed and squeezed her ass.

Her grin was so big, it lit *him* up. "You can't hide how you feel about me anymore. We're too close."

"Can you *feel* that I want you to get on birth control? Because now that I've had you with nothing between us, there's *no* going back."

Her eyes narrowed. "My body, my choice."

"Of course, I didn't mean—"

She shut him up with a kiss and a giggle. "I'm kidding. I have an appointment this week. We're on the same page. But as delicious as this was, we are *not* taking chances like this again. You'll have to make do *wrapping it before you tap it* until I'm protected."

Free-falling didn't begin to describe what was happening to

him. "You're the boss, baby girl."

"Oh, *I'm* the boss?" Her eyes brightened. "In that case, we'd better get cleaned up, because I'm starved."

He raised a brow, his cock twitching at the idea of being inside her mouth.

"Don't look at me like *that*, you sex maniac. You're taking me out for a burger and fries." She traced a tattoo on his chest with her index finger, and her expression turned seductive. "If you're lucky, *you* can be my dessert."

TRACEY TOLD HIM about the bridal expo as they got dressed. If she kept strutting around in her bra and panties like a sex kitten, they wouldn't be leaving the bedroom. "The place was mobbed, and everything was so beautiful. I think Finlay said she signed eight clients with weddings over the next six months, and Josie got a slew of orders for the holidays and a few bridal showers. Penny found a few gorgeous wedding gowns and a few places she's considering for their babymoon."

He tugged on his jeans and leaned against the dresser to watch her combing her wet hair in front of the bathroom mirror. "What's a babymoon?"

"It's a vacation couples take before their baby is born. Penny and Scott don't want to leave their baby to go on a honeymoon right away, so it makes sense to enjoy the alone time before their baby is born."

"Is that what you're looking for, sparky? A white wedding, babies, and all that hoopla?" He might be falling fast, but he wasn't headed down any aisles anytime soon.

She put down the comb and walked into the bedroom with a contemplative expression. "Someday, maybe?" She grabbed a T-shirt from the chair and put it on. "To be honest, that stuff kind of scares me, and I have a lot to accomplish before I'm ready for that."

"Why does it scare you?"

She pulled on her jeans. "Because people change. I'm not in a rush to put myself in that position."

He should be relieved by that, but it bothered him. He took her hand, drawing her into his arms. "You think I'd change like that? That I'd ever manhandle you?"

"No. I never worry about that. But hurting someone isn't always physical." Worry rose in her beautiful eyes. "I know how you feel about me, but I also know there can't be many bounty hunting jobs around here, and you've lived by your own rules forever. You might get restless and resent me for feeling like you have to stick around."

His jaw tightened. "I can't promise you I won't get restless, but I *can* promise you that I won't resent you for it. The first time I kissed you, I committed to being with only you, the same way you committed to being with only me. I made that decision because I wanted *you* more than I've ever wanted anything else, and I don't regret it. I'm a loyal motherfucker, Trace. To you and to the club. Those bonds don't break. But I gotta be honest with you. I don't see myself walking down an aisle or living behind a white picket fence. I think I'll always feel the need to hit the open road at times. How often, I can't say. But as long as we're together, where I go, you go."

"And if I don't want to leave Peaceful Harbor for long stretches of time?"

Well, hell, he hadn't thought that far ahead. "You're asking for a crystal ball, and I don't have one, baby girl." He sat on the bed and pulled her down on his lap. "Is that what you need? To have all the answers now?"

"No. I have a lot to figure out, too. Like I said, I'm not in a rush for more."

"Then we're cool with the way we are?"

She smiled. "Yes, I just wanted to bring it up."

"Good. Can I help you figure anything out?"

"I don't know. I was at the shelter the same time as Josie, and now she's got this great business, and Sarah went from a worse situation than mine to having her own hairdressing clients. Roni has dance, Finlay has catering, and Penny has her ice cream shop. I'm not jealous or anything. I'm happy for them. They're inspiring. But it made me realize that I don't have anything of my own."

"What do you mean? Like a job? You want to own a business?"

"Not specifically. I don't know what I want. That's the problem. I love my job at the bar, and I can't imagine my life without it. But I think I'd like to do more. I'd like to do something that helps others. Something I can be proud of. I just don't know what that might be."

"Lior told me he's tried to get you to teach with him."

"I know, and I love working out with him. But while those classes help, I know they don't teach what women really need to know. Not like what you're teaching me. I wish I was good enough to teach *that* to women. That would be helpful, and it's something I'm really passionate about. But I only just started learning."

"Isn't that what goals are for, baby? You're making great progress. If you want it bad enough, you'll get there."

"Maybe one day, but I still can't teach it alone. The only reason it works is because you and Lior are there to work through scenarios with me."

"You mean to scare the shit out of you until you get so pissed you tear us apart?"

She grinned. "I am getting good, aren't I?"

"Damn right you are." He slid his hand to the nape of her neck. "I'm here, baby girl. Lior's here. You keep kicking ass every week, and who knows what'll happen." He pulled her into a slow, sensual kiss, their connection so strong, he knew it was the right time to share his news. "But I think there's something bigger you need to figure out first."

"What's that?"

"You know that recon mission I went on today?"

"Yeah."

"It was for you. I found your mother."

"You *found* her?" she asked incredulously.

"Yes, and I'm sorry for going behind your back. I didn't want to give you false hope in case I couldn't track her down."

"That's okay. You *found* her!" Tears dampened her eyes, and she threw her arms around him. "I didn't think I'd ever see her again. Where is she? How is she?"

He wiped her tears with the pad of his thumb. "She's in Annapolis, and she's safe. She works in a garden center. But, babe, she's married. Her name is Michelle Kline-Braham."

"She's *married*? Did you see her? Talk to her? Did you meet her husband? Is he a good guy? Please tell me he doesn't hurt her."

She'd gone years without seeing her mother, and her first thought was for her mother's safety. How could this spectacular woman ever think he'd want to be away from her? All he wanted was to make her dreams come true.

"I only saw them from a distance, and they looked happy. I did a background check on her husband, Anthony. He's clean. No priors, not even a parking ticket. He's a high school teacher with a great reputation."

She exhaled with relief. "Thank goodness."

"But, baby, he's been married once before. His wife had an affair and took off. He has sole custody of their two teenage daughters, Anna and Malia, which means—"

"My mom has a whole new family," she said with disbelief.

"But that doesn't negate you."

"I know." She stared vacantly at the floor.

He turned her face toward his, her teary eyes cutting him to his core. "Baby, I have her address. You can see her, talk to her, work things out."

"I want to do that."

"Then why are you crying? Talk to me, Trace. Are you sad? Happy? I'm not great at reading tears."

She smiled, tears spilling from her eyes. "I'm both, and I'm scared. What if she doesn't want to see me? What if she's moved on, and she really did mean the things she said to me?"

"Then you apologize, and you tell her that you wished you had listened but that *you've* moved on, too. That you're not that naive teenager who trusted someone she shouldn't have." His throat thickened as more tears slid down her cheeks. "Tell her you know you were wrong, but that everyone makes mistakes and you want to fix things between you two. You tell her how much you love her and that you're *worthy* of her love, and you don't walk away until she hears you."

Tracey buried her face in his neck, crying. He wrapped her in his arms and kissed her head. "I'll be there with you, baby girl, whenever you're ready to go."

Her head popped up. "I want to go next weekend. After working out with Lior on Saturday if we can get the time off. I can talk to Dixie. It shouldn't be a problem now that we have Dana on board, and maybe you can talk to Jed about taking your shift?" She wiped her eyes. "At least that way I'll know for sure."

"I'll make it happen. We'll go right after the gym." He kissed her. "She's your mom and she loves you, Trace. That's why she tried to use tough love."

"I was too stubborn for it to work."

"I know a little something about being stubborn. You know that girlfriend I told you about? A few months after I started seeing her, my mom warned me not to get too attached. She thought she had wandering eyes. But I was so arrogant and stupid, I didn't listen. Everyone fucks up, babe. That's how we learn. Some lessons are just harder than others."

Tracey's stomach growled, and she put her hand over it, laughing softly.

He was glad to see her smiling. He gave her a quick kiss and tried to keep that smile in place. "Speaking of hard lessons. You need to eat, and if you keep sitting on my lap in those skimpy panties, the only thing you're gettin' is dessert, right here in this bed."

She put her arms around him. "Dessert before dinner sounds good to me."

He made a growling noise, which he'd learned she loved and, in one quick move, shifted her onto her back on the bed and came down over her, both of them laughing.

"Laughing looks good on you." She leaned up and kissed him.

"Know what looks good on you?" As he lowered his mouth to hers, he said, *"Me."*

Chapter Thirteen

BY THE TIME Saturday rolled around, Tracey was a nervous wreck about seeing her mother. Diesel had her home phone number, but Tracey didn't want to try to reconnect over the phone. She needed to see her mother in person, and she was pretty sure she'd fall apart when she did, which was why she wanted to take this slowly. Diesel found out her mother was working Saturday afternoon, and they planned to stop by the garden center so Tracey could get a glimpse of her. If she fell apart, then once she pulled herself together, she'd talk to her.

At least that was the plan, but her brain wasn't exactly functioning at full capacity. She'd barely been able to concentrate all week, and working out had been a bust. She'd tried, but she'd been too sidetracked to be productive. She'd talked with Josie and Izzy about seeing her mother, and they'd both offered to go with her, which she'd briefly considered. But Diesel had become her person. She couldn't pinpoint exactly when that change had taken place, but he'd become the one she trusted with her secrets, her sadness, and her celebrations.

She looked across the cab of the truck at her rugged, big-hearted man, admiring his clean-shaven jaw, which was working double time as if he was nervous, too. Like most days, he wore his baseball cap backward. His black T-shirt strained over his biceps. His jeans were faded, his black leather boots scuffed and marred. She liked that he never tried to impress her, or anyone else for that matter. He was as genuine as a person could get, never cushioning the things he said or playing games with people's emotions, and those qualities were among her favorites. She'd also realized that he was among the *most* communicative people she knew.

He reached for her hand, giving it a reassuring squeeze. "Nervous, baby?"

"Yeah. Can you distract me? Tell me a story or something?"

"A story? Like *Once upon a time*?"

"Anything. Tell me the story behind your hat. Did your mom give it to you?"

He nodded, keeping hold of her hand. "How'd you know?"

"I figured it out the first time you introduced me to Adrian. When we talked about your mom, you fidgeted with it."

"It was her lucky hat. She'd had it since before I was born. But she almost never wore it. She kept it by her bed on a hobbit snow globe. I asked her where she got it once, and she said someone who was all about elfin magic had given it to her on her first hobbit adventure."

"Wow, that's an old hat. When did she give it to you?"

His jaw clenched again, and he put both hands on the steering wheel, turning off the main road onto a side street. "After she got her final diagnosis. She said she saved all the magic in it for me. But I wouldn't take it. If the damn thing had any magic in it, I wanted her to have all of it."

"*Aw*, Diesel." She got choked up. "You really are the sweetest guy."

He gave her a disapproving look.

"You can be tough and still be sweet. When did you start wearing it?"

"After her funeral. When I left home, I took a backpack full of clothes, the hat, and a few other things."

"Do you think there's magic in the hat?"

"There must be." He stopped at a red light, reaching for her hand again. He kissed her knuckles. "I found you."

"See? Sweet and romantic."

He tugged her hand, so she was leaning across the truck, and put it on his crotch, smiling wolfishly. The light changed, and he turned the corner. A minute later, he pulled into the lot for Lowry's Garden Center, a massive red barn flanked by two enormous greenhouses, sending her nerves into a frenzy. She looked at the people milling around the entrances, checking out lush plants, bountiful flowers, interesting pots, and beautiful garden statues. It was easy to picture her mother working there. But was her mother the same person now? Or had she changed as much as Tracey had?

Diesel parked and turned in his seat, giving her his full attention. "You've got this, baby girl."

His encouragement was everything. She drew in a deep breath, blowing it out slowly. "We'll see. I sure wish I had a little magic right now."

He took off his hat and put it on her head. A lump lodged in her throat. She had a momentary thought about wanting to look good for her mother, but if ever there was a time when she needed a little extra *something*, it was right then. Plus, the smile lighting up Diesel's face bolstered her confidence.

"You're damn cute in my hat, sparky." He leaned in and kissed her. Then he climbed out of the truck and came around to help her out.

She shifted on the seat, and when he reached for her hand, she pulled him closer. "No matter how this turns out, I want you to know how much I appreciate you for finding my mom and being here for me. I'm so nervous, I feel like I'm going to throw up, but I know I'd be even more nervous if you weren't by my side."

His hands slid up her legs as he leaned in. "You're my girl, Trace. We're a team. Where you go, I go. If you puke, I'll be right there to clean you up."

She laughed. "Now, *that's* commitment."

"I take care of the people I care about." He winked, lifted her off the seat, kissed her, and set her on her feet. He slung an arm over her shoulder, but he didn't move toward the garden center. She knew he was giving her time to pull herself together, his dark eyes scanning the parking lot.

She took a moment to try to prepare, but it only made her more nervous, so she put her arm around Diesel and nodded, indicating she was ready. He held her a little tighter as they headed toward the garden center. Every step made her heart beat faster. She fisted her hand in the back of Diesel's shirt, trying to focus her nervous energy in that one spot, but it was like trying to rein in a swarm of bees. She reminded herself she was only going to get a glimpse, then she could escape.

They entered the barn, the scents of plants, dirt, and fertilizer stirring memories as he led her through the barn and into a greenhouse. Tracey's mind raced, her eyes darting to the faces of the women around them, suddenly wondering if she'd recognize her mother. Would her mother recognize her? She'd had long hair and bangs when she'd left home. The murmurs of customers competed with the sounds of registers dinging and shopping carts' wheels rattling on the concrete floors. It was so overwhelming, Tracey felt like she might pass out. She couldn't do this. She wasn't ready. She stopped walking and turned to Diesel, her gaze sweeping over the crowd. Just as her hand landed on his stomach, her eyes landed on her mother walking down the aisle toward them. Goose bumps chased over Tracey's body, tears welling. Their eyes met, and her mother stopped cold, her jaw dropping, brow furrowing in disbelief. Tracey couldn't move, could barely breathe. Everything around her turned to white noise.

Tears spilled down her mother's cheeks. Tracey gulped air into her lungs, the room tilting around her. Suddenly she was sprinting down the aisle, and her mother was running too. They collided in a tangle of tears and hugs, sobs slurring their words.

"*Tracey?* Oh God. Tracey!"

"Mom."

"My baby. I've missed you so much." Her mother hugged her tighter, their hearts thundering. "Oh, my sweet girl."

"I'm sorry," Tracey cried. "I'm so sorry. I should have listened to you."

She didn't know how long they stood in the middle of the greenhouse embracing, sobbing, apologizing, but at some point, her mother said, "Let me look at you," putting a few inches between them. She put her shaky hands on Tracey's cheeks, like she did when Tracey was little.

"It's really you." Tears fell like rivers down her mother's cheeks "You're safe." She pulled Tracey into her arms again. "I thought you...I feared the worst."

"I'm sorry." Tracey couldn't stop crying. She was devastated by the worry she'd caused her mother and relieved that her mother didn't hate her, but as the people around them came back into focus, she felt Diesel's presence behind her and remembered this was her mother's workplace. Trying to pull herself together, she drew back and wiped her eyes. "I shouldn't have come to your work. I can come back when you're off."

"Don't be silly. I get off in ten minutes. My boss will let me leave now. Just give me one second. Don't leave, okay? Promise me you won't leave?"

"I won't. I promise." Tracey watched her mother rush over to a man standing by a register, motioning to Tracey. Her mother held up one finger in Tracey's direction and disappeared around a corner. Tracey reached for Diesel, the smile in his eyes matching the one in her heart. "She doesn't hate me."

Tears threatened again, and he pulled her into his arms. "I'm so happy for you, baby."

"I can't believe it. Thank you. *Oh God.* Thank you." She took his hand as her mother hurried toward them with a purse slung over her shoulder, curious eyes moving to Diesel. "Mom, this is my boyfriend, Diesel. He's the one who found you for me."

Diesel nodded. "It's a pleasure to meet you, ma'am."

"Diesel? That's an interesting name," she said affectionately.

"It's a road name, ma'am. My given name is Desmond Black."

"He's a biker," Tracey explained. "They all have road names."

"Well, Diesel the biker, how can I ever thank you for bringing my sweet girl back to me?" Her eyes teared up, and she opened her arms, going in for a hug.

Tracey held her breath, thinking of how uncomfortable Diesel would be, but he wrapped her mother in his arms. "Seeing you two together is thanks enough."

"I'm not sure that's true, but I sure am grateful." Her mother smiled up at him, then looked at Tracey. "Can we go for coffee and catch up? Do you have time?"

"Yes. We'd love to."

"We have so much to talk about." Her mother took Tracey's and Diesel's arms, and marched them toward the door. As they walked past a few of her mother's co-workers, who were watching them curiously, her mother called out, "I'm going for coffee with my daughter!"

TRACEY AND HER mother sat in a booth at a cute café around the corner from the garden center. Her mother pointed out the front window to Diesel leaning against his truck, arms crossed, chin low. "He didn't really have to make phone calls, did he?"

"No. He wanted to give us time alone."

"That was nice of him. He's a looker, honey, and I like the way he opened the doors for us and called me *ma'am*, although it made me feel my age. But that's a lot of muscle, sweetheart, and I don't know much about bikers, so I have to ask. Is he good to you?"

"He's more than good to me. I know he looks intimidating, but beneath all that armor is a heart of gold. He's not just good to *me*, Mom. He's good to everyone close to him. You should have seen him shopping for birthday presents for our friends' kids. He spent more than an hour picking out dolls and GI Joes, because he wanted them to be just right. It's a Western-themed birthday party, and the other night he surprised me with a cute pair of cowgirl boots and a hat." She was so nervous she was rambling. She gazed out the window at Diesel and took a deep breath, feeling calmer already. "I wasn't sure I'd ever want to be with another man after Dennis. But then we got together, and now I can't imagine my life without him in it."

"Oh, sweetheart. I'm so glad you're happy." Her mother glanced at Diesel. "He brought us together. I guess that should have told me everything I needed to know. But the things people say about bikers had me a little worried."

Tracey tried to put her mind at ease, telling her about the Dark Knights and the good things they did for the community. She wasn't sure where to start talking about her history with Dennis, so she went backward, telling her mother about how she and Diesel worked together and about the attack. Her mother reached across the table, holding her hands as she relayed the details of the aftermath, including how Diesel had cared for her. Her mother asked a dozen questions, and reliving that night was painful, but Tracey wanted her mother to know the truth, and she reassured her she was okay. She told her about learning self-defense with Diesel and Lior, and when she could put it off no longer, she told her about what had happened with Dennis.

They both cried, and her mother moved into the booth beside her to embrace her. She stayed there, the two of them sitting sideways, each with one knee bent on the bench between them, their arms draped over the back of the seat, holding each other's shoulders. Tracey told her how she'd ended up at the shelter and about getting to know the Whiskeys and her other friends.

"Thank God you made it out alive. I want to meet all those wonderful people and thank them in person." Her mother wiped her tears. "I'm so sorry, sweetheart. I never should have given you that ultimatum. I've regretted it every day since. I never stopped trying to call you. Even after your phone was disconnected."

"It's my fault. I shouldn't have left. I should have taken your calls. I wish I could go back and make different choices. I was afraid to look for you when I first got to the shelter because there was so much water under the bridge, I thought we'd both drown in it."

"*Honey*, nothing could drown us."

"I know that now. I finally got up the courage to call you earlier this year. But I couldn't find you. Your number was disconnected. I even looked online, knowing I wouldn't find you there. I thought maybe you were hiding from me."

"I would *never* do that. Your father got out of prison a few years ago, and he came after me. I had no choice but to leave town and start over, and phones are like trackers these days. I had to get rid of mine and get a new number. But it had been years, Trace, and you never reached out. I thought you were done with me."

"Never. I was messed up, Mom, in survival mode. I'm so sorry." Sadness engulfed her, warring with panic over her father going after her mother.

"It's okay. I've been there, baby. I hate that you went through that."

Tracey pushed past the sadness, not wanting to get mired down in it, and focused on her bigger worry. "Did he find you? Did he hurt you again?"

"No, but he tried. He grabbed me on my way out of the grocery store and tried to force me into his car. Luckily, there were some men who heard me screaming and ran over to help.

Your father took off, but I was terrified he'd come back. I left town right then. I didn't even go home to get my stuff. I was afraid he'd be waiting for me. I ended up here, in Annapolis, and once I got settled and felt safe, I called the police to report what happened."

"Did they arrest him? Is he in prison?"

"They never had a chance. He got into a high-speed chase the day after he attacked me and flipped his car over a retention wall, into oncoming traffic. He was killed instantly."

"Oh my God. Was anyone else hurt?"

"A truck driver slammed into his car, but luckily the driver wasn't badly injured."

"Thank goodness. Does it make me a horrible person that I'm relieved he's gone?"

"No, honey. He never brought anything good into your life, and he hadn't been the guy I fell in love with in decades, if he even ever was. Has Dennis ever looked for you?"

"I don't think so."

"Good. And now you have Diesel, who seems very watchful."

Tracey glanced out the window at him, talking on his phone as he paced by the truck. As if he sensed her eyes on him, he looked over, lifting his chin in acknowledgment. "I do, and he is fiercely protective of me. But I've learned there's a big difference between *protective* and *controlling*. Diesel never tries to tell me where to go, how to act, or what to wear." Although sometimes he'd warn her that certain outfits might lead to him dragging her into the back room at work. She took careful notes and wore those outfits strategically, like the other night when she'd worn the red-and-black plaid miniskirt he loved and they hadn't even made it up to his room in the clubhouse before doing deliciously dirty things. It turned out she *loved* being bent over a pool table by him. Who was she kidding? She loved every sexy thing they did.

But this was not the time to think about those things.

"Diesel told me you have a new husband and two teenage stepdaughters. Are you happy? Is he good to you? How did you meet him? I want to know everything."

Her mother smiled. "He's wonderful, and so are the girls. I was at work at the garden center a few months after I moved. Tony and his girls, Anna and Malia, came in to get supplies to start a garden. They had *no* idea what they were doing, and I helped them figure it out. They came back the next day, and the next, and gosh, Trace, the way he was with his girls just melted my heart. They came in the next weekend, and the girls, who were eleven and thirteen at the time, asked if I would come by their house and make sure they were doing it right."

"Were they matchmaking?"

"Yes, they were." Her mother laughed. "And I'm so glad they did. Tony has been raising them since they were five and seven. He's a wonderful, patient, loving father. He jokes a lot. He's not that funny, but he thinks he is, and the girls are sweet. I keep waiting for the rebellious years to hit, but they haven't yet. Anna is a little mouthy at times, but she's fifteen, so that's to be expected, and Malia, who's thirteen, gets on her about it. It's really cute. You won't believe this, but they both play soccer, just like you did. Tony coached their teams when they were younger."

"I'm so happy for you, Mom." She had to ask the burning question. "Do they know about me?"

"*Of course* they know about you. Everyone in my life knows about you. You are the only reason I kept your father's last name. I thought you were done with me, but I never gave up hope."

Tracey lowered her eyes. "I gave up hope that you'd want me in your life. I'm so glad Diesel didn't let it stay that way. I'm sorry, Mom." Tears slipped down her cheeks again, and her mother embraced her.

"It's okay, honey. Let's not dwell on that. We're together now, and that's what matters most."

Tracey sat back, wiping her tears. "Do the girls and Tony hate me for leaving you?"

"No, honey. But the girls were pretty mad at me for thinking tough love would do anything but chase you away. I should have known better. I was just like you at that age, which is probably why I fought so hard to try to keep you by my side. We can't change the past, but thanks to Diesel, we're blessed to have a chance at a future." Her phone chimed with a text, and she pulled it out of her purse. "It's Tony. I called him on the way here to let him know I'd be late. We don't have to stop talking. But do you and Diesel have plans tonight? Tony's picking up steaks to grill for dinner, and I would love to get to know Diesel better and for you to meet my—*our*—family."

Just the words *our family* brought more tears. "We'd love that."

"Do you need to check with Diesel?"

"No, Mom. He just wants me to be happy." As she said it, the truth of her words hit her.

"Oh, honey." Tears brimmed in her mother's eyes, bringing more tears to Tracey's. They laughed and hugged. "We're a mess."

"No, Mom. We *were* a mess. Now we're just happy."

Chapter Fourteen

"I WAS SO nervous, but you were right. She loves me unconditionally…"

Tracey had been gushing about her mother for the last ten minutes, jumping from one part of their conversation to another as they followed her mother to her house. Diesel was thrilled for both of them. He'd wanted to find a way to open that door so she could heal that rift since she'd first told him about it, and seeing them together was everything. Even if it dredged up a longing for his own mother. Before Tracey, he would have fought those feelings with everything he had, but now he welcomed them.

"I feel like I've been given a new lease on life, and that's because of *you*," she said, drawing him from his thoughts. She was beyond adorable, wearing his baseball cap and an elated smile that outshone the sun. "How can I *ever* thank you?"

He gave her a coy grin.

"I'm down for that. *Win-win*." She laughed, but as her mother pulled into the driveway of a modest two-story home with beautiful gardens out front and Diesel parked at the curb, her expression turned serious. "What if I don't fit in with them?

Do you think I will? I still can't believe my mom doesn't hate me. She said the girls didn't, but what if they do? They play soccer. Did I mention that already?"

"Yeah, about ten times." He took her hand, wishing he could take away her trepidation. "You're the most likable person I know. If they've got a problem, that's on them, not you." He motioned to Anthony coming out the front door wearing dress slacks and a blue polo shirt, waving to her mother. "Let's go."

He came around to help Tracey out, and with his arm protectively around her, they went to meet her stepfather. Diesel sized him up as they approached. He was about six feet tall, well built, with closely shorn hair and a short beard. He had one arm around his wife, and his kind eyes told Diesel he'd probably earned that good reputation he'd heard about.

"Welcome home, Tracey. I'm Tony, and I'm so glad you're here." He said it like they were old friends, and hell if the look on Tracey's face didn't get Diesel choked up. Tony extended his hand. "I'm a hugger, but the girls told me not to freak you out."

Tracey smiled. "It's okay. We can hug." She embraced him. "This is my boyfriend, Diesel."

"I'd offer to hug you, too, but you kinda scare me." Tony laughed and shook Diesel's hand. "Michelle told me you were a big man, but *wow*. What did your mama feed you?"

"Whatever was in the cupboard, sir."

"Please, call me Tony." He hiked a thumb over his shoulder. "The girls are out back kicking a soccer ball around. They're anxious to meet you both. Would you like to meet them?"

"Yes, I'd really like that," Tracey said, taking Diesel's hand as they headed toward the backyard. "Your gardens are beautiful."

"That's all your mother's doing," Tony said. "I love flowers, but I'm better at killing them than growing them."

As they came around the side of the house, the younger girl yelled, "They're here!" and she ran toward them. She was tall and skinny, with a head full of braids and a sweet, happy face. "Hi! I'm Malia, and that's my sister, Anna, over there." She hugged Tracey as her sister sauntered over with a cautiously curious expression, holding the soccer ball under one arm.

"Hi. I'm Tracey."

"We know. We've been waiting forever to meet you." Malia beamed up at Diesel. "And you're her boyfriend, Diesel, which is the coolest name *ever*. Dad said you're a biker and that's your road name. I want a road name."

Anna, who was also tall and thin but had thick, curly hair, rolled her eyes. "You're not a biker. They don't give road names to kids."

"Actually, I give some kids road names." Diesel looked at Malia. "How about we call you *kicks*? And since your sister is tough, like Tracey, we can call her *spitfire*." That earned a smile from Anna and a squeal from Malia.

"Yes! *Perfect*. I love them!" Malia hugged him, and he patted her back awkwardly.

Tracey laughed. "Diesel's not much of a hugger."

"Why not?" Malia asked.

"*Malia*, let the man be," Tony said.

"But you always say hugs are what keep our hearts beating. He's a big guy," Malia said. "I bet his heart has to work *really* hard."

They all laughed, even Anna, who was still eyeing Tracey. Anna shifted the soccer ball to her other hip. "I heard you played soccer, too."

"I did, a *long* time ago," Tracey said.

Malia tilted her head. "Your mom said you were really good."

"She was. She scored a lot of goals, just like you girls," Michelle said.

Anna stood up taller. "Want to show us what you got?"

"I haven't touched a soccer ball since high school."

"It's like riding a bike." Anna twirled the ball on her index finger.

"Okay, but don't laugh at me if I suck." Tracey followed them into the yard, with Malia chatting up a storm.

"Anna can be a little tough at first," Michelle said.

"So can Tracey." Diesel watched her kicking the ball around with the girls, remembering how she used to give him hell before they'd gotten together. She was still tough and snarky, but now it came with a halo of something deep and playful. He looked at Michelle. "Are you close with Anna and Malia?"

"Very close," Michelle said.

"The girls' mother left when they were young, and she has no contact with them," Tony explained. "They fell in love with Michelle right away, just like I did."

"Then it sounds like Anna has a reason to be tough," Diesel said. "She's lost one mother. She doesn't want to lose another."

Michelle looked at him thoughtfully. "I didn't think about that. You're probably right. What's your family like, Diesel? Are you close to your parents?"

He shifted his attention back to Tracey, laughing with the girls as she showed them some fancy footwork. "It was just me and my mother. We were close, but she passed away a long time ago."

"I'm sorry to hear that," Tony said.

"You must miss her very much." Michelle touched his arm, bringing her eyes to his. "I know you're not a hugger, but I never thought I'd see my daughter again and you brought her back to me, and you have no mother to tell you how remarkable of a man you are." Tears welled in her eyes. "Can I please just—"

Diesel gathered her in his arms and embraced her.

"Thank you," Michelle said through her tears, holding him tight. "Thank you for bringing my baby back."

Diesel steeled himself against the emotions swamping him.

"So you *are* a hugger after all," Tony said as Michelle stepped out of Diesel's arms. "A *selective* hugger. Good timing, my friend. Good timing."

They could thank Tracey for that.

"Hey, you guys! Come play with us!" Malia hollered, waving them out to the grass.

"Dad's got steaks to grill," Tony called out. "They ran me ragged, practicing this afternoon."

"I'll play! If you gentlemen will excuse me." Michelle ran toward the girls.

"How about you, *Unleaded*?" Anna shouted, and the girls cracked up.

Tracey mouthed, *Sorry*, grinning like she was on top of the world.

Diesel chuckled and shook his head. "I think I'll help grill those steaks."

"Maybe later, then!" Malia ran off with Tracey and the others.

"She's not going to let up," Tony said.

"I'm not a soccer player."

"She doesn't care. When Malia wants something, she has a way of worming her way into your heart until you can't help but give in."

He looked at Tracey running around with her mother and stepsisters, laughing and teasing each other, and he couldn't look away. "She reminds me of another special girl I know."

MUCH LATER THAT night, after a wonderful dinner and an evening spent getting reacquainted with her mother and learning all there was to know about her new family, Tracey lay with Diesel in his bed at the clubhouse, basking in the aftermath of their lovemaking. The window was open, night sounds whispering through the curtains as she scrolled through the pictures she'd taken at her mother's house. She was wearing Diesel's shirt, but a gentle breeze chilled her bare legs, and she snuggled closer to her personal heater, clad only in his boxer briefs.

He kissed her head. "I'm going to start leaving the window open more often."

"Sounds good to me." She came to a picture of her mother and Tony sitting on the patio behind their house, holding hands. "Look how happy she is. She seems so much more relaxed than she used to be. I know a lot of that is because my father is gone and she's no longer scared. But I think it's also because of Tony and the girls. They're good for her."

Diesel hugged her against his side. That was his way of agreeing with her. Tracey wasn't just used to his idiosyncrasies—she loved them. There was something wonderful and intimate about being so in tune with a person she could read his thoughts.

As she scrolled through more pictures, she came to a few where Diesel's gaze was a little tortured and his jaw was tight. She'd noticed that several times throughout the evening, and she was pretty sure he'd been thinking about his mother. She wanted to ask him about it, but part of falling for Diesel was knowing when to bring up the parts of his life he kept closest to his heart, and this was not the time.

She continued looking through pictures, chuckling at some, studying others, wanting to soak in as much of everyone as she could. She'd taken a bunch of pictures of their gardens, too. "My mom used to dream of having a beautiful yard with gardens and flowering trees. I'm so glad she has it." She came to a picture of Diesel sitting at the patio table beside Malia with a slice of pie in front of him, fork at the ready. Malia was grinning from ear to ear, caught spearing his pie with her fork. Diesel's brows were furrowed, his eyes narrow, like he was attempting a scowl, but his kissable lips were quirked up at the edges in the cutest smile. Tracey could stare at that picture all night. She'd thought she was falling in love with him, but tonight she knew beyond a shadow of a doubt that he was put on this earth not only for his mother, whose world clearly had revolved around him, but for *her*.

"Who's *this* smiling guy?" She lifted the phone so he could see it better.

"Some asshole," he grumbled.

She set her phone on the nightstand, shifting so she could see him, her chin resting on his chest. "I used to think you could be jerky, but now I know you were just trying to hold back from going after me."

His lips quirked. "I can be an asshole, sparky."

"Sure, when people do things that warrant it."

He palmed her ass, giving it a squeeze. That, she'd learned, meant he wasn't sure she was right but he wasn't going to argue the point.

"I'm going to get that picture printed out and frame it, along with a dozen others, and hang them all up at the house before they get there next Sunday." Her mother had asked if they could come back tomorrow, but they'd promised to attend Kennedy and Lincoln's birthday party. Her mother wanted to see where Tracey lived and worked, and her stepsisters—*she had sisters!*—wanted to see all the places Tracey had told them about, like Penny's ice cream shop, Adrian's father's pizza place, and the harbor, so they made plans for her mother's family to visit them next Sunday. The girls had confided in Tracey that between now and then, they were going to work on getting their parents to let them take a ride on Diesel's motorcycle, which her mother and Tony were a little uncomfortable with. Tracey had wondered if she'd feel funny hearing the girls refer to her mother as their parent. But she didn't. Her mother had more than enough love for all of them.

"Print a few extra copies for here, too."

"You want evidence of us *here*? In your bachelor pad?" she teased. "Where your biker friends might see it?"

He smacked her ass, making her laugh.

"It's funny how much can change in a month, or even in a day. Yesterday it was just the two of us. I mean, we have our friends and they're like family, but now we have my mom, Tony, Anna, and Malia. We have a real family."

He hugged her tighter, and she kissed his chest, taking advantage of their closeness to ask the hard question. "Was today difficult for you?"

"I was happy for you."

"I know you were, but that's not what I asked. Did seeing me with my mom make you miss yours more? Because I missed her for you. I felt an ache in my chest, wishing you could have had more time with her and wishing I'd had a chance to meet her."

He hugged her again, pressing a kiss to her forehead, his lips lingering there, and she felt his heart beat a little faster. He looked at her, his stormy eyes holding hers.

"It's okay to admit it. It won't take away from the excitement of the day," she reassured him.

His brows twitched, like it was even harder to admit than when he'd told her about his mother's passing.

"Diesel, I..." *Love you* was on the tip of her tongue, but she didn't want to scare him off. "I care about you and I want to know what you feel." She shimmied up his body and whispered, "You know you can trust me with your secrets." That earned a genuine smile *and* a butt squeeze.

"I thought about her a lot today, baby girl. I wished she was there with us, playing her guitar, getting to know you and them." He shrugged. "But wishin' won't make it happen, and I don't want to bring you down."

"When you open up to me like that, it brings us closer together. That could never bring me down. It lifts me up."

"*God*, Trace," he said with disbelief, a little gruffly. "The things you say."

She traced the ink on his shoulder. "Do they sound weird?"

"They sound *unreal*, but coming from you, they feel real."

"Because they are real, but I know what you mean, because it's just like your feelings for me. You may not tell me in words, but you say it in other ways, and I hear it and feel it loud and clear. *That* lifts me up."

His brows twitched again, and he brushed the back of his knuckles down her cheek. He didn't say anything for a minute or two, and when he did, his voice was husky, emotional. "After dinner, when your sisters were showing us their yearbooks, I missed the sense of *home*. That feeling when you walk in the door, kick off your boots, and everything just feels right and comfortable. I haven't had that feeling since before my mom got sick, because after that things went to shit. But then I looked at you, and I didn't miss it anymore."

He'd stunned her speechless again, her heart scrambling to climb out of her chest and get to him. She tied a ribbon around his confession and tucked it away.

"So yeah, babe. It's funny how quickly things can change. One day I'm working at Whiskey Bro's, thinking I can hang there for a while, help out the Whiskeys, and the next day you walk in and knocked me on my ass, making me feel like my fucking heart is going to explode."

"Really? Because you gave me dirty looks, and they weren't the good kind."

"*Yes*, really. You messed me up. I had no idea what the hell was going on, which is probably what you saw when I looked at you. You were so beautiful with that pixie haircut and big hazel eyes, scared as a mouse but tough as nails. I couldn't look away. I wanted to wrap you up and protect you from everyone and everything. Then Red asked if I could keep an eye on you, and man, as time went on, I wanted more than my eyes on you. I thought I was losing my mind. You were this tiny flick of a woman, nothing like the chicks I knew, and you were what? Twenty-four then? I was thirty, and that didn't sit so well with me, either. But then I got to know you, and none of that mattered. Then that wedding changed everything. Watching you in that slinky little dress, thinking about how screwed I was, but at least I was keeping it under control."

"Not really," she teased. "Izzy and Dix and everyone else kept telling me you wanted to bend me over the pool table."

He laughed. "Well, they weren't wrong."

"I know that now. But remember at Thanksgiving when you cornered me and asked if I had a date for the wedding, I was so confused."

"That makes two of us."

"And then at the wedding, I thought you were going to ask me to dance."

"That night changed everything. I was keeping my distance until Rhys set his sights on you from across the dance floor. *Jesus.* Suddenly I realized you were everything I wanted and all that mattered."

That made her feel good all over. "Maybe I *should* thank good ol' Dr. Rhys, because the night I went out with him changed everything for me, too. When I was getting dressed for our date, I remember thinking that after too many years of just surviving, I had *finally* found myself. I had a good life, and I was ready for something more. That was *huge* for me. Two years ago, I wasn't sure I'd *ever* get back on my feet, much less be ready to trust someone enough to get close to them. I was proud of how far I'd come. I didn't *need* a man. I was happy with my friends, my job. I was working out and getting stronger. I was happy with who *I* was." She ran her finger absently over his chest as she spoke. "And that attack could have sent me spiraling backward. But you were there, reminding me not to let them break me." As she said it, something dawned on her. "It's no wonder the night I went out with Damon I kept wishing *you* were my something else. I was wrong about thanking him.

You're the one who deserves the gratitude. You gave me the courage to go after what I *really* wanted, not him. You're the reason I walked through that clubhouse door to give you a piece of my mind, and you're the reason I ended up giving you my heart."

He arched a brow. "Because I pissed you off?"

"Yes, but you also turned me on. You've taken my good life and made it great. Even if you did screw me out of being asked to dance for the first time in my life."

His jaw clenched. "You wanted to dance with Rhys?"

"I wanted to dance with *you*, but you were so intent on scaring him off, you didn't even notice."

"I'll be right back." He stepped off the bed and picked up his phone, turning his back to her. He set the phone on the nightstand, and "The Promise" by When in Rome began playing.

Diesel turned, a small smile curving his lips. "Dance with me, baby girl."

It wasn't a question, but as he pulled her up to her feet and into his arms, it was very *Diesel*, which was so much better. As they danced, Diesel whisper-sang about protecting her and not knowing the right words to say, bringing a lump to her throat. He held her tighter, his big body cocooning her, his heart beating against her cheek. She listened intently, not wanting to miss a single word as he sang about always being there, asking her to give him time to figure out what he could say that would make her fall for him, and singing about walking the world for her if that's what it took. She didn't know how he knew the song or if he'd found it just for her, but every single word was perfectly *them*.

She looked up at his handsome face, her knees weakening at

the way he was looking at her as he sang. They weren't doing a fancy dance, and she wasn't in a pretty dress, but she couldn't imagine a more perfect dance—or a more perfect man.

Chapter Fifteen

BEFORE AGREEING TO stick around and help the Whiskeys at the bar, Diesel hadn't attended a child's birthday party since *he* was a kid. The Whiskeys had been roping him into celebrating everything from birthdays to Valentine's Day ever since. Kennedy and Lincoln's party was one for the record books.

Truman and Gemma's backyard had been transformed into something out of the Wild West. All the kids wore Western boots and hats. The girls were adorable in frilly dresses and skirts, and the boys looked like little men in their plaid shirts and jeans. A HAPPY BIRTHDAY banner was strung over the table of gifts. A barrel full of hobby horses anchored one side of the patio, and a stuffed rocking horse was set up for the little ones in the grass. Bones and Dixie were throwing balls at milk jugs that were painted like cows near Maggie Rose and Axel, who were giggling up a storm as they toddled in and out of the mini city made up of massive cardboard boxes painted to look like brick buildings with JAIL, JUICE SALOON, BANK, GRUB, and CLUBHOUSE written in old-time lettering above the cutout windows or doors. Truman and Quincy were taking pictures of Hail and Bradley, the oldest boys at seven and five.

The boys were sitting on bales of hay in a photo area in the grass, holding up frames that Gemma and Crystal had made with WANTED across the top and REWARD 10,000 KISSES along the bottom. Kennedy walked beside Nick Braden, shouting instructions at her brother, Lincoln, and Lila, Bones and Sarah's almost-three-year-old daughter, as Nick and Trixie led them around the yard on miniature horses. The horses were all dolled up with pink and blue ribbons in their manes and tails, fancy saddles, and tiny Western hats between their ears.

Diesel was hanging out with Jace, Moon, and Bullet, who was holding his adorable baby girl, Tallulah, while their other friends mingled on the lawn and chased after their kids. All the adults had dressed for the occasion, too. Bear had gone so far as to wear chaps and a brown leather vest, which Diesel was enjoying giving him shit for. Even Red and Biggs were rocking the Western look. Biggs, like Diesel and Bullet, wore his black leather vest with the Dark Knights patches on the back. *Gotta represent.* Tracey had convinced Diesel to wear a cowboy hat, a big-ass belt buckle with a horse's head on it, and his cowboy boots, all of which reminded him of home.

He looked across the yard at Tracey chatting with some of the girls. She was so damn sexy in tight jeans, a flannel shirt tied just above her waist, and the cowgirl hat and boots he'd bought her. She glanced over, flashing that sweet smile, turning him inside out. She'd been bouncing off the walls to share news of her reunion with everyone, and she'd done it first thing when they'd arrived. Every time she talked about it, she got happier, and damn, that was a great sight.

"You guys recognize that look on Diesel's face?" Bullet asked.

"It's the look that makes a guy stick around," Jed said.

"And want some of *these*." Jace took Tallulah from Bullet, nuzzling her and making cooing noises.

Diesel felt a smile tugging at his lips, but he didn't say a word as they cracked jokes like he was part of their secret husband society or some shit. He wasn't ready for kids, but he sure as hell was sticking around.

"Anyone else planning on taking their hat into the bedroom tonight?" Jed waggled his brows.

Diesel scoffed. "With Tracey lookin' like that, she'll be lucky to make it indoors."

The guys laughed.

Diesel lifted his chin in Red's direction as she headed over in black jeans and a black button-down shirt with silver trim, her red hair tamed by her cowgirl hat.

"Can you believe how big our family has gotten?" Red looked out at the kids chasing one another around the yard and everyone else laughing and having a good time.

They used the term *family* so easily, encompassing everyone within their close-knit, though vast, circle. Diesel cherished that word like the most sought-after designation in the universe. Ever since his mother died, no matter where he was, he'd always felt like an outsider. But thanks to Tracey, he was starting to realize he'd put himself on the other side of that invisible line. That was fine when it was just him he was worried about. In fact, it was what he needed. But Tracey had spent years isolated against her will, with no contact with friends or family, and he never wanted her to feel alone again. He knew if he wanted that for her, he needed to step over that line and try to let the people who had been so good to him—invited him for New Year's Eve, Thanksgiving, Christmas, and all the holidays in between—into his life in a more meaningful way.

Like family.

Red's gaze moved over Bullet, Jace, and Moon, coming to rest on Diesel. "And now that you've decided to stick around, our family is even bigger. I'm so glad you're staying, sweetheart."

She was looking at him with an expression so similar to his mother's, it brought a flood of unexpected emotions. That was happening a lot lately. "Thanks, Red. I'd do anything for Tracey."

The guys eyed each other, big-ass grins spreading across their faces.

"Dude, you waited so long to make a move, I was beginning to wonder if you had a heart under all those muscles." Jace chuckled.

"I'm still shocked that Tracey saw through all your grunts and growls," Bullet added.

Diesel glowered at him.

"Brandon Whiskey." Red's use of Bullet's given name earned Bullet's full attention. "You were not exactly all fluff and sugar before Finlay came into your life."

The guys chuckled, and Red pointed at Jace. "And you, Mr. Stone, have nothing on Diesel. How long did you wait to get together with my daughter? A *lifetime* is my recollection."

"Too damn long is right, Red," Jace agreed.

"Don't mind them, Diesel. I've always known your heart was as big as the sky. I've known you since you were a boy, when Biggs and I would head out to Colorado to see Tiny, and you and your mama would come around for Friendsgivings or whatever was going on. You watched out for her even when you were too young to do a darn thing. You love *hard*, sweetheart, and your mama was so very proud of you. I have no doubt you would've given your life to save her if you could have. That's one reason I chose you to watch over Tracey when she started working for us."

"Was there another reason?" Diesel asked.

"Yes, there was. When you made your way here after your mama died, you'd changed. You'd lost a big piece of yourself, and rightly so. Every time after that, when you'd ride into town, I'd pray you'd found peace. Then I'd see you, and that emptiness was still there. But when Tracey came into the bar, that spark in your eyes reappeared as big and bright as when you were younger, like magic."

"It's called a boner," Bullet said under his breath.

The guys chuckled, but Diesel was stuck on the things she'd said. He'd had no idea that anyone other than his mother had noticed the things he'd done as a boy.

Red silenced the guys with a stern look. "I raised three boys and a feisty girl. I'm well aware that physical attraction was part of it, but it wasn't all of it. No sir." She turned her attention back to Diesel as Bear and Bones joined them. "I thought you and Tracey might need each other. You two aren't as different as everyone thinks."

"Has Mom had too much to drink?" Bear asked.

"*No*, I have not," Red said, without taking her eyes off Diesel. "You had both suffered devastating losses. They weren't the same, but they had a similar impact, making you both put up walls to protect yourselves from getting hurt. You were a lone wolf, and she was a bird trying to find her nest."

"Okay, I take it back," Bear said. "You're making sense."

"Trace is more like an owl," Diesel said evenly. "She's much too wise for a bird."

"Wait a second, Red." Jed looked between her and Diesel.

RUNNING ON DIESEL

"Are you saying you were trying to hook them up?"

Red smiled. "Let's just say I trusted my instincts, and it paid off. Look at our girl over there." Everyone looked across the yard at Tracey. She and Roni were dancing with Lincoln and Lila in their arms. "Tracey has come out of her shell, and thanks to you, she's found her family. And I think you, my big, badass boy, are slowly coming out of your shell, and maybe you've finally found your missing piece, too. That's a beautiful thing."

Diesel was surprised to find he was getting a little choked up.

"Hell yeah, it is," Bullet said. "Not to mention, you saved me a boatload of painful interviews."

"You would've been wasting your time anyway." Bones clapped a hand on Diesel's shoulder, then quickly removed it. "Nobody can replace the man who won out over Peaceful Harbor's most eligible bachelor."

"Are you talking about Rhys?" Jace asked. "The guy who was eyeing my girl at the bachelor auction?" Dixie had coordinated the last charity bachelor auction, and she'd put herself up on the auction block.

Bones laughed. "I forgot about that."

"Bikers *two*. Rhys *zero*. Am I right, big man?" Jace held up his fist and knuckle bumped Diesel.

"You paid thousands of dollars to win our sister in that auction," Bear reminded him.

Jace smirked. "I'd've paid twice that amount."

"I'm sure you would have. Now, how about sharing my grandbaby?" Red reached for Tallulah, but Jace snuck in another kiss on the baby's cheek first.

"Diesel! Diesel! Diesel!" Kennedy ran over in her frilly white dress and denim vest, her dark hair bouncing around her face.

"It's time for cake, and Mom said I can sit with my boyfriends."

"I think you mean *boyfriend*, sweetheart," Bullet corrected her.

"Nope! I'm in love with a biker *and* a cowboy, and Mama said that's okay while I'm young. So I'm never gonna get old!"

Everyone laughed.

"Tru and Gemma are in for years of trouble," Bear said.

"That's okay, Uncle Be-*ah*. Daddy said some days me and Linc are so much trouble we could give Mama gray hair. But Nana Red said you were bigger trouble than we could ever be, and her hair's still red! *Bye!*" Kennedy tugged Diesel toward the long table on the other side of the yard, where the girls were setting out plates for the cake. "Nick! C'mere! Cake time!" She waved the brawny cowboy over.

Diesel and Nick exchanged a head shake, but there was nothing they wouldn't do for the sweet little filly who had them wrapped around her finger.

As everyone gathered around the table while the kids took their seats, Diesel eyed Tracey standing with Josie a few feet away and motioned for her to come to his side.

Tracey glanced at Kennedy and shook her head.

He mouthed, *Get your hot little ass over here.*

She laughed, said something to Josie, and came to his side, grinning adoringly up at him. He hugged her against him with the arm Kennedy hadn't claimed and spoke into her ear. "How could I have missed you when you were just across the yard?" He couldn't believe how easily the words came, and leaned in for a kiss.

Kennedy hollered, "Daddy, is Diesel allowed to kiss another girl if I'm his girlfriend?" making everyone crack up.

Truman chuckled. "Only if it's Tracey, princess."

"I'll be your boyfriend, Kennedy, and I won't kiss another girl," Hail offered, inciting *aww*s from the girls and *Attaboy* from Jed.

"Okay!" Kennedy let go of Diesel's hand. "I'll always love you, Diesel, but you can love only Tracey now."

Christ, this kid. Had she read his mind? "Thanks, Ken."

"I love *Booful!* I kiss her." Lincoln had a wicked crush on Roni and had called her *Booful*—because Quincy called her beautiful, and he'd been too young to pronounce it—ever since he'd met her. He leaned toward Roni, lips puckered, his russet hair falling into his eyes as Roni kissed him.

"Little man, first you steal my name for her, and now you steal my kisses?" Quincy teased.

"I share her kisses with you," Lincoln said. "I love you, too!"

It was cuteness overload around these kids, and Tracey was dreamy-eyed over them.

"How about we sing 'Happy Birthday' and stop talking about kissing?" Biggs suggested, and all the kids cheered.

They sang "Happy Birthday," and Kennedy and Lincoln made wishes and blew out the candles. Everyone clapped and cheered. Diesel watched their friends passing out plates of cake, and his mind traveled back to his younger years, when his mother was still alive, remembering birthday parties with Tiny's family, and suddenly he didn't feel like such an outsider anymore. Tracey snuggled against his side and went up on her toes to kiss him, and he was hit with another revelation. Red was right. He'd lost a piece of himself when he'd lost his mother, but with Tracey, he'd found more than just that missing piece.

He'd found true happiness.

Tracey grabbed a plate with a slice of cake on it and offered him a forkful. "Want some?"

His mother's voice sang through his mind. *We need a little elfin magic, Dezzie. What d'ya say?*

"I want a hell of a lot more than some." *I want forever.*

Chapter Sixteen

TRACEY LAY IN bed early Saturday morning, snuggling with Diesel as he slept, thinking about how much her life had changed since coming to Peaceful Harbor. If someone had told her a year ago that she'd reunite with her mother and fall madly in love with Diesel Black, she'd have wondered if they'd ever met the growly man. But now she knew that she was the only one lucky enough to *really* know him. As much as she loved that, he had so much love to give, she hoped one day he'd see how much everyone else cared about him and open up to them, too.

She glanced at the picture on the nightstand of the two of them that Anna had taken right before they'd left last weekend and had texted to Tracey. They were standing by his truck in front of her mother's house, and she was tucked beneath his arm, her hand on his stomach, her head resting against him. Diesel was kissing the top of her head, and she had a drunkenly happy look in her eyes, caused as much by the reunion with her mother as by Diesel. It was one of Tracey's favorite pictures. They'd made an extra copy that Diesel now carried in his wallet, which made her beyond happy.

Her gaze moved to the other pictures they'd had printed and set around the room. She knew her mother and her family would be happy to see the pictures she'd hung at her house when they visited tomorrow. When they were hanging them, Diesel had asked Tracey why she'd never decorated her room. She hadn't thought about it before, and she'd realized she'd been at a standstill. She'd had her feet firmly planted in her new life, but she hadn't been able to move forward in the little ways that counted until she'd gotten answers about her mother. Diesel had built that bridge for her.

She knew she was helping him cross the bridge from his past to his future, too. It was evident in everything he did and said. They'd had a busy week, but after their workout with Lior on Wednesday, they'd snuck in a quick trip to the Whiskeys' old cabin and had taken a walk by the creek. Diesel told her about all the places he'd traveled and the bounty hunting he'd done, and he'd surprised her by sharing what he'd missed most about his mother—her smile and hearing her play the guitar on the porch late at night when she thought he was sleeping. It seemed easier for him to talk about her now, and Tracey was glad.

She pressed a kiss to his warm chest, trailing her fingers down his stomach. Dirty thoughts danced in her mind. Would she ever stop wanting him so much? She sure hoped not. She'd started taking birth control, and while sex with Diesel was always incredible, making love without anything between them brought it to a whole new level.

"Don't stop there," he said huskily.

She lifted her face so she could see him. He always looked rested and relaxed in the mornings, before his body had a chance to remember it was another new day and he needed to be on guard. "I thought you were sleeping."

"You think I can sleep with your mouth on me?" He squeezed her butt.

Oh, how she loved the things he said and did! She slicked her tongue over his nipple, earning a hungry growl that ignited her from head to toe. He swept her beneath him, his dark eyes and big body pinning her to the mattress. He had that move down to a science, and she went willingly, *eagerly*, every single time.

"You woke me up, baby girl."

"If this is the punishment, I'm going to do it a lot more often."

A slow grin eased across his handsome face, but it was the knitting of his brows and intensity of his stare that had her holding her breath. "I mean it, Trace. I was blowing through life with blinders on, never slowing down to enjoy any of it. You took those blinders off and slowed me down. You make me want things I never imagined wanting and see things from a whole different perspective. You changed my world, baby, and one day I'm going to change yours."

She gazed up at him, her heart so full she could barely contain it. "Don't you know you already have?"

As he lowered his lips toward hers, he said, "How'd I get so lucky that you're mine?"

He didn't give her a chance to answer, taking her in a merciless kiss that went on and on, her desires twining together with the words he'd said, sweeping her into a frenzy of want and need. His erection pressed against her center, and she lifted her hips as he entered her.

Lord have mercy.

He deepened the kiss as they found their rhythm, his every thrust stroking the secret spot that made her toes curl under and beats of ecstasy pulse through her. She pushed her hands down his body, grabbing his ass, earning another potently *male* sound. His hips pistoned harder, *faster*, taking her impossibly deeper. He fisted his hands in her hair, ravaging her mouth, messy and demanding, possessing *all* of her. They were on fire, and she *chased* those flames with everything she had, groping, clawing, biting his shoulder, his neck, anywhere she could take purchase.

Her name fell roughly from his lips, drenched in lust. *"Trace."*

He reclaimed her mouth feverishly, his strong arms pushing beneath her, lifting and angling her hips as he slowed them down, driving in painfully slow and deliciously deep, then grinding his hips and starting over again in a maddening rhythm. Just when she fell into sync, he quickened his efforts in gradual waves, each increase stealing her breath, making her greedier, *needier*. He held her tighter, kissed her rougher, taking her to the edge of a cliff. Pinpricks raced up her limbs, spreading like wildfire through her chest, and exploded into a shower of fiery sensations as her world spun away. Diesel was right there with her, giving in to his own powerful release. Their skin was slick and heated, their breathing ragged and choppy, but their hearts hammered out the same frantic beat as they rode out their passion.

They collapsed in each other's arms, and Diesel kept her close as they caught their breath. He turned them on their sides like he did so often, their bodies moving as one so he could hold all of her. His hand slid to her bottom, his thigh moving over hers as he kissed her. When their lips parted, Tracey's world stilled at the emotions staring back at her.

"I hope you never stop looking at me like that," she whispered.

The tender, lingering press of his lips told her he never would.

AFTER A STEAMY, sexy shower, Diesel whipped up breakfast in the kitchen of the clubhouse and Tracey pranced around in a sports bra and skintight workout pants, chatting about her mother's visit tomorrow. He thought he'd be used to her sexy outfits by now, but it didn't matter what she wore. Every minute she wasn't in his arms was a test of his willpower.

"Do you think I should get something for the girls? I'm going to the grocery store after we work out with Lior. I could head over to the mall and pick something up for them first."

They were meeting Lior at nine. Tracey wasn't scheduled to work until two o'clock, but Diesel had to be there at eleven, so he was going to work out with them for an hour first. He was glad she was taking the full two-hour workout. She'd been a bundle of nervous energy all week about her mother's visit. She'd been a wild woman during Wednesday's workout and had blown both Diesel and Lior away with how far she'd come.

"They're coming to see you, babe, not to get presents."

"I know, but do you think I should? Or will it seem like I'm trying too hard, or trying to buy their friendship? I'm just so happy to have them in my life."

He took her hand and pulled her closer, loving the way her eyes lit up. "I think you should do whatever makes you happy. If you want to buy them something, do it. But if you're doing it because you're afraid you need to in order to win them over, you're wrong." He kissed her, and then he lifted her hand and kissed her palm. "Time with you is the best gift you can give them, and I think they know that."

She sighed. "I know you're probably right. But I'm just so excited about seeing everyone, I want to pick a little something up for them. I know we only spent a few hours with them, but I feel like Anna and Malia are my sisters. How can that be?"

"Because you want it to be."

Her smile faltered. "You think I'm being silly?"

"No. I think you're being the big-hearted chick who roped me in." He set her plate on the table. "Eat up, sweet thing. We'd better get going so we're not late."

After they ate, they grabbed her gym bag and kissed as they headed outside.

"Now, there's a welcome sight." Biggs closed his car door and made his way toward them.

Diesel lifted his chin in greeting.

"Hi, Biggs." Tracey waved.

Biggs leaned down to kiss her cheek. "How're you doing, darlin'? On your way to kick this guy's ass?"

"I'm going to try."

"Don't let her kid you, Biggs. She's a beast. What're you doing here?"

"I gotta get some boxes out of the basement. Bud's birthday is coming up, and Chicki's been bugging Red for pictures of the old days. You know how Chicki is. When she gets a hair up her butt, she doesn't let up." Bud Redmond had grown up with Biggs and had been a member of the Dark Knights forever. His wife, Chicki, owned the salon where Sarah worked, and she was one of Red's closest friends.

"Biggs, you can't be carrying boxes up those stairs. How many boxes are we talking about?"

"No idea. We have all sorts of shit down there. Ten? Twenty maybe."

"*Twenty* boxes?" What was he thinking? "Where are your boys?"

"*Eh.*" Biggs waved his hand dismissively. "They're busy with their families. I don't want to bother them with this."

Diesel hated to disappoint Tracey, but he wasn't going to let Biggs carry boxes while wrestling with a cane. "I'll get the boxes."

"*Nah*, you're on your way out," Biggs said. "You got stuff to do. I can handle it."

Diesel knew better than to argue with him, but that didn't mean he'd give in. He looked at Tracey, but before he could get a word out, she said, "I was just going to offer you up." She rose on her toes and kissed him. "I'll see you at two. Don't let Biggs carry too much."

Damn, he loved her. "Thanks, babe. I'll make it up to you." He gave her ass a swat, earning an eye roll that made him and Biggs chuckle.

Tracey pointed at Diesel. "I'm going to start saying goodbye to you by smacking *your* ass."

Biggs laughed. As she climbed into her car, he said, "Your little gal doesn't take any guff, does she?"

"No, sir." *It's one of the things I love about her.*

They headed inside, making their way through the main room to the kitchen. Biggs looked around as he pulled open the basement door. "I didn't know the counters could shine like that. Did you fix that cabinet and put those doors on the pantry?"

"About a year and a half ago." He'd also organized the cabinets and pantry. "No use having things if you're not going to take care of them. I'm surprised one of the guys didn't put them up for you."

Biggs stroked his beard. "Guess they never come in the kitchen, either. With the second fridge in the meeting room, this room doesn't get much use unless someone's staying here. Did Tracey organize the pantry?"

"No. That was me."

"Damn, son. Guess you had time on your hands." Biggs opened the door to the basement, and they were met with a musty, cold scent. He flicked on the light and headed downstairs.

Diesel followed him down. "Who's in charge of the annual maintenance of this place?"

"We all are. When something goes wrong, we fix it."

"The kitchen tells me otherwise. You should put someone in charge of it, Biggs. This place will last a lot longer if it's properly cared for. I'm sure Crow or one of the other guys can handle a once-a-year inspection and take care of the stuff that goes wrong. I've been changing the air filters every three months, but when I got here, they were in shit shape. When's the last time you had the roof checked or the HVAC serviced?"

"I'm not sure."

"I'll come up with a system and get my arms around it." Diesel stepped into the basement beside him. On the far side of the room, there were rows of precariously stacked boxes, some with open flaps, others crushed. Between stacks were old chairs and a coffee table with more boxes on them. Antlers from a deer head poked out from behind a tower of boxes, and off to the side were plastic containers overflowing with tinsel and holiday decorations.

Diesel cursed under his breath. "Getting my arms around

this is another story. What is all this shit?"

"I don't know what's in all the boxes, but my family and several club members have stuff down here. All the club minutes and records dating back to when my grandfather founded it are down here collecting dust. The records are in the white boxes."

"That's your system? White boxes?" Diesel looked at the various brown cardboard boxes—from beer and alcohol cases to television boxes, and Lord knew what else. Long wooden shelves lined the back wall, and more sets of metal shelves sat off to the side littered with tools and other miscellaneous items, as if someone had once thought about organizing. But he didn't see white boxes anywhere, which meant they were probably buried in the middle of the stacks.

"You know how it goes. You think you've got a system. You have your boys carry a box or two down here and there, and before you know it, twenty years've gone by and you've got *this*. Hell, Tiny's got stuff down here from before he moved out West. You know that story?"

"I might have heard it." Diesel adjusted his baseball cap, and began looking for markings on the boxes as Biggs told him the story he'd heard a handful of times.

"Tiny and I were riding cross-country. It was summertime, hot as hell, when we stumbled upon the Roadhouse. Wynnie had just graduated college, and she was there celebrating with her sister and friends. Tiny took one look at her, and I kid you not, he said, *I'm gonna marry that chick.*" Biggs chuckled. "I rode back alone that summer. Wynnie was going to grad school in the fall, and Tiny got a job at the ranch, which was originally owned by her grandfather. It was just a horse rescue at the time, and he put a ring on her finger a few months later. That winter Axel and I packed up Tiny's stuff and drove it out to him in a

U-Haul. Whatever didn't fit has been down here ever since."

Great. "Biggs, none of these boxes are marked. How're we going to find the pictures Chicki wants?"

"Guess it's a bigger job than I anticipated. I can take care of it, son."

"No way, old man. But rather than carry all this upstairs, why don't you do it down here and organize as we go? Kill two birds with one stone. We've got packing tape and labels in the bar. Give me a few minutes to grab them and I'll be right back." He narrowed his eyes at Biggs. "*Don't* try to lift any boxes."

Biggs held one hand up. "*A'right, a'right.* Grab me a bottle of water while you're up there?"

"Already planning on it."

When Diesel returned with the supplies and water, Biggs had already moved and rummaged through five boxes. The ornery bastard. Diesel set up the chair by a coffee table, so Biggs wouldn't have to stand as he rifled through boxes. An hour later, Diesel had cleared a path to the shelves, and they'd worked their way through, marked, and shelved a number of boxes, organizing by club business or member.

Diesel tore open another box, as Biggs said, "We just struck gold. Grab a chair, and get over here, D. I'll show you some pictures of me and Tiny back in the day."

Diesel pushed to his feet, set a chair backward beside Biggs, and straddled it.

Biggs was holding a handful of old photographs. The top picture was taken outside of Whiskey Bro's. There were a bunch of guys wearing black leather jackets and vests, jeans, boots, and serious expressions. A few stood on the porch, slouched against the building, cigarettes hanging from their lips; others were leaning over the railing. Most had longer hair and scruffy beards, a sign of the times. There was no mistaking Biggs sitting on the third step, elbows resting on his knees, skull rings on three fingers, his keen eyes and gritty attitude as tangible as the picture itself. His thick hair and beard were dark as night, his young, powerful arms snaked with bright, not-yet-weathered ink. Tiny was also easily recognizable, not just for his size, but for that relaxed mask he wore so well. The man could look lost in thought, and in the space of a second he'd become as lethal as venom. He was sitting on a chopper motorcycle in front of the bar, looking at the camera. His bushy hair and beard were a shade lighter than Biggs's. A red bandanna was tied around his forehead, his posture was rounded, and his arms inked.

"That's you on the steps, right? And Tiny on the chopper?"

"Yup, and that's Bud leaning on the railing with the sunglasses, mustache, and ridiculous-looking fiddler cap."

Diesel chuckled. "He looks like a porn star. You look damn good, Biggs. You must've been younger than me in that picture."

"A few years. Late twenties. Tiny was living in Colorado then. He came into town for a rally on that chopper. He loves that damn thing."

"He still won't let Dare near it," Diesel said.

"I wouldn't, either. I love my nephew, but he does some scary shit. He'd probably build a ramp and try to jump over a truck on the damn thing."

"You're not wrong." Dare had always been a thrill seeker. But he'd taken it to new, terrifying levels ever since the death of his lifelong friend, who had been engaged to their other best friend—leaving her a shell of the woman she'd once been and leaving Dare to test the fates every chance he got.

"See that angry dude?" Biggs pointed to a clean-shaven,

thick-chested guy with his hair brushed back James Dean style. He looked a good bit younger than the other guys, but like he could take them out without breaking a sweat. He was leaning against the front of the porch, his thumbs hooked into his belt. The casual stance contrasted with the threatening look in his eyes. "That's Axel during those rough years I told you about, after that motorcycle accident. He did a lot of bad shit for good reasons, and sometimes he did bad shit for bad reasons. But God help the men who ran red lights in front of him. He'd catch up to them, haul their asses out of their cars, and teach 'em a lesson."

If cancer were a person, Diesel would've done the same thing to it.

"It took a lot of years, but eventually he learned to harness that rage and channel it elsewhere." Biggs nodded as he spoke, as if he were reminding himself as well. "Riding the open road and working on motorcycles and cars was the only thing that calmed the beast."

"I get that."

"Unfortunately, son, I believe you do, and I'm sorry about that. I know how hard it was to watch your mom let go. I was there with Axel when he took his last breath, and I swear he took a few of my years with him when he went."

Diesel clenched his jaw, knowing that feeling all too well.

"But you've found someone to fill that hole your mama left behind, and that's a blessed thing. Axel never let himself find true happiness. That was a damn shame because he really pulled himself together and became one of the best men I ever knew. He was the VP of the club and took over when I had my stroke, and he was more of a mentor to Bear than I could ever be."

Biggs set the picture down, and as they looked through

others taken around the same time, he told more stories about his family and longtime friends. Diesel was floored by the depths of his relationships. Biggs had decades of memories collected while building a life where everyone in it mattered. Diesel thought about how Tracey had embraced their friends as family and had wasted no time getting to know her stepfather and stepsisters and putting up their pictures. It was crazy how a few pictures had kept those people, and the time they'd shared, in the forefront of his mind. Seeing them had made him long for pictures of his mother and their life together.

Diesel pushed those thoughts down deep and moved those boxes to the shelves, putting two more on the table. As he looked at pictures of Biggs's family and friends, a pang of guilt settled in his chest. He'd been there for two years, and other than Tracey, he knew little more than the basics about the people he worked with every day, the people he'd spent the holidays with. If he hadn't met Tracey, what kind of memories would he have when he was Biggs's age? One beat-up photograph in his wallet and some vague memories of people he'd known peripherally?

Biggs tapped his arm, waving a handful of pictures. "These were taken out your way, a few years after Tiny moved there."

As Diesel took them, his gaze skimmed over the box, catching on a picture that all but stopped his heart. He reached for it, his chest constricting at the image of his mother sitting on the back of a motorcycle, smiling like she was the happiest girl in the world. She was so young and effervescent, it was hard to reconcile that version of her with the image he held in his mind of her dying days. She wore a white tank top, jeans, and sandals, and her arm was around a muscular dude with bushy dark hair and tattooed biceps. His sunglasses and thick facial hair hid all but his cheekbones, but while his mother had never looked happier, the man's expression was unreadable.

Diesel's gaze moved to the black baseball cap his mother held in her other hand. In the distance behind them was a sign for the Hobbit Shop. His mother had taken him to that shop a dozen times. He turned the photograph over and read the messy, faded ink. *My elfin magic, Ruthie.* The date was scrawled beneath it—almost ten months before Diesel was born. His pulse spiked, confusion and anger brewing inside him. His mother's voice stomped through his head. *I love Tiny and his crew, but your mama does not date bikers.*

Had she lied to him? He shoved the picture toward Biggs. "Who's this?"

"That looks like Axel, when he was just a kid. Twenty-two, -three maybe. He always carried a camera when he traveled. That looks like your mama, doesn't it?"

"Sure as hell does, on the *back* of his bike."

"Don't let that fool you. Axel had a different woman warming his back everywhere he went."

So he fucking used her? "Were they together?"

"I didn't even know they knew each other, son. Why do you look like you want to kill me?"

He turned the picture over, showing Biggs the date.

"What…?" His brows knitted, and Diesel saw the moment understanding hit. "*Oh*, hell."

Biggs leaned forward, looking in the box where he'd found the picture, and plucked out a few more, handing them to Diesel. There was a selfie of Axel and his mother smiling. Axel wore the black baseball cap and his mother's cheek rested on his shoulder. They were outdoors, and though Diesel couldn't see her guitar, he recognized the strap on her shoulder. The other pictures had more selfies of the two of them taken in different locations, some of them kissing, others laughing or serious faced, but in every one of them, there was a light in his mother's eyes that shone brighter than he'd ever seen. There was another picture of his mother sitting in a hotel room wearing only a far-too-big black Dark Knights T-shirt and the baseball cap, smiling sweetly with a dreamy expression. She was holding one hand out toward whoever had taken the picture. He turned the pictures over, reading the dates on each, and realized they'd spent several days together.

Fucking Axel.

Diesel pushed to his feet and paced. "How could you not have known about them?"

"Son, my brother and I were close, but we didn't talk about the women he got together with."

"This date," he seethed. "He could be my *father*."

Biggs stroked his beard, nodding. "Or it could be a coincidence."

"There's got to be more pictures." Diesel began digging furiously in the boxes. "Do I look like him? He was a big motherfucker, like me."

Biggs studied him. "It's hard to tell, son. It's been a lot of years, and we see what we want to see."

Diesel glowered, speaking through clenched teeth. "I don't want to see myself in a man who used my mother and left her to raise me alone." He shoved the box and paced like a caged animal, questions, memories, anger, and *hurt* consuming him. He shook his fist at Biggs, clutching the pictures. "*Who* would know about these? Who can tell me what happened?"

"I don't know. That was thirty-plus years ago. But you've got to calm down, son."

"Calm *down?*" Diesel fumed. "If this shit means what I think it means, my mother lied to me my entire life, and your brother used her and never looked back. I'll fucking calm down when I get answers."

Biggs pushed to his feet, leaning on his cane, his face a mask of concern. "I think your best chance of that is in Colorado."

"I'll be back in a few days." He took the stairs two at a time. He stormed out the front door and climbed on his bike, peeling out of the parking lot at breakneck speed, feeling like he did before each of his underground fights—like it was him against the world. He sped over the bridge toward the airport, determined to find the answers that he prayed his mother and Axel hadn't taken to their graves.

Chapter Seventeen

TRACEY WAS PUTTING the groceries away when Izzy sauntered into the kitchen in a miniskirt and tight long-sleeve shirt with I'VE BEEN GOOD. WHERE'S MY SPANKING? emblazoned across the front.

"Did you buy out the store?" Izzy eyed the bags littering the counter.

Tracey set the cake she'd bought in the fridge. "I couldn't help it. I want everything to be just right when I see my mom and everyone. I swear, Iz, I'm getting more excited and nervous by the second. Thank goodness Diesel can cook, because I'd probably burn everything."

"I still can't believe you nailed the baddest guy around and he cooks, cleans, *and* gives ten-star orgasms."

"He does laundry, too, but even if he didn't do any of those things, I wouldn't care. Wait. I take that back. I need those orgasms."

They both laughed.

Izzy helped her put the rest of the groceries away while they chatted about tomorrow's visit. When they were done, she reached for her phone in her back pocket to send Diesel a message and realized she'd left it in the car. "Shoot. I left my phone in the car. I'll be right back."

She headed outside with a bounce in her step, grabbed her phone, and checked her messages. There was a text from Red and one from Diesel. She read Diesel's first. *On a flight to Colorado. Back in a few days.* She read it again, sure she'd misunderstood. What the hell? He was going to miss her family's visit? Forget text messages. She called him.

The call went straight to voicemail.

She typed a response with shaky hands. *I just got your message. What's going on?* She tried to make sense of him suddenly up and leaving and remembered what he'd told her. *It'd take someone ripping my fucking heart out for me to leave you.* Panicked, she opened Red's message. *Honey, is Diesel okay?* Her stomach plunged, and she called Red as she headed inside.

"Red, what's going on?" She sounded as frantic as she felt.

"Have you spoken to Diesel?"

"*No.* He texted and said he was on a flight to Colorado."

Izzy came out of the kitchen and must have heard the panic in her voice, because she rushed to her side, mouthing, *What's wrong?*

Tracey held up her index finger, listening to Red.

"He and Biggs found pictures of Axel and his mother, and from what Biggs said, the dates on the back of them made Diesel think Axel might be his father."

"Ohmygod." Tracey grabbed Izzy's wrist. "Where's he going in Colorado?"

"*What* is going on?" Izzy asked frantically.

"My guess is Redemption Ranch to talk with Tiny," Red said. "But Biggs talked to Tiny after Diesel left, and it didn't sound like he had any answers. I was going to send Bullet after him, but Biggs told me not to. Tracey, this is bad. Diesel thinks his mother might have lied to him."

"Oh, *nononono*." Tears welled in her eyes, her heart breaking for him. "I have to get to him. He can't do this alone. Red, can I have a few days off?"

"Of course. Go, honey. I'll take your shifts and have Babs watch the grandbabies for me." Babs was the wife of a Dark Knight, and she filled in as the kids' babysitter when Red couldn't do it. "Do you want me to get Dixie to go with you?"

"No, thank you. I have to go. I'm sorry." She ended the call, and Izzy was all over her.

"What's going on? Is Diesel okay?"

"I don't know. Red said he found out his mom might have lied to him about his father. *Izzy.*" Tears spilled from her eyes. "If she did, he'll be crushed. I have to get to him."

"Okay. What can I do?"

"I have to pack. Can you get online and book me a flight to whatever airport is near Hope Ridge, Colorado?"

"I'm on it." She scrolled on her phone, following Tracey to her bedroom. "What about your mom?"

"Ohmygod." Tracey spun around. "I have to call her." Her stomach lurched. "How can I blow her off for Diesel? That's what I did last time, and I lost her for years."

"This is different," Izzy insisted. "Call her. She'll understand. She met him. She knows how serious you two are."

"Right. Okay." She paced, anxiety fracturing her thoughts as she called her mother.

"Hi, sweetheart."

Her cheerful voice sent Tracey down to the edge of the bed. "Hi." Too nervous to sit, she popped to her feet, her heart racing. "Mom, I have to leave town for a few days. Diesel got some potentially devastating news, and I really need to be with him."

"Is he okay?"

"I don't know. I doubt it. He took off for Colorado, and I need to find him."

"You don't know where he is?"

"No. Maybe. I think so."

Her mother was quiet for a beat. *"Trace,"* she said carefully. "Are you sure he wants to be found? He seems to be an *intentional* man who thinks through his actions."

Tracey closed her eyes against a rush of tears. "He is, but I don't think he's thinking straight right now. He's been lied to and hurt before. His mother is the only person he ever counted on to be honest, and she might have lied to him about his father. I know it sounds like I'm blowing you off for a guy who doesn't want to be with me because he took off, but that's not what this is. Diesel *loves* me." The words came out too fast for her to stop them. He'd never said that, but she felt his love, as real and viscerally as she knew he needed her with him while he faced this trying time. "He's been alone forever, and now everything he thought he knew might be turned upside down. He was there for me when I needed him most, and I'll be damned if I'm going to let him suffer alone. I'm sorry, Mom, but I have to try to find him. Please don't hate me."

"I could never hate you, sweetheart. And now I understand why you're going. Diesel told Tony that before you, he hadn't had anyone special in his life since his mother passed away. He said he didn't know how to be a good partner, but he'd learn."

Fresh tears fell, and Tracey couldn't choke out a single word.

"Even big, strong bikers need a little help sometimes, honey.

Go. I'll tell the girls we had a schedule conflict, and we'll do it when things are settled. I love you, Tracey, and I'm proud of you. I'm not going anywhere. I promise."

Relief engulfed her as she ended the call, and she sank to the edge of the bed to try to regain control.

Izzy sat beside her. "You're all set. I texted you the flight details. It's a nonstop flight. You'll be there by six o'clock Colorado time. I have to go to work, so I ordered you an Uber to take you to the airport. They'll be here in ten minutes. What should we pack?"

"It doesn't matter what I bring." Reality weighed on her like a lead coat. "If she lied to him, it'll break him."

"Then it's a damn good thing you'll be there to put him back together."

DIESEL SPENT TOO many hours on that damn plane, dwelling on questions for which he had no answers and trying to shut out the gnawing in his gut over Tracey, who didn't need to be dragged down by his shit. By the time his boots hit the ground in Colorado, he was fit to be tied.

Renting a motorcycle took forever, but there was no way he could stand being trapped in a car. As he sped toward Redemption Ranch, the brisk fall air whipped over his skin, and the afternoon sun began its descent. The long ride took the edge off, but as he neared the entrance to the ranch, anger and hurt threaded their way through him again, tightening like a python in his chest. He focused on the road as he drove through the main gate, passing under the wooden beam with an iron *RR* across the top—the first *R* was backward. He passed pastures and corrals, the familiar scent of horses and the crisp air of *home* stirring a wealth of emotions.

Pushing them all away, he tried to figure out where Tiny might be on a Saturday afternoon. The property had several houses, barns, other outbuildings, and indoor and outdoor riding arenas. He headed for the main house, which served as the offices for traditional therapeutic services and also was the residence for several staff members. As he cruised toward the house he saw a paintball battle going on in the field, people darting behind sandbag bunkers and stone walls, around barrels, upright tires pinned to the ground, and other obstacles and barriers.

Diesel drove toward the field to look for Tiny, who had been known to drag anyone who was having a hard time out there to work off some steam. As he parked, he saw Birdie at the far edge of the field. Her blue mask was pushed up and she was taking a selfie with her back to the field. She wore full camo, splattered with orange, red, and blue paint, and carried a black-and-blue rifle in her free hand. Two people wearing red masks and carrying red-and-black guns were sneaking up behind her as she lifted her chin in a snarky pose for the selfie. They nailed her with red paintballs and howled with laughter.

Birdie shoved her phone in her pocket and spun around, hollering, "Can't you see I'm *out?*"

The others pushed their red masks up, revealing Cowboy's and Sasha's amused faces. They hadn't spotted Diesel, and it was just as well. He was in no mood for chitchat or Birdie's and Sasha's high-energy hugs. They all knew he preferred not to be touched, but like Malia, they refused to believe anyone didn't need hugs.

"You're still inside the field." Cowboy pointed the tip of his gun at her foot, which was still in bounds. He and Sasha high-fived.

Birdie lifted her gun and shot them, then took off running as she pulled down her mask. Sasha ran after her. Cowboy caught sight of Diesel climbing off his bike and headed over. He was the largest of the Whiskey men, thick and hard bodied from years of working the ranch. He wore his fair hair short and his beard neatly trimmed.

"Dude, good to see you." Cowboy offered a hand and pulled Diesel closer, but not too close, clapping him on the back. "I heard you weren't coming back for a while."

"I wasn't planning on it. This isn't a social visit. Is your old man around?"

"Yeah, he and my mom are at the north barn, checking on the rescues we got in last night."

Diesel nodded and headed back to his bike.

"Hey, D," Cowboy called after him, and Diesel turned, jaw tight. "Anything I can do?"

"No. Thanks."

"If you're sticking around and want to hang with us later, we'll be at the Roadhouse."

Diesel nodded again and climbed on his bike. He drove toward the north barn to talk with the people who had always been there for him and his mother. To the man who had mentored him in more ways than he could count. He fucking hoped they hadn't lied to him, too.

He found Tiny and Wynnie in the barn with Doc, discussing the sickly horses in the nearby stalls. Diesel's questions suddenly seemed almost pointless compared to animals that were probably on the verge of death and had been rescued from

God knew what kind of hell.

"Diesel," Doc said with surprise. He was tall and fit, not burly like his brothers, a real charmer, and he looked the part in a dark blue Henley as he raked a hand through his short brown hair.

He lifted his chin in acknowledgment. "Doc." Tiny's serious expression told Diesel that unlike Doc, Tiny and Wynnie already knew why he was there. Diesel was thankful Doc hadn't been clued in. He didn't need everyone's nose in his business.

"Sweet darlin', it's *so* good to see you." Wynnie came toward him with open arms, layered blond hair bouncing above the shoulders of her yellow top. She gave him a quick embrace and kissed his cheek, worry hovering in her eyes.

Her familiar scent should have brought comfort, but the idea that he might have been lied to stood between them like a villain, and he couldn't muster any degree of warmth.

"We've missed you, son." Tiny stood eye to eye with Diesel, his gruff voice carrying a slightly cautious edge. He wore a familiar red bandanna tied around his forehead, and a Dark Knights T-shirt stretched over his gut.

Diesel swallowed the bile rising in his throat. "You and Wynnie got a minute?"

"Always. Let's step outside." Tiny lifted his chin in the direction of the barn doors. "We'll be right back, Doc."

Diesel's gut knotted. His heart hammered against his chest as he followed Tiny and Wynnie out of the barn, the pictures burning a hole in his pocket. There was a part of him that didn't want the answers he sought, but he needed them.

Tiny walked a good distance away from the barn before stopping, his wise eyes landing on Diesel the way they had when Diesel was thirteen and had started hanging out with some questionable kids. Back then, Tiny had steered him to the ranch, doling out lessons in responsibility, giving him purpose for those hours when his mother was at work and he'd had to fend for himself. Had he taken Diesel under his wing due to a sense of duty rather than simply extending kindness to help a single mother?

"Biggs called," Tiny said evenly. "I know why you're here, son."

Diesel handed him the pictures. "What do you know about these? The dates are on the back."

"Oh, honey," Wynnie said in a soft, pained voice. "We didn't even know your mother and Axel were ever together."

Diesel eyed her, looking for hidden signs of lies, but there was nothing but grief and empathy looking back at him. He shifted his attention to Tiny. "That true?"

"Pretty much. I knew they'd met at the Roadhouse when Axel blew through town and we were there with a few brothers." By *brothers* Diesel knew he meant other Dark Knights. "Your mother was working, and I saw him flirting with her, but I didn't think much of it. He was always playin' around, and he made no attempts to hide who he was from the women he was with. Biggs said he told you about what Axel had gone through."

Diesel nodded.

"Axel was in rough shape." Tiny sounded as if his brother's anguish had been his own. "You remember how angry you were after we buried your mother? How you took off on your bike with that damn backpack, and we didn't see you for more than a year?"

He'd never forget the unrelenting dragons that had chased him down the highway and had continued chasing him...until recently.

Until Tracey.

But he couldn't go there now, couldn't think of her sweet face and loving words when his whole life might have been built on a lie.

"That's where Axel found his solace, too, on the open road. He was a brokenhearted kid struggling to get through each day. I worried he'd do something stupid like drive off a cliff, but while he was stronger than that, he was still human. When he was on his bike, he was okay. But off it? He went from one woman to another, trying to keep from falling into the abyss of his grief. That's not to say if he and your mother got together, that she wasn't special to him. She very well could have been, and he wouldn't have told a soul, because he didn't believe he deserved any kind of happiness after losing his girl. I don't have the answers you're looking for. But honestly, D, I can't imagine my brother taking pictures with *any* woman, much less keeping them. Maybe that should tell you something." He looked at the pictures, bushy brows slanting. "I sure miss the bastard."

Wynnie put her hand on Tiny's back as he handed the pictures to Diesel.

Diesel stared at the pictures, feeling a kinship with Axel's grief. But that didn't lessen the uglier emotions coursing through him. He knew all about trying to fill a void any way he could, but the idea that *that* was all his mother was to the guy who might have been his father only made him angrier.

He lifted his gaze to Wynnie, hoping for some kind of answer. "She didn't say anything to you when she was in therapy?"

Wynnie shook her head. "I wish she had. I'm sorry, sweetheart. I asked her if there was any other family we should be talking with to help them prepare, to help you move on, but she said there was no one. When I asked about your father, she said they were just two kids having fun, and he wasn't interested in anything more. I pushed her on it and told her he might have changed over time. I tried to get a name. I was worried it might come to this one day. But she'd said it wasn't in the cards."

That wasn't good enough anymore. He needed to know the truth.

She took his hand. "Honey, I can see how this is tearing you up. You need to remember that your mother was just a kid herself when you were born, younger than Birdie is right now." Birdie was twenty-five. "You know how it is at that age, all those hormones runnin' wild. You meet someone and hit it off and ride the high as long as it'll carry you. But I cannot impress upon you enough that your mama had made peace with whatever the situation was with your father, and she didn't come out the other side a broken girl. She came out stronger, with a beautiful baby boy to love, and she loved you with *everything* she had. Your mother had no regrets at the end. Not a single one."

Swamped with too many emotions to deal with, he needed an escape. "Thanks. I'll get out of your hair."

"Stay," Wynnie pleaded. "Let's catch up. It's been too long. Red told me you have a girlfriend now, and I'd love to hear about her, and how you're doing."

"With all due respect, Wynnie, another time would be better."

"Okay, but you have to let me..." She moved in for a hug, and this time he hugged her back. "We love you, baby."

He was too choked up to speak.

"Son, before you go, I want you to know two things. Regardless of whether Axel was your father or not, he was messed up for a lot of years, but he was a good, kindhearted man who suffered from a tortured soul."

Diesel could relate to that and nodded in understanding.

"I don't give a rat's ass about whose sperm made you. As far as I'm concerned, you are and always have been *family*. Now I'm going to hug you, and you're going to deal with it." Tiny hauled him into a tight embrace, speaking low, like he did when Diesel was a kid. "You might be solid muscle, but I'll still squash you like a peanut."

Diesel smiled despite his heartache.

"Where're you heading?" Tiny asked as he released him.

"The cabin." *To look for answers.* He couldn't say *home*, because nothing felt like home without Tracey.

"Don't you leave town without coming back to say good-bye, you hear me?" Tiny said sternly. "You've got family here, boy, and they want to see you."

"I'm not good company right now," Diesel warned.

Tiny threw his shoulders back, looming over him like a mountain. "They don't give a damn if you're mad, sad, or sittin' on cloud nine. Times like these are what family is for. You got that?"

He answered with a curt nod.

Tiny didn't even blink. "I don't think Wynnie heard your answer, son."

Wynnie winked at Diesel. "He's our Diesel. Of course I did. Loud and clear."

Chapter Eighteen

DIESEL TORE THROUGH his mother's bedroom, rifling through the drawers he hadn't been able to face after she'd died. The hell with sadness. He needed answers. He emptied boxes from her closet, finding crayon drawings he'd made as a child, school pictures, his tiny clay handprint, Mother's Day and birthday cards he'd made and the ones he'd bought as he'd gotten older. There were report cards and school awards and notes he'd written to her as a kid. She'd saved all of them, but there was nothing about Axel, or any other man.

Anger pounded inside him as he stormed into the hall and stood in front of the closed door to the hobbit room. The room where his mother had taken her last breath. He reached for the doorknob, memories slamming into him of his mother's jerking body, the sounds of desperation she'd made in her last moments.

His hands curled into fists, grief stacked up inside him, filling every crack and crevice until he couldn't breathe. He couldn't do it. Couldn't go in there and face it all again. He stalked into the living room, throwing open the cabinets by the television where his mother had kept what she'd called her most precious memories, and yanked photo albums from the shelf, shaking them out and flipping through the pages, looking for what? Another picture of Axel that wouldn't tell him shit? Rage and despair warred with all-consuming guilt inside him as he threw the albums to the ground, then did the same with her guitar notebooks, where she wrote songs and lyrics.

Coming up empty, he stood amid the mess, knowing damn well where he'd find the answers, but couldn't bear the thought of tearing apart the room that had meant so much to her. To *them*. A roar of frustration ripped from his lungs, and he went a little crazy, tearing out drawers, looking under cushions, storming into the kitchen, emptying more cabinets and drawers in search of the ghosts of his past.

Breathing heavy, barbed wire twisting in his chest, he forced himself to return to the closed door. He swallowed hard, telling himself to let it go, that it didn't matter who his father was. The answer wouldn't bring his mother back. He could never hear her side of the story.

Fuck.

Driven by a bone-deep need to know if the woman he'd trusted most in this world had kept something so important from him, he threw the door open, adrenaline pumping through his veins. He stood stock-still at the sight of the hospital bed and the walls they'd painted with forests and creatures year after year, until every inch was covered. Eyes peered out from behind leaves and vines, like *he* was a villain there to desecrate the sacred space he'd helped bring to life.

His gut fisted, and he lowered his eyes to the floor, blazing a path to the closet, gutted at the sight of her guitar. *Sit and sing with me, Dezzie.* He shoved that memory down deep, storming past the guitar, and yanked boxes from the closet shelves. He rummaged through knickknacks, books, more childhood drawings, Popsicle stick figures, and handmade ornaments, memories of his mother's excitement when he'd given her those gifts pecking at him like woodpeckers. *Jesus.* He tossed box after box to the floor, dug through coat pockets and drawers, until he'd gone through every last thing. In a fit of anger, he pushed the dresser over, his heart stopping at the sight of a thick red journal duct-taped to the bottom of it.

Hit with an onslaught of disbelief, he fell to his knees, unable to do more than stare at it. Guilt pummeled him. His mother was *allowed* to have secrets. He gritted his teeth against the voice in his head telling him to get on his motorcycle and drive until he could no longer feel—and then keep going until he was so fucking numb he'd never be able to feel again.

But Tracey's beautiful face appeared before him, her sweet smile tugging at the parts of him he'd thought had long ago died, her trusting eyes reminding him of all the reasons not to follow that voice in his head. He'd spent a lifetime boxing himself out of the lives of everyone who had cared about him so he'd never get hurt again. He didn't want to live like that anymore. He wanted a life with Tracey, with friends, building memories, a future. But after all she'd been through, she deserved a man free from demons. A man who knew who he was, and if Diesel knew one thing about himself, it was that he wouldn't sleep until he knew the truth.

He tugged the journal free, tearing off the tape as he pushed to his feet and pacing as he opened the cover, gutted anew at the sight of his mother's swirly handwriting. He swallowed hard, trying to stop a lump from forming in his throat as he turned the pages, entering his mother's private world.

Her diary began two years after she'd left home at eighteen, but it read like a highlight reel of a movie, narrating the life of a young girl who had left her home in Nebraska with stars in her eyes and a hopeful heart in search of something better. There were mentions of hitchhiking that made Diesel cringe for her safety and friends she'd made along her travels. She'd worked as a waitress here and there and spent weeks traveling in a van with a group of other twentysomethings. Her writing carried the voice of a girl who was seeing the world through new eyes. *Every time I laugh, I'm reminded of the emotional jail my parents had kept me in, which makes me want to cling to that laughter and be even happier...If I ever have a kid, I'm going to make sure it knows what joy feels like every day of its life...I think I'm in love with this world. There's so much good in it.*

Diesel skimmed the parts that talked about hookups before the month he'd have been conceived, but he lingered over details of her first days in Colorado when she'd met Manny, who was now Alice's husband, who she described as a nice guy with a lot of hair. When she'd mentioned she was looking for a job and a place to stay, Manny had brought her to the Roadhouse. *I was scared at first because there were about ten bikers there. But Manny introduced me and explained that he had recently joined a new motorcycle club called the Dark Knights, and I got to meet the guy who founded it! His name was Tiny, but he was huge, and kind. I like him, and I like it here. I think I might stay.* She'd met Manny's then-girlfriend, Alice, and described her as a strong-willed blonde. They'd given her a job as a waitress and had let her stay in the cabin she'd later bought from them.

Diesel flipped through the pages, learning about how much his mother liked her job, how tired she was by the end of each night, and how Manny's father had moved away the next year and had given him the bar.

And then he saw the first mention of Axel, his muscles flexing as if readying for a fight as he read the entry.

I was walking into work, and the hottest guy I'd ever seen was climbing off a motorcycle. He was big and eyed me up like I was his favorite flavor. But behind those flirtatious eyes, he seemed sad. I know all about sad, and I felt an instant connection to him. He must have felt that way, too, because we stared at each other all night. I had the overwhelming urge to show him that life could be better than whatever was making him sad. His name is Axel. That might not be his real name, but I like it. It's strong like him, and different. Kind of mysterious and kind of poetic.

She wrote about him flirting with her every time she passed by his table and how he'd stuck around until closing time and had driven her home. Diesel read about how they'd sat by a fire in front of the cabin, and his mother had been enamored by stories of his travels, which he likened to the Hobbit after meeting Gandalf, only instead of joining a group of dwarves to reclaim a kingdom, he'd gone on a personal journey to reclaim his life.

It was no wonder she'd felt a kinship to him. She'd done the same damn thing.

I told him about my awful parents and how far I've traveled, and he told me about how he'd lost the love of his life.

As Diesel read his mother's entries, it became clear that Tiny was right. Axel had been honest with her about not looking for anything more than a good time. His mother had also told Axel her truth, that she'd hoped to one day find her soul mate, who wanted to build a magical, happy life. Diesel took comfort in their honesty. He continued reading about how Axel had been on his way out of town, and his mother had had the next three nights off. They'd embarked on what sounded like a whirlwind few days of exploring towns, having sex, and sharing secrets, or as his mother wrote, *a journey of two souls coming together that filled me with enough happiness for a lifetime.*

Diesel sank down to the floor, leaning his back against the bed. At least if Axel *was* his father, it wasn't from a shitty hookup. He'd made her happy. That was something.

He continued reading and took that last comment back when his mother described her tearful goodbye, and in later entries, wishing Axel would call and heartbroken when he didn't. His mother wrote about how she'd considered asking Tiny for Axel's number, but she kept circling back to Axel's confession about not wanting to be tied down.

Diesel gritted his way through entries spanning weeks of disappointment, descriptions of waking up nauseated, a panicked entry about a positive pregnancy test, and her fears of losing her job. His muscles corded tighter with every word. Several painful entries detailed weeks of trying to figure out what to tell Axel the next time she saw him and more debates about telling Tiny the truth, which she'd nixed because *Axel was sad enough without my adding guilt to his already overburdened heart.* She described talking to her unborn child and the excitement and worry when she started to show. She wrote about telling Alice that she was pregnant and answering her questions about the father.

He doesn't want a family, and I'll never put my child through what I lived through. Better this baby is loved by me, wholly and completely, than resented by a man who never wanted it.

Every word drove Diesel's pain for her deeper.

It finally happened. Axel came into the bar tonight, but he was with another woman. I nearly died. I had practiced what I'd say for so long, I knew it by heart, but when he came over and looked at my belly, my mind went blank and I could barely remember how to breathe. He said, "Hey, Ruthie. That's a good look on you. I guess you found your soul mate after all. Better him than me. I'd fuck a kid up somethin' awful." My heart cracked right down the middle, and I realized my mistake. I romanticized what we had, instead of believing what he'd said. I thought we'd connected so deeply, I could pull him from his grief. But now I know that nobody can do that for someone else. But you're NOT a mistake, baby, and I'm strong. Even stronger because of you, so I held my chin up high, put my hand on my belly, and said, "Yes, I have." A relieved smile appeared on Axel's face, the kind you flash when you're happy for someone but also glad you're not pulled downstream with them, and he said, "It must've been that elfin magic. That's one lucky baby. Best of luck to you both." He walked away, slid into the booth beside the other woman, and slung an arm over her shoulder.

And you know what, baby? I was okay with that. It's just you and me, and I swear to you right here and now that I'm going to be the best mother that has ever walked this earth. You will be loved more than life itself.

TRACEY HAD BEEN a nervous wreck all day, vacillating between being brokenhearted for Diesel and upset that he'd thought sending a text and taking off without any explanation was okay. As the cab pulled into Redemption Ranch, she felt like she might throw up. If Diesel wasn't there, she'd have no idea where to look. She didn't even know where he stayed when he was in Hope Ridge. What if her mother was right, and he didn't want to be found? What if he'd discovered everyone had lied to him? A heaviness settled in her chest.

Scratch the part about her mother.

If everyone had lied to Diesel, *she* knew he *wouldn't* want to be found, and that reality was suffocating. She rolled down the window, and the cool Colorado air whisked in. Thank goodness she'd worn a sweater. She'd been barely thinking when she'd gotten dressed.

"Where to, ma'am?" the driver asked, pulling her from her thoughts.

She had no idea where to look for him. "Is there a main office or something?"

"There's a main house, but it's Saturday evening. I'm not sure if it's open."

"That's okay. Let's start there." As they drove down farther onto the ranch, she gazed out the windows at horses in the pastures and mountains in the distance, remembering the views from the Whiskeys' old cabin by the creek. No wonder it reminded Diesel of home.

The car slowed to a stop, drawing her attention to the motorcycle doing a wheelie and barreling toward them. The cabdriver pulled onto the shoulder, giving the motorcyclist the road, but about thirty feet away, the driver lowered the front wheel and waved. He pulled up beside the car and took off his helmet, revealing a handsome dark-haired, bearded man with piercings in his ears, septum, and nostril and tattoos snaking down his arms. He eyed Tracey through the open window and cocked a brow. "Hey there, beautiful. Lookin' for me?"

"Um...Not unless you're Tiny."

He scoffed. "There ain't nothing tiny about me, darlin'."

"I didn't mean *that*."

He laughed. "I figured that much. What's a pretty girl like you want with my old man?"

Relieved she'd found someone who knew Diesel so quickly, she got out of the car, not wanting the driver to hear what she had to say.

The shameless flirt on the motorcycle whistled.

She ignored that. "You're Tiny's son?"

"Dare Whiskey at your service." A slow grin curved his lips. "And I do *service* well."

"I'm sure you do, but I don't need servicing. I'm Tracey, and I'm looking for Diesel Black. Have you seen him?"

"Oh shit. You're Diesel's old lady? Sorry about that, princess."

The respect in his voice for Diesel made her happy, and she hoped the fact that he'd heard about her was a good sign. "It's okay. Have you seen him?"

"No, but he was here. He's at his place. I can run you over there. I wanted to check on him anyway."

"Are you sure you don't mind?"

"I'd do anything for D, which means I'll do anything for you. Are your bags in the trunk?" Dare knocked on the driver's window.

"No. They're in the back." She reached into the open door to grab her bags and thanked the driver as Dare paid him. When the driver pulled away, she handed Dare money for the fare. "Thank you."

"Put that away, little lady. I only take money from women when they're stuffing it in my waistband."

"You're a *stripper*?" What kind of friends did Diesel have out here?

He chuckled. "Every woman in town wishes. I just like to

get my groove on. Leave your bags on the grass and climb on the back. We'll go get my car."

"Okay, but can you please not do a wheelie? I'd definitely fall off."

"You're Diesel's, darlin'. Taking a chance with you would be a death wish."

They picked up Dare's car from his place, which was on the grounds of the ranch, far from the rest of the houses. His garage was bigger than his cabin and full of shiny classic cars and trucks, dented and worn vehicles, motorcycles, and ATVs. They took a black, souped-up old Chevelle with a loud engine and enormous tires, picked up her bags, and headed to Diesel's place.

Dare was kind and funny, making small talk as he drove, but Tracey's mind was all over the place. She was worried about Diesel and could barely muster responses. When he turned off the beaten path, driving down a secluded gravel road toward a rustic cabin with a tin roof and a motorcycle parked out front, her nerves flamed again. The cabin and a small shed sat on a clearing surrounded by woods, with an iron fire pit off to the side. The grass was long but not overgrown, as if someone had cared for it while Diesel was gone. There was a rugged simplicity to the cabin, and it was easy to imagine Diesel's childhood in such a serene place. Unfortunately, it was equally easy to imagine it swamped with despair.

As they climbed out of the car, Dare's eyes narrowed, and she followed his gaze to the front door, which was on the side of the house and wide open.

"Stay here." Dare's command left no room for negotiation.

She followed him anyway, despite the stern look he cast her way. When they reached the door, Dare put an arm out to keep her back, his chest puffing out, face stern as granite. "Do *not* come in here until I check it out."

Tracey's heart raced as Dare stepped inside. She peered in at a small living room and kitchen, both of which looked like they'd been ransacked. Couch cushions were upended, cupboards emptied, drawers rifled through, the contents littering counters and floors. The hair on the back of her neck stood on end as Dare moved down the hall, peering into rooms. He stopped at the second room on the right, his shoulders dropping, and she knew something was wrong. She ran down the hall, pushing past him, and entering the room painted with forests, hobbits, elves, and wizards, some messy and childlike, others so real, she felt like she'd entered another world—until her eyes hit Diesel, sitting on the floor with his back against a hospital bed, surrounded by overturned boxes, scattered papers and photographs. His knees were bent, elbows resting on them, his forehead in one palm and a journal dangling from his other hand.

Tracey ran to him and dropped to her knees. "Diesel, what happened?"

His grief-stricken eyes met hers, his jaw clenching. He shot a questioning look at Dare.

"She showed up at the ranch, man."

"Don't look at *him*," Tracey snapped, emotions bowling her over. "Look at *me*. What do you *think* I'm doing here? I was worried about you!"

His eyes narrowed, and he lifted his chin in Dare's direction, another silent message passing between them. This one she could read, a thank-you and a request for space.

"I'll leave your bags out front, Tracey. D, you know how to reach me."

"Thank you," Tracey said as he walked away. With her heart in her throat, she moved closer to Diesel. "What happened? Did you do all of this? Are you okay? I got your text, and Red said you think Axel might be your father?"

He stared at her, silent seconds exploding like bombs. Just when she didn't think she could take it anymore, he said, "Yeah." His eyes fell to the journal, his fingers holding a page open as he handed it to her. "It's all here."

She took it and began reading, her heart breaking anew with every entry as she learned about Axel losing his first love, Diesel's mother thinking she'd found hers, and pages of excitement and heartache later, his mother realizing it had been unrequited, or misdirected, but not a mistake, and that was what was most important. She closed the journal and set it on the floor. "He was your father."

Diesel nodded. "Biggs and Tiny both said he was messed up for a long time, but then he became one of the best guys they knew, and my mother never gave him a chance to decide if he wanted to be part of my life." Pain and sorrow laced his words with an underlying anger she understood. "She had three chances to tell him. She saw him twice when I was little, and she never told him the truth, and she never saw him again after that." He made a fist and rubbed it with his other hand. "I trusted her my whole life, and now what? It's all shot to hell? What the fuck, Trace? What do I do with that?"

She took his hand. "You do the only thing you can. You forgive her. It sounds like she was doing the best she could with the information she had. You read what he said to her, that he'd mess up a kid."

He looked away.

Tracey touched his cheek, bringing his grief-stricken eyes

back to her. "Diesel, we all make mistakes. Big, awful mistakes. But think about where your mom was in her life back then. She was so young, and she knew what it was like to live with parents who didn't want her. Only a selfish mother would knowingly put their kid in that situation. She was looking out for your best interests, not trying to pull the wool over his eyes."

"What if he would have changed if he'd known?"

"Would you have? From what I just read, it seems like you unknowingly followed in your father's footsteps after your mom passed away. You took off just like he did after he lost his girlfriend, and you said you never looked back, never stayed in one place too long. If one of the women you'd had sex with had gotten pregnant, could you have suddenly changed your ways and stuck around? Become a good parent? Because I've watched our friends with their babies, and babies change *everything*. They take up all your time and energy, and you need a *lot* of patience and love to be that selfless. Even people who plan to have kids complain about how hard it is. I think it's a blessing in disguise that Axel knew himself well enough to realize and to tell your mother up front what he wanted and for your mom not to have thrust it on him."

Diesel's whole body seemed to tense up, his brows slanting.

Tracey hated what she had to say next, but Diesel dealt in truths, and she'd never lie to him. "We'll never know if he might have changed. That sucks and it hurts a lot. But what we do know is that your mother loved you enough to protect you from the heartache she'd lived through. The heartache she'd *run* from. She kept you safe and built a good, happy life for you. She surrounded you with people who cared about you, and it sounds like, from what you've told me and from the little I've just read, she built her world around you."

His expression softened, and she climbed onto his lap. "I wish I could turn back time for so many reasons, but the past is like a summer storm. It's already done its damage and spread its light. It's become a part of us, a part that we can't change, but we can learn from it." She touched his jaw, feeling the tension ease as he leaned into her hand. "Want to know what I think?"

He raised his brows.

"I think you have a lot of Axel in you. Everyone says he became a great man, even after all he'd lost, and so did you. That goodness must run in the genes."

Diesel's arms circled her, his lips tipping up at the edges. "How do you do that, baby girl?"

"What?"

"Flip things around? Take the anger out of me and turn it into something else?"

"I don't know. I guess I've been the one who made the big mistakes, and I thought they were for good reasons. I'm just showing you the other side of it. Something good came out of this, Diesel, but you're too close to see it. You have *family*. Real, true family, here, and in Peaceful Harbor. People who have been in your life and loved you without knowing you were blood related. I know your mom hurt you by lying, and that kind of hurt may take some time to heal, but she was protecting you, and I hope you won't let this change how you feel about her."

"It feels like a lie, even though it wasn't. She never said she didn't know who my father was. She said he was someone who believed in elfin magic, and he did." He picked up pictures from the floor beside him and handed them to her. "That's them. See the hat? I think he bought it for her at that store behind them."

"Now I know where you get your honesty from." Tracey kissed him. "You know, it's okay to be mad at your mom and mad at him. Whatever you're feeling is okay. This'll take time to process, but at least now you know the truth, and you don't have to deal with it alone. You have me, and I don't know the Whiskeys who live here, but I know you have the support from the Whiskeys in Peaceful Harbor and the rest of our friends there."

He nodded, eyes serious.

She looked around the room, her heart swelling with love and aching for him, too. "Your mom did so much for you, Diesel, but she forgot to teach you one very important thing."

"What's that?"

"You said we were partners. *Where I go, you go.*"

"We are," he said firmly.

"Don't give me that, Mr. One-Sided. You took off alone to do something really hard, like you didn't trust me to be there for you, and that hurt—and pissed me off."

"Trace, I didn't want to bring you down."

"Don't give me that crap. That's what relationships *are.* It means we're there for each other no matter what. You were there for me through awful things, and I want to be there for you, too."

"You don't get it. This was different. How could I be the man you need if I didn't know who I was?"

She took his face between her hands, holding his stubborn gaze. "You *always* knew who you were. You're Desmond 'Diesel' Black, son of Ruthie Black, a mother who adored you. You're a Dark Knight, a good man who helps others, a bounty hunter, bartender, lover, and friend. And now you know you're a *true* Whiskey, joining the ranks of more of my favorite people." She paused to let that sink in. "And you're *mine*, Diesel. And I'm yours. But if you want it to stay that way, you can't leave me behind because you want to protect me, or because you think you're strong enough to weather *any* storm. You're the strongest, most resilient man I know, and I know you can weather really bad storms." She looked around the room. "Hell, Diesel, you *are* the storm." Bringing her eyes back to his, she softened her tone. "But even badass bikers need someone to lean on sometimes, and when you love someone, you're there for them no matter what. I'm here for you, Diesel. When it's hard, when it's easy, and every time in between. Do you want that? Do you want me to stick around for a while?"

He pushed his hands into her hair and hung on tight, his eyes drilling into her. "More than you could ever know." He crushed his mouth to hers, kissing her like he was pouring everything he had—heartache, confusion, and a sea of other emotions—into their connection. When their lips finally parted, he kept her there, lip to lip. "I'm sorry I hurt you. I love you so fucking much. I want you to stick around for a hell of a lot longer than a while, baby girl, but I've been alone for a long time. I can't promise I won't screw up like this again."

To Diesel, honesty *was* love, and she was so full of his, she could taste it. "Well, I *can* promise that I'll call you on it every time until you realize you're no longer a lone wolf."

He smiled and touched his forehead to hers. "I don't know where to go from here."

She didn't know if he was talking about their relationship, or the other parts of his life now that he knew Axel was his father, but either way, her answer was the same. "That's okay. We'll figure it out together."

Chapter Nineteen

DIESEL PACED THE yard in front of the cabin Sunday morning with his cell phone pressed to his ear, talking with Tiny, telling him everything he'd learned. He and Tracey had gone over the significant parts of his mother's diary last night after they'd cleaned the cabin, and they'd talked about all of it. Well, Tracey had talked and he'd mostly nodded or shaken his head, but it had helped, hearing her thoughts on what his mother must have been feeling. She was right about his mother protecting him and about it probably being a blessing in disguise that Axel had known he couldn't handle fatherhood. Diesel could have spent his life trying to win the love of a man who wasn't capable of giving it. The way Tracey admired his mother's strength had made him see his and Tracey's relationship more clearly. She had been hurt by his actions, and she'd *still* flown across the country to be there for him. He'd told her he might fuck up, and she was still there, believing in him, loving him. Last night, while she lay sleeping in his arms, he vowed to do everything within his power to make sure he never hurt her again.

He finished relaying the details to Tiny. "So it looks like

your brother was my old man."

"How're you feelin' about that, D?"

"It's a lot to process, but I'm glad I know. I wish Axel had known, but I can't change that."

"Yeah, I understand. But your mama did the right thing. Axel didn't clean up his act until he was about thirty, and by then who knows what it might have done to him. Guilt's a funny thing, and like you, Axel had a big heart. He might never have forgiven himself for not being able to be the man she thought he was. Maybe she saved all of y'all some heartache."

"I hadn't thought about that."

"Life's a funny thing, D. It'll knock you on your ass more times than you can count, but now we know you're *blood*. I say you come over for a barbecue and celebrate. We'll eat by the main house. I bet Simone would love to see you again."

Celebrate. As unexpected as that was, it was damn good to hear. "You mind if I bring Tracey?"

"Boy, if you don't bring that little filly Dare's been telling everyone about, nobody's gonna believe she exists."

Diesel laughed. "Tracey told me Dare hit on her."

"Yeah, he told us. That was before he knew she was your girl. You coming over or what?"

"We'll be there, and, Tiny, thanks for keeping an eye on me through the years and being there for my mom."

"Like I told you, you've always been family. We take care of our own. You mind if I give the others the good news? Or do you want to tell them?"

"And open myself up to all those hugs?" He scoffed. "Go for it. We'll see you soon."

After they ended the call, Diesel rolled his shoulders back and called Biggs. His craggy voice came through the phone like a wave of unexpected comfort. Diesel felt like his whole life had been unexpected lately. He laid it all out for Biggs, and much the same way Biggs handled everything else, he seemed to take it in stride. Diesel apologized for the way he'd taken off, and Biggs took that in stride, too.

"There's something that's been bugging me. Do you have any idea why Axel stopped going to Colorado? According to my mother's journal, she never saw him after I was three or four."

"I've been thinking about this since you took off like a bat outta hell. I don't have a concrete answer for you, but I'd be lying if I said I never wondered if someone out there had gotten under his skin. Don't take my word on this, because Lord knows I'm just a rambling old man. But if your mother, or any woman, had gotten to him in those messed-up years, he'd've stayed far away once he realized he was hooked. It would've just about killed him knowing he'd fathered a son and wasn't strong enough to raise him. But knowing Axel, dying a slow death of guilt was better than screwing up a kid's life."

Diesel didn't know what to think about that, but as Tracey had said, that summer storm had already hit.

"What's your plan, son? Are you comin' home, or sticking around there for a while?"

Tracey walked out on the porch, gorgeous in jeans, a wine-colored sweater, and the cowgirl boots he'd given her. She smiled and waved, stirring all the emotions that had swamped him last night when they'd made love and again this morning when the sun had crept in through his bedroom curtains over her peaceful face as she'd lain asleep in his arms. She'd truly become his *home*, his grounding force, his light at the end of what had been a very dark tunnel. When she'd spoken with her mother last night, Tracey had put him on the phone because her mother had said she'd needed to hear that he was okay with her own ears. For the first time in his life, he wondered if a person could have more than one place where they felt like they belonged, and man, that was a hell of a good thing to wonder about.

"We'll be back Tuesday afternoon." Diesel wanted to pack a few of his mother's things to bring back to Maryland. "I texted Bullet, and he said the bar's covered."

"How about you swing by my house around six?"

"I can do that." He winked at Tracey, closing the distance between them.

"A'right. You need anything?"

"No, sir." He pulled Tracey in close. He had everything he needed right there in his arms and everything he never knew he wanted at his fingertips.

"You give my love to your brave little lady and my pain-in-the-ass brother."

"Will do. Thanks, Biggs. See you in a couple of days." He pocketed his phone and pressed his lips to Tracey's.

"How'd it go?"

"Fine. *Good*, actually. Tiny invited us to a barbecue. Do you want to meet the Whisk—" Reality hit like a gust of wind, lifting him higher. "You want to meet my family, baby?"

"Your *family*? Gosh, I'm not sure. That sounds serious." The tease lit up her eyes. "Are you sure we're ready for that?"

He crooked his arm over her shoulder, tugging her into a kiss. "Get your sexy little ass on that bike while I lock up the cabin." He swatted her butt, and she giggled as he headed into the cabin.

He walked through the living room, seeing flashes of memories of his mother smiling from the kitchen and playing her guitar on the living room couch, but mixed in with them were images of Tracey as she'd gushed over his baby pictures and lingered over pictures of him and his mother. He went into the hobbit room, sensing the two of them again. Tracey had asked a million questions about that room, wanting to know the stories behind each of the paintings. He loved her even more for wanting to keep his mother's memory alive.

As he reached for the guitar, his mother's voice whispered through his head with the words she'd said before the cancer had stolen her coherence. *Promise me you won't be sad for too long, that you'll grab life by the horns and blaze your own happy path. You were my elfin magic, Dezzie. Promise me you'll find yours.*

He looked around the room he'd torn apart, the room in which his world had been turned inside out and then righted again. "She found me, Mom. And hopefully now she'll find a little of you, too." He put the guitar into its soft transit case, and then, guitar in hand, locked up the cabin and headed for his girl.

Confusion filled Tracey's eyes. "What're you doing with that?"

"If you're ever going to travel the world with a guitar on your back, you've got to learn to play." He put the straps over her shoulders, so the guitar rested on her back, and tightened it around her.

"Travel the world?"

"Play at festivals, play in the yard. Whatever you want to do."

"But that's your mom's guitar."

"It was, and now it's yours. I bet if you ask nicely, Sasha will teach you a thing or two."

She stared at him, wide-eyed. "*Diesel.* Are you sure?"

"I've never been more certain of anything in my life." He grabbed his helmet, rethinking what he'd said. "Actually, I have. I love you, Tracey Kline, and I will love you until I've got no more breath to give." He kissed her smiling lips and straddled the bike. "Now put that helmet on. It's not nice to keep family waiting."

TRACEY NOTICED A lot more vehicles on the road than there were yesterday. A slew of them fell into line behind them as Diesel followed a motorcycle onto the Redemption Ranch property. He drove to an impressively large house made of stone, wood, and glass with a sign out front that read REDEMP-TION RANCH THERAPEUTIC SERVICES. There were dozens of people pouring out of cars and milling about on the lawn, where men and women were setting up tables and chairs and children were chasing one another around and kicking balls. Diesel parked in the packed lot, and the other motorcycles and vehicles behind them parked along the road.

Tracey looked around as they took off their helmets, notic-ing a sea of leather jackets and vests boasting Dark Knights patches. "Are we interrupting a club event?"

"No. I think Tiny put the word out." He locked their hel-mets to the bike, hung the guitar over one of his shoulders, and draped an arm around her.

"About what?"

"He said he was going to tell the others about Axel and that we should celebrate. I thought he meant with the family."

As people waved and called out to Diesel, Tracey couldn't stifle her grin, excitement bubbling up inside her. "He did. Only in your language, they're called a brotherhood."

He leaned down to kiss her. "Don't give me crap about my language."

"I'll give you crap about whatever I want." She went up on her toes for more kisses.

"Diesel!" A petite brunette ran toward them in an oversized *Flashdance*-style sweatshirt that hung off one shoulder, a black miniskirt, black fuzzy boots, and a polka-dot scarf tied around her forehead.

Trying to keep pace with her was a cute blonde wearing jeans, a blue sweater, cowgirl boots, and a hat. Behind her trailed a very large man with a gray beard and a pendulous belly, wearing a black leather vest and a bandanna tied around his head. He was holding hands with a pretty middle-aged blonde with a layered shag haircut and a warm smile, and they were looking at Diesel like they'd never seen anything better.

The brunette launched herself into Diesel's arms. "I've missed you!" As he set her on her feet, she punched his arm and smirked. "Hey, *cuz*. Dad told us the exciting news. I guess it's a good thing we never hooked up."

Diesel's brows slanted. "What...?"

The brunette cracked up.

"Birdie! This is his *girlfriend*." The cute blonde rolled her eyes. "Ignore her. I'm Sasha, the normal one, and she's Birdie, the *other* one."

"I prefer the *cute* one." Birdie wiggled her shoulders.

Diesel shook his head. "Birdie, Sasha, this is my girl, Tracey."

"Hi. It's nice to meet both of you." Tracey already loved

them.

"I can't wait to get to know you better," Birdie said. "I want all the *deets* on you and the big man. Diesel, are you playing guitar now? Serenading your better half?"

"No. Tracey wants to learn, and I was hoping Sasha might have time to show her a thing or two later."

"I'd love to!" Sasha hugged him. "I've missed you, and for the record, I always knew you were one of us."

The large man and the older blonde joined them. The woman embraced Diesel, saying something that Tracey couldn't hear, but whatever it was, it made him smile.

He eyed the grizzly of a man. "Is this what you meant by telling the *others*? Putting the word out with the club?"

"They're your family, too, son." The man hauled him into a rough embrace, clapping him on the back.

"Brotherhood," Sasha and Birdie said teasingly.

"Give him a break, girls. He just learned he's got Whiskey blood," the man said.

Diesel took Tracey's hand, giving it a squeeze. "Tiny, Wynnie, this is my girl, Tracey. Trace—"

"I know," Tracey interrupted. "I'm so excited to be here and meet your family."

"Please tell me you're not opposed to hugs." Tiny cocked a brow.

"No, sir. I like them."

"Get on in here, darlin'." Tiny embraced her so tightly she could barely breathe and said, for her ears only, "I'm glad you came after him. He's a good man."

She warmed all over with the love they had for Diesel.

"Welcome to our home, sweetheart." Wynnie hugged her. "I have heard so many wonderful things about you."

"You have?" Tracey looked at Diesel.

"Not from him," Birdie said. "Diesel doesn't gossip. Dixie's been raving about you forever. She knew y'all would end up together, and now I understand why. I've never seen *Growly* look so happy."

Tracey laughed. Diesel scowled.

"Actually, it was Red who did the gossiping," Wynnie clarified. "She thinks the world of you, Tracey. Come on, let's introduce you around."

Diesel put his arm around Tracey and whispered, "Sorry about all this," as they followed Wynnie and the others.

"Don't be. I love them, and they obviously love you."

She was introduced to dozens of people, including the rest of the Whiskey family. They grew them handsome and rugged out there. If she'd thought Dare was a flirt, he had nothing on Doc and Cowboy, who made remarks about being available when she got tired of Diesel. Diesel's scowl made them laugh, which led to a round of hilarious banter between the burly men. Cowboy, Dare, and Doc razzed Diesel about being their cousin, and Diesel seemed like some of the weight he'd carried on his brawny shoulders was lifted.

As the day wore on, hamburgers and hot dogs were grilled, tables were filled with sides and desserts, and drinks were handed out. Tracey met too many people to remember them all, but one thing stood out above all else. They all adored Diesel and knew him well enough not to try to hug him—at least the adults did. Children ran up for hugs or high fives, and Diesel was sweet with them. There were handshakes, nods, pats on the back, smiles, and long conversations about time missed between visits.

Tracey loved watching him with the people he'd known

forever, who had taught him what it meant to be a man, a Dark Knight, and regardless of what Diesel called them, treated him like he'd always been family.

"Baby, there's Manny and Alice, the couple who owns the Roadhouse. I want to introduce you to them." Diesel led her across the lawn, toward an attractive middle-aged couple standing by the food table.

"There he is! The man of the hour," Manny called out. He had deeply tanned skin, short salt-and-pepper hair, and pitch-black brows. He shook Diesel's hand and clapped him on the back as the other guys had.

"Hi, Manny."

"Diesel, sweetheart." Alice, a thick-waisted, pretty blonde, leaned in and kissed his cheek, giving it a quick maternal pat. "Oh, how I have *missed* this handsome face."

"Hi, Alice," Diesel said.

"You can *hi* everyone else, Desmond Black, but I changed your diapers and wiped your bottom. I deserve a hug."

He hugged her. Tracey had never seen Diesel blush before. Who knew her brawny man could get embarrassed?

Alice looked at her warmly. "And this pretty gal must be Tracey."

"Yes. I've heard a lot about you. It's nice to meet you."

"And we can't wait to hear more about you." Alice gave her a gentle hug.

Manny moved in for a hug, too. "It's a pleasure to meet you, Tracey. How long are you two in town?"

"We're leaving Tuesday." Diesel's expression turned serious. "I just discovered what you did for my mom when she first came to town, and I want to thank you for giving her a chance and watching out for her, for giving her a place to live. I appreciate you keeping her safe."

Manny and Alice exchanged a loving glance, and Manny said, "Do you know how I met your mom?"

"No."

"I was coming back from Denver and stopped for gas, and she was coming out of the station looking at a map. She had the whole thing unfolded, and she was turning it around like she didn't know which way was up. She had a backpack and that guitar you're carrying across her back. Her long brown hair was wild and tangled, and her eyes were full of joy. I'm telling you, it radiated off her like the sun." He laughed softly. "I asked her where she was headed, and she said she'd heard of a place called Hope Ridge, and she had a feeling if she could be happy anywhere, it would be there."

Diesel nodded. "That sounds like her."

"Ruthie was quite a woman. A talented artist, incredible with people, and just a pleasure to be around. She could brighten anyone's day." Manny lifted his chin toward Diesel. "Especially this one's. When he'd get in a mood over homework or whatever kids get moody about, she'd play that guitar or tell him a story, and he'd light up like a Christmas tree."

"She sure did." Diesel lowered his voice. "Did my mother ever tell you that Axel Whiskey was my father?"

Manny cocked his head, dark brows knitting. "No. She never told us who your father was. When we got the text from Tiny calling us over to celebrate his nephew—*you*—we put two and two together."

"I wondered, though," Alice admitted. "I remember Axel coming in with another woman when Ruthie was a few months pregnant with you. Something about the look in her eyes that night had led me to ask if there was anything between them.

But she'd said there wasn't, and that was that."

Diesel nodded. "Well, I appreciate all you did for her, and for me."

"Sweetheart, you're family. We're always here for you." Alice glanced over their shoulder. "Looks like Charlie's Angels are on a mission."

They followed her gaze to Simone, Sasha, and Birdie heading their way. Simone looked different than she had last December, when Diesel had first brought her to Redemption Ranch. Tracey had met her only once, but she remembered an excruciatingly nervous, painfully thin girl with gaunt cheeks that accentuated the scar running down the left side of her face. Her cheeks were fuller now, her auburn hair was longer, shinier, full of natural wave and curl. She looked healthy and happy.

Alice touched Diesel's arm as the girls neared. "We'll catch up with you later."

As Alice walked away, Diesel gave Simone a quick once-over. "How's it going, Simone? You look good."

"I feel great. This place, Sasha, Birdie, and the rest of them, were *exactly* what I needed." Simone even sounded healthier and stronger.

"That's what guys say after they go out with one of us," Birdie teased, earning a scowl from Diesel, which made Tracey and the other girls laugh.

"Have you guys eaten yet?" Sasha asked.

Tracey shook her head. "Not yet, but I'm getting hungry."

"We haven't, either. Let's get food while you guys catch up with Simone," Sasha suggested. "Give Tracey a break from being dragged around the yard."

Tracey was about to say she never needed a break from Diesel, and she loved meeting the people in his life, but his knowing glance told her that he already knew all that. His theory about saving his breath by keeping his thoughts to himself must have been wearing off on her, because she no longer felt the need to say it. "Sounds good."

Tracey grabbed a plate. "Simone, do they work you hard on the ranch?"

"Cowboy would like to work her *hard*." Birdie smirked.

Simone rolled her eyes as she put salad on her plate. "I like the work I do here, and yes, it's hard some days. But that cowboy-hat-wearing tyrant is the bane of my existence."

"Why is that?" The protective nature in Diesel's voice did not go unnoticed. Neither did the way he eyed Cowboy as he sauntered over.

Cowboy leaned over Simone's shoulder, speaking gruffly. "What'd I tell you about eatin' like a bird? Load up that plate, girl. You're gonna need the fuel for chores later."

Simone flashed a deadpan look at Diesel. "Does that answer your question?" She turned to Cowboy with fire in her eyes. "Not all of us need to eat like a horse in order to care for them." She lifted her chin and stalked off.

Diesel arched a brow as Cowboy watched her go and said, "She's a pistol, isn't she?"

"Careful, Cowboy. It's those fierce ones you have to look out for." Diesel's gaze slid to Tracey, lust and love eating up the space between them. "What starts as a spark can lead to full-on combustion, and you'll never be the same again."

"Our wise cousin has spoken." Cowboy winked at Diesel.

"Cowboy, you better keep your finger away from Simone's trigger." Sasha glared at her older brother. "Hooking up with anyone involved with the ranch will *not* end well. Just ask Doc."

"What happened with Doc?" Tracey asked.

Diesel and Cowboy exchanged a glance she couldn't read, and Cowboy said, "Let's just say he fell for the wrong girl and bought himself a whole heap of trouble."

"We don't talk about Juliette," Birdie whispered to Tracey. "Hey, *Big D*. Just a heads-up. After we eat, we're going to steal Tracey so Sasha can teach her to play a little guitar and I can get the scoop on you two. If you got a problem with that, take it up with someone who cares." She flashed a mischievous grin. "Being cousins is *fun*."

Lunch was delicious and their conversations were enjoyable, with just enough kisses sprinkled in from Diesel to make Tracey feel like she was walking on air. After they ate, the girls whisked Tracey away. Sasha was a patient teacher as she helped Tracey learn the basics about guitar and Birdie peppered her with questions about her and Diesel. As the afternoon blended into early evening, many of the guests left, though a handful stuck around. Diesel and the guys built a bonfire, and Tracey and the girls gathered blankets and set them out on the grass around the firepit.

Everyone settled onto the blankets, and Diesel hugged Tracey against his side, kissing her cheek. His gravelly voice coasted into her ear. "You doin' okay, baby girl?"

"Better than okay. But more importantly, how are *you* doing?"

"Good. Really good."

"Do you feel any different being with everyone now that you know about Axel?"

"Yeah, I think I do. But it's more than just because I know about Axel." He leaned closer. "It's you, baby. You make everything better, and you make me want to be part of something bigger. Something special."

"From what I saw today, you've always been part of something big and special. I thought you belonged with the Whiskeys back home, but you belong here, too, with these people who love you and knew your mom."

"And you belong near your mom and your new family, near Biggs and everyone out there, because as you've said many times, they're your family, too."

She swallowed hard, wondering if he'd want to build his life here, which she'd totally understand. "Does this feel more like home to you?"

He pressed his lips to hers. "You're my home, baby girl."

"You know what I mean," she said with a happy heart and a sliver of worry.

He pulled her onto his lap, eyes stern as he pressed his hand to her cheek, brushing his thumb over her lips. "I said, *you're* my home, Tracey. Where you go, I go. Your mother is back East. The people who became your family—and mine—are back there, too. The life you built is in Maryland. The life we're building together is there. There's plenty of time to come back and visit here, but your dreams of helping other women have already started there. You've got a foothold, and you're on your way to the top. I want to climb that mountain with you, baby. I already spoke to Lior about it, and he's all in, if and when you're ready."

Tracey could hardly process all he'd said, and he must have seen how overwhelmed she was, because he said, "You don't think I'd forgotten about your dreams, do you?"

Her heart skipped. "You'd teach with me?"

"I'd do anything and everything with you." Holding her gaze, he pushed his hand into her hair, those dark eyes turning wicked and seductive, sending shivers of heat searing through her core before he even said a word. "And I do mean *every-thing.*"

As he sealed his mouth over hers, Birdie hollered, "Get a room!" causing laughter and teasing.

"Y'all are right. Enough of this family stuff. I'm taking my girl home." Diesel pushed to his feet, pulling Tracey up with him, and threw her over his shoulder. Everyone whooped and hollered as she shrieked, and Diesel blazed a path toward the motorcycle.

"Attaboy! Do it like a Whiskey!" Dare hollered.

"The guitar!" Sasha shouted.

Diesel didn't slow down. "She won't be needing it tonight!"

"Diesel!" Tracey laughed. "They did all this for *you!*"

He lowered her to her feet, grinning like a lovesick fool, and *wow*, that was a great look on him. "That's great, sweet thing, but I'm ready to do *you*. So either get your pretty little ass on that bike, or I'll strip you naked and bend you over it right here and now."

"You wouldn't dare with everyone watching."

A wolfish grin appeared on his handsome face. "You're right, but there are no neighbors at my cabin."

Thrills bubbled up inside her. "Now, that's an idea I'd like *you* to get behind."

His eyes flamed, and a sexy growl rumbled out as he grabbed her by the waist, lifted her off her feet, and plunked her down on the bike. They quickly put on their helmets, and he climbed on in front of her. Her heart thundered at the thought of him taking her rough and untethered in the moonlight, unleashing all his power after such an emotional time. She wrapped her arms around him, running her hands down his chest, feeling his beautiful muscles, his heart hammering as fast as hers. She dragged her fingers lower, clutching his arousal through his jeans, heightening her anticipation, and because she loved him wild and hungry for her, she couldn't resist saying, "Better hurry before I change my mind."

She'd never seen him drive so fast.

The vibrations of the engine, the promise of their illicit tryst, and the feel of *Diesel* worked their magic, and by the time they arrived at the cabin, she was a needy, greedy girl. He climbed off the motorcycle as they tore off their helmets, and he turned her roughly, wedging himself between her legs, taking her in a penetrating kiss as demanding as it was delicious. She rose off the motorcycle, desperate for more, and he kissed her harder as he worked open her jeans and pushed his hand into her panties. His thick fingers thrust inside her, and she moaned into his mouth, rocking along the length of them, his thumb wreaking havoc with that secret spot that took her up on her toes. She clung to his shoulder with one hand and tugged open his jeans with the other. She was just as eager for him, and fisted his cock, earning the hungriest growl she'd ever heard. Lust spiked through her as she worked him with her hand, and he took her up, up, *up*, until she shattered into a million blinding lights, crying out in the darkness as he reclaimed her mouth, fierce and aggressive.

He tore his mouth away and pushed down his jeans, burying his hands in her hair. "Suck me, baby."

God yes. She sank to her knees, taking his steel cock in her mouth, loving him with everything she had—hands, mouth, teeth—earning one appreciative sound after another. Moonlight glittered in his eyes as he watched her pleasure him. It never failed to blow her away how seeing desire in his eyes, feeling it in his body, excited her. Her sex grew wetter, needier with every lick and suck. She felt him swell in her hand, and he tugged her up by the hair, the pain taking her pleasure higher. He crushed his mouth to hers, feasting, their tongues thrusting. He tore down her jeans and spun her around, giving her ass a slap, then grinding his cock against it as his teeth closed over her neck, sending prickles of desire like hot needles rushing over her flesh.

She clung to the motorcycle, moaning and mewling, grinding her ass against him, arching as he tore her sweater and bra off. The cold air sliced over her skin, and he palmed her breasts, squeezing her nipples so hard she felt it between her legs. "Oh God. *Diesel.* I need *you.*"

She didn't have to ask twice. He entered her in one hard thrust, sending her belly to the leather seat, and she *loved* it. She wanted it harder, deeper, *rougher.* She wanted him wild and free. "*Fuck me*, Diesel. Don't hold back."

He bent over her, his fingers curling tight and possessive over her ribs, and he placed the tenderest of kisses to her shoulder. She glanced over that shoulder, and he lifted lust-drenched eyes and a wicked grin that made her insides catch fire, and then he took her harder, faster, rougher, shaking the motorcycle with each blissful invasion. His teeth found her neck, and holy mother of orgasms, sensations charged through her like a stampede, obliterating her ability to do anything more than hang on and take everything he had to give—and she fucking loved it. Thunder and lightning crashed inside her, burning, seizing, *ravaging*, and just as she hit the peak, he gritted out her name, following her into the storm with renewed power. Their bodies jerked and thrust, sounds of their lovemaking mixing with the sound of the bike jarring with every piston of his hips. Their cries of passion carried in the breeze, easing as they came back down to earth.

He kissed her shoulder, cheek, and neck. His strong arms embraced her, and his greedy hands cupped her breasts again. "God, Trace. Sex with you should be illegal."

She giggled.

He rose to his full height, turning her in his arms, kissing her slowly and sensually. "I didn't hurt you, did I?"

She shook her head, so drunk on him she felt like she was floating.

"Good." He kissed her again, sweet and tender, and then he dressed her, before pulling up his jeans. With an arm securely around her, he led her to the cabin. "Because now that we've taken the edge off, I'm going to make love to you all night long."

"Did you just say *make love*?" she teased as he unlocked the door. "Who *are* you?"

"The way you screw with my head, I have no idea anymore. But I'll be fucking Fred Flintstone if it'll keep you by my side."

"Fucking Fred won't keep me by your side." She sauntered past him into the cabin. "But if you're into that…"

He glowered, striding toward her like a tiger stalking prey. "You're in *big* trouble, sparky."

She felt giddy. "I was counting on it."

Chapter Twenty

DIESEL RETURNED TO Peaceful Harbor a different man from the one who'd left. He felt in his bones a need to put down roots instead of a desire to flee at the thought of it. But the changes he was undergoing ran deeper than where he rested his head at night. He was no longer a lone wolf. He had Tracey to think about, and now he had family, too, all of which meant greater consequences for his actions. As he stood on Biggs and Red's porch Tuesday evening, recognizing the four motorcycles out front as Bullet's, Bones's, Bear's, and Dixie's, guilt tightened like a noose around his neck for the way he'd taken off, leaving Biggs in the basement with a job half-done and Bullet to pick up the pieces and rearrange the schedule to cover his shifts. If he had any chance of building a life there, a life with Tracey, he needed to get that shit under control, regardless of knowing they would always have his back.

Red answered the door. "Welcome back, darlin'."

"Thanks. Biggs asked me to stop by."

She motioned for him to come inside. "You okay, honey?"

He nodded, but the knots in his stomach said otherwise as he followed her into the dining room. Bullet and Bones sat on one side of the table, Bear and Dixie on the other, and Biggs at the head. The room fell silent, five sets of serious eyes turning to Diesel. The men crossed their arms like he was the enemy, not part of the family. Suddenly he saw the situation from another side, and those knots in his gut tightened. Did they think he expected something from them because he'd found out he was family? *Shit.*

Biggs motioned for him to sit in the empty chair at the other end of the table. As Diesel sat down, Red slid into the seat to his right, beside Bear, and patted Diesel's hand. Only then did he realize she hadn't tried to hug him when he arrived.

Biggs sat back, but there was nothing relaxed about the stare he had fixed on Diesel. "Your flight okay?"

"Yes, sir. Listen, I know this is a crazy situation, but it doesn't change anything. I'm not looking for handouts."

"You're wrong, son," Biggs said sternly. "This changes *everything*, and if you think otherwise, I'm afraid we're going to have a problem."

There were unsettling nods from the others.

Diesel steeled himself against his mounting discomfort. "With all due respect—"

Biggs held up a hand, silencing him, and pushed to his feet, cane in hand. "Listen to me, boy." He put a hand on Dixie's shoulder. "I've made mistakes where family's concerned, and I don't intend to make another one." He continued walking toward Diesel. "My brother is gone, and I thought that was all we'd get of Axel." He stood beside Diesel. "On your feet, son."

Diesel stood tall, willing to take whatever Biggs dealt.

Biggs stepped closer. "You're my brother's son, and that makes the rest of us lucky sons of bitches to be in your presence." He pulled Diesel into a manly embrace, speaking roughly into his ear. "Welcome to the family, D."

Relief and disbelief bowled Diesel over as he processed what Biggs said, his gaze moving over the others, who were trying to stifle smiles. "Y'all were *fucking* with me?"

They burst into laughter, and Diesel uttered a curse as they got up, all speaking at once.

"We're a lot to handle, but you know you love us." Dixie hugged him.

Bullet pushed his way in. "Get used to it. You're a Whiskey now."

"Welcome to the family, cuz." Bones clapped him on the back.

"I got the best of Axel, and those years should've been yours," Bear said with a tinge of guilt.

As much as Diesel would have liked to have gotten to know Axel and maybe even been taken under his wing, he didn't begrudge the closeness Axel and Bear had shared. "No, man, it's all good. I'm glad he was there for you."

Bear gave him a quick embrace. "When you're ready, I've got lots of stories to share."

"I look forward to hearing them all."

Red hugged him, all sappy eyes and sweet, maternal smile, tugging at those parts of him Tracey had unearthed. "Honey, you've always been like a son to us, and this just makes it even better." She motioned toward several boxes on the floor behind him. "We went through Axel's things from the basement of the clubhouse and what we had here. It's not much. Mostly books and such. I put together a few photo albums and other things we thought you might want."

That lump that had been popping up like a groundhog in his throat all weekend reappeared. He glanced at the boxes as

Bear lifted the flaps of one of them and pulled out a book.

"I don't know how interested you'll be in these, unless you're into Bilbo Baggins." Bear turned the book around, showing him the cover of *The Hobbit*.

They had no idea how very big of a deal that book was. Diesel cleared his throat to try to regain control of his mounting emotions. "As a matter of fact, I am. I appreciate you putting this stuff together, and I'm really sorry for taking off the way I did and leaving you hanging."

"We get it," Biggs reassured him. "But there *are* a few things that go along with being part of this family that you need to hear. The first is that we've cut you in as a partner in the bar and the auto shop."

"Whoa, Biggs. What're you talking about?" There was no hiding the shock in his voice.

"The bar is a family business, and Axel left the shop to the family. You're part of this family, son."

Diesel was overwhelmed by his generosity. "Thank you, but I don't need a handout. I'm cool working for you all."

"Don't you give me that handout shit," Biggs snapped. "This is family business, not charity."

"Biggs, it's too much." He looked at the others, hoping for support, but they were shaking their heads, clearly in agreement with Biggs. "You all paid your dues. You worked your asses off to keep the businesses going."

"So have you." Biggs limped closer. "Every time you've come to town, for more years than I can count, you've put in time for us. You stepped in when we needed you most these last couple of years, and you've given nearly seven days a week to our family—to *your* family. Which brings me to our next order of business. Tiny, Reba, and I have been holding on to a piece of our past that was important to all of us, but mostly to Axel. It's not much, just a little cabin across town where we grew up, and until he was too weak to do so, Axel used to go there when he needed to think. Tiny said he told you about it when you first left Colorado."

"Yeah, he did. I've been going there since my first trip to Peaceful Harbor." *Just like Axel.* He liked knowing that.

Biggs nodded. "It's yours now, son."

Rendered speechless, Diesel shook his head, sure he misunderstood what Biggs was saying.

"Funny thing is, every few years we talked about selling it," Biggs said with a thoughtful expression. "We never could let it go. Now we know why. It's been waiting for you."

"Biggs, I can't..." *Shit.* Emotions clogged his throat. "You don't even know what my plans are."

"I don't give a damn what your plans are. The cabin is ours, and we're giving it to you. What you do with it is your decision."

"I can't accept it free and clear like that. But I am stickin' around, so I'll buy it from you. I've got plenty of money, and I *love* that place."

"Your money's no good here, son." Biggs's stroked his beard. "Red, straighten this boy out."

Red handed Diesel a manilla envelope. "We've already had the paperwork drawn up for the businesses and the house. I'm afraid you're not walking out of here until you sign."

Bullet, Bones, and Bear stood in the entrance of the dining room, arms crossed.

Diesel scoffed. "You know I can take you all out, right?"

"My ass you can." Bullet smirked.

Bones and Bear exchanged an amused glance. "You can try."

"Would you all stop fluffing your feathers?" Dixie handed Diesel a pen. "We love you, and we want you to have a home here. Now sign the damn papers so you can get home to Tracey and I can get back to the bar before Dana quits."

Diesel gritted his teeth against the warm fuzzy chaos going on inside him. "I don't know what to say."

"You don't have to say anything, honey. We know you love us," Red reassured him.

With a curt nod, he pulled the papers out of the envelope, trying to reel in his emotions. As he read the documents giving him a percentage of the businesses and ownership of the cabin, his heart expanded. He looked at the people he was lucky enough to call family, and this time he held nothing back. "Thank you. I do love you all." He looked at Bullet. "Even your sorry ass."

They laughed as Diesel signed the papers, and then they moved in for more hugs and kind words. That family stuff was awfully touchy-feely, but he had a feeling he'd better get used to it.

When he finally left, he was still in a state of shock. He straddled his bike and called Tracey.

"How did it go?" she asked anxiously.

"I'll tell you when I see you. Meet me out front in five." He pocketed his phone and drove straight to her place. She was waiting on the sidewalk, sexy and beautiful in jeans and a sweatshirt, her eyes dancing with curiosity. He handed her a helmet. "Climb on, sparky."

She straddled the bike. "Aren't you going to tell me how it went?"

"Soon. Put your helmet on and hang on tight."

He drove to the cabin, and as he set their helmets down, he

took Tracey's hand.

"What are we doing here?"

"Checking out the place." He dangled the keys to the cabin from his finger.

Her eyes widened. "Where did you get those?"

He looked at the girl who had changed his life with doses of sweetness and sassiness and enough love to pull him from the wrong side of that invisible line and make him never want to go back, and his heart poured out. "My *family* gave it to me. It's ours, baby girl, and I can't wait to see you fill this yard with gardens and have your family over for steaks and soccer and see you smile every time you walk through that door."

Her jaw dropped. "*What?* You want to move in together?"

He gathered her in his arms and kissed her. "Damn right. I love you, Trace. I want to wake up with you every morning, put up pictures of our families on the walls, and do dirty things to you in the moonlight on the porch."

She laughed, but the joy glittering in her eyes told him she wanted those things, too.

"Come on. Let's go check out our new home." He slung his arm around her shoulder and headed for the door.

"You know, a girl likes to be *asked* to move in, not told."

God, I love you. "This *is* me asking, baby girl." He lifted her into his arms and carried her up the porch steps, silencing her laughter with a long, slow kiss.

Chapter Twenty-One

"HOW MUCH TIME do we have?" Diesel called out from the bathroom where he was shaving.

They were getting ready for Penny and Scott's wedding. It had been six months since Diesel had found out that Axel was his father, four months since they'd moved into the cabin, and two months since Penny had given birth to Liam Wilson Beckley, their adorable baby boy.

Tracey pulled on her underwear. "We have to leave in forty-five minutes. I'm going to grab a snack. I always get hungry at weddings." She slipped on his dress shirt and headed out of the bedroom.

In the kitchen, she grabbed a container of yogurt from the refrigerator, smiling at the meticulously organized shelves and drawers. Everything in Diesel's life had a place, and she was so glad to be part of it. Sunlight spilled through the French doors, bathing her bare legs in warmth as she sat at the table to eat. Diesel and the guys had cleaned the place inside and out, refinishing the hardwood floors, adding more windows, replacing appliances and tiling, and building a deck off the kitchen that faced the woods and their private path to the creek.

They'd christened every room—and the deck.

Diesel had finished the basement and turned it into a gym with enough space to practice self-defense. They'd worked out an agreement with the gym, and they'd been teaching self-defense classes for five weeks, sometimes with Lior, sometimes without, but always together. They offered free classes to the women at the Parkvale shelter. They both still worked at the bar, sneaking kisses, doing dirty things after hours, and loving every second of it.

Tracey heard Diesel moving around in the bedroom and glanced in that direction, her eyes catching on her guitar propped up beside the couch in the living room. He'd surprised her before Thanksgiving with a month of guitar lessons from a local musician, and he loved listening to her play as much as she loved playing. She looked at the pictures of their families and friends decorating the walls. Many of which were from his childhood. Tracey swore the pictures of his mother added more than a little dash of magic to their life. They'd brought her hobbit snow globe and other items from Colorado, and Diesel smiled every time he saw them. For a man who had lived life on the road, never staying long enough for grass to grow beneath his feet, he sure knew how to make a warm, loving home. She looked up at the ceiling, sending a silent thank-you to his mother.

She had a feeling their mothers would have been best friends. They saw her mother's family often, and out of the blue, her mother had started calling Diesel *Dezzie*. Her mother hadn't known that was what *his* mother had called him, and Tracey had clued her in and asked her not to call him that. But Diesel had chosen to show his softer side and had happily approved of the nickname. He'd even used some of those saved-up words of his to tell her mother and her family a few lovely stories about his mother. Anna and Malia had spent a weekend with Tracey and Diesel last month, and they'd loved the creek and riding on his motorcycle. Although Diesel had become as protective of them as he was of Tracey, and he wasn't too thrilled about Malia's declaration that she wanted to date a biker. He'd given her one of his sternest looks and said, *You know you're not dating for at least another ten years, right?* Tracey and the girls had enjoyed a good laugh over that.

"Babe, have you seen my shirt?" Diesel came into the kitchen looking like sex on legs, wearing only dark blue dress pants and a blue tie draped around his neck. His eyes swept over her, and he prowled toward her. "Is that *my* dress shirt?"

"You always say what's yours is mine."

He leaned over, boxing her in with one hand on the table, the other on the back of her chair, bringing his delicious lips a breath away from hers. His heated gaze moved down her face, to the exposed swell of her breasts, then slowly trailed back up, taking in the shirtsleeves pushed up to her elbows. "I'm going to have to iron that again."

"Oopsie." She tugged one end of his tie, sliding it off from around his neck, and wrapped it around his waist, using the two ends to tug him closer. "Maybe I can make it up to you."

His eyes darkened, and a growl rumbled up his throat, causing her nipples to pebble. He brushed his lips over hers. "We're going to be late."

"Not if we're fast."

She rose up to kiss him, and he scooped her off the chair, ravaging her as he carried her into the bedroom and loved her senseless. They showered and dressed quickly. Tracey straightened his tie, her breath catching at how utterly gorgeous he looked.

"You keep looking at me like that, and we're going to miss the wedding."

She felt her cheeks heat up. "I can't help it if you look hot."

He grabbed her butt, hauling her in for a toe-curling kiss. "Not half as hot as you. But we're going to be late if we don't get a move on." He turned her around to zip her dress, placing several kisses along her spine before pulling up the zipper, sending shivers of heat coursing through her again. He turned her in his arms, eyes serious. "Don't even think about dancing with Rhys."

"Don't tell me what to do." She giggled and kissed him. "He's not even going to be there. Besides, there's no room on my dance card. It's got your name in every slot."

"Damn right it does. Let's go."

"I just have to find my earrings."

"Better hurry, sparky. I'll go start the truck."

As he left the bedroom, she called after him, "Grab their gift!" She put on earrings and the pretty diamond infinity necklace Diesel had given her for Christmas. Biggs and Red always invited everyone over for Christmas Eve, and this year they'd invited Tracey's family, too. Diesel and Tracey had left a few days later to celebrate New Year's with his family at the ranch in Colorado. It turned out they were very much like Biggs and Red, and they celebrated with everyone on the ranch. Tracey had gotten close with Sasha, Birdie, and Simone, and it was hilarious watching Simone try to avoid Cowboy, while Birdie did everything she could to make it impossible, and in turn, Sasha did everything *she* could to help Simone by foiling Birdie's attempts.

Tracey grabbed her heels and flew out the front door, holding on to the porch railing as she put them on. Diesel whistled, stalking toward her on the slate path between the gardens her mother and sisters had helped her plant last weekend.

He reached for her hand as she came off the last step. "Baby girl, you are too gorgeous for words. But something is missing."

She looked down at her blue dress, which she'd bought to match his tie, and the high heels that brought her a little closer to his lips. "What did I—"

Diesel slid a gorgeous ring on her left ring finger. "There. Now we can go."

It was all she could do to stare at the blue diamond surrounded by a flower-petal design of white diamonds and two gold twisted vines around a slim diamond band. She blinked up at him with damp eyes, dumbfounded. *"Diesel...?"*

"What? You don't like it?"

Tears slid down her cheeks. "I *love* it. I love you, and our home, and our yard. I love our *life*. But is this...? Are you...?"

"Shit. I forgot you like to be asked." He cleared his throat, his love wrapping around her like an embrace as he got down on one knee, holding her hand in his. "Baby girl, everything about you, about *us*, was unexpected, and not a minute goes by that I don't thank my lucky stars that out of all the men in the world, you chose me. You are the *peace* I never knew I was missing. We've got roots, sparky, but I want *more*. I want you to have a fancy white wedding with all the trimmings, and one day I want to have tough little boys who growl and adorable little girls who give them hell for it. I want to listen to you playing our song on the guitar until we're old and gray and to think back on the memories we've made and the incredible life we've had."

He must have been saving up all his words for this very moment. More tears spilled down her cheeks.

He rose to his feet, his loving eyes holding hers. "Tracey, my love, my life, my *everything*, will you be mine forever? Marry me, take my name, and fill our house with more happiness than we could ever hope for."

"Yes!" bubbled out with more tears, and she threw her arms around his neck and kissed him. He spun her around as they laughed and kissed. "We're getting married!"

"Damn right we are."

He set her on her feet, gazing deeply into her eyes. "I love you, sweet thing. Now get your fine ass in that truck before I carry you back inside and tear that pretty dress off."

She giggled and couldn't help teasing him. "You know a girl likes to be asked to get into a truck, not told."

He swatted her ass, and she squealed, running for the truck, but he caught her around the waist, sweeping her into his arms, and kissed her. With the spring sun warming their cheeks and a heart full to near bursting, she said, "Ring or no ring, there's only you, Diesel Black. There's always been only you."

Ready for the Whiskeys at Redemption Ranch?

Fall in love with Dare Whiskey and Billie Mancini
in **THE TROUBLE WITH WHISKEY**

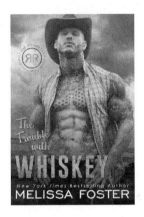

She's the only woman he's ever loved, and the one he could never have...

Years after losing one of their best friends to a dare gone wrong, Devlin "Dare" Whiskey continues to live up to his name, endlessly testing fate, while Billie Mancini buries the best parts of herself. Billie is beautiful, tough, and determined not to go back to the adrenaline-driven lifestyle she once craved like a drug and now fears like the devil. But Dare is done watching her pretend to be something she's not and takes on his most important challenge yet—showing the woman he loves that some dares are worth the risk.

Read the book in which we first meet the Whiskeys at Redemption Ranch, SEARCHING FOR LOVE, a deliciously sexy, funny, and emotional second-chance romance.

Zev Braden and Carly Dylan were childhood best friends, co-explorers, and first loves. Their close-knit families were sure they were destined to marry—until a devastating tragedy broke the two lovers apart. Over the next decade Zev, a nomadic treasure hunter, rarely returned to his hometown, and Carly became a chocolatier, building a whole new life across the country. When a chance encounter brings them back into each other's lives, can they find the true love that once existed, or will shattered dreams and broken hearts prevail?

Have you read The Wickeds: Dark Knights at Bayside?

The Wickeds are cousins to the Whiskeys

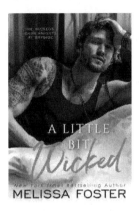

What do a cocky biker and a businesswoman who has sworn off dating bad boys have in common? According to Chloe Mallery, not much. But she couldn't be more wrong...

Justin came into the Wicked family after a harsh upbringing by a thieving father. He's gone through a lot to become a true Wicked, and he's made them proud. Now he's ready to show the woman he loves exactly what type of man he is. But Chloe has worked hard to move past her difficult upbringing, and she's wary of getting involved with a man who looks like he's walked right out of it. When tragedy strikes, will their trying pasts draw them together, or will Justin's protective nature be too much for Chloe's independent heart to accept?

Remember to download your Whiskey/Wicked family tree here:

Whiskey/Wicked Family Tree

www.MelissaFoster.com/wicked-whiskey-family-tree.html

Love Melissa's Writing?

If this is your first introduction to Melissa's work, please note that the Whiskeys are just one of the many family series in Melissa's Love in Bloom big-family romance collection. All Love in Bloom romances can be enjoyed as stand-alone novels. Characters appear in other family series, so you never miss out on an engagement, wedding, or birth. Discover more Love in Bloom magic and the collection here:
www.MelissaFoster.com/love-bloom-series

Melissa offers several free first-in-series ebooks. You can find them here:
www.MelissaFoster.com/LIBFree

Downloadable series checklists, reading orders, and more can be found on Melissa's Reader Goodies page.
www.MelissaFoster.com/Reader-Goodies

More Books By Melissa Foster

LOVE IN BLOOM SERIES

SNOW SISTERS
Sisters in Love
Sisters in Bloom
Sisters in White

THE BRADENS at Weston
Lovers at Heart, Reimagined
Destined for Love
Friendship on Fire
Sea of Love
Bursting with Love
Hearts at Play

THE BRADENS at Trusty
Taken by Love
Fated for Love
Romancing My Love
Flirting with Love
Dreaming of Love
Crashing into Love

THE BRADENS at Peaceful Harbor
Healed by Love
Surrender My Love
River of Love
Crushing on Love
Whisper of Love
Thrill of Love

THE BRADENS & MONTGOMERYS at Pleasant Hill – Oak Falls
Embracing Her Heart
Anything for Love
Trails of Love
Wild, Crazy Hearts
Making You Mine
Searching for Love
Hot for Love
Sweet, Sexy Heart
Then Came Love

THE BRADEN NOVELLAS
Promise My Love
Our New Love
Daring Her Love
Story of Love
Love at Last
A Very Braden Christmas

THE REMINGTONS
Game of Love
Stroke of Love
Flames of Love
Slope of Love
Read, Write, Love
Touched by Love

SEASIDE SUMMERS
Seaside Dreams
Seaside Hearts
Seaside Sunsets
Seaside Secrets
Seaside Nights
Seaside Embrace
Seaside Lovers
Seaside Whispers
Seaside Serenade

BAYSIDE SUMMERS

Bayside Desires
Bayside Passions
Bayside Heat
Bayside Escape
Bayside Romance
Bayside Fantasies

THE STEELES AT SILVER ISLAND

Tempted by Love
My True Love
Caught by Love

THE RYDERS

Seized by Love
Claimed by Love
Chased by Love
Rescued by Love
Swept Into Love

THE WHISKEYS: DARK KNIGHTS AT PEACEFUL HARBOR

Tru Blue
Truly, Madly, Whiskey
Driving Whiskey Wild
Wicked Whiskey Love
Mad About Moon
Taming My Whiskey
The Gritty Truth
In for a Penny
Running on Diesel

THE WHISKEYS: DARK KNIGHTS AT REDEMPTION RANCH

The Trouble with Whiskey

SUGAR LAKE
The Real Thing
Only for You
Love Like Ours
Finding My Girl

HARMONY POINTE
Call Her Mine
This is Love
She Loves Me

THE WICKEDS: DARK KNIGHTS AT BAYSIDE
A Little Bit Wicked
The Wicked Aftermath

SILVER HARBOR
Maybe We Will

WILD BOYS AFTER DARK
Logan
Heath
Jackson
Cooper

BAD BOYS AFTER DARK
Mick
Dylan
Carson
Brett

HARBORSIDE NIGHTS SERIES
Includes characters from the Love in Bloom series
Catching Cassidy
Discovering Delilah
Tempting Tristan

More Books by Melissa

Chasing Amanda (mystery/suspense)
Come Back to Me (mystery/suspense)
Have No Shame (historical fiction/romance)
Love, Lies & Mystery (3-book bundle)
Megan's Way (literary fiction)
Traces of Kara (psychological thriller)
Where Petals Fall (suspense)

Acknowledgments

I hope you enjoyed Diesel and Tracey's story. The Whiskeys: Dark Knights at Peaceful Harbor series is not ending. Izzy and others will get their happily ever afters. Be sure to sign up for my newsletter for updates.
www.MelissaFoster.com/News

If you'd like to find out more about my writing process, get sneak peeks into stories and characters, and chat with me, please join my fan club on Facebook.
www.Facebook.com/groups/MelissaFosterFans

Follow my author pages on Facebook and Instagram for fun giveaways and updates of what's going on in our fictional boyfriends' worlds.
www.Facebook.com/MelissaFosterAuthor and
www. Instagram.com/MelissaFoster_author

If you prefer sweet romance, with no explicit scenes or graphic language, please try the Sweet with Heat series written under my pen name, Addison Cole. You'll find the many great love stories with toned-down heat levels.

Thank you to my meticulous editorial team, Kristen Weber and Penina Lopez, and my exemplary proofreaders, Elaini Caruso, Juliette Hill, Lynn Mullan, and my last set of eyes, Justinn Harrison and Lee Fisher. And as always, thank you to my family for your endless support and for allowing me time to disappear into my fictional worlds.

Meet Melissa

www.MelissaFoster.com

Melissa Foster is a *New York Times, Wall Street Journal,* and *USA Today* bestselling and award-winning author. Her books have been recommended by *USA Today*'s book blog, *Hagerstown* magazine, *The Patriot,* and several other print venues. Melissa has painted and donated several murals to the Hospital for Sick Children in Washington, DC.

Visit Melissa on her website or chat with her on social media. Melissa enjoys discussing her books with book clubs and reader groups and welcomes an invitation to your event. Melissa's books are available through most online retailers in paperback and digital formats.

Melissa also writes sweet romance under the pen name Addison Cole.

Free Reader Goodies: www.MelissaFoster.com/Reader-Goodies

Made in the USA
Coppell, TX
13 September 2021